a novel by

THOMAS CONWAY FISHBURNE

~

For Dana, without whose faith,
love and encouragement this book could never have been written

~

Thanks to Dr. D.B. Shelnutt, Jr. for his continued
encouragement and inspiration.

Additional thanks to Leamon and Kim Hall, Robert T. Price, and Mary
Barnard for their assistance and suggestions.

"To be, or not to be— that is the question:
Whether 'tis nobler in the mind to suffer
the slings and arrows of outrageous fortune,
or to take arms against a sea of troubles
and, by opposing, end them."

Hamlet, Act 3, Scene I by William Shakespeare

TABLE OF CONTENTS

PROLOGUE

A DAY LIKE today was a rarity for mid-January in Atlanta. The sun was bright, there was no wind, and the temperature was hovering around an unseasonably warm 63 degrees. Like most of his fellow motorists, Danny Chambers was enjoying this pleasant change in the weather by driving with his window open.

The heavy bass thumping of the rap music coming from the car directly in front of him, a late-model Ford Mustang with over-sized tires and a gorgeous pearlescent green, after-market paint job, almost drowned out the sounds from his radio. The Georgia vanity plate read "CISCO-JR." The car sat very low to the ground, and Danny assumed it was equipped with the hydraulic lifters that seemed to be all the rage with kids nowadays.

The Mustang's horn began to blow in a rapid string of staccato bursts, causing Danny to look up again at the traffic light. The turn arrow for their lane was now glowing bright green, and he could see that the car in front of the Mustang, a white SUV, was not moving.

Great, just great, he thought to himself. *This light is short enough as it is, and if that SUV doesn't get moving pretty soon, I'm going to end up sitting through another sequence of lights and be late for my date.*

Without warning, the driver's door of the Mustang swung open violently, and a short, muscular youth wearing jeans that hung down over his hips and a tight, tank top jumped out. The young man raced up to the SUV in front of his Mustang, reached through the driver's window, grabbed the woman behind the wheel by the hair, and began to scream at her.

For a split second, Danny thought he had stumbled into a reality TV show or a movie shoot, but he quickly realized that neither scenario meshed with the intensity and brutality of the attack taking place in front of him. He threw the gear shift into park, opened his door, and jumped out. His heart was pounding as he ran toward the struggle, and in his loudest—and he hoped most commanding—voice, he shouted, "Hey, stop that! Leave her alone!"

The woman's assailant never looked back. He continued to scream at her. By now he had pulled her upper body almost through the open window and was striking her in the face with his fist. Danny came up beside them, grabbed the young man's shoulder, and shouted again, "Stop it! Stop it! You're going to kill her!"

Still, the attacker refused to acknowledge his presence. He continued to pull the woman, whose face was now a mask of blood, through the window. Danny let go of the young man's shoulder and grabbed him around the waist with both arms, pulling back as hard as he could. Over the boy's shoulder, he saw the woman press a small silver cylinder into the back of her assailant's forearm. The boy screamed and released his grip. Suddenly, all of Danny's force, no longer counterbalanced by the boy's hold on the woman, catapulted him and the boy backward toward the narrow concrete median which separated the east and west bound lanes of the road.

Danny's heel caught on the curb, and he fell on his back. His head struck the concrete hard, causing him to let go of the boy, who sailed over him and into the oncoming traffic. In a blur of sounds, Danny heard the horns, then the screeching tires, then the horrible thump. He looked over his shoulder and moaned, "Oh my God"

෴

CHAPTER ONE
DANNY

DANNY CHAMBERS SHIFTED his six-foot-two inch tall, 195-pound body in the hard wooden chair outside his supervisor's office. Some days he felt ten years younger than his forty years; other days, like today, sitting on this rock of a chair, he felt ten years older. The chair was positioned next to the closed door of the office of the principal of Robert E. Lee Senior High, where Danny taught three history classes and two gym classes, and coached junior varsity football. This particular chair was meant to be uncomfortable because it was usually reserved for students who were about to have justice meted out to them by Jonathan Evans.

Today Danny was just as nervous about his meeting with Evans as any student caught smoking in the rest rooms would have been. *Heck of a way to start the week out* he thought to himself. *Monday morning and I am waiting to see the principal.* This was the day Danny would find out if he had been approved by the school board as assistant principal and dean of boys at Robert E. Lee.

The Principal's administrative assistant, Mary Lou Barnard, was obviously busy, so Danny decided against making idle conversation. He stared out the window across the hall at the pine trees swaying gently in the breeze. Through the open window, he could hear the noises coming from the outdoor basketball courts where students in a morning gym class were shooting hoops. *Those kids don't have a care in the world*, he thought to himself. High school had been a wonderful time in Danny's own life, and he wondered if these kids knew just how good they had it right now.

Just then, Mrs. Barnard made a clucking noise. When Danny looked back at her, she was staring at her computer screen and shaking her head as if she were looking at something she didn't like or agree with. She was an attractive, big-bosomed woman in her mid-fifties, who didn't appear to need much makeup and was proud of her graying hair. *She must be very, very good at her job to have outlasted three principals before Jonathan Evans,* Danny thought.

Being assistant principal and dean of boys would be huge boost for Danny's career, and he was as nervous as a bridegroom as he waited for Principal Evans to call him in. Jonathan had recommended him for the position, but the board still had to approve the appointment. Evans had told Danny not worry, that the board's approval was just a formality. But Danny Chambers knew all about "formalities," and he knew that nothing was a certainty in this world except that you didn't get out of it alive and that you had to pay taxes until then. Evans had sent him a note asking him to drop by at half past ten that morning. Danny looked at his watch. It was already twenty until eleven. *It can't be a good thing that he's making me wait.*

Two years earlier, when Danny was assistant head coach and offensive coordinator for the Robert E. Lee Varsity Football team, the head coach had announced his retirement and picked Danny as his successor. The coach had told Danny that the board's approval was just a formality. But the day before the board was to meet, one of the school's more illustrious alumni, a man who had played football at Lee, then went on to play for the hometown Georgia Tech Yellow Jackets, and later had spent three years in the National Football League with the Atlanta Falcons, had thrown his hat in the ring.

Danny not only lost out on the promotion, but the new coach said he felt it would be best if Danny worked with the JV squad in the future instead of the varsity. He told Danny that there would be less conflict between them if they didn't work so closely together. Danny had simply looked the handsome young athlete, who was at least ten years his junior, in the eye and said, "Whatever you think is best, Coach." And that had been the end of that.

Danny had taken that setback in stride just as he had taken every other one in his adult life. He had just put it behind him and moved on. Sheila, his wife of eighteen years, had not taken it so calmly, she had ranted about the unfairness of it all, and the loss of the pay raise that would have come with the job, for several days until Danny finally had to ask her to please drop it. Being reminded of it every day was becoming more painful than losing out on the promotion, he told her. Danny Chambers was a man who was comfortable with who he was and with his place in the world. He firmly believed that if you lived your life the right way and had faith in the Lord, things would always work out—if not in this world, then certainly in the next. Sheila sometimes felt that Danny's good nature and his faith allowed others to make a doormat of him at times. But Danny never wavered. *We just need to do what we know is right and keep our faith, and we will do just fine,* he told her whenever things looked bad.

He went over this mantra as he sat waiting to meet with Evans: *Whatever happens today, life goes on. Maybe I'm a better coach and teacher than I would be an assistant principal? Whatever happens, it is God's will and we will be just fine.*

Finally, the door opened and a white-faced student scurried out and disappeared through the waiting room doors. *If that boy had a tail, it would be tucked firmly between his legs right now,* Danny thought.

Jonathan Evans stepped out and extended his right hand.

"Come on in, Danny. The smell of burning flesh has just about cleared out from the roasting I gave that young man." They both were laughing as Danny followed his boss into the spacious office. Evans was a tall, elegant man who would have looked equally at home behind the CEO's desk of a Fortune 500 company or delivering the headlines on the evening news. He wore a well-tailored suit that was probably five or six years old but still fit him like he had just purchased it. He was taller than Danny, perfectly tanned from his weekends of year-round tennis, with just a touch of gray at the temples. He was also one of the nicest men Danny had ever worked with or for.

"I'm sorry you had to wait," said Jonathan. "When I sent you the note, I had no idea I'd have to deal with Billy Skinner again today. That boy is headed down the wrong road. You want a cup of coffee, Danny?"

"Thanks, I've already had my quota of caffeine for the day. Two cups before ten in the morning is all I ever allow myself. More than that, and I get a little jittery in the afternoon and have trouble sleeping at night."

Evans poured himself a cup from the carafe on the credenza behind his desk and sat down. Danny sat across from him.

"I won't keep you in suspense, Danny. The board approved you. You're the new assistant principal. Congratulations. I know you'll do a terrific job."

Danny stood up, his face first showing surprise, then genuine jubilation. Grinning broadly, he said, "Wow! That's just great, Jonathan. I can't thank you enough for backing me for this opportunity. I won't let you down. I promise."

"I never thought for a moment that you would, Danny. I guess you know that your new position means a 16 percent pay raise. You will, however, need to keep coaching the JV Team until we can find a suitable replacement."

"Actually, Jonathan, I wasn't sure what the raise would be. I never checked. It would have been easier that way if I didn't get the job. As far as the JV goes, I love the kids, and I would really like to stay on as coach indefinitely."

"I'm sure you would, Danny, but that won't be possible. Your new duties won't leave you time for coaching. I hope that's not going to be a problem." Danny shook his head to indicate that it would not be.

"Danny, there is one potential problem that we need to discuss. I hope it will not be serious, but, knowing you as I do, I think we need to discuss it."

Danny felt a chill run through his body. "I hope it won't be serious either Jonathan and I am anxious to hear what it is." he responded.

"Danny, it's about your religious faith." Jonathan said in a definitely apologetic voice. "That's where the problem might come in."

∿

CHAPTER TWO
CISCO

FRANCISCO RAMOS, STREET name Cisco Ram, opened his eyes and looked up at the expensive, ornate ceiling fan over his bed. The fan was not moving, but to Cisco's wine-addled brain, it appeared that the entire room was. He sat up on the side of the bed and reached for his cigarettes. He lit his first of the day, took a deep draw on it, and began to cough. The cough lasted almost a full minute. When it was over, there were tears in his eyes. *Damn*, he thought, *I got to get that cough checked out. Cisco don't have no time to be sick. Cisco is a busy man. Cisco has people depending on him.*

It was a Monday morning, but Cisco did not have to worry about getting up for work. Cisco did not have a job. The people who worked for Cisco had jobs. Their job was to do whatever Cisco asked them to do and to bring Cisco money. How or where they got the money did not matter to Cisco. All that mattered was that they brought it all to him and kept him at arm's length from the law. If they did that, then he would give some of the money back to them. How much depended on how much they had brought him and what kind of a mood Cisco was in.

Cisco Ram was the leader, the boss, and the undisputed king of the Latino Death Lords. The Latino Death Lords, the LDL, were his family. They supported him, and he led them with an iron fist. The LDL were involved in every type of income-producing street crime imaginable, including drugs, prostitution, bookmaking, numbers-running, and contraband—flat-screen TVs, computers, and cell phones. Anything that could be stolen and resold was in play. All these endeavors brought money into the LDL treasury and, eventually, into Cisco's pocket. One of his favorite sources of income came from extortion. It cost him nothing, the risk was minimal, and everything that came in was pure profit. He simply let the word get around to the owners of the Hispanic businesses that had sprung up all over Atlanta, that if you wanted your store to be safe, you should hire the Ramos Security Agency to keep it that way.

The Ramos Security Agency was just one of several quasi-legitimate businesses that Cisco owned. Though the RSA signs displayed prominently in the merchant's windows, may have deterred a few petty criminals, the only thing the agency actually protected the stores from were the Latino Death Lords. His clients eventually came to understand this arrangement, even if they did not like it. Cisco made sure that these solicitations for offers of "protection" never came directly from him, always from one of his trusted lieutenants: *Cuchillo*, *Borracho*, or *El Carnicero*. They were the nominal heads of all his businesses that involved anything even slightly illegal.

The Knife, The Drunk, and The Butcher all served Cisco well. They were not stupid men, but it never seemed to occur to them that they took most of the risks and Cisco took most of the money. Each of the men felt honored to be listed as manager, president, or whatever other title Cisco chose to give them. It also, never occurred to them that Cisco was rarely, if ever, around when anything illegal happened. Threats were made, punishments were dealt out, and crimes were committed in his name, but never in his presence. Like a ruler on high, Cisco simply said what he wanted done, and one or more of these three made it happen.

Cuchillo, the most intelligent and self-educated of the trio, had once seen a movie in which the Pharaoh of Egypt, after he gave an order, would say, "So it shall be written, so it shall be done." *Cuchillo* liked to use that phrase when Cisco sent him out to do a job.

Cuchillo was fiercely loyal to his boss, so much so that none of the others dared to utter a hint of dissatisfaction with anything Cisco said or did. He obeyed Cisco's commands immediately and without question. Once, when Cisco was having a heated discussion with the leader of a rival gang, **Cisco** had told the man that he and his associates would be well-advised to stay clear of the LDL and it's territory because the members of the LDL would do whatever Cisco instructed them to do, no matter how illegal or dangerous, and that included sacrificing their lives for him.

The man had laughed at him and said he did not believe Cisco's men would willingly die for him. Cisco took out his cigarette lighter, held the flame in front of him, and told *Cuchillo* to put his hand on it. Without hesitation, *Cuchillo* put his hand on the flame and held it there for five seconds before Cisco withdrew the lighter. They had no more problems with that particular gang.

The three men were intensely jealous of Cisco's friendship, each picturing himself as Cisco's most trusted and closest confidant. Cisco used this to full advantage. Lately, whenever he was alone with *Cuchillo*, he would say, "Cuch, you know you're my right-hand man. The others are good men, but you are the best. You are like a second son to me. But you must never tell the others how I feel. It would only hurt them and cause the family trouble. But you will know it. You and I will always know that you are the one I will count on when things get tough."

He had, of course, been saying the same thing to *Borracho* and *El Carnicero* whenever he had them alone. It was this desire for his approval that drove them to take the risks they did. Cisco had found each of these men when they desperately needed a friend, and he had seen in them a blood lust and a killer instinct that he could use. Just like their leader, each of the three was devoid of a conscience or moral compass, and no act of violence or depravity was beyond them. Cisco thought of them as his *Tres Tiburones...* his three sharks. Man-eating sharks to be exact.

❧

CHAPTER THREE
THE KNIFE IS BORN

MANUEL OCTAVIO OSORIO liked his nickname: *El Cuchillo*, the Knife. He had given himself the name one night on the docks of Veracruz, a major port on the Mexican coast of the Gulf of Mexico, when he was only fifteen years old.

He was born in Mexico City, but the family had moved to Veracruz when his father had decided it was in their best interest to leave the capital. *La policia,* who had been looking for his father for several years after he had been implicated in a murder-for-hire scheme, and multiple assaults, did not know the Osorios had left Mexico City. Even if they had known, they would not have stood in his way. Octavio Osorio was bad news, and there was a good chance that someone, most likely a policeman, was going to get hurt, if and when the authorities ever did find him. As far as they were concerned, if he was gone, good riddance. He was now the problem of some other police force.

Manuel's mother was a part-time prostitute and full-time alcoholic. She rented her body out when the family needed money. Sometimes, her husband worked with her to rob her customers before or after she had sex with them. Before or after did not matter to Manuel's mother or father.

Manuel's older sister had run away from home when she was thirteen and Manuel was ten. He had not seen or heard from her since. Manuel learned early on that the only life that had any value was your own. If the price was right or if it was necessary for his own survival, he would have sold his mother or father to the nearest policeman. He would hold on to this belief until he met Francisco Miguel Ramos.

Manuel's life of crime started at age seven, when his mother began to teach him how to pick pockets. His sister had been supplementing the family income this way for three years, and Manuel was expected to do the same. By the time he was eleven, he had moved on to shoplifting and other petty theft. By the time he was thirteen, he was breaking and entering homes and businesses, and bringing in more money than his mother's prostitution did.

When the family moved to Veracruz shortly after his fifteenth birthday, he began to steal cargo from the docks. One night, as he and another boy were trying to open a crate of video games that was too large to be dragged out the warehouse window they had come in though, they were surprised by the night watchman, a middle-aged man named Tomas Valenzuela. He was a burly man with a huge belly and big arms who was frequently drunk and had a reputation as an exceptionally cruel person who liked to fight when he was drinking. He was surprisingly fast for his size, but not as fast or as agile as these young boys. As he tried to block their escape, one went to his left, the other to his right. The tail of Manuel's loose-fitting shirt snagged a nail protruding from a crate, and he was held up for just a moment. That was all it took for the big man to put him in an inescapable headlock.

Manuel screamed for his friend to help him, but these two young thieves had not worked together long enough to form any bond of loyalty, and the other boy was out the window and gone before he even knew Manuel had been caught.

"So, little man, you have come into my warehouse to steal the things I am paid to protect? You don't care if I lose my job, do you, *muchacho*? You don't care if I lose my job do you?" All the while, he was squeezing Manuel's head tighter in his powerful arms.

"So, what am I to do with you, little thief? Should I call *la policia*? I think not this time. They will maybe just call your whore of a mother or your drunken father and then let you go."

Manuel was stunned that the man knew who he was and knew about his parents. From the moment he realized the man had him, his mind had begun to formulate the story he would tell the police. He knew he did not need a story for his parents. But now, this fat old fool was saying something about not calling the police?

"Yes, little man, I think I will teach you a lesson about stealing and just give you a good beating. But, so that your beating will also be a good lesson to others as well as to you, we need an audience." He dragged Manuel out of the warehouse, around a corner to the main street, and into a bar filled with sailors and longshoremen.

"Hey, *hombres*, look what I caught," he shouted as he came through the door dragging Manuel, who was still in a headlock. "A little rat trying to steal the cheese from your labors." Everyone in the room stopped to see what the commotion was.

"I think it's time we give these little *bastardos* a lesson about stealing from us, don't you think, hombres?" There was a murmur of assent from the crowd.

Manuel was small for his age and did not appear anywhere near fifteen years old. Maybe if the man had known his age, he might have done things differently. Instead, he chose a punishment fit for a child.

"Help me get his pants off, *hombres*, so I can give him a good beating." Several of the men grabbed Manuel by the arms and others by his feet so the night watchman could release his headlock.

"Bend him over that table," he ordered.

The men had pulled Manuel's trousers and underwear down, exposing his buttocks and genitals. Some of the women began to laugh. Tears of rage and shame were pouring down Manuel's face.

"Let me go," he screamed.

But it was too late for that. One of the men grabbed his arms and stretched him over the table while others he could not see, held his feet down on the floor.

"Nice arse," said one of the British sailors, laughing.

"Go ahead and bugger him," roared another, convulsing the crowd with laughter.

Valenzuela removed the thick leather belt that held up his own pants and slapped it loudly on the table, inches from Manuel's face.

"Are you ready for your lesson, *muchacho*?" he asked.

"Give him twenty lashes!" yelled a skinny woman at the bar.

Suddenly, the belt landed with another crack, this time on Manuel's bare butt. He jerked and squealed in pain.

"One," the skinny woman counted.

The belt landed again.

"Two," she continued. This time the crowd picked up her chant.

Manuel twisted his head frantically, searching for any source of aid. He saw a man who lived above his parents' small apartment. He saw another man who also stole from the docks. Then he saw his mother. She was sitting on a sailor's lap at a table in the back of the barroom. She appeared to be in an alcohol or drug induced trance. When their eyes met, she just smiled and resumed kissing the sailor's neck and fondling his crotch.

Eighteen more times the broad leather belt came down on the boy's defenseless buttocks and thighs. Manuel passed out after the thirteenth lash, but not before he had committed to memory the face of the man holding down his arms. The mop of thick gray hair, the drooping mustache, and the bushy beard were seared indelibly into Manuel's brain as he lost consciousness.

∽

The cold water startled him awake, as if from a dream. Then he swallowed a mouthful and realized he was not dreaming. He was underwater and in danger of drowning. After the beating was over, the men had thrown him into the harbor between two rusted freighters.

Manuel kicked hard with his legs and fought to reach the surface. When he broke through, gasping and sputtering, he saw the silhouettes and heard the laughter of several men who were still standing on the dock. The pain in his legs and buttocks was excruciating, and as he tried to swim toward a rope hanging off the dock, one of the men threw an old life preserver down to him.

"A life boat for a drowned little rat," he shouted, and the others laughed. Then they all turned away and went back to the bar.

Manuel finally made it to the rope and, with painful deliberateness, pulled himself back up on the planks. He lay on his stomach gasping for a few moments before he realized that somewhere along the way, he had lost his shirt and was completely naked. He rolled over, got to his feet, and stared at the entrance to the bar. Tears were running down his face again. But not from pain. This time they were tears of pure, unadulterated hatred. He started to yell out a threat but thought better of it and, moving as quickly as his injuries would allow, disappeared into the shadows.

He stole a pair of pants and a shirt he found hanging on a porch to dry. They were still damp, but he didn't care. Then he headed for the only safe place he could think of: the church. He knew the nuns would tend to his wounds and look after him. Two days later, he returned home.

He and his mother never spoke about the fact that she had simply sat and watched while he was being brutalized. He never asked her why she had not come to his rescue. She never even acknowledged that it had happened. That was fine with Manuel. The last thing he wanted to do was relive that night. He didn't know if his mother had been too drunk to recognize him, or if she simply didn't care. It made no difference. She had turned her back on him in his time of greatest need.

Manuel had never carried a knife because the police and the courts treated armed criminals more severely than unarmed petty criminals. Manuel had never felt the need to have a weapon of any kind for fear of going to prison instead of a juvenile facility. But, just one week after the beating, at two o'clock in the morning, he crept into his parents' room and, while they slept, pulled a six-inch switchblade knife out of his father's pants, which were hanging on a post at the foot of the bed. His mother and father were sleeping soundly, probably drunk, and neither one stirred when he removed the knife. The same pocket contained a wad of money that consisted of both *pesos* and U.S. dollars. Manuel took the dollars and left the pesos.

He left the room as quietly as he had entered and then left the house through the window of the room he shared with his younger brother, Juanito. Every night since he had healed from the beating, he had gone back to the dock outside the bar where it happened. Every night, he wore a large, floppy *sombrero* and sat in the shadows near one of the freighters, watching the patrons come and go. The bushy-bearded man who had held his arms down came every night at the same time. He would arrive at five minutes before midnight, and he never left before three in the morning. Manuel also knew that the fat night watchman from the warehouse worked from midnight until seven o'clock in the morning, Monday through Saturday.

Now, one week after his humiliation, he sat in the shadows and waited. He was wearing a Seiko watch with an illuminated dial that he had stolen several years before but never allowed his mother or father to see. He always kept it hidden in his trouser pocket whenever they were around and only wore it when he was away from home. Manuel loved the watch, and he knew that if his father ever saw it, he would either take it for himself or sell it on the street.

Tonight he consulted it frequently while he waited. At ten minutes after three in the morning, the bar door opened, and the man with the bushy beard came out. He paused for a moment and breathed deeply, as if he were trying to exchange the smoky bar fumes in his lungs for the cleaner air of the night. Then he started down the pier toward the main street that would take him to his small house on the outskirts of town. Manuel silently followed. When the man reached an especially dark part of the pier, he stopped to light a cigarette. Like a spirit of the night, Manuel materialized beside him.

"Hey, hombre," he whispered. "You wanna meet my sister?"

The man turned to look at him through rum-soaked eyes.

"What's that you say?" he asked, slurring the question.

"I say it's time for you to pay for your sins, hombre."

"Who are you? What do you want?"

The words came to Manuel like a bolt from heaven.

"I am *El Cuchillo*, and what I want is your blood as payment for your many sins."

The man flicked his cigarette lighter and held the flame down toward Manuel's face. Just as a glimmer of recognition entered the man's eyes, Manuel drove the long blade of his father's knife into his side and dragged it across the girth of his huge belly. The man gave out a small cry and dropped to his knees, trying to hold the blood and intestines in with both hands. Manuel stepped behind him, grabbed a handful of his thick gray hair, and jerked his head back.

"You remember me now, don't you, old man?" he whispered into the man's ear. "I will see you in hell." Then, still holding the bearded man's head back by the hair, he ran the razor-sharp blade across his throat. Blood from the new wound mixed on the cobblestones with the blood that was still oozing from his stomach. But, none of it touched Manuel. He let go of the hair, and the man made a gurgling sound as he fell forward on his face and then lay still. Manuel stood there for a moment, feeling nothing but exhilaration. He grabbed the man's feet, dragged him to the edge of the pier, and pushed his body into the water below. Then he walked back down the pier toward the warehouse.

Tomas Valenzuela had worked as a warehouse night watchman on the docks of Veracruz for almost twenty years. He had never married and lived alone in a boarding house nearby. He started his shift at midnight each night and got off at seven o'clock in the morning. He usually started drinking as soon as he left work, and was often unconscious by noon. He got up at eight or nine o'clock in the evening and fixed himself beans and rice or sometimes a couple of eggs. He had no girlfriends, but was a frequent patron of the prostitutes who worked the waterfront bars. When he was drunk, he was known to beat these women violently, so unless they had a pimp to protect them, many of them kept their distance. Occasionally, a new girl would come to town and have to learn about Tomas Valenzuela the hard way.

When Manuel got back to the warehouse, he reached behind a pile of empty crates and loose boards near the door and pulled out a baseball bat he had hidden there earlier in the day after he had stolen it. Gripping the bat firmly with both hands, he went up to the warehouse door and tapped on it lightly. There was no response, so he tapped a bit harder. This time, he heard someone cursing softly inside.

"Who is it?" asked the voice behind the door.

"Just checking to see if you were sleeping on the job again, you fat old fool," Manuel said. His words had the desired effect. The door jerked open violently, and Valenzuela stepped out into the dim light of the street lamps. When he did, Manuel hit him in the groin as hard as he could with the bat. The big man grunted in pain and fell back into the warehouse. Manuel followed him in and closed the door. The watchman was rolling on the floor in agony, cupping his genitals with both hands.

"You're not laughing now, are you?" Manuel asked as he leaned down into the man's contorted face. "Time for your lesson, fat bastard. But, I don't wear a belt, *amigo*, so I'll have to use this bat." He began to strike Valenzuela's legs and shoulders. The man cried out, and Manuel hit him in the throat. The night watchman began to gag, but the boy continued to flail at him with the bat, striking him exactly twenty times all over his body. When he finished, the man curled up into the fetal position, groaning and whimpering like a child.

"That was a pretty good lesson, *amigo*, don't you think? Too bad there was no one here to see it. Now I must leave, but you can join your friend bushy beard in hell." Manuel knelt and plunged his father's knife through the man's right eye into his brain. The groans and whimpers stopped, and the night watchman lay motionless. Manuel picked up his bat, cautiously peeked out the door to see if anyone had heard, then vanished into the night.

Twenty minutes later, he was back in his parents' room. They were still sleeping in the same positions. He knelt beside his mother and shook her gently.

"Mama," he whispered. "Wake up, Mama." But she did not move. He shook her again with more force. "Mama, please wake up. I need you, Mama. Please wake up." No response. He shook her harder. Finally, her eyes opened slowly and she tried to focus.

"Manuelito, is that you? What is it? Why did you wake me?"

"Mama, I need your help. I am in bad trouble, Mama."

"Go away and let me sleep. I don't care if you're in trouble. Maybe tomorrow."

He put one hand over her mouth and, for the third time that night, *El Cuchillo* left his calling card. He drew the blade slowly across her throat. She tried to sit up, but her strength was quickly drained, and she fell back. A gusher of blood quickly saturated the front of her cotton gown.

"Too bad for you mama. I gave you one last chance. Juanito will be better off with no mama, than with you," he said softly. "Now all debts are paid."

He held the knife by the blade and rubbed the handle in his mother's blood. Then he went to the other side of the bed and put the bloody weapon in his father's outstretched hand.

"*Buenos noches, Padre*," he whispered. "Better you than me."

Manuel Octavio Osorio had now cut all ties with Mexico and his family. *El Cuchillo* had begun his journey toward the United States and, though he did not know it, toward Francisco Miguel Ramos.

CHAPTER FOUR
LATINO DEATH LORDS

THE LATINO DEATH Lords had more than a hundred official members. Only those who had passed Cisco's tests of loyalty and viciousness were granted full membership. He saw himself as the Field Marshal, the three sharks as his generals, and below them the foot soldiers. The generals had large groups of soldiers who reported directly to them. The gang was organized like a mafia-based crime family. Cisco's favorite movie was *The Godfather,* and he pictured himself as the younger Don Corleone that Robert DeNiro portrayed in the sequel rather than the older man Marlon Brando played in the original movie.

There were always a dozen or so gang wannabes hanging around the club house trying to impress Cisco. Occasionally, one of the sharks would tell a member-in-waiting that if he were to perform a certain chore or commit a certain crime, he would gain favor with Cisco, which could earn them a spot as a full-fledged member of the gang. Cisco never spoke to these people except in passing, and when one of them did a deed the sharks told them to do, they were instructed never to mention it to Cisco. The sharks always assured these stooges that they would make sure that Cisco knew who had done him this favor. Sometimes, this promise was kept; other times, the would-be gang member simply disappeared—permanently. In these instances, the "service" the stooge had performed had brought with it a sufficient enough threat of criminal prosecution, to make the perpetrator a serious liability. After these disappearances, one of the sharks would circulate rumors that the missing "associate," as Cisco called them publicly, had gotten homesick and gone back to Mexico, been busted by the cops, or run over by a truck. The associates never realized that Cisco never even knew what they had done for the gang. They also never realized that they were as expendable to him as a bullet from his Glock automatic.

There was also no shortage of female friends of the LDL. They could never assume the status of a full member, but they did have their roles. They provided home-cooking at the gang's "club house," escorted various members when the gang went bar-hopping on Saturday night, and—unless they were the official property of a particular gang member—made themselves available for sex to any full LDL member at any time. Even though many of these women were young, pretty, and willing, Cisco seldom took advantage of them. He had other tastes. In fact, their willingness turned him off. Cisco liked to take his sex when he wanted it and from someone who was not a willing participant. He had seen his first pornographic movie at age thirteen in the back of a bar in Ciudad Acuna, Mexico, his hometown. The movie included a graphic scene of sexual assault. After it was over, Cisco left the bar and beat up, then raped a twelve-year-old girl who had spit at him in school that day. It was his first experience with sex, violent or otherwise.

He was now thirty-six, and he had kept a record in his head of every rape. To date, there had been sixty-seven. In Mexico, there was always the risk of an enraged husband, brother, or father, not to mention *la policia*. But here in the United States, the girls he assaulted were almost exclusively illegal aliens, and they suffered the rapes in silence rather than go to the police and risk deportation. In the early days of the LDL, a husband or boyfriend would occasionally try to defend the honor of an assaulted girl. But after a few of these men disappeared or were found dead or near dead from a beating, attempts at retribution ceased.

ॐ

CHAPTER FIVE
RODRIGO THE DRUNK

RODRIGO GUZMAN GREW up around the bars, brothels, and pool halls of Juarez, Mexico. He relished the excitement and the action of this back-alley life and developed an affinity for alcohol. He had enjoyed the buzz of being drunk from the time he was twelve years old. Back then, he would often bring a bottle of rum that he had stolen from his uncle to school and drink from it during lunch. He drank after school, and he drank at night, which meant he had to steal money to pay for his habit, which also meant he was continually in trouble with the authorities.

The first time Rodrigo's teacher called his home and spoke to his Uncle Pablo about his behavior, Pablo begged the teacher not to throw him out of school and promised he would deal with the boy. Pablo did not care one way or the other whether Rodrigo finished his education, or got any education at all, but he did not want the boy under foot all day.

He did speak to Rodrigo the day the teacher called. He spoke to him with a jockey's whip he had found one day at the Juarez Horse Racing Park. He beat Rodrigo until the boy screamed for mercy, and then he locked him in the storeroom behind his small house. He left Rodrigo there from four o'clock in the afternoon until eleven that night. It was chilly and stuffy, but there was enough oxygen coming through the slat-board wall for the boy to breathe. Other than field mice, spiders, and assorted insects, there was nothing else in the room but stacks of old newspapers and magazines, and some rusty tools.

Once or twice a month, the school would call, and the punishment would be repeated. Finally, his uncle, who was sick and tired of having the boy steal his liquor and whatever petty cash he could find in the house, could take it no more. The next time the school called, he told them to go to hell and that he didn't care what happened to the boy. He also told them not to bother calling again because he was throwing Rodrigo out of the house for being a thief. When Rodrigo came home that afternoon, Pablo told him to take whatever clothes he had and get out. He told him that if he ever came back, he would beat him within a inch of his life and lock him in the storeroom for a week.

He had lived with his uncle for the past two years because his mother was dead and his father was in prison. Now he was being thrown into the street. Rodrigo did as he was told, and at dusk he found himself sitting beside his small bag of clothes, on the curb in front of a McDonald's restaurant. He had no money, no friends, and no family to turn to. He was fourteen years old. When the shift changed, one of the departing employees handed the boy a bag that held two cheeseburgers, an order of French fries, and a Coke. Rodrigo said, "*Gracias*," opened the bag, and ate. He spent the night in a box in the alley behind the restaurant.

The next day, he got a job sweeping and cleaning the bathrooms at a brothel that served a clientele that ranged from local men to college boys and servicemen who came across the border from El Paso, Texas each night. After everyone had gone home for the evening, the woman who ran the place, Rosita Vasques, let him sleep in one of the rooms the whores used to entertain customers. That meant that he usually got to bed around four in the morning. The owner rousted him by nine each day so he could begin his chores.

Rodrigo did what he was told, kept his mouth shut, and watched. He watched everything that went on in the business. He made a mental note that Senora Vasques usually took the night's receipts home with her when she left. But she always waited for her large, ill-tempered son, a Juarez policeman, to finish his shift and escort her and her money home.

One night, her son didn't show. The woman called his cell phone several times but got no answer. She asked Rodrigo, who was the only person left in the brothel, if he had called or if anyone else had called or left a message about him. Rodrigo told her he knew nothing about any calls or messages. When she went into her office and closed the door, Rodrigo dropped to his knees and peeked through the keyhole. Rosita was kneeling on the floor by the far wall. As the boy watched, she pried a section of baseboard free and stuffed a large wad of bills into the wall. By the time she had replaced the board, gathered up her things, and exited the office, Rodrigo was already in one of the whore's rooms, feigning sleep. As soon as he was sure she had left for the night, he went down to the office, jimmied the lock on the door, and went in. The boy had been a smoker since he was nine, so he always had a cigarette lighter or a book of matches with him. He used the lighter to illuminate the section of baseboard where he had seen the woman hide the money.

Rodrigo was not stupid and he had decided that, unless this stash contained enough money for him to disappear into the United States, he wasn't about to give up his job and a place to sleep by stealing it. He had no way of knowing how much might be in the hole, but he had decided that if it wasn't at least the equivalent of $500 American, he wouldn't take it.

He pulled the board from the wall, reached in and found the wad. With his hand full of money, he moved over to the window and cracked the curtains just enough so that some of the light from the street lamps and the moon could seep into the room. He began to count the money on the floor in front of him. To his amazement, she had secreted away $793 in American currency, as well as Mexican *pesos* worth at least another $300 American. Rodrigo knew that Rosita was a dangerous woman to have as an enemy, especially since her son was *la policia.* He knew that if he took her money, he could never return to Juarez. He didn't care. There was nothing for him here anyway. He tucked some of the money in his pockets and the rest in the bag with his clothes. By the time Senora Vasques came in the next morning and discovered that she had been robbed, Rodrigo Guzman had found his way into the United States of America. He would spend the next six years of his life moving from one Texas town to another. When he was twenty years old, he decided that things were getting boring in Texas and headed east. Before the year was out, he was in Atlanta, Georgia. Six months later, he was a full-time member of the Latino Death Lords.

Over the eight years that followed, he had made himself invaluable to Cisco by doing whatever Cisco told him to do, whenever he told him to do it, and by keeping his mouth shut. Rodrigo drank less these days but still enough that one day Cisco began calling him *Borracho,* the Spanish word for drunk. Of course, since it was Cisco's idea, Rodrigo didn't object, and the name stuck. Cisco had become his god, and he would do anything for him.

Prior to meeting Francisco Miguel Ramos, Rodrigo Guzman had been a petty criminal whose exploits seldom would have merited notice even in the smallest of newspapers. By the time he had reached the upper echelons of the LDL hierarchy, Rodrigo had become *Borracho*, and *Borracho* was an extortionist, a hijacker, a carjacker, a rapist, and a murderer. He might have become all of these things on his own, but his entrance into Cisco Ram's world certainly accelerated his evolution.

CHAPTER SIX
THE BUTCHER COMES TO GEORGIA

EDUARDO AGUILAR WAS a rarity in Mexican street gangs, especially in the Latino Death Lords of Cisco Ram. Eduardo was not a Mexican. He had come to the United States from Cuba when his father had escaped the country, bringing with him Eduardo's mother and his three sisters. While his parents worked, Eduardo watched over his sisters.

When he was seventeen and his sisters were old enough to take care of themselves during the day, his father forced him to find a job. His efforts were lackadaisical until one day with the help of a friend, he stumbled into a job in the meat department of a large grocery chain. Eduardo learned to cut meat. It was tough, bloody work, but he discovered that he liked it. He seemed to have a natural talent for it, and the money was good. His friends began to call him *El Carnicero*, the butcher, and he liked that, too. By the time he was twenty years old, he was a skilled meat cutter and had moved from his parents' home to live with two friends.

Eduardo, now known to his friends as "Eddie", had always been sociable and soon realized that if he wanted to be a part of the vibrant South Beach nightlife, he would need more money than a meat cutter could make. So, the butcher began to sell cocaine for a man he had met through some friends. Normally, he would not have trusted the man, who was Columbian, but several of his acquaintances were already working for him, and Eddie was envious of the wads of cash they always seemed to have, so he signed on. Eddie knew his father would be very angry if he found out that his son was breaking the laws of this wonderful country that had given Eddie's father a fresh start, so the young man was careful to never show any outward signs of his newly acquired wealth when his father or mother were around.

Eddie might have remained a minor cog in the extensive South Florida drug business except for an unfortunate incident involving his sister Olga, was a beautiful young woman of eighteen who had always been close to her brother. So, when she came to him and told him that three boys from the *barrio* had gotten her drunk and taken advantage of her, Eddie was incensed. To make matters worse, Olga told him that the boys were now telling all their friends that Olga Aguilar was a *puta.*

To have his sister violated was bad enough. To have her labeled a whore was more than Eddie could take. He waited for three weeks before he acted. He found the addresses of each of the three boys and where they hung out. He watched the boys on weekend nights to become familiar with their activities. He discovered that the same boy drove the group around on their weekend jaunts and that he took the same boy home first every time. One night, Eddie waited at the first boy's home, hiding in the bushes near the street. When the car stopped at the curb and the door opened to let the boy out, Eddie stepped out of the shadows and said, "Olga Aguilar is my sister, you bastards." Then he shot each one of them in the chest as fast as he could pull the trigger of his pistol. Then he ran down the street, turned the corner, and got into his car. He drove away, leaving two boys to die in their car and one in the street. As he crossed one of the many bridges on the intra-coastal waterway, he tossed the pistol out over the railing into the water and headed home.

Unfortunately for Eddie, one of the three victims did not die immediately. He was able to tell Miami-Dade detectives that even though he couldn't see the shooter's face in the darkness, the shooter had said he was the brother of a girl named Olga Aguilar. Eddie was arrested and charged with two counts of first-degree murder and one count of attempted murder. Two days after Eddie's arraignment, the third boy died.

Eddie's attorney requested and got a dismissal of all charges due to lack of evidence. Since the authorities had only the statement of the young man that his assailant stated that he was the brother of Olga Aguilar, the defense argued successfully that anyone who had a grudge against Eduardo Aguilar could have shot the boys and covered himself by saying he was Olga's brother.

Eddie's attorney pointed out that the police had no murder weapon, no eye witness and no one to connect Eddie to the murders. The judge agreed, and Eddie was released.

The next day, he got a visit from one of the Miami-Dade Police Department detectives who had investigated the case. The detective told Eddie that he may have skated for the time being but that the whole department would be watching him from now on. Sooner or later, he said, Eddie was going to break the law, and the police would be there to put him away. Eddie had no reason to doubt him. He figured that if he wanted to continue the lifestyle to which he had become accustomed, he would need to live it somewhere other than South Florida. He packed his belongings and made the seven-hundred-mile drive north to Atlanta.

Once he got to Atlanta, he had no trouble finding employment as a meat cutter. While working at a grocery store, he met a few LDL members. Eddie didn't know which gang these people belonged to, but he could tell they were definitely gang members. He casually began to mention to some of them that he was looking for a more interesting and lucrative way to make a living. Finally, one of the gang members arranged for him to meet Cisco. The two men hit it off right away. As soon as Cisco was able to check Eddie's background through his contacts in the Miami area, he invited him into the gang. The first time they met, Cisco had asked him what his friends called him, and Eddie had told him he was known as *El Carnicero*. When Cisco asked why, Eddie had smiled and said, "Because I like to chop things up with a cleaver."

That was good enough for Cisco. Over the next five years, *El Carnicero* proved to be a resourceful and merciless instrument of the Latino Death Lords. Although he no longer worked in the grocery as a butcher, he still used his cleaver whenever Cisco told him to. In less than two years, he had become one of Cisco's most trusted aides.

∾

CHAPTER SEVEN
FAITH IS NOT A PROBLEM

DANNY STARED AT Jonathan Evans in shock. For a moment he was speechless. Then he stood and said, "My faith? How is my faith a problem?"

Evans also rose to his feet and held up both his hands, palms out, as if to apologize. Then he said, "Now Danny, you know me as a brother in Christ but, there are others who don't think that school administrators, especially those in higher positions, should be too vocal about their own faith. Ever since the Supreme Court in *Murray vs Curlett* threw out prayer in public schools, there is always, and I mean always, someone watching what the schools do in regards to religious matters."

"I do not attempt to push my faith on anyone Jonathan, especially at school," Danny protested.

"I know that Danny. But I also know that you are not shy about being a Christian. We are not talking about a simple prayer with your team before a football game. We are talking about people who would like to get any mention of religion, especial Christianity, permanently banned in the schools. You are a strong Christian man and you profess your faith to anyone who will listen. It could get you in trouble is all I am saying."

"No more trouble that that high school sophomore did at Columbine when she was murdered for admitting her Christianity," Danny said, becoming a little heated.

"Danny, just calm down. I am telling you this for your own good. I just don't want to see you do anything to hurt your career."

"Jonathan, if someone does ever take issue with anything I say in regards to my religious faith, will it be a problem for the school?"

"Probably only in the sense that it would bring pressure on me to dismiss you from staff if it was a serious enough complaint," Evans responded.

"Good, then we don't have a problem because if it ever becomes a serious enough issue to put you in that position, then I will resign before you have to ask me to leave."

"Danny, I am so sorry that we had to have this discussion. I hope you know that I think the world of you and would never do anything to hurt you. It was just something that had to be said."

"Jonathan, I am not angry with you, nor do I blame you for this situation. We live in the world we live in. I am not the first nor will I be the last person who is asked to keep his faith to himself. All I can promise you is that I will do my best not to let this be a problem."

"I can't ask for anything else Danny. Now, can we get back to the details of your new job. Like maybe the effective date of your pay raise," Jonathan said with a smile.

As the two men sat back down to discuss the details of the new position, Danny was silent for a moment then he returned Jonathan's smile and said, "Jonathan, I truly believe that my life starts a whole new and exciting chapter today."

Unfortunately for Danny, he had no idea just how true his words were and that the day's life changing occurrences were not quite complete just yet.

⌒⌒

CHAPTER EIGHT
THE REALTOR

HOLLY ANNE LANGMAN stood outside the restaurant with her cell phone in one hand and a Marlboro Menthol cigarette in the other. She listened impatiently to the voice on the other end of the line. Holly was a real estate agent, and she was speaking to a mortgage loan officer from one of the largest banks in Atlanta. He was delivering the bad news that her latest prospective buyers did not qualify for the $540,000 loan that they would need to buy the home she had convinced them to buy.

"Come on, Troy. Between the two of them, the Stevens make almost $225,000 a year. How can they not qualify?" Her voice was husky from too many cigarettes.

"Holly, you know I'd do this for you if I could, but the underwriters won't budge," the loan officer said. "The truth is, the Stevens have no business trying to buy a $600,000 home. They have too much credit card debt, some late payments on their current mortgage, and she's only been at her new job for two months. I know you must have asked them some of this before you sent them to me."

"Of course I asked them about their credit. They said it was fine except for a few dings here and there." She flipped the butt of her cigarette away and reached into her purse for another.

"Well, either Mr. Stevens is a stone-cold liar, or he has no idea what good credit looks like. Sorry, Holly. This one just won't fly."

"Fine. Fine. Thanks for trying," she said sarcastically and pushed the button to end the call. *Damn. Damn. Damn. I needed that commission.* Holly's share of the commission on the sale would have been just over $10,000, and the sale would have made her the number one agent in her office. *Well, I still have lunch today with Walter Davis. I have a feeling he and his wife are ready to take the plunge, and that house in Sugarloaf is perfect for them. It's a steal at $999,000, and I know they have the money and the credit. If I can just get them out there to see it, I may get it on the books by the end of the month to lock in the top spot in the Million Dollar Sales Club. Jamaica, here I come.*

What troubled her was that Walter Davis was already twenty minutes late for their lunch meeting. She opened her cell phone and found his work number. She lit yet another smoke and punched *Send*. His secretary answered after two rings.

"The office of Walter Davis. May I help you?"

"May I speak to Mr. Davis, please?" Holly asked.

"May I tell him who's calling?"

"Holly Langman. We have a lunch on for today."

"Just a moment, please." Ten seconds later, Walter Davis came on the line.

"Good morning, Holly, or I guess good afternoon would be more appropriate. I'm so sorry, but I have to cancel our lunch."

"I'm sorry to hear that, Walter. Perhaps we could reschedule for tomorrow?"

"Actually, I've changed my mind about buying a new home. My wife and I have been getting so much static from our teenagers about having to leave all their friends and move to a new school that we've decided to just do some renovations and stay where we are until the kids graduate. I do want to thank you for all your efforts, though. I have some folks in my office, so I really have to go, Holly. Have a good day." He didn't wait for a reply.

"Good-bye," Holly said numbly to the dial tone. She mentally calculated the hours she had wasted riding around one neighborhood after another with the Davis couple. Then she thought about a lost commission for the second time that day. *Damn teenagers. Who cares if they have to make new friends? I have to make a living, and this day has gone completely to hell in less than ten minutes. It can't possibly get any worse.* Her appetite having vanished with the commissions, she tossed her latest smoke into the flower pot by the door and headed for her new SUV, a white Ford Explorer.

CHAPTER NINE
JUNIOR

CISCO RAMOS HAD one child: Francisco Miguel Ramos, Jr. Junior's mother had died of a drug overdose when he was two years old. Though there were rumors that Cisco Ram had administered the overdose himself, after learning that his wife was involved with another man, no one had ever repeated them to Junior.

The boy was cocky, spoiled, and, even though he was in the tenth grade, functionally illiterate. He did not want to be in school, and he put forth minimal effort. The public school system was overcrowded as it was, and Junior's school, located in a now largely Hispanic section of east Atlanta, even more so. As a result, he simply got passed on every year to the next grade. If it worked for the football and basketball players, Junior figured, it would work for him.

Who needed school anyway? He saw the money his father brought in and the power he wielded, and he knew that was his future. He was only in school because his father said that until he was eighteen, he would at least have to show up for school. His father liked to tell friends that his son was going to graduate from an American high school with an American diploma.

Francisco Junior was already as mean and crazy as his father. He was just barely five-foot-four with his shoes on and tried to compensate with body-building. Other than wearing lifts in his shoes, he could not make himself taller, but he could make himself stronger. Strong enough that the other kids would save their cracks about his height at least until he was out of earshot. He had been body building for two years, and the results were striking. His chest was thick with muscle, and his arms looked like two jackhammers.

The muscles combined with his small stature made him look like a fireplug. Because of his physique and skin color, some of the kids at school referred to him as "the little brown stump." This was, of course, was a sobriquet which was used only behind his back.

No one dared say such a thing to his face because he would fly into a rage and go on the attack. He would often end up pounding even larger boys bloody, and if he couldn't do it, *Borracho, Cuchillo,* or *El Carnicero* would finish the job later. Most of the boys who ended up tangling with him had learned that it was better to take their lumps from Cisco Junior than face one of his father's friends.

Though he did not yet share his father's predilection for rape, Francisco Junior was not beyond using his reputation for viciousness to get a girl in bed. When he was thirteen, his father had sent one of the LDL "mamas" to deflower him, and Junior now availed himself of them as often as he could. But he was not naïve. He knew the girls slept with him because of his father. He wanted girls to sleep with him because of who *he* was, not because of who his father was.

Recently, Junior had become enamored with a tall, willowy blonde in his home room, at school, named Meredith Stanford. She was a beautiful young woman who got along well with every other student she came in contact with and was easily one of the most popular girls in school. She dated the captain of the junior varsity basketball team and had been voted Queen of the Sophomore Class. Meredith had boys flocking around her and all the girls envying her, so when Junior approached her before homeroom one day, she was not at all surprised.

Junior asked her to be his date for the school dance that was to be held that coming weekend. The girl politely told him she already had a date and that she was, in fact, "seeing" someone. This was not what Junior wanted to hear. Never shy about anything, he told her she didn't know what she was missing and that what she really needed was some "Latino heat." He promised her that after one date with him, she would forget all about any other boy in school.

Meredith then made a tragic mistake. She began to laugh. She looked around to see who had put this little Hispanic boy up to this. There was no shortage of witnesses, but she couldn't tell from their expressions if any of them were in on it. She looked back at Junior.

"Is this like a joke or something?" she asked, smiling at him. The other kids were all beginning to laugh and snicker, some openly, some covering their mouths with their hands.

Junior's hands clenched into fists. "A joke? Are you calling me a joke? You stuck-up skank. You don't diss me. I'll show you who's the joke." He took a step toward her, but before he could reach her, a teacher stepped between them.

"What's going on here?" she asked.

"Nothing," Junior said sullenly, looking away from Meredith and the teacher. "We were just talking."

"Yes ma'am, we were just talking," Meredith chimed in, sorry she had laughed and hoping to avoid any further embarrassment for either of them. "It was a misunderstanding about who I was going to this weekend's dance with. No big deal. Honestly." The teacher looked from one teenager to the other.

"That doesn't sound like a big deal to me, either," she said. "So everyone just move along and forget about this." Meredith turned and walked away immediately, but Junior saw the smirks on the other kids' faces. His face turned bright red, and he ran out of the building.

That night at the gang's clubhouse, a forty-year-old four-bedroom, three-bath house in one of the seedier sections of east Atlanta, Junior beat up one of the gang's regular girls. *Cuchillo* had to pull him off her, and when he asked him what was going on, Junior told him what had happened at school.

Cuchillo, a skinny little 15-year-old when he left Veracruz, was now an attractive young man of twenty-three, with teeth as white as ivory and skin as smooth as fine leather. At five-foot-ten, he matched his leader in stature, if not authority. He had been with Cisco for almost seven years now, and, though *Cuchillo* was the most trusted and deadly of the three generals, he was always on the lookout for ways to curry favor with his boss. *Cuchillo* saw Junior's humiliation as one of those opportunities.

After hearing the details from *Cuchillo*, Cisco called a meeting with his other sharks.

"Find out her name," he commanded. "Then go get her as soon as you can—without attracting attention. Bring her here to me and tell no one, especially my son."

Three nights later, Meredith and her boyfriend, Sammy Wright, went to the movies. At eleven thirty in the evening, as they walked through the deserted parking lot behind the theater, a black cargo van pulled in front of them, and four men jumped out. A fifth man stepped out from behind a car where he had been hiding and grabbed Meredith. Before she could scream, he put one hand over her mouth and the other over her eyes. When her boyfriend whirled around to protect her, *Cuchillo* drove a stiletto under his ribs and into his heart. The boy slumped against a car and slid to the ground without uttering a sound. Meredith was already in the back of the van. There were no witnesses, and the entire episode had taken less than thirty seconds. The young basketball player would bleed to death in less than five minutes. Not wishing to draw any attention, the van drove slowly out of the parking lot and disappeared in the traffic.

Meredith had a wad of cloth in her mouth and a bag over her face. She had not seen any of her attackers, and no one had said a word. After driving around for twenty minutes to make sure that no one had seen the attack and tried to follow them, *Borracho* pulled the van down the driveway and behind the club house. With one assailant holding her by the shoulders and the other by the legs, they hustled Meredith through the back door, down a flight of stars, and into what Cisco liked to call the Game Room.

Meredith heard a door close and a deadbolt click into place. Someone removed the bag from her head and the gag from her mouth, and she stood there squinting in the bright lights for a moment. Then she started screaming. Cisco walked over to her and slapped her across the face. The screaming stopped.

"You can scream all you want after I leave," he said. "No one will hear you. This room is soundproof so our games don't bother the neighbors. But your screaming bothers my ears, so don't do it again while I'm here."

Meredith wiped the blood from her mouth. "What do you want with me? Why are you doing this?"

"We want *you*, girlie," said Cisco. "We want your body for my son to play with. You know my son, don't you?"

"I don't know you—or your son," she said defiantly. "This is a mistake. Please let me go."

"You sure you don't know my son? The joker?"

Her face contorted in terror with the recognition of who this man was and why she was here. "I was surprised that he asked me out, that's all. I was only kidding. I didn't mean to hurt his feelings."

Cisco snorted and said, "Well, he'll be here in a few minutes, and you can tell him yourself. But I think you're gonna have to do more than say you're sorry." He laughed wickedly. "*Much* more than just say you're sorry." He turned to *Cuchillo* and *Borracho.* "Put the gag back in and tie her on the bed. I wish I had a little ribbon to tie around her neck. She's going to make such a nice present for my son."

Meredith was sobbing now. "Please don't hurt me. I'll have sex with your son...I'll have sex with all of you...Just don't hurt me. You can let me go when you're done."

"Oh, we're gonna let you go, *senorita*," Cisco said mockingly. "When my son is through with you, I have some friends in South America who will pay a lot of money for a pretty *gringa* like you. You'll be some good amusement for the workers in the coca fields of Columbia for a few years. Then, when your looks are gone, you'll work in the fields. But one thing is for sure: You will never see your mommy and daddy again."

Before Meredith could say anything else, the gag was stuffed back in her mouth, and she was being dragged towards the bed.

A moment later, there was a knock on the door, then Junior's voice. "Hey, Papa, it's me. The butcher says you wanted to see me."

"Yeah, just a minute. I have a surprise for you." Cisco said.

By now, the girl was on the bed. Her hands tied to the headboard and her feet to the footboard.

"Okay, Junior, come on in." Junior walked into the room and immediately saw the girl on the bed. Her head was turned away from him, so he did not recognize her. "A special, early birthday present for you, my son."

The boy looked at the girl and then at his father. "Come on, Papa, you don't have to do this. I can get chicks on my own."

"You couldn't get this one," Cisco said. He walked over to the bed, grabbed Meredith's head, and jerked it around to face his son.

Junior registered no emotion at first. Then he smiled.

"Well, my son, what do you think of your present?"

"Very nice, Pops. Very nice."

"She's all yours to do with whatever you want."

Junior began to unbuckle his belt. "First I'm gonna give her a good beating. Then she'll be ready for some true Latino heat."

His father motioned to the others. "Come, *muchachos*, let's get out of here and give these lovebirds some privacy." Cisco and his men could hear Meredith screaming as the door closed behind them.

∾

When his daughter had not returned home from her date by one o'clock in the morning, which was thirty minutes past her curfew, Bill Stanford called her boyfriend's house. Sammy's dad seemed less concerned, even though his son also should have been home before that hour..

"You know how kids are these days, Bill," said Sammy's father. "They're probably just at a party or something and lost track of time."

"I don't think so. Meredith keeps her cell phone on all the time and has always been very good about letting us know when she's going to be late. She hasn't called, and she isn't answering her cell."

"Hold on a minute Bill." Stanford heard the man yell to his wife to call Sammy's cell. He came back to the phone a minute later. "That's strange. Sammy's not answering his cell, either."

"Do you have any idea where they were going?" Stanford asked. Once again, he could heard the man consult his wife.

"Marge says that Sammy mentioned maybe going to see the new Batman movie at the Odeon Cineplex."

"Well, maybe I'll take a ride up there just in case they had car trouble or something," Stanford said. "I'll call when I find them."

Meredith's father wrestled with the idea of going out to look for his daughter for fifteen or twenty minutes. First deciding that he should go, then changing his mind and telling himself that he was just being silly and over cautious. Finally, he realized that he was not going to get any sleep until he knew where his daughter was, so he might as well go look for her. He didn't really believe that the kids were stranded in the parking lot of a movie theater, but he felt he needed to do something. He took off his pajamas and threw on an old pair of jeans and a Georgia Bulldog sweatshirt. Halfway down the stairs, he heard the phone ring.

"That's probably Meredith now," his wife said from the top of the staircase.

Stanford picked up the phone in the kitchen.

"This is Detective Donnie Walsh of the Norcross Police Department. I'm trying to reach the father of Meredith Stanford."

"This is her father," Bill Sanford said nervously. "What's wrong?"

"Mr. Stanford, have you heard from your daughter this evening since she left your home with Sammy Wright?"

"No, we haven't, and we're getting pretty worried. Has she been in an accident?"

"We don't know where your daughter is, Mr. Stanford. We just got your name from Sammy's parents. Sammy's body was found in the parking lot of the Odeon Cineplex twenty minutes ago. He had been stabbed. Your daughter wasn't there."

⚭

CHAPTER TEN
QUESTIONS FOR JUNIOR

THE FRIDAY NIGHT murder of Sammy Wright and disappearance of Meredith Stanford was front-page news in Atlanta over the weekend. On Monday morning, detectives from the Gwinnett County Sheriff's Department arrived at the school and began to question students and faculty. Several students and one teacher reported that a Latino boy named Francisco Ramos had been involved in an altercation with Meredith several days before she disappeared.

The detectives were familiar with the name Francisco Ramos and his street name, Cisco Ram. They knew he was the reputed head of one of the most vicious Latino gangs in Atlanta. When they matched the suspected boy's home address from the school files with the known addresses of Cisco Ram, they made the connection. Francisco was immediately summoned to the principal's office. He became sullen and uncooperative as soon as the detectives identified themselves.

"Where were you last Friday night, Francisco?" Detective Walsh asked.

"How do I know man? I don't remember three days ago. Why?"

"Well you better start remembering," Walsh said.

"OK, maybe I was at the gym. Yeah, I was at the gym on Friday night."

"What time did you leave the gym, son?" the second policeman asked.

"About ten—and I ain't your son," Francisco responded sarcastically.

"That's right, he's not your father. Your father is a piece of Mexican scum named Cisco Ram, isn't he?" Walsh said. It was a statement of fact more than a question.

The principal tried to step in, but the second detective laid a hand on his chest and motioned him back. Junior started to say something, then decided against it. He sat with his arms folded across his chest and stared at the floor.

"Did you see Meredith Stanford last Friday night, Francisco?" Walsh asked.

"Hell no, I didn't see that stuck-up anglo bitch. Why would I waste my time on her when I got plenty of *chicas*?"

"Are you sure you didn't see her on Friday night, *muchacho*?"

"No, man. I done told you I didn't see her, so leave me alone."

"Don't you even care why we're asking? Or do you already know?"

"No, man. I don't know, and I don't give a damn why you want to know. All I know is that I was at the gym last Friday night, and I got nothing to do with her."

The detective glared at him and Junior began to squirm a little in his chair. Finally Walsh said, "Her boyfriend was killed Friday night, and she's nowhere to be found."

"What the hell does that have to do with me?"

"Several people saw you ask her out recently, Francisco, and they all said you were very angry when she turned you down."

"Who said that? I never asked her out. I was just killing time talking to her about homework."

The detective turned a chair around, straddled it, and moved it in front of Francisco's chair. He was a big man, and his massive arms engulfed the chair back. He leaned in closer, and Francisco tried to back his chair away, but the other detective was standing directly behind him.

"You weren't talking to her about homework, kid. You were asking her out on a date and she turned you down cold and laughed at you, didn't she, Francisco?" Walsh persisted. He was taunting the boy now. "I bet that really pissed you off and embarrassed you didn't it?"

The school principal had seen enough. He pushed his way past the detective who had been holding him back.

"I think this is getting out of hand now," he said. "I need to call Francisco's parents and get them down here before this goes any further."

Walsh stood up. "No need for that, sir. We can continue this later down at the station, and Francisco can bring his whole family if he likes." He started for the door, then stopped and looked back at Francisco. "You know something about this, kid, and I'm as sure of that as I am that my mama loved me. I think you're dirty, boy, and if you are, rest assured that I'm going to get you. In fact, I'll probably send a patrol car to pick you up later today, so don't leave the area."

After the policemen had left, the principal told Francisco that it would be best if he didn't return to class today. The boy glanced at him, said, "No kidding," and walked out the door.

As Junior drove home, his bravado was replaced by genuine dread. No one had told him that Meredith's boyfriend had been murdered or what was going to happen to Meredith when he had finished with her. *Cuchillo* had merely told him the next morning that every thing was going to be cool and not to worry. His old man had always protected him, and Francisco assumed that his father had some plan to do so this time. For all Junior cared, the *gringa* could rot in hell. He had heard enough stories to know that the women who were victims of his father's attacks could be scared into not reporting the crimes and figured this would be the case with Meredith as well. He had not even had time to consider what the repercussions of the kidnapping and sexual assault might be. Now the cops were talking about murder as well. It seemed to him that the smart thing to do was to wait and see what his father's plan was. He was confident that the great Cisco Ram could handle these dumb *gringo* cops. No worries. He decided to go to the gym and pump some iron.

ↄ∿

CHAPTER ELEVEN
COLLISION COURSE

LATER THAT MORNING, Junior was sweating through a workout at a local gym where his father had bought him a membership, when the cell phone on his hip began to vibrate. He finished his set of bicep curls, took off his gloves, and sat down on the weight bench. He flicked the phone open. It was his closest pal, Jose Palacios.

"Speak to me, bro. What it is?" At sixteen years of age, Cisco Junior still imitated everything he saw the cool set do on TV or in the movies. His current fascination was black rappers.

"Francisco, you know that Anglo kid, Tommy Leland, the one you got into it with in gym class last week?"

"Yeah, Essa, I know the gringo punk. So what?"

"Well he's right here in the Spalding Soda Shoppe, having lunch with his chick, and telling her and his friends how he punked you out in gym class."

"You kidding me, *amigo*? He's saying he punked me out?"

"It's true, man. I just thought you'd want to know."

"Okay, Essa, you tell the little bitch that I'm on my way there now, and you tell Leland to wait for me or *he's* the punk. Make sure you say it in front of all his friends, too. I'm on my way." He snapped the phone shut and headed for the locker room.

"First the cops and now this Anglo punk. Damn, but I'm gonna kick somebody's ass before today is over," he muttered to himself as he entered the shower area.

Twenty-five minutes later, he was sliding into his new Mustang, a present from his father on his sixteenth birthday. He had owned the car exactly one day short of a year and had averaged driving it for two to three hours a day. The first thing he had done after his father gave him the car, was to have it repainted a brilliant green and to have a new stereo system and over sized speakers installed.

He usually did not drive fast because his father had warned him what would happen to his hot car if he lost his license for speeding. But today, as he pictured the grinning face of Tommy Leland and thought about his adversary sitting with his stuck-up Anglo friends making fun of him, he floored the accelerator, throwing gravel all over the cars parked near him, and raced out of the school parking lot.

As he pulled out on to Pleasant Hill Road, he could barely contain his rage. He didn't realize it, but the steroids he had been taking to build up his body were kicking in. The combination of his violent personality and "roid rage" were fueling a fire that only beating up on someone or something could put out.

᠙

Holly Langman was also in a foul mood when she pulled out of the restaurant parking lot. She eased into the flow of the traffic and hit the speed dial for her office. Her assistant answered.

"Miriam, did you finish that MLS sheet for me? The properties over $500,000 in west Gwinnett County?" Holly asked impatiently. She had only made the request that morning and knew that there was no way the poor girl could have completed the task already, but she needed to take out her frustration on somebody.

"No, Holly, I'm sorry, but I haven't even gotten started yet. We had a staff meeting and…."

Holly cut her off. "I don't give a damn what kind of meeting you had. You are my assistant. The houses I sell pay your salary." She swung over to the left-turn lane for Buford Highway and stopped for the red light. "You will do *what* I tell you to do *when* I tell you to do it, or I will be finding a new assistant—meetings or no meetings. Do you hear me?"

Holly lowered her window and put a cigarette in her mouth. She usually didn't smoke in her car because the lingering odor of cigarette smoke was offensive to most of her clients. But this was a special occasion. She was mad, and she wanted a cigarette.

"Ask Bill Jeffers if he can sit on that open house for me this Sunday," she ordered her assistant. "Tell him I'll owe him one. Go do it now. I'll wait."

As she touched the tip of the cigarette with the car lighter, the end of it, a burning cherry of fire, fell into her lap. With her phone in one hand and the lighter in the other, she tried to brush the hot ash off her skirt with the back of her phone hand. Then she heard the driver of the car behind her begin to blow his horn. As she frantically tried to brush the hot ashes away, the horn sounded again and again. She looked up to see that the turn arrow was green, but she didn't have a hand free for the steering wheel. *Could this day get any worse?* she thought. She put down the phone and swept the remaining ashes to the floor. Then, without looking in her rear-view mirror, she stuck her left hand out the window and extended her middle finger. She cursed loudly and pushed the cigarette lighter in for a second try.

❧

Danny Chambers finished his conversation with the principal then paused for a few minutes in the outer office to chat with some of the staff. Before he could leave, Evans came out of his office and announced Danny's promotion to the group. Everyone liked and respected Danny, and the news was met with a loud round of applause followed by handshakes, hugs, and slaps on the back. It was another ten minutes before he could extricate himself from the crowd and get to his car. The first thing he did was pull out his cell phone and call his wife Sheila. When she answered, he said, "Hello, I'm calling for the wife of the new assistant principal at Robert E. Lee Senior High School. Is that lady available?"

"Oh, Danny, you got it!" Sheila screamed. Before he could say anything else, she went on, "And, yes, that lady is not only available but ready for whatever you have on your mind."

"You're such a shameless hussy," he teased. "How about we save that for later. But I would love to take you to lunch for a little preliminary celebrating."

"Okay, Mr. Spoilsport, if that's all you have time for right now, I'll give you a rain check for the rest of the celebration. You just say where and when."

Danny laughed. "Well, I'm near Buford Highway right now, so I'll meet you at J. Alexander's at one o'clock."

"It's a date, cowboy. See you there." Sheila made a kissing sound into the phone, and they both hung up.

Danny turned the key in the ignition, put the car in gear, and made his way out of the parking lot. "Okay, Lord," he said out loud, "please, just once, no major lunch-hour traffic jams." He fiddled with the radio dial of his five-year-old Honda Accord, scanning from NPR to country music to an oldies station, vainly searching for something of interest. He entered the turn lane on Pleasant Hill Road and waited to make a left onto Buford Highway. It was twenty-five minutes until one in the afternoon, and traffic, as usual, was mind-numbing.

The music from Danny's radio was almost drowned out by the heavy thumping of rap music coming from the car in front of him. A green Mustang with a vanity plate that read: CISCO-JR.

∞

CHAPTER TWELVE
ON TELEVISION

THE ATTRACTIVE YOUNG woman inserted the tiny earpiece into her left ear, adjusted it for a snug fit, then let her honey-blond hair fall back, to cover it.

"Mason, are we ready to go live?" she said to the burly cameraman standing just to her left.

"Ready when you are, Lindsey."

"Good. Let's start on your count in five seconds."

The cameraman dutifully counted backward from five. When he silently mouthed the word "one," the woman began to speak.

"Good afternoon, Atlanta. This is Lindsey Adams reporting live from Duluth for Channel 14 Live Action News. We're at the scene of a major traffic jam that was caused by a fatality at the intersection of Buford Highway and Pleasant Hill Road. Traffic has not moved on Pleasant Hill for almost forty-five minutes, but it may begin to clear soon. Reports are still sketchy, but what we do know is that a young Hispanic man was killed when he was struck by a delivery van in the eastbound lane of Pleasant Hill Road at approximately twelve forty this afternoon. The victim apparently left his vehicle at the stoplight and got into an altercation with the driver of the vehicle in front of him while they were both waiting to make a left turn from Pleasant Hill Road onto Buford Highway. It also appears that a third person was involved. He has been identified as Daniel Chambers of Norcross. Witnesses say Mr. Chambers attempted to intervene when the victim attacked the woman who was driving the car in front of him."

The camera panned the intersection while the reporter continued to talk. "As you can see, a Gwinnett County fire truck is just leaving the scene. The woman who was attacked was taken to Gwinnett Medical Center, and Mr. Chambers is still being interviewed by the police. If I can get a word with him when they're finished, I'll try to find out exactly what happened here. All we know for sure is that a young man, whose identity is being withheld pending notification of his next of kin, lost his life after some sort of disagreement with another motorist, tying up this corner of Gwinnett County for almost an hour. This is Lindsey Adams for Channel 14 Live Action News."

಄

Danny was sitting in the back of a police car giving his account of what happened to a uniformed officer when his cell rang. "Oh jeez," he said, "that must be my wife. I was supposed to meet her for lunch, and I completely forgot in all the excitement."

"That's understandable, Mr. Chambers," the officer said. "Go ahead and talk to her. I think we're done here for now, but here's my card. If you remember anything else, please call me at the precinct or on my mobile."

Danny looked at the card, which read: Jimmy Sapp, Patrol Sergeant, Gwinnett County Sheriff's Department.

"Thank you, Officer Sapp. I'll certainly call if I think of anything else."

"I have a few more things to do here at the accident scene, so if you want to sit here in the patrol car and take your call, I doubt anyone will bother you."

Danny said, "Thanks," and the policeman got out, leaving him alone in the patrol car. He answered the call and started to tell Sheila what happened.

"Oh Danny, are you all right?" she asked before he could finish. "You're not hurt, are you?"

"No, I'm doing okay," he said. "Physically, at least."

"What do you mean?"

"I mean that because of me, that boy is dead. I keep thinking there might have been something else I could have done." Sheila could hear the deep sadness in his voice.

"If you hadn't acted when you did, that poor woman could be dead instead of that psycho kid—maybe both of you."

"If I had stopped to think for a second or two, I might have come up with a better plan than just rushing in and starting a wrestling match with a kid in the middle of the street."

"Well, if I was that woman in the car, and the kid, as you call him, was pounding on me and trying to drag me out the window they way you described, I sure as heck wouldn't have wanted my guardian angel to stop and think for a while."

Danny knew she was just trying to make him feel better, but her argument did make some sense.

"I'll be fine, Sheila. Just let me finish up with the police here, and then I'll be home. Do me a favor. Call the school and tell them what happened and that I won't be back today. Tell Johnathan I'll be in to see him first thing in the morning."

"Okay," she said. "I love you."

"Love you, too. See you soon." He hit the End button on his cell and clipped it back to his belt. As he stepped from the patrol car, a voice said, "Excuse me, sir, could I have just a moment of your time?" Danny turned to see an attractive young woman in a smart business suit with a microphone in her hand. She had been waiting patiently behind the police car. Danny had been interviewed by sports reporters enough times to know that where there's a microphone, there's usually a camera nearby. He looked to his right and, saw a man aiming a large video camera at him. His first instinct was to walk away, but he figured they had probably shot some tape of him when he was in the back of the police car. *Maybe my best move here is to go ahead and talk to them,* he thought, *so they don't get the wrong idea and think I'm being charged—or worse, arrested.*

He did not respond to her invitation. He simply turned back to face her and smiled.

"My name is Lindsey Adams, and I work for Channel 14," she said brightly.

"Hello, Ms. Adams, I'm Danny Chambers."

"Mr. Chambers, I've been told by some bystanders that someone saved a woman's life here today by pulling a would-be carjacker off of her. Would you be that hero, sir?"

"I don't know anything about a carjacking, Ms. Adams, and I'm no hero. I just saw that the lady looked like she needed help, so I tried to pull him away from her."

"Other witnesses said the man was savagely beating this woman and trying to pull her through the window of her vehicle. Is that correct?"

"I guess that about sums it up. At least, that's what it looked like to me."

"Where were you when the altercation first started, Mr. Chambers?"

"I was sitting in my car behind the young man who was killed, and he was one car behind the lady in the white SUV. I was on my way to have lunch with my wife when I heard the boy begin to blow his horn repeatedly. Next thing I know, he jumps out and starts pounding on this woman, and...well, I guess you know the rest."

"Mr. Chambers, we don't get many real-life heroes these days, and I know our viewers are going to want to know a lot more about you," she went on breathlessly. "Would you mind telling me what you do for a living?"

"Ms. Adams, if you keep calling me a hero, I'm going to have to leave," Danny said with a smile. "I already told you that I'm no hero. I'm just a high school teacher slash football coach and soon-to-be assistant principal. That's all there is to me. Nothing special and certainly no hero."

"Where do you teach, Mr. Chambers, and what subjects?"

"I'm at Robert E. Lee Senior High, and...."

Sergeant Sapp came to Danny's rescue. "I'm sorry, young lady, but I have a few more questions for this gentleman, so I'm going to have to pull him away from you." He took Danny's elbow and guided him back toward the intersection.

"I really don't have anything else," the sergeant said, "but you looked like you needed someone to bail you out."

"You're so right, officer. Thanks. Now if you'll just walk me to my car, I can get the heck out of here before she catches up to me again."

When they reached Danny's car, the two men shook hands, and Danny drove away. Lindsey Adams watched Danny leave, then she turned back to her cameraman.

"Did you get it all, Mason?" she asked.

"Every heroic bit."

"Good, good, good," she said. "I think we have something special here, Mason. I can just feel it. Let me brush my hair, and we can shoot the last of my on-site comments again."

"Ready when you are," the cameraman said and began the countdown: "Three, two,...."

෧෨

CHAPTER THIRTEEN
THE MORGUE

BORRACHO WAS LOUNGING at the clubhouse. He had just finished eating a pizza and was washing it down with a beer when a live report from Gwinnett County interrupted the courtroom drama he was watching on TV. He sat up straight in his chair and turned the volume up. He heard the reporter say a young Hispanic man was dead in a bizarre incident. He wasn't sure what bizarre meant, but dead was dead. He settled back in his chair. *Why should I give a damn about this?* he thought. *I don't know any young Hispanics that I give a damn about. Except Junior, of course. But he's in school now.*

"Come on," he shouted at the TV, "get this crap off so I can watch my show, man." At that moment, the camera panned the scene, and *Borracho* saw Junior's green Mustang. The car was empty, and a policeman was standing beside it writing something in a note pad.

"*Cristo* no, no," he kept repeating as he ran through the house to the room Cisco Ram used as an office. The door was closed, but Borracho didn't stop to knock. He pushed the door open and found Cisco sitting at his makeshift desk.

"What the hell, *hombre?*" Cisco barked. "You know don't come busting in on Cisco like that. You gone loco, man?"

"Boss, you better call Junior," he said breathlessly. "I just saw his car on the news, and I think something bad might have happened."

"What the hell are you talking about?" Cisco yelled.

"That's all I know, Boss."

Cisco punched a button on his cell and waited for a few moments.

"Damn, I got his voice mail," he said.

"Didn't you tell Junior he better always take your calls—no matter what he was doing?"

"Shut up. I know what I told him." Cisco stood up. "Maybe he's at home. Let's go, man, and you tell me again everything you heard and where this bullshit went down."

The gang's clubhouse was located in one of the poorer sections of town, but Cisco's home was not. He lived in an upper-middle class neighborhood in Decatur in an old, but luxurious house. He had a full-time maid, a gardener, and a pool service to take care of his property. Aside from his three lieutenants—and rarely even them—he never allowed anyone from the gang near his home. As far as his neighbors knew, his name was Jose Flores, and he owned several authentic Mexican restaurants. He seldom went into his yard, always parked in his garage, and never attended neighborhood social functions, so most of them had never seen his face other than through the tinted windows of his car as he passed by.

When the two men pulled into the driveway and Cisco didn't see his son's car, his heart sank. He raced into the house, calling out the boy's name over and over again. No one was there but the maid, who told him that Francisco Junior had not been home since he had left for school that morning.

"So he's not here," Cisco muttered. "That proves nothing. Let's go to the scene of the accident. Maybe we can find out more there."

They turned to leave but never made it out of the house. When they got to the front door, two uniformed policeman were coming up the walk.

"We need to see Francisco Ramos," one of the officers said. "Is he here?"

"That's me," Cisco answered. "What do you want?"

"Mr. Ramos, is Francisco Ramos, Jr. your son?" the officer asked.

"Yeah, he's my kid." The blood was pounding in Cisco's head, and he steadied himself on a railing by the door.

"Does your son drive a late-model green Ford Mustang with 'Cisco Jr' on the license plates?" the officer continued.

"Yeah, that's my son's car. I gave it to him for his birthday a year ago."

"Could we come inside, Mr. Ramos? I'm afraid we have some very bad news."

Cisco grabbed the railing with both hands and held on as pictures of Junior at different ages flashed through his mind. The two officers stepped inside and calmly told Cisco that they strongly believed that his son had been killed in a traffic accident and that he needed to come down to the morgue to identify the body. Then they explained that the accident had happened after his son had gotten out of his car and attacked a woman driving the car in front of him at a stoplight. At that point, Cisco interrupted the officer.

"How do you know it was my son? Maybe someone stole his car, or he lent it to a friend?" Cisco asked in an almost pleading voice.

"We can't be 100 percent positive sir until a family member identifies the body. But, the deceased was driving your son's car, had your son's driver's license in his wallet and appeared to look exactly like the picture on the license."

Cisco's heart sank again. He said, "So what happened? This woman killed my son? Some old lady killed my son?"

"No, sir. Your son was trying to pull the woman through the window of her car when a bystander intervened and tried to pull him off her. We don't have all the details yet, but it appears that your son and the bystander tripped on the median, and your son rolled into the oncoming lane of traffic. He was hit by a truck and apparently died instantly of massive trauma to the brain."

"What about the bystander?" Cisco asked. "Is he dead, too?"

"No, he managed to stay on the median and wasn't injured. The woman your son attacked was taken to the hospital for treatment and observation. It looks like he gave her quite a beating."

Cisco slumped into a large chair and stared out the window toward the street. Tears rolled down his cheeks, but he didn't make a sound for several moments.

"My boy is dead," he finally said softly. "My boy is dead."

The policemen stood up and gave him a chance to absorb what had happened.

"Whenever you're ready, Mr. Ramos, we need you to come down to the county morgue and make a positive ID for the records," said one of the officers. Cisco simply nodded his head several times.

"Yeah, okay," he said absently. "I'll come down in a while."

The officers offered their condolences and left. When they were gone, Cisco said to *Borracho*, "Go find *Cuch*. Tell him to find out who the woman Junior beat was, and, more important, find out who the good Samaritan was. I want the son-of-a-bitch who killed my boy."

As *Borracho* stood to leave, Cisco held up his hand.

"You don't tell nobody—and I mean nobody—that you saw me cry today, man. You tell anyone at all, and it's gonna go hard on you."

"Come on, boss. It's cool. He was your son, man. It's okay if you cried a little." Cisco grabbed him by the front of his shirt and pulled him so close that their faces were only inches apart.

"No, it ain't cool, and it ain't okay. You tell anyone, and I will cut you bad, *hombre*, real bad." He let go of the man's shirt and *Borracho* backed out of the room without saying another word.

Two hours later, Cisco, accompanied by his trusted sharks, walked into the Gwinnett County Morgue. The exterior looked like most municipal buildings, but the inside was darker and quieter. The smell of chemicals was pervasive, even in the lobby and waiting room. Cisco went over to the information desk and stated his business. The bored-looking old black man sitting behind the desk wrote Cisco's name in his log book, told him to take a seat, and went back to reading his newspaper. Ten minutes later, a somberly attired young woman with unnaturally bright red hair came over and introduced herself.

"Mr. Ramos, I'm Helen Starling, assistant county medical examiner. I'm so sorry for your loss."

Cisco looked at her through red eyes and merely nodded.

"Are you ready to identify the body now, sir?"

Once again, Cisco just nodded.

"Yeah, we ready," said *Cuchillo*.

"I'm sorry, but only one of your friends can accompany you to the viewing area, Mr. Ramos. Is that all right?"

At last, Cisco spoke. "Yeah, it's cool. In fact, I don't want no one with me. I'll go by myself."

Cuchillo started to object, but Cisco cut him off with a look and a raised hand. The sharks returned to their seats, and Cisco followed the young woman through a door and down a long flight of stairs, disappearing into the pale green bowels of the building. He returned ten minutes later alone, his eyes even redder than before and still moist. He blew his nose into a white silk handkerchief and stuck it back in his pocket. He did not speak to his friends, pushing past them out the door and into the parking lot.

Cuchillo caught up to him. "Boss, you okay?"

Cisco turned and looked at the men. "His head was smashed. My boy's head was smashed like a Halloween pumpkin. It didn't hardly look like him anymore, but it was." The tears began to flow again, and *Cuchillo* put his arm around Cisco's shoulder.

"Come on, boss, let's get out of here. I'll buy you a beer, man."

∾

Three days later, *Cuchillo* came to Cisco's home to report his findings. It was raining hard, and the wind was pushing the water across the street and lawns in sheets. Lightning repeatedly etched the sky like a giant piece of shattered windshield glass. Cisco was sitting on his back porch drinking a beer and smoking a cigarette when *Cuchillo* approached him.

"Boss, this guy, Daniel Chambers, is a school teacher. He also coaches football. He's married and has a couple of kids—a girl and, get this, a son the same age as Junior. The bitch was a real estate agent. Her name's Holly Langman. She was….."

Cisco held up his hand up to signal silence. After a moment, he corrected *Cuchillo.*

"You mean he has a son the same age my Junior *was* when this hero killed him, don't you, *Cuch*?"

"Yeah. I'm sorry, boss."

Cisco turned and stared at him. "Essa, when are you going to tell me something I don't know? If I just sit here and watch the TV or read the damn paper, I'll know more about this hero than you've told me." Cisco picked up a folded section of newspaper from the table beside his chair and threw it at him.

"Have you read this crap, *Cuch*?" Cisco asked. *Cuchillo* bent down to pick up the scattered newspaper.

"Read what, Cisco?"

"The article on the first page about this hero? What the hell do you think I'm talking about?" *Cuchillo* tried to reassemble the paper and find the front page.

"I don't read the paper too much, boss," he said.

"Well, you should read it, *amigo.* Then you could be intelligent like me. Read the article now, and read it out loud so I can hear it again. I want to hear it again so my blood will boil again, and I can imagine how I will deal with this hero."

Cuchillo finally found the front page and the article:

Norcross Man Is Hero...Again, read the headline of the story by Joe Goddard, senior staff writer for the *Atlanta Record. Cuchillo* began to read it to Cisco:

Daniel Chambers, assistant principal and dean of boys at Robert E. Lee Senior High School in Norcross, was a hero for the second time in his life last week. Chambers likely saved the life of a woman who was being violently beaten by a teenage gang member. According to witnesses, 16-year-old Francisco Ramos, Jr., was striking Ms. Holly Langman about the head and face while attempting to drag her through the window of her car when Chambers, who was in the car behind Ramos, came to the woman's aid by pulling the assailant away from her. In the ensuing struggle, Ramos was struck by a vehicle in the oncoming lane of traffic and died at the scene.

"I have no doubt in my mind at all that if it hadn't been for Mr. Chambers quick action, that vicious animal would have killed me," said Ms. Langman from the hospital bed where she is recuperating from injuries sustained during the incident. "I have no idea what caused that boy to attack me, but I do know that Daniel Chambers was a hero sent from God that day."

This is the second time the popular teacher and coach has been cited for heroism. While serving as a medical evacuation helicopter pilot in Operation Desert Storm in March of 1991, Chambers was awarded the Silver Star from the U.S. Army.

Chambers, who was attached to a unit of the Georgia National Guard from Fort McPherson in Atlanta, was credited with saving the lives of six severely wounded soldiers by flying into heavy enemy fire on two consecutive missions to rescue the men and take them to an Army field hospital. According to Army records, the doctors who worked on the six soldiers said it was almost certain that none of them would have survived had Chambers not risked his own life by flying during daylight hours to reach them instead of waiting for cover of darkness. Chambers received both a Silver Star and a Distinguished Service Medal for his service during Operation Desert Storm.

Cuchillo paused for a moment then started to read again, but Cisco cut him off.

"That's enough. Do you believe this man? Every time I turn on the TV, all I see is his face. All I hear is his name. They're calling him a hero, and they're calling my boy an animal."

Cuchillo didn't know if he was supposed to respond, but having been silenced twice by his boss already, he decided to keep his mouth shut. Cisco went on.

"Can you believe this? My son is dead, and when they talk about him, they're calling him a dangerous criminal, a vicious animal? Well, it's not going to end this way, *Cuch*. No, not this way. This hero is gonna pay for what he did to my boy—and pay hard."

"You damn right, boss," *Cuchillo* chimed in. "He's gonna pay. What do you want me to do?"

"I don't want you to do anything yet," he said, "and you tell the others the same. No one touches this man or his family until I say so. I'm going to make him sweat and sweat some more until I decide where and when to deal with him. This hero is going to wish he was never born." He had been staring out at the rain the whole time, but now he turned and looked directly into the shark's eyes. "You hear me good, *Cuch*? Nobody—and I mean nobody—touches him until I say so."

"I hear you man. I hear you."

Cisco drained the beer in his hand and crushed the empty can in his fist. He scowled at *Cuchillo*.

"Go get me another beer and then leave me alone," the boss said. "I need to think."

CHAPTER FOURTEEN
THE FIRST CALL

DANNY'S CHILDREN HAD always been in awe of their father. Now they had a new reason to admire him. Daniel Jr., his 16-year-old son who everyone called "DJ," had asked his father to retell the story of the fight several times. Once, when he brought some school friends over, Danny had refused, telling his son and his friends that the death of a 16-year-old boy was a tragedy, not something to glorify.

Danny and his son had always been close, and their shared love of football brought them even closer. Danny often said that if he had a dollar for every pass he had thrown to DJ, he could retire early. Saturday afternoons in the fall had always been a day for Danny, Sheila, and the kids to attend a Georgia Tech game in downtown Atlanta or make the hour-long drive to Athens to see the Georgia Bulldogs play.

Since DJ played at Lee on Friday nights and Saturday afternoons were reserved for college football, Danny tried to spend as much time with Melissa and Sheila as he could. In addition to the whole family attending their respective Sunday School classes and then morning worship service, it had been their tradition to go to the matinee at the local multiplex on Sunday afternoons, a tradition Danny could see was slipping away. DJ had a girlfriend and seemed to prefer her company to that of his parents when it came to going to the movies. Even Melissa, at only thirteen, was starting to find things to do with her friends on Sundays.

Both kids had strict weeknight curfews and were always in bed early, lights out by eleven o'clock on school nights. Danny made it a point to visit a bit with each of them before the lights went out. Sometimes he longed for the days when he read stories to them while they snuggled together under the covers on a cold winter night. But he knew that growing up and away from mom and dad was part of God's plan for his children, so he tried to be philosophical about it.

∽

The first phone call came at five minutes after three in the morning, four days after the incident. Danny had not been sleeping well since the boy's death, and he grabbed the phone before it could ring a second time.

"Hello," he said, clearing his throat.

"Daniel Chambers, please," an official-sounding voice said.

"This is he."

"Mr. Chambers, this is Deputy Alan Swanson of the Gwinnett County Sheriff's Department. I'm afraid I have some very bad news. Your son was killed in an automobile accident about an hour ago on Buford Highway. He was pronounced dead at the scene. I'm very sorry."

Danny's heart froze. He gasped for breath. Half-awake now, Sheila was pulling on his T-shirt.

"Honey, what is it?" she asked.

He ignored her and tried to collect himself. "That's impossible. My son went to bed at eleven o'clock tonight. I spoke to him."

"I'm sorry, sir, but he wouldn't be the first teenage boy to sneak out a window and go joyriding," said the voice at the other end of the line.

At the mention of her son, Sheila flew out of the bed and down the hall. Danny sat there numbly on the side of the bed, with the phone in his hand. *This is the phone call every parent fears most—but would it be a phone call? Surely, someone would come in person to deliver such devastating news, wouldn't they?* The voice was saying something about DJ being drunk and several other teenagers in the car also being killed. Danny was too petrified to move. And then Sheila was back.

"DJ is asleep in his bed," she said, trying to catch her breath. "Or he was asleep until I woke him when I turned on the light." Danny put the phone back to his mouth.

"There's been some mistake," he said. "My son is here, and he's fine."

The voice on the other end of the phone changed. It no longer sounded like the same person with whom he had been speaking. Now the voice was low and guttural. The speaker had a distinctly Hispanic accent.

"Yeah, Hero, there was a mistake all right—and you made it. You killed my son, Hero. So I called you tonight to give you a little taste of what it will feel like when this phone call comes in for real, and your boy is as dead as mine. Think about it, Hero. I'll see you around."

The call ended before Danny could reply. He hung up the phone and looked at Sheila.

"What did they say?" she asked frantically. "What did they want?"

"It was a crank call," Danny told her. "Probably some kids. They said DJ got arrested, and I should come and bail him out. Then they started laughing and hung up."

"Well, it isn't funny," Sheila said. "If that number came in on the caller ID, somebody's mother is going to get a call from me tomorrow, I promise you!" She headed downstairs to check the phone with caller ID. Danny mumbled something about that being a good idea and walked into the bathroom. He stood over the toilet for several seconds before his stream began to flow. He couldn't relax, and he couldn't forget what the voice had said about the next time, when the call would be for real and not a crank.

"Darn, the caller ID is showing 'unknown' so I guess I won't be calling any mothers in the morning," he heard Sheila say. "Those kids probably were calling from a pay phone."

"Yeah, you're probably right," Danny said, his head still in a fog. He flushed the toilet and went back to bed. But he didn't sleep anymore that night.

∽

CHAPTER FIFTEEN
THE SECOND CALL

DANNY'S NEWFOUND NOTORIETY was causing him some discomfort at school. He often caught students and other faculty members staring at him as he moved about the school or sat in the faculty lounge eating his lunch. Combined with the onslaught of newspaper reporters and television cameras, all of this was becoming disruptive to the point that, after two days of it, Principal Evans banned all media from the school grounds, which included the parking lot where Danny parked his Honda.

The second threatening call came three days after the first, this one as the family sat down to dinner. When the phone rang, 13-year-old Melissa leaped up to answer it, hoping it was the boy who was her latest crush.

"Not during dinner, Mel," Sheila said. "Tell whoever it is you'll call them back after you finish your homework." Melissa picked up the phone, listened for a second, then hung it up. "They hung up?" her mother asked. "I bet it was some girl who has a crush on DJ," the girl said.

As soon as Melissa returned to the table, the phone rang again. This time, Sheila answered but heard only a dial tone. The phone rang again ten minutes later.

"Let me get it this time," Danny said. He picked the phone up and said, "Hello?"

"About damn time you answered the phone, Hero. Don't let the kid answer it again. You killed my son, Hero, so I'm going to kill yours."

"What do you want me to...." Danny was cut off by the caller.

"Don't interrupt me again, Hero. Bad for your wife's health. You're already a dead man, Hero. No need to take her with you. Like I said, you killed my son, so you gotta die. But it would be too easy for you to just die, Hero. So I'm gonna kill your boy first. Then, after you suffer like I'm suffering, say, in a few weeks or months, I'm gonna kill you. Have a good night, Hero." And then a dial tone.

Before he put the phone back in its cradle, Danny pretended he was still talking to someone.

"I don't want to buy any aluminum siding, pal. Don't call here again. If you do, I'm gonna report you." He slammed the phone down.

"Those people aren't supposed to be calling us at home anymore, are they, Danny?" Sheila asked. "Didn't we opt out or something like that to get our number removed from these lists?"

"Yeah," he said, "but some guys just don't listen. I'll report it tomorrow."

CHAPTER SIXTEEN
G . B . I .

THE NEXT MORNING, Danny took Patrol Sergeant Jimmy Sapp's card to work with him. After he had a cup of coffee, he told his assistant he didn't want to be bothered for a while, went into his office, and closed the door. He dialed the precinct number and was bounced over to Sgt. Sapp's voice-mail. Danny left a brief message about the previous night's phone call and asked the sergeant to return his call as soon as he could. It was almost noon when Danny's phone rang, but it wasn't Sgt. Sapp.

"This is Lieutenant Don Livingston with the Georgia Bureau of Investigation. May I speak to Daniel Chambers, please?"

"This is Danny Chambers."

"Mr. Chambers, I received a call from a colleague in the Gwinnett County Sheriff's Department this morning, Sgt. Jimmy Sapp. I believe you left a message for him about a phone call you received last night?"

"Yes, sir, I did. But what does this have to do with the GBI?"

Livingston gave a brief history of the agency and why it was involved: "Mr. Chambers, the GBI grew out of law passed by the governor in 1937 that created the Department of Public Safety, the same law that created the Georgia State Patrol. This law created a plainclothes investigative division that later became the GBI. The bureau is not connected with the FBI, but it does, in some respects, operate the same way. We help local police and the court system and get involved in specific cases when asked by the local authorities. We also have departments within the bureau that deal with specific threats to the public safety."

"Okay," Danny said, "that all sounds interesting, but why did Sgt. Sapp call you? There hasn't even been a crime committed yet, has there?"

"Mr. Chambers, I head the Anti-Gang unit at the GBI, and if the call you got last night was from Francisco Ramos, then it has everything to do with the GBI, and we need to talk soon. Have you had your lunch yet?"

"No, I hadn't given lunch a thought. Too much on my mind, I guess."

"You're up in Norcross, right?"

"Yes, but I can meet you wherever you say."

"There's a Denny's at Exit 27 off I-285," suggested Lt. Livingston. "Can you be there by one o'clock?"

"Yes, sir, I can be there by one. How will I recognize you?"

"What are you driving?" the agent asked.

"A five-year-old Honda Accord, Georgia license plate AEL-4350."

"Fine. When you get there, just sit in the car. I'll find you."

"Okay," said Danny. "See you at one, then."

Danny arrived at the restaurant first and sat in his car listening to the radio, trying to understand why he was in this situation and if it was part of some greater plan the Lord had for him. He was completely lost in thought when someone tapped on his window, causing him to flinch. He jerked his head to the left to see who it was.

"Sorry, Mr. Chambers, I didn't mean to startle you," said a very dark-skinned African-American man, who appeared to be in his late forties or early fifties. He wore a dark gray suit, a white shirt, and a regimental tie.

Danny thought the man looked the part of a career law enforcement officer. He was about five-foot-nine, a solid one hundred eighty-five pounds, close-cropped hair with tinges of gray at the temples, no facial hair, and dazzling white teeth.

"No problem, lieutenant. I was just somewhere else for a minute there. I'm Danny Chambers," he said, extending his hand as he got out of the car. They shook hands and said, "Nice to meet you" simultaneously, causing them both to laugh. Then the lawman turned serious.

"I'm pressed for time, Mr. Chambers. Do you want to talk while we get something to eat?" The man's voice was deep and stern, and Danny immediately decided that Livingston was not much for small talk. Danny nodded, and they went inside the restaurant. The hostess seated them in a booth, and a waitress took their drink orders.

"No disrespect meant, lieutenant," Danny said, "but you look like you should be a police chief rather than a lieutenant."

Livingston smiled. "I don't know if I should take that as an insult or a compliment, so I'll take it as a compliment, Mr. Chambers."

"It's Danny. As I said, I meant no disrespect."

"Okay, call me Don. Not Donny. Not Donald. Just Don. And you are correct, sir. I am a bit long in the tooth to be a lieutenant. I spent twenty years in the Marines as part of the military police. I retired as a Master Gunnery Sergeant and went to school on the G.I. Bill. I have a criminology degree from Georgia State University. Upon graduation, I was offered an investigator's position with the GBI, an offer I suspect was a result of my skin color. But I can live with that. Worse things have happened in my life because of my skin color."

Lt. Livingston was direct and honest, and Danny took an immediate liking to him. He began to feel hopeful that this man could help him deal with Cisco Ramos. After the waitress took their orders, Livingston got down to business.

"Sgt. Sapp filled me in some, but it would really help if you just start at the beginning, Danny, and bring me up to date." By the time the food came, Danny had finished his story, including the two phone calls.

"So, what's the Georgia Bureau of Investigation's part in all this, Don?"

"Mr. Chambers, my grandmother taught me never to talk with my mouth full, and I really want to get into this club sandwich. What say we eat, and then I'll tell you what I can?"

Danny's appetite had reappeared, so he readily agreed. While the two men dug into their food, Danny tried to make small talk about sports and their families, but the lieutenant, as Danny had deduced early on, was an uninspired a conversationalist, so he decided to stay focused on the food. Fifteen minutes later, Livingston washed the last of his sandwich down with iced tea, wiped his mouth, and leaned in toward Danny.

"You finish eating, Danny," he said, "and I'll do the talking for a while." Danny nodded and took another bite.

"By our best estimate, and, mind you, it could be way off, more than a hundred adult street gangs are currently operating in the state of Georgia, most with operations or affiliates in the Atlanta area. There are black gangs in the Atlanta city limits, along with Chinese, Vietnamese, Puerto Rican, and Mexican gangs—not only in Atlanta proper but in every outlying city as well. Not to mention the skin heads and white supremacist groups. Believe it or not, the Russian Mafia is also alive and kicking here. Whether you live in Norcross, Alpharetta, Stone Mountain, Roswell, or anywhere else around here, there are gangs."

Lt. Livingston went on to tell Danny that while gangs do spend some of their time fighting with each other, they understand that this is a waste of their time and manpower, so they tend to get along unless one of them gets into the other's territory or business.

"At least, this is true of the larger gangs. The smaller ones are always fighting with someone because it's how they identify themselves and their cultures. It's a way for them to feel important.

You don't see them or hear about them until violence erupts or a big case comes to trial, but they're out there. They spend most of their time terrorizing their own people. They're into drugs, prostitution, and everything else from petty theft to murder for hire. Another favorite is extorting money from small businessmen for protection—protection from them, that is. Drug-dealing is where the big money is, and they're all in it one way or another. They have affiliations with national gangs, and most of the gangs operate as part of larger gangs in the prison system. Cisco Ram and his Latino Death Lords are loosely tied to the major Mexican gang known as Los Aztecos."

Danny was getting an education he would rather not have received, but he was fascinated. He kept eating, and Lt. Livingston kept talking.

"The vast majority of whites, blacks, Hispanics, Asians and other ethnic groups who live in this country are as law abiding as you or I. But, the tiny minorities who make up the gangs are as evil, vicious, violent, and mean as anything you can imagine," the lieutenant said. "They do not observe the social niceties of the mafia, whose members are forbidden, by their own warped code of honor, from attacking or retaliating against the women or children of their enemies. These gangs know no law but their own, and for every one we throw in jail, another one pops up. They operate successfully because the people they hurt don't believe we can beat the gangs, or even protect them from the gangs even if they try to fight back or testify against them."

"It sounds a bit hopeless," Danny said when Livingston took a breath. "I mean, how do you fight something like this?"

"We do have our successes," said Lt. Livingston. "Every once in a while someone will testify, and every once in awhile we get a man or—if you can believe it—a woman on the inside. Even more rarely, a gang member who's been sentenced to death by the gang for some transgression will escape and come in to testify. That's how we put away the ones we do."

"What about this guy who's been calling and threatening me?" Danny asked. "What are the odds that you can stop him?"

"Unfortunately," said Livingston without batting an eye, "Cisco Ram is one of the most violent and sadistic characters we know of, and we can't pin a thing on him. He's been arrested several times and even indicted twice, but aside from a few petty crimes he committed as a youth, he's always been found not guilty or the case has been dropped due to a lack of credible witnesses. Everyone who ever agreed to testify against him either developed a case of amnesia, disappeared or turned up dead, before the trial. We've arrested more than a few LDL members, but none of them was close enough to Cisco to deliver any meaningful testimony against him. He gives all his orders through his three top lieutenants. No one else has ever heard him make a threat, order anything illegal done, or seen him commit a crime. Unless we get one of his three top guys, *Los Tres Tiburones*—the three sharks as he calls them—to testify, we're going to have a very tough time tying him to anything."

"So I guess you're saying that if Cisco Ram is coming after me and my family," Danny said, setting aside the remainder of his lunch, "I'm in a lot of trouble."

"I can't lie to you. Danny. The answer has to be yes."

"Can you help me?" The gravity of the situation had finally gripped Danny. "I mean, I know these gangs are a problem, but I never knew it was this bad."

"Danny, saying that the gangs are a problem is like saying Custer had a problem with some Indians along a river in Montana. As for helping you,

I hope we can. We'll do our best. I not only want to protect you and your family from Cisco, but I want Cisco. I mean, I really *want* Cisco."

"What do we do first?"

"I want to get a recording device on your phone so we can record the threats as they come in. If we can match Cisco's voiceprint to these calls, we have the beginnings of a case against him. Nothing to put him away for too long, but at least a start."

"How's that going to work? Will there be a policeman in our home sitting beside the phone all the time, like in the movies?"

Livingston's face gave no indication that he saw any humor in Danny's comment. "No, nothing as dramatic as that. We'll just hook the recording device up to the phone line, and you can activate it when a call from Cisco comes in. The rest of the time it will be inactive."

"Let's do it!" Danny said. He felt better knowing he could at least take some action rather than sit around and worry about his safety and the safety of his family.

"I'll need a judge to sign off on this so that anything we get will be admissible in court," Livingston cautioned. "But with Cisco's background, that shouldn't be a problem."

"Is there anything else you can do in the meantime, or anything else I should do?"

"Well, I can't put your house under surveillance, if that's what you're asking. We just don't have the manpower. Have you told your wife and children what's going on?"

"No, I didn't want to alarm them until I had a better idea of how serious this threat was."

Livingston frowned. "It's serious, Danny, and it's time for you to tell them. You'll all need to be very careful from now on. Don't put yourself in any dangerous situations if you can avoid it."

"What do you mean?"

"How many children do you have, Danny?"

"Two. My son DJ is 16, and my daughter Melissa is 13. Why?"

"How do they get home from school?"

"They ride the school bus."

"And is your wife there every day when they get home?"

"Yes, Sheila doesn't work outside the home."

"So, you're saying your kids stand unguarded at a bus stop every morning and every afternoon, and your wife is home by herself all day until the kids get back. Even then, you have a woman and two teenagers in a house that is probably no more secure than the typical suburban home. Your wife has to go to the grocery, the laundry, and any number of other places during the week, doesn't she?"

"Of course she does."

"That's a lot of opportunity for someone who wants to harm one or all of them, Danny."

Danny was trying not to show the fear that was beginning to grip him, but his face betrayed him. "So, what are we supposed to do—live in a cave or a fortress somewhere until this animal is put behind bars?"

"Actually, if that were possible, that would be great," Livingston said without a trace of irony. "But we both know it isn't. I'm just pointing the need for you and your family to take certain precautions."

"Such as?"

"Do you have a security system?"

"No."

"Get one. Tell the kids to stay together and watch for strangers around the bus stops, the house, and near school. Tell your wife not to go out any more often than she needs to and to be very aware of anyone around her or her car when she's out. Tell her to shop with someone, if possible. Do your wife and children all have cell phones?"

"Sheila does, but I don't think kids the age of mine need a phone, even if everyone else seems to think so," Danny said defensively.

"Tell your wife to keep her phone with her all the time, and get phones for the kids. Have all of them set so the internal locator signal is always on."

"What does that mean?"

"Almost all cell phones now come with a transponder device that can be tracked as long as the phone is on. The device can be set to work all the time or only when you dial 911. Tell your wife and kids to make sure their phones are on anytime they leave the house. One more thing—and this is very important—as soon as you get the new phones, call me with the numbers then send me a written request asking a judge to give me an open subpoena to ping the number anytime to obtain a location."

"What does all that mean, Don? A subpoena?" Danny was feeling overwhelmed.

"Yeah, a subpoena. Law enforcement can't just start pinging someone's phone trying to locate them without permission from the courts. It's considered an invasion of privacy. Trust me on this, Danny, and let's hope there never comes a time we need to use the locator. But if we do, having the court's and your permission may mean the difference between life and death."

"Fine. Fine. I trust you, Don. What else?"

"Do you own a gun?"

"No. And, lieutenant, I don't think my Christian faith would allow me to use a gun on another human being, even to save my own life."

"I understand, Danny, but I must emphasize that these people are serious about hurting you. But let's set aside your life for a moment. If they get the chance, these people will make good on their threats to your family. Before this is over," said Livingston, "you may have to make a decision between your feelings about hurting another human being or the safety of your family."

"That would be a hard decision to make. My faith is the core of my life, and my family *is* my life."

"Then let me say it again in a different way. Before this is over, you may need to choose between killing someone or watching your family die. I suggest you do some praying and some soul-searching about this," Livingston said. "By the way, do you even know how to fire a gun?"

"I was in the military," said Danny. "I spent some time in Iraq."

Livingston raised an eyebrow. "You were in the military, but you don't think you can use a gun to protect yourself?"

"I flew Medical Evacuation choppers,"said Danny, growing tired of the all questions. "It's a long story."

"Don't quote me on this, Danny, because if you do, I'll deny it. But if I were you, I'd buy a shotgun. You may have doubts about whether or not you can use it, but don't you think it's better to have it and then decide not to use it than the other way around? I'd teach my wife how to fire it, and I'd keep it where I could get to it in a hurry. Keep the shells accessible as well, but not with the gun—and not where the kids can find them."

"Is all this legal?"

"It's legal to purchase a shotgun in the state of Georgia without a waiting period and without a permit. It's what I'd do if I were you," Livingston said grimly.

Danny sat there silently for a moment, and the agent seemed to be finished with his suggestions.

"I really have to get back to school, Don. Is there anything else I should know?"

"Not that I can think of at the moment. We'll get someone out to your home with the recorder as soon as possible. Call me if you hear from Cisco." Livingston paused. Danny didn't think the expression on the lieutenant's face could get any more grave, but it did. "In the meantime, Danny, be careful."

෨෨

CHAPTER SEVENTEEN
DIAMOND GIRLS

THE CITY OF Atlanta sits at the geographic center of the Atlanta statistical metropolitan area, but accounts for less than 10 percent of its population. The ring of smaller cities that surround it—Stone Mountain, Doraville, Norcross, Sandy Springs, Marietta, Austell, College Park, Lithonia, and others—stretch out from the city of Atlanta like spokes on a wheel.

Doraville, to the northeast, was once home to a large General Motors assembly plant that employed thousands of highly paid blue-collar union workers. The city was peaceful and clean, not unlike hundreds of other factory towns around the United States. But when hard times fell on General Motors, they soon fell on Doraville. The plant was eventually closed, and many of the skilled workers moved elsewhere in search of jobs that would match their union incomes. Housing became a buyer's market, and new residents flooded in. Most were of Asian or Latin descent, and their cultures soon became the dominant cultures of the tiny Atlanta suburb. Korean, Chinese, and Vietnamese markets and restaurants sprang up in every strip mall. Mexico provided the vast majority of Latin immigrants, but Panama, Guatemala, Honduras, and El Salvador, among others, contributed as well. Mexican restaurants seemed to be on every corner.

The women typically found work at hotels or in private homes as maids or cooks. The men learned construction skills and became part of the Atlanta building boom. Those who did not acquire such skills became gardeners and yardmen, euphemistically labeled, "landscape technicians." Most of these people worked hard and sent as much of their money as they could back to their families back in their native countries. Those who had been criminals in those countries, became criminals in their new country and continued to prey on their own kind. Women who wanted to earn more than a housekeeper's pay often chose to work in strip clubs, and Atlanta, like most major cities, had its fair share of those establishments. Atlanta, in fact, had been home to one of the most infamous clubs in the country. The Gold Club had made national headlines when it closed down after the owners were charged with offenses ranging from money-laundering to prostitution. Several high-profile professional athlete's marriages hit the rocks when the club's list of clients was made public.

Maria Elena Santana worked at a strip club. Tiffany's Diamond Girls was the most elegant of all the clubs in Atlanta, and the girls who performed there made the most in tips. Maria was one of the top earners. She was 23 years old and had a 4-year-old daughter whose father, a young Anglo named Johnny Winters, was serving five-to-seven years in the Florida State Penitentiary at Raiford for drug-trafficking. Maria, who danced under the stage name Tequila, was born in Mexico City and lived there until she was 15, when her father brought her, his wife, and Maria's three brothers to the United States to find a better life. Instead, the family had been in Atlanta for less than a month when her father was found with a knife in his back. A knife driven there by another Mexican expatriate who wanted the job Pedro Santana y Palacios had secured in the maintenance department at a Marriott Hotel. Marriott was considered a good employer that paid a fair wage and treated their people well, even helping new immigrants learn English.

The man who killed Pedro simply wanted to work where his girlfriend worked. There were no openings in the maintenance department, so he made one. The morning after he stuck a knife in Pedro's back, he applied for a job in maintenance. Two days later, he was hired.

After Maria's father died, the family remained together. Her mother took a job as a maid at the same Marriott, and her three older brothers found jobs in construction. Maria was sent to public school. She was a good student and quickly learned to speak English. Over time, she grew tall and beautiful. She dreamed of going to college to study fashion design, but before that could happen, she met Johnny Winters.

The handsome, athletic, blond swept her off her feet and into his bed less than two days after they met at the local Starbucks. He told her he was a successful importer-exporter and promised she would never have to worry about money again after they were married. She moved into his apartment despite the heated objections of her mother, and she and Johnny set up housekeeping.

Johnny did not actually export anything. He did, however, import illegal drugs. Maria discovered she was pregnant a week after Johnny was arrested. When she went to her mother with the news, her mother called her a whore and told her she could not come home. Maria was so ashamed that she walked silently down the steps and out of her mother's life. Because of the difference in their ages, Maria and her brothers had never been close. She was on her own now.

If meeting Johnny Winters had been bad luck, meeting Francisco Ramos was a disaster. At a time when she was most vulnerable—pregnant, alone, and penniless—Cisco Ram came into her life like a knight on a white charger. He got her a job as a receptionist at an apartment complex and let her move into one of the bedrooms in the gang's clubhouse. This wasn't where Cisco lived, but once she had settled in, he began to spend more nights there. Initially, Maria did not know she was living in the midst of a gang. It just seemed like a big, happy family, the head of which had taken a liking to her.

By the end of her first week, she and Cisco had become lovers. And although she did not enjoy his style of lovemaking, she felt indebted to him. If he could get pleasure from her body, she reasoned, it was a small price to pay. She would soon realize she had let the devil himself into her life and her bed.

At first, Cisco and the family treated her well. But after the baby arrived, everything changed. Cisco pushed her hard to get her body back in shape. When she did, he took her to Diamond Girls and put her to work. The day manager was a business associate of Cisco's, in the sense that Cisco supplied him drugs, so he was glad to do a favor for the man who provided his cocaine and weed.

Maria emphatically refused to become a nude dancer, but Cisco changed her mind. He took her down to the playroom and stripped her naked. While *Carnicero* and *Borracho* held her face down on the bed, he beat her on the buttocks and thighs with a thin leather belt. Being careful not to break the skin and damage his valuable merchandise, Cisco still managed to inflict immense pain. After the beating, Cisco forced her to have sex with him. When he was finished with her, she lay there exhausted and in agony.

"Now, bitch, you know what happens when you say no to Cisco," he said sternly. "This will happen every day until you say yes and take the job. If you go to the police, I will kill your mother, your brothers, and you. If you try to run away, I will kill your mother and your brothers, and then I will find you and kill you. After I find you and kill you, I will take your daughter and raise her to be my whore. Now, I'm going to let some people come and talk to you and tell you who I am. I know you think you know me but, you don't know the real Cisco Ram. You know only what I wanted you to know. They will tell you that everything I say is true. I have done these things before, and I will do them again. As for me and you, I don't care about you. You are not my woman. From the first moment I saw you, I knew that after you dropped that baby, you could make me a lot of money."

Maria lay on the bed and cried for a long time. Later, some people she had never seen before came to talk to her. They all said the same thing: Don't cross Cisco. He's a savage and a killer. Whatever he asks you to do, you do it. When they left, she cried some more. The next day, she told Cisco she would become a dancer. Three days later, when the red whelps on her legs and buttocks had disappeared, Cisco took her to Diamond Girls. As soon as they went into the manager's office, Cisco got down to business.

"Okay, girl, my friend don't have all day," he said. "Get your clothes off and show him what you got."

Maria had not anticipated this and hesitated for a second. Cisco took a menacing step toward her.

"You want me to help you strip down, girl?"

"No, no," she said, instinctively raising her hands to protect herself. She slowly unbuttoned her blouse, pushed her skirt down to the floor, and stepped out of it. She stood before them in her bra and white cotton panties. She knew what they expected now, but she was slow to move.

"Damn you, girl," Cisco shouted. "I told you not to waste this man's time. Get naked, and I mean naked *right now*."

The manager was becoming uncomfortable with the confrontation happening in front of him and he quickly said, "No, that's good man. I am in a rush this morning and I can see the merchandise just fine the way she is. No need to take off anything else right now."

"She does what I tell her to do whether you think it is necessary or not."

Maria stared down at the floor and reached behind her to unsnap her bra. When it hit the floor, she removed her panties. She stood there in silence, hands at her sides, still looking at the floor.

The man whistled. "I lot damn, Cisco, she looks just like Jennifer Lopez. This girl will make us a lot of money, if you can get her to cooperate."

"Oh, I can get her to cooperate, my friend. That's my specialty."

"Okay, buy her some outfits to dance in and get her here tomorrow at eleven o'clock, and we'll get her started."

Three years later, Maria was earning $4,000-$5,000 a week and giving half of it to Cisco. She no longer had any inhibitions about dancing nude. During her first six months at the club, Cisco had beaten that out of her. She considered herself just a piece of meat and understood that her body belonged to someone else. She no longer cared if men stared at her body and pawed at her while they told her how pretty she was. What did it matter? The only thing she cared about was her daughter. Portia was 4 years old now and had never seen her father. She didn't know he was in jail. When she finally asked her mother about "Daddy," Maria said he was an American soldier who had been killed in Iraq. She showed Portia a picture she had found of a young blond boy in a soldier's uniform and told her it was her father.

Sometimes the only way Maria could get through another day at Diamond Girls was to think about being home with Portia. Maria knew there would come a time when she could no longer compete with the new, younger girls for tips and would be of no value to Cisco. So, she saved her money and hoped that when that time came, she and Portia could get away from him for good.

∽

CHAPTER EIGHTEEN
THE THIRD CALL

WHEN DANNY GOT back to his desk after his meeting with the GBI agent, the phone rang. He picked it up and said, "Danny Chambers."

"Hey, Hero, how you doing today?" Sometimes Danny thought he might be talking to Cisco Ram himself; other times, someone else. The lieutenant told him it was a common ploy to get several voices involved in calling the victim, so he could never testify for sure what Cisco had said or what threats he might have made, and which ones came from someone else. This time, he thought it really was Cisco.

"I'm okay, I guess," Danny said calmly. "What do you want from me? Why do you keep calling me?"

"Hero, you don't sound happy to hear from me? Aren't you happy to hear from me, Hero?" Before Danny could respond, the voice went on, "Well, no matter if you're happy or not. You asked me what I want from you? Here's what I want: You come to meet me today, and we can talk this over, you know, maybe settle our differences? What do you think, Hero?"

"I don't know if I want to meet you today—or ever. I just want you to leave my family and me alone. People tell me you're a killer."

"I'm a killer? I'm a killer?" The voice rose an octave. "*You're* the killer, Hero. You killed my son. Or have you forgotten that already?" As quickly as the rage had surfaced, it disappeared. The voice was relaxed, measured again. "You don't have to worry about me hurting you, Hero. I said I was going to kill your son and then wait a few weeks for you to suffer like I'm suffering and then kill *you*. Isn't that what I said, Hero? I said I was going to take your son from you just like you took mine. But I'm thinking that over, Hero, and maybe we don't have to do it that way. So, why don't you meet me today at, let's say, maybe five o'clock?"

Danny hesitated a moment, but he knew that sooner or later, somewhere, sometime, he would have to face this man.

"All right, I'll meet you at five o'clock. Where do you want to meet?

"You know a place called Diamond Girls, Hero?"

"I've seen it, but I've never been inside. Yeah, I know where it is."

The voice became playful. "You've never been in it? You gotta be lying, man. Everybody has been to Diamond Girls. But if you're not lying, Hero, then you're in for a treat, my friend, a big treat."

"I don't want to meet you there," Danny said abruptly. "Pick somewhere else."

The voice became menacing again. "If you want to talk to me about this situation with your son, Hero, we do it today. We do it at five o'clock, and we do it at Diamond Girls, or we don't do it—*ever*. You hear me, Hero?"

Danny started to answer but the voice cut him off.

"Be there at five, or you can forget about saving your son's life, Hero. You hear me? I know what you look like. I will find you there." Cisco terminated the call.

Danny put the phone back in its cradle and sat looking at his clenched fist. He had been gripping the phone so tight his knuckles were white, and he struggled to unclench his hands. He had not lied to Cisco when he said he had never been inside Diamond Girl's. In fact, he had only been in one strip club in his life and that was back in college when he and some other guys on the football team had sneaked out after bed check at an away game in New Orleans. Danny had gone along with his teammates but, once he entered the club, he had drank a single beer and then slipped out and gone back to the hotel.

Danny was a rarity in the modern world, an attractive, physically fit, heterosexual male with a perfectly normal sex drive whose wife was the first and only woman he had ever slept with. Danny and Sheila dated through high school and got married during his sophomore year of college. The football coach had a strict rule about not keeping married players on the team, but Danny told him that Sheila was pregnant, and they had to get married. The coach knew Danny needed the scholarship to get through school, so he gave the young man a break and let him stay on the team as long as he kept the marriage quiet.

Sheila wasn't pregnant, but Danny knew this ruse was his only chance of getting married and staying on the team and in school. He liked and respected his coach, and it hurt Danny to have to lie, but he loved Sheila and wanted to live together with her as man and wife. A month after a very small and quiet wedding, he told the coach that Sheila had miscarried.

In their eighteen years of marriage, Danny had never cheated on Sheila, and though he was aware that a lot of pretty girls seemed to be attracted to him, he had never even considered it. Danny didn't think of himself as particularly good-looking. In fact, he hadn't thought much about his physical appearance since his teen years when, like all adolescent boys, he was obsessed with avoiding acne, attracting girls, and finding out all he could about sex. He had also been paranoid about being skinny. Early on in high school, he realized that skinny boys got bullied and had to fight a lot. Muscular boys didn't get picked on, and they usually only fought with other boys when they felt like it. This seemed to Danny the better way to go, so he went out for the junior varsity football team and began working out in the school weight room vigorously and often. By the time he headed off to Valdosta State to play football, he was a solid two hundred fifteen pounds on a six-foot-two frame. As for his curiosity about sex, between having received "the talk" from his father, reading books, listening to his friends, watching TV, and going to the movies, Danny had pretty well figured it all out without ever actually having done it. By the time he and Sheila began to date seriously, his Christian faith was sufficiently strong to counteract his youthful male hormones. Though their make-out sessions sometimes got quite heavy, Danny or Sheila always stopped the proceedings before they went too far.

Sheila had always told Danny how much she adored his baby blue eyes, lustrous dark hair, and perfectly formed sparkling white teeth. Danny was always embarrassed when she said these things and usually laughed it off by saying something like, "You can thank the Good Lord for the blue eyes and the dentist for the teeth." It sometimes amazed his wife that her hunky husband not only loved only her but seemed totally oblivious to the effect he had on women of all ages.

That was because Danny's world was firmly anchored in his family and his love for his wife, which far surpassed any desire for another woman. Once, when he was out of town attending a coaching seminar, one of the other coaches suggested they go to the bar after dinner and see if they could pick up some girls. Danny begged off, saying he needed to get to bed early. The coach called him a sissy and told him Sheila would never know. Danny looked the man in the eye and simply said, "But I would." Then he went to bed. That group never again brought up the subject of picking up women around Danny.

Danny still thought his wife was the most desirable woman in the world. He wasn't afraid of being tempted in Diamond Girls; but he would be embarrassed to be seen there. However, he knew he had to go and hoped the meeting would be brief and private. He parked his car in the back of the club and self consciously walked in the front door of Diamond Girls promptly at five o'clock that afternoon.

Now what? he thought. *Do I have to pay a cover charge? Do I seat myself?* As he stood in the darkened foyer of the sprawling club, with waves of raucous music, hooting, and cheering washing over him while he waited for his eyes to adjust to the dim light, an attractive young woman in an evening dress approached him.

"Hi, I'm Autumn, your hostess," she said. "Welcome to Diamond Girls. Is this your first time with us?" Danny mumbled that it was, and Autumn continued on with her welcome speech. "Well, so you don't have to fumble around for bills to tip the ladies or pay for your drinks, you can purchase books of Diamond Dollars in denominations of $1, $5, $10, $20, or $50 using any major credit card. I can seat you now and take your credit card and your first drink order all at once. You'll have a pocket full of Diamond Dollars before you know it."

Her smile is brilliant even in the low light, Danny thought. He tried to pull himself together. "Uh...uh...not just yet, Autumn. I'm supposed to meet someone here, and I don't know how long I'll be staying. Can I just stand here at the door until my party spots me?"

Autumn gave him a sardonic grin. "Oh, you mean stand here and look at all these beautiful, almost naked women without spending a dime?" she asked in an exaggerated southern accent. "Why, that just wouldn't be polite, now would it?"

"No, I'm sorry," Danny said, turning red. "That's not what I meant. Can I just get something to drink and sit down at the bar, then?" Autumn said that would be just fine for starters and led him to the bar. The bartender slid a bowl of pretzels in front of him.

"How are you doing today, sir?" he asked.

"I'm fine, just fine," Danny responded. "How about you?"

"Hell, man, I couldn't be any better, could I? I get paid to stand here all day, look at beautiful babes in their birthday suits, and talk to nice people like you? Couldn't get much better. What can I get you?"

Danny had no moral problem with alcohol. He had had a few in his college days and a few more during his time in the military. He didn't think it was forbidden by the Bible, and he was sure Jesus Christ had turned water into wine, not grape juice, when the host of the wedding party ran out of wine. Danny also doubted that Jesus passed around a cup of grape juice and told His disciples to drink it in remembrance of Him. But, alcohol was expensive, and he did not particularly like the taste of beer, which he figured was the cheapest option. He didn't mind an occasional glass of wine with dinner if it was a special occasion, but he was driving tonight and didn't know how long Cisco was going to make him wait. One beer might lead to two, and the thought of spending ten or twelve bucks of his hard-earned money on beer while he waited for a crazy man didn't appeal to him.

"I'll have a Diet Coke," Danny said finally.

"Okay, buddy, but the soft drinks cost as much as the beer," the bartender said sympathetically.

"That figures," Danny said. "But I'll still take the Diet Coke."

"Coming right up," the bartender said as he moved down the bar toward the soft-drink dispenser.

When the soda arrived, Danny took a sip and looked around the room. There must have been at least fifteen gorgeous women dancing on tabletops, or sitting at tables or in booths, drinking with their customers. Danny was thankful that Georgia had recently prohibited smoking in public places. His primary recollection of the strip club in New Orleans was the smell of stale liquor mixed with the fragrance of cheap perfumes and a suffocating cloud of cigarette smoke.

He couldn't see anyone near him who resembled the man in the photos the police had shown him of Cisco Ram, and everyone else was hidden by the darkness and the writhing bodies of the tabletop dancers. He decided to keep his eyes on the television over the bar and prayed silently that Cisco would arrive soon. Forty-five minutes passed. Finally, at ten minutes before six, Danny decided he had waited long enough. He motioned to the bartender to bring his check. When the man walked up, Danny said, "I have to go, friend. What do I owe you for the Diet Coke?"

"Well," the bartender said, leaning in, "seeing as how you're wearing a wedding ring, I guess you're married, so you ain't gay. And seeing as how you haven't been looking at my ladies, let's just say this one was on the house. Next time you come by though, I'll let you buy me a beer. How's that work for you?"

"That'll work. And thanks for the Coke. You have my promise that if I ever come back in here, I'll buy you a beer, and a cheeseburger to go with it."

The bartender laughed, and Danny slid off the bar stool and headed toward the door. When he reached the foyer, he felt a hand on his shoulder.

"Hero," said a voice from behind him. "Where you going, man? We haven't had our talk yet."

Danny turned around. "Are you the man who's been calling me?"

"Calling you? Yeah, I called you to arrange this meeting, if that's what you mean, Hero," Cisco said evasively.

"Why can't you just leave me alone? Your son's death was a tragedy, but it was an accident. I never meant to hurt anyone." Danny started to ask the man why he was so late but decided there was no point.

"Hey, Hero, calm down, man. Just calm down. That's why we're here. Just to do some talking and try to straighten this out. Come on back in and let me buy you a beer."

Danny eyed the man suspiciously. He was taller than Danny expected for a man of Mexican descent, and he was barrel-chested, with short but powerful-looking arms. His hair was jet black and combed straight back from his forehead. He was clean-shaven except for a thin mustache that was as dark as his hair. The mustache covered his entire upper lip and hung down the sides of his mouth like a Fu Manchu. Danny's experience as a football coach put the man at about five-ten and easily two hundred pounds. *This is not a guy I want to meet in a dark alley,* Danny thought to himself.

Cisco led Danny back into the lounge, but instead of going to the bar or one of the tables, he led Danny up a small flight of steps to the area where private dances took place. They sat down in a dimly lit booth with opaque curtains that could be drawn to completely enclose its occupants. A waitress soon materialized to take their orders—a beer for Cisco and another Diet Coke for Danny.

"Why did we have to meet here?" Danny asked when the waitress was gone. "This doesn't seem like a good place for a serious conversation."

Cisco leaned back and lit a cigarette. "We met here because I like the place," he said matter-of-factly. "I like beautiful women with no clothes on, and I like the music and the beer. Is that all right with you, Hero? By the way, don't worry about the cigarette. I know there isn't supposed to be any smoking in here, but the manager is a friend of mine and he doesn't care. What's the worst that could happen to me if the no-smoking cops come in, anyway?" He laughed at his attempt at humor, but Danny just stared at him.

The drinks were delivered by a different waitress, one who was dressed like one of the dancers. After she set the drinks in front of them, she sat down next to Danny.

"This is my friend Tequila," Cisco said. "She's gonna sit with you for a minute while I make a phone call." Before Danny could protest, Cisco was up and out of the booth. Danny wasn't sure what was going on. The girl picked up Cisco's beer and took a sip. Danny studied her as she drank. She was a stunning young woman, with long dark hair pulled up in a bun and perfect teeth that matched the color of the pearls on her choker. At the top of her left breast, she had a small tattoo, a skull with the letters "LDL" above it. Below the death's head was the word "Mexico." Her outfit was similar to a two-piece bathing suit that had been augmented with thousands of tiny sequins and hundreds of tassels. Her breasts seemed on the verge of spilling out of her top, which only made Danny more nervous.

"Do you like what you see, *senor*?" Tequila asked, putting the beer down.

Danny's face turned red. "No...I mean yes...you're very pretty," he stuttered. "I didn't mean to stare. I just don't know what's going on here. I was supposed to have a meeting with Mr. Ramos, but he was late...and now he's gone again....and...." He realized he was jabbering like a school boy, so he shut up.

"Relax," she said. "It's all right if you look at my body. That's what men come here to do, isn't it?"

"Yes, I guess so...I mean, yeah, yeah sure...that's why guys come here." He knew he was stuttering again and tried to change the subject. "That's an interesting tattoo you have."

She looked at him for a moment. "It's not a tattoo, *senor*," she said with no trace of humor. "It's a brand." She stood up suddenly and, before Danny realized what she was doing, reached behind her and unsnapped the top of her costume. A second later, she reached down and unsnapped the sides of the bottom of her costume and pulled it away from her body. Except for a tiny G-string, she was totally nude.

Danny got up to leave. "No, no thank you," he said, averting his eyes. "I don't want a dance. I have to go now."

Tequila put her hands on his shoulders and pushed him back down in the booth. He was surprised at her strength, and he felt her nails bite into his flesh. "No, you cannot leave yet," she insisted. "I *must* dance for you. If I don't, Cisco will beat me tonight. Please, do not go."

"What are you talking about?" Danny asked, trying to make sense of the situation. "Why would he beat you if you don't dance for me? All I know is if he isn't back soon, I'm leaving. And I don't need a dance."

Even in the dim light, Danny could see tears welling up in the young woman's eyes. "He's not coming back, *senor*. He told me to give you a very special and very sexy dance before you left. He said his friends would be checking on us to make sure I did. He said if I let you leave without a dance, he would go very hard on me tonight. *Senor*, I have been with Cisco for many years, and I know what hard means. It means he will beat me and then give me to his friends for the night. That's how he is. Please stay."

"Why have you stayed with him, then? If he does these things to you, why don't you leave and call the police?"

Tears streamed down her cheeks. "I cannot do either," she said softly. "He will hurt people I love, and the police cannot protect them. That's how it is. He owns my life and will continue to own it until I am of no more use to him. Please. They may already be watching us. I must dance for you or face Cisco tonight. It's like I told you, *senor*. The image on my breast is not a tattoo. It's a brand."

Danny stared at her for a few seconds without speaking. He wanted to say something, but he couldn't think of anything appropriate. *This poor girl is in the same situation I am* he thought. Finally, he just shrugged his shoulders and slumped back down in the booth. She was either an Oscar-caliber actress or what she was saying was true: Cisco Ram was terrorizing her just like he was terrorizing the Chambers family. Danny could easily understand how helpless she felt.

The girl swung her left leg over Danny's legs and sat in his lap, facing him. She straddled his thighs like she was riding a horse. Music played almost continuously in the club, so she didn't have to wait long for a new song to start. When it did, she put her arms around the back of Danny's neck and began to grind her pelvis into his groin and tried to pull his face down between her breasts. He let her pull his face close, but not close enough to touch her breasts.

Danny was in a daze. He couldn't believe this was happening. He was not aroused by the dancer's movements; he was shamed by them, just as he knew she was shamed by having to perform this way. He knew she must have danced like this for many men, but this was different. She was being used by Cisco to embarrass and hurt him. He closed his eyes and thought of Sheila and the kids at home. They would be sitting down to dinner soon and wondering where he was.

As the song was about to end, Tequila reached down and grabbed Danny's crotch. She could feel that he had not been excited by her gyrations.

"You do not like my dancing?"

His face flush with humiliation, Danny just stared into her eyes and said nothing. A moment later, the girl climbed off his lap and quickly began to reassemble her costume. She did not look at him.

"Why?" Danny muttered. "Why did he do this?"

"Because he hates you. He knows many things about you, *senor*. His friends have been checking up on you. He knows you are a man of faith. He knew you would hate being here and that you would hate having me rub my body over you. He thought you would be even more ashamed when your body responded to me. He knows a lot about you, *senor*, but maybe not as much as he thinks. But I fear for your son because I know Cisco will try to kill him." She left him alone with nothing but the smell of her perfume on his body.

∽

When Danny got home, he went straight to the kitchen and pulled some cold cuts out of the refrigerator to make a sandwich. Sheila, who had been upstairs helping Melissa with her homework, came in and stood beside the table.

"Why were you so late, Danny? And why didn't you call? You always call, and I was worried when you didn't." She stared at him while she waited for his response.

Danny turned around to face her, holding the half-prepared sandwich on a plate. In eighteen years of marriage, Danny had rarely lied to Sheila, and never about anything important. The lie about the late-night phone call telling him DJ was dead still bothered him. He realized on the drive home that this was not something he could, or should, hide from Sheila any longer, even though he knew it would make her frantic with fear for her son. He knew the GBI agent was right about alerting his family to the danger they faced.

"Sit down, Honey," he said solemnly. "I need to start from the beginning."

∽

CHAPTER NINETEEN
SHOTGUN

THE NEXT DAY, an agent from the Georgia Bureau of Investigation called Danny at work and asked if he could come by and install the recording device on their phones. Danny said he would meet him at the house at four o'clock then called Sheila to fill her in. He had given Jonathan Evans the whole story that morning, and Jonathan had asked Danny if he thought his presence at the school might pose a risk to the students. Danny told his boss he didn't think it would, because if Cisco came after him, it was unlikely he would do it in a public place like a high school. Now he had to ask Jonathan's permission to leave early.

On his way home, Danny stopped at a huge sporting goods store that carried everything from camp stoves to shotguns. It was the shotguns that interested Danny. He found the department that sold guns and knives and walked along the counter, checking out the dozens of shotguns and rifles on the wall. A heavyset man with a ruddy complexion, full black beard, and a big smile on his face approached him.

"What can I help you with today, sir?"

"I want a shotgun," said Danny.

"What are you gonna use it for?" the salesman asked.

The question made Danny a little nervous. "Nothing illegal, that's for sure," he said, faking a laugh to disguise his uneasiness.

The man grinned at him. "Betcha if you were, you wouldn't tell me, anyway, would you?" Before Danny could answer, the salesman went on. "Just kidding, pal. What I meant was, do you want the gun for hunting or self-defense?"

Relieved, Danny said, "Home-defense."

"Well, sir, you've come to the right place. Personally, I'm a big fan of the 12-gauge for protecting home and hearth. A 12-gauge will stop just about anything or anybody, and it doesn't require you to be much of a shot. Hell, if you can aim a water hose, you can aim a 12-gauge. Another good thing about it is that bad guys are just flat-out afraid of it. Now, there *are* a few dimwits out there who'll keep coming at you if you have a handgun, but trust me, pal, when they see Mr. Remington or Mr. Mossberg staring them down, they lose interest in whatever they're up to in a hurry."

Danny was amazed at how fast the man could talk, so as soon as there was an opening, he said, "Okay, I'm sold. What's the best model for me?"

The man looked him up and down. "If I might ask, sir, what do you do for a living?"

"I'm a high school football coach and a teacher," Danny answered, already forgetting he was now the Assistant Principal. "Why do you ask?"

"Well, coach, I'm an honest man, and I don't want to sell you more than you need or can afford. If you're a high school coach, you don't make a lot of money, so the Remington 870 Express Pump is all you need. She's made by a great manufacturer, so the quality's there, but she doesn't have a lot of frills. Holds four shells, which is usually enough to handle most situations, and if it isn't, then another two dozen probably wouldn't help anyway. The 870 has an eighteen-inch barrel and weighs a little over seven pounds. The whole dang gun is barely a yard long. I can set you up with one for $299.95, and I'll throw in a box of double-oughts." He walked over to one of the gun racks, unlocked the security bar, and removed a shotgun. He returned to the counter and handed it to Danny. "That's it, and a real winner, if you ask me. Hardly weighs a thing, does it?"

"Well, if you say so. Once you get beyond an M-16 or a Colt 1911 Model .45-caliber automatic, I know next to nothing about guns."

"M-16, huh? You ex-military?"

"Yeah, I did my time."

"What branch?"

"Army, but I really don't like to talk much about it, and I'm in kind of a hurry. So, if we could just wrap this up...?"

"In a hurry? You're not going to go right out and shoot someone with this nice new gun, are you?"

Danny was catching on to the man's sense of humor, or at least he thought he was. "No, not today," he said, grinning. "But maybe tomorrow."

The man burst out laughing. "Will that be cash or credit?"

Three hundred dollars was a lot of money to pay for something he hoped he would never have to use, but Danny knew this was not the time to be frugal.

"Can I take it with me today?" he asked.

"You betcha you can. Just step this way so we can do a little paperwork for the government, and you'll be all set."

When Danny got home, he found the GBI agent standing on the front porch, saying his good-byes to Sheila.

"Oh good, here's my husband now," she said when she spotted him. "Danny, I was hoping that you'd get home before the sergeant left."

The policeman extended his hand. "Hello, Mr. Chambers, my name is Sgt. Rodney Brown. I just finished installing the recording device on your incoming phone lines."

"Thank you, sergeant," said Danny. "What do I need to know about how they work?"

"The device is very simple," said Sgt. Brown, "and I went over this with your wife. Basically, it's on all the time, unless you turn it off. It begins recording as soon as you pick up the phone to receive a call. If the call is not of a threatening nature, you just press the pound sign on the phone, and the recording stops and is erased. If the call is threatening in any way, just keep talking and everything that's said, on both ends, will be recorded."

"Great," said Danny. "That sounds easy enough, doesn't it, Honey?" He put his arm around Sheila's shoulders.

"I have to go now," the sergeant said, "but if you have any problems, just call us. You have my card and Lt. Livingston's, I believe. If you get a threatening call, call us as soon as you break the connection. It's important to keep the caller on the line as long as possible. Even though at this point we're not trying to trace the call, the more conversation we can get for the voice analysis, the better."

"We understand, Sergeant, and thank you for coming out so promptly," Danny said. Neither he nor Sheila spoke as they watched the agent get into his car and drive away, but both of them were thinking the same thing: *The next time a policeman knocks on our door, will he be telling us that one of our children is dead?* They went back in the house, and Danny sat down at the kitchen table. Sheila poured two cups of coffee from the pot she kept going all day every day and sat down across from him.

"What are we going to do, Danny?"

"I don't know, Angel, I really don't. But I know this much: the first thing we have to do is to talk to the kids, especially DJ. He needs to know what's going on. They both need to be very, very careful from now on until this thing is over."

"Until it's over? When is it going to be over, Danny? How will we know when it's over? This man could terrorize us for the rest of our lives if he wants to."

Danny wanted to offer her some words of comfort, but he didn't have any. Sheila was right. This could go on for a long time. He had a bad feeling that it would go on until Cisco had exacted his revenge or until Cisco was dead. But this was not something he was ready to share with his wife.

"Where are the kids now?" he asked.

"DJ's in his room studying, and Melissa just called from Erin's house. They're watching something on TV or doing Facebook. I told her to be home by six for dinner, though."

"Well, it'll be dark by six o'clock, and I don't want her coming home in the dark. Call her at Erin's and tell her I'll be there to pick her up in fifteen minutes."

"Do you really think that's necessary? Erin only lives two blocks away."

Danny did his best to keep his voice calm and pleasant. "Yes, my love, I know where Erin lives. Unfortunately, I *do* think it's necessary. We're going to have to change the way we do a lot of things for a while. Please go ahead and call while I get something from the car." As Sheila dialed the phone, Danny went into the garage, opened the trunk of his car, and took out the shotgun. He worked the slide action to make sure it was unloaded, then he brought it into the kitchen.

Sheila was still on the phone dealing with an obviously unhappy daughter and when Danny came back in, she had her back turned to the door from the garage. When she hung up the phone and turned around, she let out a shriek and her hand flew to cover her mouth when she saw the weapon.

"Oh, my Lord, Danny! Has it come to *this*?"

"Yes, it has come to this," he said soberly. "I need you to be strong, and I need to show you how to use the gun. Please don't argue."

"Why do I have to learn to shoot a gun?" she asked, already knowing the answer to her question.

"Because one day you and this gun may be the only thing between our children and death." Sheila's face turned white, and she slumped into a chair. At that moment, DJ walked into the room, stopping short when he saw the shotgun in Danny's hands.

"Whoa, Dad, are you taking up hunting in your old age now that you won't be coaching football anymore?" he said, laughing.

"No, Son, I'm not taking up hunting. I'm afraid this is a lot more serious than that. Have a seat. I need to talk to you and your mother."

"Why does DJ have to be involved?" Sheila asked. "I don't want him learning to shoot a gun."

"DJ is already involved. He just hasn't been told yet. And he has to learn to shoot for the same reason you do. He may have to defend himself, you, or Melissa—or even all of you before this is over."

"Before *what's* over, Dad?" The boy had always been an obedient child, and he had taken a seat beside his mother as his father had directed. "Does it have something to do with that kid's death?"

"Yes, DJ, it has everything to do with it," said Danny. "Hold your questions, and I'll tell you all I know. But prepare yourself, Son. This will not be pleasant to hear." The boy took his mother's hand and held it on top of the table, a gesture intended to comfort her rather than himself.

"DJ, a man named Francisco Ramos, a criminal known on the streets as Cisco Ram, is the father of the boy I accidentally killed. He has been calling the house and threatening to take revenge on me for his son's death. One of the things he has threatened is that he might kill you or Melissa." Danny knew this would be a shocking news, but there was no way to sugarcoat it.

DJ needed to know how serious this was so he could take the necessary steps to protect himself. The boy was bright, and he quickly cut to the heart of the matter.

"So he wants to kill me, your son, because you killed his son." It was a statement, not a question. It grieved Danny's heart to hear the words coming from his son's mouth.

"That's about the size of it, Son," Danny said. Then he tried to put a positive spin on things. "But we already have the police and the Georgia Bureau of Investigation involved. They're monitoring our phones and doing their best to keep an eye on Ramos. I'm having an alarm system installed in the house, and now we have this shotgun. We will all be extra careful, and we will all protect each other. I promise you, Son, that I will not let this man hurt any of you."

Sheila started to protest. "How can you promise...?" Danny silenced her with a look that said, *I love you, but please shut up for now.*

"I'm going to put the shotgun away now," Danny said. "I have to go get Mel, and I don't want her to see it. Later, when she's gone to bed, I'll do my best to show you both how to load and fire it without actually firing it. Do your best not to scare Mel anymore than she will already be when she gets home. I'm going to give her what I think she needs to know on the way back from Erin's. After dinner tonight, the four of us are going to sit down and talk about personal and household security. DJ, you'll be a man soon, and I'm afraid this is going to accelerate your maturity."

"Dad, in some societies, I would already be considered a man and a warrior," DJ said proudly. "I know this is serious stuff, but I want you and mom to treat me like an adult, an adult who can help, not a kid, okay? Besides, I'm the one he's threatening to kill."

That evening, after the dinner dishes were cleaned and put away, Danny called his family into the den. "All right, kids," he said, "I have some good news for you. Tomorrow, everyone gets a cell phone." He stopped there and just looked at them. Sheila knew this was coming, so she did not comment. The two teenagers leaped to their feet in unison and cheered.

"That's great, Daddy," Melissa said, "but why did you change your mind? You always said we were too young to need cell phones?"

"Princess, this is for your safety, not for your social life. Because of what I told you both today, we need to change a lot of things we do, and you two having cell phones is just one of the changes. So, here's the deal. You each get a phone, but they will come with a very small number of minutes. I want you to be able to call for help if you need it, but I don't want you spending hours on a cell phone. As for you, DJ, no using it while you're driving, unless it's an emergency. I want all of you—and that includes Mom—to keep your phones on and with you at all times."

"No can do, Dad," DJ interrupted. "You know we can't have cell phones turned on during school hours."

"I'll speak to Dr. Evans about yours, DJ, and to your principal, Mel," said Danny. "I'm sure that once they understand the situation, and as long as you have them on vibrate and don't use them except in an emergency, it'll be all right." Danny resumed laying out the battle plan. "We will have an alarm system installed in the house tomorrow or the next day. It stays on all the time. That means that you'll have to be very careful when you come in and remember to rearm the system behind you—no exceptions. Does everyone understand?"

"Dad, what if we're inside the house and open a door to go out?" DJ asked. "Won't the alarm go off?"

"No, it will chime, which means you'll have about fifteen seconds to punch in the code to disarm it. It would be better for you to get in the habit of putting in the code before you open the door rather than waiting for the chime, though. One more thing: the windows will be part of the system, so you can't open a window to smell the fresh air or shout at a friend you see walking by. We have to make sure that the alarm is on and that the doors and windows are locked at all times. Even if you're the last one out of the house, you have to set the alarm so no one can sneak in while we're gone. Are we clear on this?"

Sheila joined in, "And do not, under any circumstances, open the door to anyone you don't know. That means if someone comes to the door to deliver something or sell something—or for any other reason—you come and get your father or me. If you're home alone, just speak to them through the door and tell them to leave whatever it is. If they say they need a signature or payment, just tell them to come back later."

"That last part is not for you, Mel, because you will never be here alone," said Danny, "at least not until all this is settled. DJ, what your mother just said is for your benefit. I'm serious about it, too. I don't want you thinking you're some big football tough guy who can take care of himself. The people we're dealing with use guns and knives, and football tough guys are no match for guns and knives." Danny went on to explain that the kids would only be riding the school bus occasionally in the future and that he or Sheila would drive them to school and pick them up, except on days when DJ drove.

"I know this is hard to live with," he said, "but it is what it is, and we have to deal with it. We can whine and complain, but in the end we have no choice if we want to be safe. You two should never be away from home alone except going to and coming from school. And then, you should be together. If you go to a friend's home to visit, *we* take you and *we* pick you up. That's all I can think of for now. Remember: phone always with you, alarm always on. I love you all."

"Daddy, how long is this going to last?" Melissa asked. "I know it's for the best, but I already feel like I'm in prison."

"I don't know, Baby, I don't know," Danny said, wishing he did. "The police are doing everything they can to end this. Until they do, we do as we always do—we pray and put our trust in God."

CHAPTER TWENTY
EVEN OUTLAWS HAVE MOTHERS

ELDEMIRA AYALA SANTOS y Garza was 16 years old when her first child, a boy she named Francisco Miguel, was born. Francisco's father was a young American from Arizona named Johnny Ramos. His parents were both from Mexico, but Johnny was born in the United States and was fluent in both English and Spanish. Johnny was 18 years old and stationed at Laughlin Air Force Base in Del Rio, Texas, when he met Eldemira in a restaurant where she worked in Acuna, just across the U.S.-Mexico border. They fell in love, and he petitioned the Air Force to allow him to marry a foreign national.

Johnny spent his days repairing jet engines and his nights in Mexico with his beloved "Mira." Before the paperwork was completed and the young couple could be married, however, two unfortunate events occurred. First, Eldemira became pregnant. Three weeks later, Johnny was killed when a huge jet engine he was working on from a cargo plane fell on him. Before his death, Johnny had informed the base commander, Colonel Richard Erickson, that Eldemira was pregnant and had asked him to do whatever he could to speed up the marriage-approval process. Ironically, the final paperwork arrived on Erickson's desk three hours before Johnny died. As a result of the commander's efforts, Eldemira was allowed to give birth to her and Johnny's son in the modern Air Force hospital at Laughlin instead of the antiquated one in her home country. Because Johnny Ramos was a U.S. citizen and Francisco was born in the United States, the infant was automatically a U.S. citizen, a fact that would have a significant impact on the future life of Francisco Miguel Ramos. Primarily because of the fact that, since he was a citizen of the United States, when he became a major criminal in his adult years, the

U.S. Government was unable to simply deport him back to Mexico as an undesirable alien.

Francisco was 15 years old when he was arrested for the first time and charged, as a juvenile, with breaking and entering. This was followed by an arrest at 16 for assault, for which he spent six months in jail, and another one at 17 for car theft, which earned him another two years of jail time.

After his release from the Mexican prison, Eldemira moved with her son to Atlanta to seek work. Because her son was a citizen, she was able to get a green card quickly.

She had done her best to support Francisco son through it all, but when he was caught in the act of stealing the silver communion plates and Crucifixes from her church, she had had enough. Francisco was surprised in the act by a priest, who tried to restrain him. The boy shoved the old man down a short flight of stairs and got away. When the police came to Eldemira's home looking for him, the priest was with them. He told her that what the authorities were saying was, unfortunately, true. Her son had stolen from the Mother Church. Eldemira told them the truth, which was that she had not seen her son since the night before. She promised to call them when she heard from Francisco. The priest and the policemen went away, doubtful that would ever happen. But two days later, Eldemira surprised herself, Francisco, and the police when she called to tell them that Francisco had come home in the middle of the night and was sleeping peacefully in his bed. The police dragged him out of bed and off to jail.

There was little the public defender could do to counter the eyewitness testimony of the priest. Francisco Miguel Ramos was sentenced to five years in prison. He was not yet 22 years old.

❧

Cisco spent three years, of his five-year sentence, in the Autry State Penitentiary in Pelham, Georgia, in relative obscurity. He wanted to be paroled on time, so he avoided any type of altercation with other inmates or the guards. He was beaten savagely the first week of his incarceration when he successfully defended himself from a gang rape by biting the ear off one of his attackers and gouging the eye of another. He told the men that the next time, they better kill him or he would find a way to kill every one of them if they ever touched him again. The men saw the madness in his eyes and took him at his word. He was soon told, not asked, to join *Los Aztecos*, the gang made up entirely of prisoners of Mexican descent. He joined out of self-defense, knowing that without the affiliation with *Los Aztecos*, he would be easy prey for the racially-based Black and Anglo gangs. Even as a member of *Los Aztecos*, he managed to avoid ever being identified by the guards as a troublemaker, and when his parole hearing came up, the all-Protestant parole board decided that stealing silver from a church did not make him a menace to society and sent him back into the world of free men.

By the time he returned to Atlanta, Cisco had come to the conclusion that it was smarter to find others to do his dirty work than to risk a return to prison. In short order, he found *Borracho* and *El Carnicero*, and the Latino Death Lords gang was born. He later brought Manuel *"Cuchillo"* Osorio into the fold. Over the following eight years, though he had been questioned about many crimes and many known criminals had been questioned about him, Cisco Ram was never again convicted of a crime. The authorities knew all about the illegal activities of the LDL and its leader, but they could prove none of it in court, primarily because none of their victims had ever testified against them, either because they lacked the courage or because they were dead.

Had Francisco Miguel Ramos ever been studied by a clinical psychologist, he likely would have been diagnosed as a classic sociopath. Even as a child, Cisco was glib and charming when he wanted to be. More often than not, he didn't. But, when he wanted something from someone, he could turn it on at will. Cisco recognized the personal rights of no one but himself. He easily made excuses for his behavior, no matter how vile, because in his mind he was different from the rest of the "sheep" in the world, as he called them. He was special, and he felt it was his right to take whatever he wanted, whether it was a woman, a car, a piece of jewelry, or a life. If the world was strong enough to stop him, fine. If not, he would have his way.

Like all sociopaths, he was an habitual liar. Cisco lied about things even when the truth might have served him better. In the mind of the sociopath, the lies they tell others are no different from the lies they tell themselves. After a while, these lies take on a life of their own and become part of a complex belief system that produces feelings of omnipotence. Cisco Ram felt that the world had somehow cheated him in his youth, and because a sociopath is never wrong, he had developed an unquestioning belief in his own intelligence, cunning, and supremacy. To Cisco, the end always justified the means, so no matter how abhorrent his behavior, it was entirely appropriate to the situation he found himself in. He never felt remorse for anything he did. The only piece of the puzzle that did not fit the sociopath profile was his love for his son.

Prototypical sociopaths are incapable of love for anyone but themselves. They are unable to put the needs or feelings of others above their own. In Cisco's case, however, the only person he cared about—the one person who was the focus of all his love—was his son. He had positively doted on the boy. Just as he could never see his own faults, he could see none in his son. That the boy had been accidentally killed while he was being prevented from savagely beating a woman who had merely flipped him off meant nothing to Cisco. He could never accept that his son's death was the result of the boy's own actions and that no one was to blame but the boy himself.

◦◦

CHAPTER TWENTY ONE
MEDEVAC

AS DANNY AND Sheila lay in bed struggling to find sleep, the phone rang. They both sat straight up in bed and looked at it.

"The kids are tucked in, aren't they?" Danny asked, fully awake.

"I checked before I came to bed," Sheila said.

The phone rang again and again. On the sixth ring, Danny answered it.

"Hello?" he said, expecting a threat.

"Hey, Hero, how you doing tonight?" It was the same voice as the previous call.

"I've told the police about your calls, so you better leave us alone before you get in real trouble," Danny said, wondering if the threat sounded as lame to the caller as it did to him.

"Leave you alone? That's no problem, Hero. I'll leave you all alone— alone and dead in your beds one night." Then came the laugh, low and mean. Danny sat there for a moment with the phone to his ear, not saying a word. He couldn't think of anything to say. The voice became a whisper. "What's the matter, Hero? Are you afraid of dying?" Danny slammed the phone back onto its cradle. It was the second time in his life he had been asked that question.

❧

Danny Chambers was a good college football player, but not good enough to move up to the pros and make a living from football. He felt he was very lucky to have received a full athletic scholarship to play at Valdosta

State University in south Georgia. Although Valdosta State was a Division II school and didn't compete at the same level as big schools like the University of Georgia or Georgia Tech, the football was good, and Danny's education was free. He knew that when college was over, his playing days would be, too. He wanted to coach, and he wanted to teach, but he also felt the need to serve his country. Young coaches straight out of college don't make a lot of money, so when a former classmate told Danny that he had joined the Army Reserves, Danny thought he might have found a way to serve his country *and* supplement his and Sheila's meager income. No one ever asked him if he would be willing to kill someone in the line of duty. It was simply assumed that anyone who volunteered to join the military would have no problem with it. Danny knew the question would come up sooner or later, but he also knew there were a lot of jobs in the Army that would not put him in a position to kill. He had narrowed his choices to military intelligence or flying medical evacuation—better known as medevac—choppers that would remove wounded soldiers from the battlefield.

Danny signed up and was soon in basic training in South Carolina at Fort Jackson. Being a well-conditioned athlete, he had no problems with the physical part of the training, and his years in college were a great benefit in the classroom. He stood out among his squad members and was quickly elevated to Squad Leader.

His platoon had just arrived at the firing range for their first day of dry-firing their newly assigned M-16 assault rifles, which were standard issue for U.S. armed forces. When he was told to assume the prone firing position, Danny said, "Sir, the officer cadet does not wish to learn to fire this weapon, sir." In a flash, the senior drill instructor's face was only inches from Danny's.

"This is the last time I will tell you this, boy," the drill instructor screamed. "I am *not* an officer. I work for a living. I am your drill sergeant, and you will address me as 'drill sergeant,' not 'sir!' Are we clear on that now, soldier?"

Danny kept his eyes straight ahead and yelled out, "Yes, drill sergeant!"

"Now what the *hell* do you mean you don't want to learn to fire this weapon? What's the matter, soldier—are you afraid of dying?"

Danny kept his eyes focused squarely on the brim of the D.I.'s hat. The South Carolina sun was beating down on the top of Danny's head, and he felt as if it were draining the liquids from his body as quickly as a knife cutting through an artery. A large bead of sweat formed on his forehead and then slowly began to make its way between his eyebrows and down the right side of his nose. No one in the company made a sound. For that one moment in time, nothing in nature made a sound. Even the omnipresent helicopter transports and gunships seemed to have all disappeared.

"I am talking to you, boy!" the drill instructor shouted. "I said, are you afraid of dying?"

"No, drill sergeant!" Daniel screamed back, his eyes still on the hat brim.

"No, drill sergeant, what?"

"Drill sergeant, the officer cadet is not afraid of dying!" Danny answered.

"Well, what the hell *are* you afraid of, boy? You must be afraid of something since you don't want to learn how to fire this very effective and very expensive piece of weaponry your Uncle Sam has given you."

"Drill sergeant, the officer cadet is afraid of killing, not dying, sir," Danny explained. This was not the answer the senior drill instructor expected, and, for just a second or two, he was puzzled. He took a step back and lowered his voice, not wanting the rest of the fort to hear his next question or its answer.

"Then what in the hell are you doing in my army, mister?" he asked.

Not noticing that the sergeant had lowered his voice, Danny screamed out his answer, "Drill sergeant, the officer cadet wants to serve his country but does not feel he must kill to do it, drill sergeant!"

"Then what the hell are you planning to do to earn your pay, boy?"

Danny gave him the answer that he had been thinking about for months. "Drill sergeant, the officer cadet wants to fly medevac helicopters to take wounded troops from the battlefield."

No other answer could have ended this confrontation so quickly and, in Danny's mind, so agreeably. Master Sgt. Booker L. Edmonds had been in the United States Army for almost thirty years and had served in Vietnam and Cambodia. During his tour in the central highlands of Vietnam, he had been wounded in the leg by shrapnel from a North Vietnam Army anti-personnel mine. His company was pinned down in a dry wash by enemy fire, and Edmonds was bleeding badly. The same mine had killed the company medic. Private 1st Class Edmonds could tell by the looks on the faces of the men around him that he was in very serious condition and that they had done all their untrained hands could do for him. He had a vision of his deceased mother's face and thought, *I will see you soon, Mama.* As he was fading into unconsciousness, he thought he heard the familiar sound of an incoming helicopter, then his life blood draining away, he passed out.

A medevac chopper, piloted by a young warrant officer fresh out of officer training, set down in the wash amidst heavy enemy fire and picked Edmonds up. The chopper took off through even heavier fire while the medics on board were doing their best to slow the bleeding. Less than ten minutes later, the Edmonds was delivered safely to a field hospital where his injuries received proper attention. Several days later, a doctor casually mentioned to him that had he been even fifteen minutes later getting on the chopper, he would have been loaded on it in a body bag instead of a stretcher.

"You were very fortunate, soldier," the doctor said. "The kid flying that chopper must have balls the size of grapefruit to go in there to pick you up in the middle of that shit storm of NVA and Vietcong machine-gun fire."

Now, looking into the dirty, sweating face of the young man in front of him, the sergeant's mind flashed back to that dry wash. The heat, the dust, the noise, the pain, and the fear of dying all came rushing back.

"Well, dammit, soldier, we can never have too many of them," he said, lowering his voice almost to a whisper, "but, if you want to finish basic training and fly those choppers, you're gonna have to qualify with this weapon. After that, whether you ever fire it at anyone is between you and Jesus." He turned away and quickly resumed his position to the side of the firing line.

"Alright ladies, story time is over so let's get back to business. Now let's see if any of you know what a prone firing position looks like?" The platoon spent another hour on the range before Sergeant Edmonds called a halt by shouting, "Everyone on their feet! Form up in squads!" When the men were properly aligned, he bellowed, "Company, *ten-hut!* You girls did not impress me today with your ability or interest, so we are going to double time back to the barracks."

While they double timed towards their barracks, Danny thought about what the sergeant said. If he didn't qualify with the rifle, he would be washed out. And just because he knew how to fire the weapon, that didn't mean he would ever have to do it, except on a firing range. He also decided that if he was going to qualify, he might as well do his best. By the time the qualifying sessions for his platoon were completed, Danny had qualified as an expert and attained the third-highest round of qualifying in his company.

With Cisco's threats still ringing in Danny's ear, he put the phone back in its cradle and went into the bathroom, closing the door behind him. That day on the firing range played over and over again in his head. Later, Sheila could hear the sound of him vomiting, but she knew it was best to leave him alone. She couldn't think of anything to say that would make him feel better.

CHAPTER TWENTY TWO
PASTOR

DR. DAVID B. Sheildman, pastor of the Victory United Methodist Church and Doctor of Divinity, was at his desk making minor changes to his Sunday sermon. David's hair was starting to gray a bit, and lately he had noticed a bit of a middle-age bulge in his mid-section. He kept his weight close to one hundred and seventy pounds by taking the stairs instead the elevator at hospitals where he visited the sick in his flock and by walking with his wife through their neighborhood. He missed the days of throwing the football in the street with his two sons. One had left for college and the other to seek his fortune as a guitar-player in a rock and roll band. College was working out well, but the band was still waiting to be discovered.

After God, his church, and his family, the pastor's abiding passion was college football—specifically, the Georgia Bulldogs. His office was a virtual shrine to his beloved "Dawgs." Bulldog banners, pennants, a picture of Sanford Stadium where his team played "between the hedges," and even an autographed picture of David shaking hands with the Bulldogs Head Coach Mark Richt adorned the walls.

He was five-foot-eleven, which to him was close enough to what his father had predicted. "My boy David is going to be a six-footer, I just bet you," he had overheard his father say to a friend when he was nine years old. "Just look at his feet." He had aspired to reach that height ever since. David idolized his father, who had also been a minister, but had always felt he would be letting his father down if he didn't hit that magic six-foot mark. So one day he simply decided that, as far as he was concerned, five-eleven and a half barefoot was six feet in shoes and put the issue out of his mind forever.

The intercom on his desk buzzed and he pushed the button to answer.

"Yes, ma'am?" he said to Joanie, his administrative assistant. Even though she was a lot younger, he was a true southerner, and "ma'am" came as naturally to him as breathing, when he addressed an adult female.

"Sir, Danny Chambers is on the phone, and he says it's very important that he speak with you right away." Shieldman had been the senior pastor at Victory for the past eight years and during that time had come to know Danny Chambers well. Danny had served on many church committees and seldom missed a Sunday morning service. His wife and children were also active in the church, and Shieldman's own son, Bobby, had played football for Chambers at Robert E. Lee.

Like most church pastors, Shieldman studiously avoided knowing how much money any member of his congregation contributed to the church, but he knew that Chambers gave ten percent of his modest income as a teacher and coach. The chairman of the stewardship campaign had mentioned it to a fellow committee member who innocently passed the percentage on to the pastor before Shieldman could stop her.

Shieldman had never known Danny to speak ill of anyone nor could he recall an occasion when anyone spoke ill of Danny. The number of people he could say that about was quite small. Danny had never turned down a request to work on any church project or to give to any special need that arose. He frequently opened his home to members of various touring youth choirs that regularly performed at Victory UMC. He had made more than one trip to the youth camp as a counselor, even when it meant using his vacation time. For these and many other reasons, David Shieldman thought a great deal of Danny and his family, so he immediately picked up the phone.

"Hello, Danny Chambers," he said. "How are Sheila and the kids?" No matter how well Shieldman knew a person, he liked to refer to them by their first and last name. When someone asked him why, he replied, "I only do that to people I love."

"But, preacher," the man protested, "you do it to everyone."

"Exactly," Shieldman said.

Danny's response to his pastor's question was uncharacteristically short and formal. "They're fine, sir. Can you meet me down at JJ's Barbeque for lunch today?"

Shieldman looked at his watch. It was twenty minutes to twelve. "Sure, Danny. I can be there by noon. What's going on?"

"I'll tell you when I see you, David, and thanks for giving me your lunch hour," Danny said and hung up. Pastor Shieldman put the phone down and leaned back in his chair. He swiveled to get his legs out from under the desk and stretched them. Whenever he sat too long, his right knee stiffened up from an old football injury. He laced his fingers together behind his neck to support his head. He had earned an undergraduate degree in mathematics at the University of Georgia before he felt the call to ministry. He attended seminary at Emory University in Atlanta, and after he was ordained, he was appointed pastor at a small church in the North Georgia Conference of the United Methodist Church. He continued to work on his studies and six years later was awarded his Doctor of Divinity.

Shieldman was a man of strong emotions and great empathy. He loved his wife and children with great passion, and he loved his church. He had time for one hobby and one hobby only: rooting for the Georgia Bulldog football team. As he reclined in his desk chair and thought about Danny Chambers, he surveyed his office walls, festooned with Bulldog paraphernalia. *Can a man have too many Bulldog banners?* he mused, then answered his own question out loud: "Absolutely not." He grabbed his suit coat off the hangar behind the door and walked out of his office. "Going to lunch, Joanie. Don't know how long I'll be. Call my cell if you need me."

❧

JJ's Original Pig Barbeque Restaurant, a home-cooking tradition in Norcross for more than thirty years, sat at the corner of Peachtree Industrial Parkway and Miller Bridge Road. Originally occupying an old two-story home, it had grown, one room at a time, over the years. Johnnie Jefferson, the founder, knocked out the wall between the living room and dining room in the old house and started with an eating area just big enough to feed sixteen people at once around two large rectangular tables. Everything was served homestyle, meaning Johnnie and his wife would bring out platters of barbecued beef and ribs, barbecued and fried chicken, white-loaf bread, baked beans, and cole slaw. Sweet iced tea washed it down, and apple cobbler finished it off. You paid Johnny seven dollars when you sat down for lunch—ten if it was dinner—and ate until you were full.

The two large smokers and huge homemade charcoal grill that filled the back yard cooked nonstop from five o'clock in the morning until after the dinner hour every day. As his following grew, Johnnie knocked out more walls and added more dining space to accommodate them. When he added breakfast to the menu in 1985, he had to build extra rooms on the back of the old house and open up some of the second-floor rooms to handle various civic organization breakfast meetings. The Rotarians and the Lions Club changed their monthly meetings to breakfast instead of lunch just because of Johnnie's famous buttermilk biscuits covered in white-sausage gravy.

David was delighted to find a parking spot as soon as he pulled in. He saw Danny sitting in his old Honda with his head bowed. As he approached the car, he could see that Danny's eyes were closed and his lips were moving. The pastor stood there silently until Danny opened his eyes and raised his head. When he saw the minister, he immediately got out of the car and shook his hand.

"Are you all right, Danny?" asked Pastor Shieldman.

"No, Pastor, I'm far from all right. Let's go inside, and I'll tell you all about it."

At Danny's request, the hostess, one of Johnnie's granddaughters, seated them in a back-corner booth as far from the rest of the diners as they could get this time of day. Both men ordered barbecue sandwiches, fries, and Cokes. Though Johnnie had expanded his menu over the years, a lot of people, Danny and his pastor included, felt that the barbeque was still the best thing in the house. By the time the food arrived, Danny had brought his pastor up to date on how his life was falling apart.

"I just don't understand why the police can't protect you and your family," Pastor Shieldman said, dipping a large, crisp French fry in the blob of ketchup on his plate. "Can't they arrest this man for something? Or at least give your family some protection?"

"Sure, they could give us protection, David—but for how long? A week? A month? Ramos says he'll wait as long as it takes. As for arresting him for something, this is still America, and until he breaks the law and someone comes forward to testify against him, there's nothing they can do. They've never been able to get this guy. Witnesses either don't survive until the trial or their memory suddenly goes blank."

"Danny, I'm so sorry. What are you going to do?"

"That's why I called you, Pastor."

"You want me to pray for you? For guidance?"

"No, David, I've already prayed and prayed. I mean, yes, of course, I need your prayers, too, but what I need most is for *you* to give me some guidance," Danny said, looking directly into his friend's eyes. "Tell me something from scripture that will help me to feel right with God if I have to resort to violence to protect my family." He picked up his sandwich, held it up to take a bite, stared at it for a few seconds, and then put it back on the plate. He looked back at his pastor with such a look of anguish that David's eyes grew moist.

"I don't think I understand, Danny," said the Pastor. "What is it you think I can tell you from the Bible?"

Danny had tears in his eyes and a lump in his throat, which he tried to eliminate with a sip of Coke. He hesitated a moment, gazing down at the uneaten food in front of him. Finally he looked up. "Jesus taught us to turn the other cheek, but I don't think I can just sit by and let this maniac hurt my family. Is that what 'turn the other cheek' means, that we do nothing while our loved ones are injured or killed?"

The minister wiped his mouth with a napkin and took a drink of his Coke. "Danny, I need to collect my thoughts for just a moment. You have to understand something. I've never had a conversation like this before. I mean that honestly. No one has ever asked me to give him a dispensation to use violence, and I need to think before I answer you."

"Well, let me put it this way, David. If a man had just killed one of your sons and was preparing to kill your daughter—and you had a gun in your hand—and the only way you could stop him was to kill him, would you just turn the other cheek and let him kill her?"

"I never thought of it that way, Danny, but I guess, if I'm being honest, I would do whatever I had to do to save her life."

"So, you're saying you would break a commandment and kill to save your family?" Shieldman squirmed in his seat and loosened his tie. He could feel himself beginning to sweat. *I owe this man the absolute truth*, he thought to himself.

"I would kill to protect my family if I was certain I had no other choice," he said.

"And do you believe you would burn in hell for it?"

"No, I don't, Danny, and I will do my best to tell you why."

"That's the burden I brought to dump on you today, David," Danny said. "Please take it from my shoulders and show me a way out of this horrible situation."

The minister took another drink of his Coke and asked Danny a question. "Have you ever heard of a man named Dietrich Bonhoeffer?"

Danny shook his head.

"Bonhoeffer was a Lutheran minister and theologian who lived in Germany during Hitler's rise to power. He was also a member of the German resistance and was involved in several failed attempts to assassinate Hitler. He was willing to break the commandment against killing to achieve what he felt was the greater good: ridding the world of a genocidal madman. He espoused a doctrine that would later be called 'situational ethics,' which basically holds that moral principals can be temporarily set aside in certain situations if love is best served by doing so. Not romantic love, but what the Greeks called 'agape' love. Agape love is the universal, unchanging, and unconditional love for all people."

"Well, I know he did not succeed in assassinating Hitler," Danny cut in, "so what happened to him?"

"The German secret police captured him, and he was hanged just weeks before the allies liberated Berlin."

"So he died for what he believed in?"

"Yes, and that's one of the reasons he felt, as did the established church, that he was not damned by his decision to take a life. He was willing to lay down his life for the life of another, or in his case, many others. As it says in the Gospel of John, Chapter 15, verse 13, 'Greater love has no man than this, that a man lay down his life for that of his friends.' Bonhoeffer lived what he believed."

Danny was scribble notes on a napkin. "What was the chapter and verse again?" he asked.

Shieldman repeated the citation and then continued, "And in Matthew, Chapter 10, verse 34 Jesus said, 'Do not think that I came to bring peace on this earth. I did not come to bring peace but a sword.' Jesus knew there would be times when the sword was necessary. Even if it pit son against father and mother against daughter. Finally, I would tell you to go to Ephesians and read Chapter 6, verses 10 through 20."

"I know that one, David," Danny said, his mood brightening. "That's the armor of God, isn't it?"

"Yes, Danny, verse 13. 'Therefore put on the full armor of God, so that when the day of evil comes, you may be able to stand your ground.' I don't think there's a clearer way to put it, do you?" Danny didn't answer, and the two men sat silently for a while. Finally, David broke the silence. "What are you thinking, Danny? Do you already have a plan that involves violence?"

"I'm not sure what I'm thinking, David. I know one thing. I can't sit back and wait for this psycho to kill my son or my daughter or my wife. The police say he's killed before and they don't doubt that he'll do it again. I guess I know what I have to do, but I don't want to involve you any further."

"Danny, I've been your friend and your pastor for a long time, and I think I know you pretty well. I have to say it's hard for me to picture you taking a life. Do you really believe you could actually *do* it?"

"I guess that's the real question, isn't it, David," Danny said, not knowing the answer himself.

"As far as involving me, anything you say to me is protected, and I would never divulge it to anyone. I'll respect your wishes, but I want to leave you with this thought. In the middle ages when the term 'outlaw' first came into use, it meant that the person who was declared an outlaw had broken the laws of man and God. This man Ramos is an outlaw in every sense of the word."

"I know that, Pastor," Danny said. "What's your point?"

"Did you also know that once a man was declared an outlaw, it also meant he was now outside the protection of the law and the protection of the church, and by extension, God?"

"No, I wasn't aware of that," Danny said, growing a bit impatient. "I still don't know why you're telling me this."

"I'm now speaking to you as your friend and as a father with children of his own," Shieldman told Danny before continuing his story. "Once a man was declared an outlaw and no longer enjoyed the protection of the laws of man or God, he could be killed by anyone who saw him. The person who killed an outlaw was not held accountable by the law or by the church. That was the most damning thing about being declared an outlaw, Danny. Cisco Ramos is clearly an outlaw. I've said all I can as your friend and as a father. Now I'm going to go back to the church and pray to Jesus that I haven't sinned against Him by sharing my thoughts."

"Pastor, I really appreciate your coming here today, and, believe me, your counsel is invaluable."

"I hope I've been some help to you today, my friend," said Shieldman.

"More than you know, David. More than you know." Danny signaled for the waitress to bring the check.

That night, Danny read and reread the Bible passages that Pastor Shieldman had given him. Then he got down on his knees and began to pray. He prayed every night, but this time he prayed like he had never prayed before. He prayed that God would show him what to do. Then he prayed for forgiveness for the sinful thoughts he held in his heart. He had been asleep for only a few minutes when the phone rang. The clock beside the bed showed eight minutes after four in the morning. Danny picked up the phone and held it to his ear, saying nothing. It was the same voice.

"You know, Hero, I've been thinking that maybe you might try to run away? You know, maybe grab up that pretty little wife of yours and those two kids and go hide out somewhere. Or maybe just send your boy away somewhere to hide." Danny didn't respond but he didn't hang up. *What would be the point?* he thought. *I can't leave the phone off the hook forever. Maybe this guy will say something that might help the police.* The voice went on.

"So, I was thinking that I better tell you something, Hero. If the boy disappears, he better take his little sister with him because if he doesn't, I'll kill her instead. But not before my friends and I have a little fun with her. If you all disappear one night and I can't find you, I will kill your mother and your father. I will kill the friends you work with. I will kill your aunts, your uncles, your cousins, and your neighbors. You know I'm telling the truth, don't you, Hero?"

Danny did not answer.

"Okay, Hero, now you're pissing me off. You are insulting me by not answering my question. If you don't answer me right now and tell me you know I will do it, I'm going to kill your next door neighbor, Mr. Burwell, tomorrow night. You want that on your conscience, Hero?"

Left with no choice, Danny spoke up. "Yes, I believe you. You're just sick enough to do it. So, yes, I believe you."

"Good, Hero. I'm glad we got this straight. Don't forget now and go so far away that I can't find you when I want you. You be a good little Boy Scout and do what I say, and maybe I'll let your son live." He laughed. "But probably not." The line went dead.

CHAPTER TWENTY THREE
EZRA

THE NEXT MORNING, still with no clear answer to his dilemma, Danny went to school to continue his new duties as assistant principal and dean of boys. It was a difficult morning. He could not concentrate for longer than a few minutes before Francisco Ramos and his threats of violence flooded into his head.

Finally, at a quarter until noon, he gave up. He picked up his lunch bag, walked down the hall to the soft-drink machine, inserted a dollar bill, retrieved his Diet Coke and change, and took the stairs down to the basement. Students were not allowed below ground, so it was much quieter there. Danny strolled past the doors of various storage rooms until he came to the room where all the schools heating and air conditioning equipment was housed.

He knocked, then pushed the door open. Sticking his head inside, he shouted over the sound of the machinery, "Anybody home?"

"Always home for you, Mr. Dan," a voice from behind one of the furnaces responded. Danny entered the room, and a small, wiry, old, black man stepped into view.

"How you doing today, Ezra?" Danny asked.

"Oh, about good as can be expected for a man my age, Mr. Dan. About good as can be expected." They shook hands and sat down at a small desk that had long ago been the only equipment a good teacher needed, aside from a piece of chalk and a ruler. Today's teachers had bigger desks, computer work stations, and Power Point projectors for their laptops. Ezra Reed inherited the ancient desk many years ago, and it suited him perfectly. He sat at the desk to eat his lunch and to fill out work orders or material requests required to make sure the school stayed warm in the winter and cool in the summer.

Although the two men had worked at the same school for a long time, they had never exchanged more than a passing "good morning" until three years before, when Danny saved the old man from a group of young toughs from another school. The Robert E. Lee Generals were hosting a Friday night football game against a team from Duluth. The Generals were winning easily, and some of the Duluth fans sneaked out to their cars during the game to drink beer. Four of them were still hanging around the school an hour after the game, looking for something to vandalize.

Ezra Reed was always the last person to leave the school after football or basketball games, and he had surprised the youths as they were about to break some windows and spray-paint a few obscenities on the sidewalk. Ezra took his responsibility to the school very seriously, and even though these four young white men had been drinking, he had tried to stop them from damaging school property.

"You boys better get on gone from around here now," he said. "Don't make me call the police on you." The boys, who had not seen him approaching, turned and stared at the old man. Their initial panic at being caught in the act quickly disappeared when they realized their adversary was an old, unarmed maintenance man. They slowly formed a circle around Ezra, blocking any possible escape, though it was unlikely that the old man could have outrun them even if he wanted to try. The largest boy, who appeared to be the leader, moved in close.

"You ain't calling nobody, old nigger," he said. "You should've minded your own business. Now, you're gonna get hurt."

It had been many years since anyone had called Ezra that despicable word to his face, and it brought back terrible memories of another time and another place. *Some things just never change*, he thought. But he ignored the slur and didn't back down.

"You better do like I tell you now, boys, and get on away from here," he warned them. "You gonna get mo' trouble than this is worth if you don't." The large boy hit the old man in the stomach so hard that Ezra staggered backwards, tripped, and fell to the pavement. The boy walked up and stood over him, then spit on the old man's shirt.

"You know something, nigger. I think I'll let you go. But before I do, I want you to crawl over here and kiss my feet." One of the other boys decided he didn't want any part of this.

"Come on, Billy," he said nervously, "let the old dude alone. Let's just get the hell out of here before anyone else shows up."

"You shut the hell up, Sam. I already told this nosy nigger that he's gonna kiss my feet, and we ain't leaving till he does." Ezra sat up and was holding his hand to his stomach.

"Ain't no way I'm gonna kiss yo' feet, boy," the old man said firmly. "Even if you kill me, boy, just ain't no way in hell."

"Well, then, if your mouth won't come to my feet, I guess I'm gonna have to bring my feet to your mouth," the boy said. Then he tried to kick the old man in the face, but Ezra saw the kick coming and rolled on his side, causing the boy's foot to barely graze Ezra's cheek.

Just then, Danny came out of the field house where he had been editing some film from that night's game. As he turned the corner and headed for the faculty parking lot, he heard voices coming from the shadows to his left. He walked over to investigate and spotted the school janitor lying on the pavement with four teenage boys standing over him.

"What's going on here?" Danny shouted. "Get away from him."

All four boys turned to face him. Danny could see that they were big kids, probably seniors or maybe even recent graduates.

"You want some of this mister?" the leader asked. Danny looked around for something to use as a weapon to intimidate them. He stooped to pick up a two-foot-long stake that was lying in the grass near the curb. He was operating on pure instinct.

"Yeah, I want some of it kid," he said with as much bravado as he could muster. "Fighting is my specialty. There are four of you and just one of me, but I promise you this: at least one of you boys will be in the hospital tonight. And by tomorrow he'll be telling the police the rest of your names. So, the way I see it, you have two choices: Figure out which one of you is going to the hospital, or get out of here right now."

The leader took a step forward, but his buddy Sam started to back away while the other two boys kept shifting their gaze from Danny to their leader and back. "I'm out of here, Billy," Sam said. "I didn't come here for this. This dude is crazy." He turned around and broke into a run. The other two boys hesitated for a split second before they sprinted away behind him.

"Get back here, you chickenshits!" bellowed Billy. His friends never looked back and were quickly lost in the darkness between the buildings.

"Well, Billy boy, it looks like it's just me and you," Danny said menacingly. "I guess they've elected you as the one to go to the hospital—*so let's do this!*" He took a step forward and Billy bolted, quickly vanishing into the night.

Danny could feel the adrenalin pumping as he knelt down to help Ezra to his feet. "Are you all right, sir?" he asked, extending his right hand. The old man looked at him and grabbed Danny's hand.

"I been better," he said. "Then again, I been worse, too."

"Come on back in the field house and let me take a good look at your face. I have some antiseptic and bandages in there."

"Sir?" Ezra seemed puzzled.

"I beg your pardon?"

"Sir," the old man repeated. "You called me 'sir.' I don't think a white man ever called me 'sir' that I can recall. I ain't ever gonna forget this night. You a mighty brave man."

"I was scared to death," Danny admitted. "I don't know what I would have done if they had decided to fight instead of run. All that stuff I said? Heck, I just heard it in a movie last week. It was the first thing that came to me."

"I expect that if they had decided to fight instead of run, one of them would be headed to the hospital right now," the old man cackled, grinning at Danny. "No, sir, I ain't never gonna forget this night."

❦

Ever since then, Danny had been coming down to the furnace room to eat lunch with Ezra at least once a week. He had developed a strong bond with the old man. He once called on Ezra to help him replace a propane furnace at the mountain cabin Sheila's father owned in north Georgia. Danny's family had vacationed there often when the children were younger, but they seldom went there anymore. The kids had outgrown it, for now at least. He hoped that he and Sheila might use it more in their "golden years" and that maybe the kids--and someday maybe even a few grandkids—would spend some time there.

Because of the cabin's elevation, temperatures in the summertime averaged as much as fifteen degrees cooler than in Atlanta. The mountain breezes and fresh air had always been attractions for Danny. It was a different story in the winter. The city of Atlanta seldom got snow, and when it did, it was usually either a dusting or a couple of inches that melted away in a day or two. In the North Georgia mountains, however, with elevations reaching almost five thousand feet at Brasstown Bald at the southern end of the Blue Ridge Mountains, snow was much more prevalent. During the spring, summer and late into the fall, Sheila's father and family friends used the cabin on occasion to fish the lake that had been created by rainwater and snow melt filling an abandoned quarry near the cabin. The old furnace had quit working and, without heat, the cabin would have been virtually useless after September. Danny and Ezra spent an entire weekend together there repairing it. The old man's knowledge of heating systems had been a money-saving godsend for Danny's father-in-law. The 38-year-old white educator and the 65-year-old black maintenance man were casual friends when arrived at the cabin, but when they left, they were like family. Since that weekend, they had been to the cabin on several occasions to fish in the freshwater lake.

Out of curiosity one day, Danny had pulled Ezra's personnel file. According to the records, Ezra Elijah Reed was born in 1943 in Tupelo, Mississippi, and he had lived in Atlanta since 1963. He had listed no next of kin. The file also indicated that he had never had any trouble with the law and had been a 'Green Beret' in the U.S. Army, serving a tour in Vietnam, during which he earned a Bronze Star for Valor. Danny once asked Ezra about it, but the old man just shrugged, saying, "Sometimes a man has got to do what he's got to do, and he don't have time to think about it. 'Cause if he thought too long, he might not do it. I believe I seen you do that very thing yourself." Danny never brought it up again.

"Well, what do we have on the menu today, Ezra?" Danny asked his friend, as they sat down at the old school desk.

"Mr. Dan, I have a can of vienna sausages, some soda crackers, and an apple." Danny detested those little cocktail wieners, but he knew they were a staple for the maintenance man.

"Wonderful, sir, just wonderful," he said. "And I can contribute two ham and cheese sandwiches on rye bread with Swiss cheese." Ezra never knew it, but on days Danny planned to have lunch with the old man, he always asked Sheila to pack an extra sandwich. The men opened their lunch bags and spread the food out on the table. Danny slid one of his sandwiches over to the old man and delicately plucked a vienna sausage from the can. He popped it into his mouth, chewed it quickly, then washed it down with Diet Coke.

They chatted comfortably, as old friends do, covering a range of topics that included the recent elections, the war in Afghanistan, the Robert E. Lee football team, and, finally, Danny's new job.

"That's mighty fine, Mr. Dan, mighty fine," said Ezra when the subject came up. "I'm very proud of you." Danny had asked him numerous occasions not to call him "Mr. Dan," assuring him that "Danny" was just fine. But growing up in the segregated Deep South had ingrained in him old habits that were hard to correct. So Ezra could never bring himself to call his white friend just "Danny."

"You know, Mr. Dan, for a man with such a fine new promotion, you seem mighty sad," said Ezra, finished up another vienna sausage. "You don't seem happy at all and not like your usual self. What's ailing you, Mr. Dan?" Danny felt at ease with this old man, and he saw no reason not to share at least some of his problem.

"Well, Ezra, there's a man who has it in for me," Danny said, getting right to the heart of the matter. "He hates me for something I had no control over. He says he's going to hurt my family and maybe even kill my son. The police say they can't do anything unless I can prove he's making the threats or until he actually does something. I think he'll do what he says, and I don't know what I'm going to do about it."

The words came out in a rush, and when he was finished, Danny leaned back in his chair and looked into the sorrowful eyes of his friend. Without saying a word, Ezra got up from his seat, walked slowly over to the old student locker he had brought down to his "office," opened it, and took out a cigar box. He came back and sat down at the desk with Danny, setting the box down between them. The stained paper cover of the box was torn in several places and it's corners were frayed. But, when Ezra opened it, Danny could see that it contained some cherished memento of the old man's life. Ezra reached into the box and gently removed a photograph. He looked at it for a moment, then gave it to Danny, who held it up to the light. It was a picture of a middle-aged black woman, a young black woman, and two children—both boys. One of the boys appeared to be about 3 years old, the other a year or so younger. The picture was black and white and very old, wrinkled at the edges, with a few cracks streaking like spider webs across the image.

"That's my mama, Mr. Dan, and my wife, Rachel, and my boys, Solomon and Jeremiah," Ezra said tenderly. "I wasn't even there when Jeremiah was born 'cause I had just left for Vietnam when he came along. Rachel sent me that picture whilst I was overseas in the war. I been carrying that picture with me ever since then. It's all I got left of all of them." Danny saw the tears in his eyes.

"Ezra, if you want to tell me what happened to them, I would be glad to listen."

"Mr. Dan, I don't tell many people this story, and I ain't never told a white man, but I think I should tell you. Maybe it will help you with your struggle, maybe not. I don't know, but here goes."

He took a mouth full of his coffee, swished it around in his mouth, and swallowed. Then he began to speak:

"It was November of nineteen hundred and sixty-three. I had just come home to Tupelo from the war in Vietnam. It weren't much of a war yet, but still, people was killin' and getting killed just the same. Anyway, I was almost 21 years old and full of piss and vinegar, as my mama used to say. I was proud to wear my uniform with all my ribbons and my Bronze Star on it, too. I strutted around shantytown wearing that uniform every day for a month while I was looking for a job. I thought maybe that uniform and them medals would help me get me a job, you see. Well, one day I heard that the feed store in town was looking for a driver, so I went on into town to see if I could get me that job. I was walking down the sidewalk, not bothering nobody, but feeling pretty good in my uniform, when a white man name of Jesse Wilburn met me coming the other way. He stopped right in front of me so's I couldn't get by him. I tried to go around him on the right, but he just moved over there and kept blocking me. So, I go to the left, and he blocked me again. Finally, I said to him, 'Let me pass, sir.' He looked me right in my eye and says, 'Nigger, if you want to go by me, boy, you walk out in the street. That's where niggers are supposed to walk, boy, in the street. Not up on the sidewalk with white folks. If you want to walk on the sidewalk, boy, get your ass on back down to niggertown.' That's what the white folks called shantytown." Ezra looked at Danny to make sure he understood before he went on.

"I said to him, 'No sir, I served my country in a war, and I can walk on the sidewalk like the next man.' He said, 'Hell no you cain't, neither. You ain't walking by me.' So I put my hand on him just a little, you know, nice and gentle, and I try to push him a little so's I can get by. When I do, he slapped me in my face. I mean, he *slapped* me—not a punch like you give to a man, but a slap, like to child. When he did that, I never did stop to think, and to this day I wish to God I had. I hit that man so hard he flew off the sidewalk into the street. I wasn't a small man back then, and I could hit pretty hard. I had my share of fights while I was in the Army with colored boys and white boys, too. Anyways, he don't get up for a second or two, and I start to walk on down the sidewalk. Somebody screamed, and I turn around, and he was coming at me with a knife." Danny was spellbound.

"I had hurt him pretty good, and he wasn't moving too fast or thinking too straight, so before he can cut me, I kicked Jesse Wilburn right between his legs. This time he goes down and don't get back up. He just lay there moaning and holding his crotch. So I go on down the street. Well, when I get to the feed store to apply for that driver job, Mr. William Tucker, who owned the store, told me he seen what happened and he says to me, 'Good on you, young man. I don't care if he's white and you're black, that Jesse Wilburn is a mean and evil man. Somebody been needing to take him down a notch for a while.' So he give me the job, and I thought that was the end of it. But it wasn't the end of nothing. No sir, it were just the beginning.

Well, I got that job at the feed store, and they was paying me pretty good for a colored man in those days. My mama was living with us in a little two-bedroom place in shantytown. Me and Rachel slept in one room, and mama and the boys slept in the other. Mama used to laugh and say that maybe instead of sleeping with the boys, she need to sleep in the same bed with me and my Rachel so's there won't be no more young'un's mouths to feed. About two weeks after I start work at the feed store, I come out to the truck one morning where it was parked behind the store. Mr. William, who owned the feed store, you know, he said if I was white or I didn't live in shantytown, he might let me drive it home at night, but he was afraid to have it parked down there in shantytown at night. I told him that was okay by me 'cause I had got used to walking in the Army. Anyways, when I get to the truck, I find a note stuck under the windshield wiper. The note says, 'Nigger, you is a dead man, and so is your nigger wife and them nigger kids. You kicked me in my nuts, and I'm gonna cut yours off, nigger.' I was scared real bad for my family, and I went right down to see Sheriff John Stuart. He wasn't such a bad man, even though he used to brag that his great granddaddy was General Jeb Stuart of the Confederate Army. Still, he seemed to treat colored folks fair, and he liked that I had been a soldier. He told me he would warn Jesse Wilburn to leave me alone, but unless I could prove it was him who wrote the note, there weren't much else he could do for me—at least until Jesse actually did something to me or my family that we could prove." Danny was amazed at how this story mirrored his own. Ezra went on.

"I said to him, 'Sheriff John, I ain't kicked nobody else excepting Jesse Wilburn, so who else gonna write that note?' He tells me, 'Ezra, we both know Jesse wrote the note. But writing a note like that ain't going to get him put in jail. All I can do is speak to him about leaving ya'll be.' Well, I didn't hear or see nothing else for a couple of weeks, and I was hoping Jesse Wilburn had just been drunk when he wrote that note and really wasn't gonna come after us. But one night, as we was sitting down for supper, a brick come smashing through the front window. The brick had a note wrapped around it tied with a string. It said, 'Nigger, don't think I've forgot you, 'cause I ain't. I'm just biding my time and making you sweat, but I'm coming, nigger, I'm coming.'

I went back down to the sheriff's office the next day. Sheriff John Stuart told me to get in his patrol car with him, that we was going to take a ride. I don't mind telling you that I was a little skeered about then, 'cause, like I told you, this was Mississippi, and it was 1963. I wouldn't be the first colored man who disappeared after getting into a police car. But I trusted that man, so I got in, and we rode out to Jesse Wilburn's farm. He was sitting on his porch eating some chicken when we pull up in the yard. He didn't get up or say 'howdy' to the sheriff or nothing. He just sat there gnawing on that piece of chicken and staring at us. Sheriff John told me to stay in the yard, so I got out of the car since it was kind of hot and went and stood under a tree by the barn. He walked up on the porch and said, 'How you doing today, Jesse?'

That Jesse Wilburn didn't look at him 'cause he was just staring at me, and he says, 'What for you bringing a nigger up in my yard? I didn't invite you out here, and I damn sure didn't ask that nigger to come up to my house.' The sheriff says, 'I don't need an invite, Jesse, because I'm the law. And the colored fella is with me.' Then he reached in his pocket and pulled out the note I found on the brick that come through my front window. He unfolded it and handed it to Jesse Wilburn and said, 'Did you write this, Jesse?' Wilburn don't even look at the note. He just says, 'Hell, no, I didn't write it. Now get that nigger off my property, and don't bring him back.' The sheriff says, 'Jesse Wilburn, Ezra says you wrote it, and I believe him, so I'm putting you on notice as of right now. If anything bad happens to this man or his family, you are the first person I'm gonna come looking for. You got that?' Jesse Wilburn jumps up out of his chair and gets right up the sheriff's face and starts screaming at him. 'John Stuart, have you started taking the word of a nigger over a white man now, you son-of-a-bitch?' The sheriff don't say nothing at first. Then he hit Jesse Wilburn right in the belly so hard that he fell back in his chair. Then he leaned over real quick and started throwing up. Pieces of chicken come flying out of his mouth and got on the sheriff's boots. The sheriff just reached his foot out and cleaned his boot on Jesse's leg, then he says, 'If you ever speak to me that way again or disrespect the law like that, I'm gonna put you in jail for a long time for assaulting a police officer. And speaking of taking one person's word against another, if it's me saying you did it and you saying you didn't, I can tell you who the judge will believe. We're going now, but don't forget what I said about this man and his family.'

We went back and was getting in the patrol car when Jesse Wilburn finally catches his breath. He stands on the top step and starts hollering at the sheriff, 'There's lots of white folks around here that ain't gonna take kindly to you taking a nigger's word over a white man's, especially when it comes election time.' Sheriff John sticks his head out the window and says, 'Since you are the white man in question, I doubt there's many folks gonna doubt who's telling the truth. Don't forget what I said today.'

On the way back to town, the sheriff told me he appreciated what I done serving my country and that if he could, he would stop Jesse Wilburn from messing with my family. Then he told me again that he couldn't do nothing until Jesse did something first. I figured I wasn't through with Jesse yet, so I started asking the people who lived in shantytown about him. Colored folks knew just about everything going on in any town back then 'cause white people just talked around us like we didn't even exist. So the maids and gardeners and delivery men heard a lot of stuff. I found out that Jesse Wilburn was a bad person. I heard when he was a teenage boy, he used to ride around at night drinking bootleg whiskey and shooting people's dogs off their porches. He raped and beat up a colored girl real bad one night behind the road house where she washed dishes, but she never told the sheriff 'cause Jesse said his brothers would kill her family even if he was in jail. That girl never did tell nobody what happened until she was in the hospital birthing a baby. The baby was half white, and the girl died, but not before she told who the daddy was. Anyway, I learned enough about the man to know he was dangerous and that he probably would try to hurt us.

Finally, me and my Rachel decided to move out of Tupelo and go somewhere else. I found out later that my mama told some of her friends, and they told somebody else, and next thing you know, Jesse Wilburn knows that we planning on leaving town soon. But I didn't know that then. While I was on my way home late one night, after making a run to the feed plant in Jackson, somebody threw three firebombs made out of jugs of gasoline into my house. Before they threw them, they had tied the front and the back door of the house shut with rope running from the handles to the porch rail. Since they had throwed the gas in through the three windows of the house, that's where the fire was burning hottest and Mama and Rachel couldn't get the doors open cause they was tied shut. That old, dry, wooden shack went up like a bonfire. Every one of them died in that fire. When I got home about one o'clock in the morning, the house was just a smoldering pile, and all the neighbors was just standing around crying. They thought I was a ghost when they first seen me cause they didn't know I wasn't home when the fire started. The next day the sheriff arrested Jesse Wilburn, but nobody could say for sure that he was the one who set the fire. Besides, it was Mississippi, and it was 1963, and he was white, and the dead folks was black. It didn't matter that the sheriff testified about the notes and everything. There was too many people on the jury who wasn't gonna send a white man to the gallows for some dead black people. That was just not gonna happen in Mississippi back then. If you send the first white man to jail for killing colored people, then who knows what's gonna happen next. The Ku Klux Klan even put up some notices about what would happen to Mississippi and the rights of white people if Jesse Wilburn got convicted. He walked out of the court room a free man in less than three hours."

Danny had been studying Ezra's face as he listened to the story. The old man's expression never changed, as if everything he was describing had happened to someone else and he was just passing on the facts.

"My God, Ezra, I am so sorry," Danny said. "Whatever happened to Jesse Wilburn? I mean, is he still alive after all these years?"

"Somebody shot and killed Jesse Wilburn with a rifle from about five hundred yards away whilst Jesse sat drinking beer on his front porch. Sheriff John Stuart said it was murder for sure. Murder done by, as he put it, 'a person or persons unknown.' He said it was a mighty fine piece of shooting, too. Maybe the shooter had some kind of military experience. Maybe the shooter had even been a sniper. Then the sheriff said he would do some investigating, but since Jesse Wilburn had so many folks who wanted him dead, it would be like looking for a needle in a haystack, so he wasn't gonna pursue it too long. A few folks thought maybe it could of been me on account of what happened to my family. One of Jesse Wilburn's cousins even told the sheriff that he knew for certain I was a sniper in the Army. The sheriff told them he didn't believe such a fine piece of shooting could have been done by a colored man, even one who had been in the military. About a month later, Sheriff John asked me to come by his office for a little talk. I was pretty skeered that once I walked into that jail, I was never coming out, but I went anyway. He asked me if I had been a sniper when I was in Vietnam. Now the sheriff had been good to me and more than fair, but I was still scared of him because... well, he was white and I was black. But I decided I wasn't gonna lie about my service, because being a sniper was the only thing I had ever been really good at. I was proud I could shoot better than a lot of the white boys. I was proud I had fought for my country. So I told him the truth. 'Yes,' I says, 'I was a sniper.' Then I figured he was gonna ask me if I killed Jesse Wilburn. But he didn't. He just sat there and looked at me for a minute, then he said he was gonna have to search the little shanty I'd been living in since my house burned down to see if I had a sniper rifle. He said he would be starting to search in about a week, since he was busy with other things right now. He winked at me and told me to go on home. I told you Sheriff John was a good man. I went home and gathered up everything I had left in this world, and took a bus to Atlanta. All I had was just a few things I had stored at my uncle's house 'cause we didn't have room for them in the shanty. That was a long time ago, and that's all I am gonna say about Jesse Wilburn. That's the end of my story. But yours ain't finished, is it, Mr. Dan? Like I said, I ain't never told a white man any of this before."

Danny picked up the remains of his lunch and tossed it into the can beside the desk. He stood up to leave and shook Ezra's hand.

"I know why you told me this story, Ezra, and I thank you for trusting me," Danny said. The old man looked at him with the same sad expression he had worn when he told the story of his family's murder. "See you next week, Ezra," Danny said as he left the furnace room. "Don't forget the vienna sausages."

⁊

CHAPTER TWENTY FOUR
LINDSEY PRESSES ON

LINDSEY ADAMS GRADUATED from Georgia State University in Atlanta with a degree in journalism when she was 22 years old. Now 25, she was an up-and-coming on-scene reporter for Channel 14, the Universal Broadcast System affiliate in Atlanta. Lindsey was a very attractive, all-American, girl next door looking young woman. She was single, ambitious, and more than a little intimidating to most of the young men who attempted to build a relationship with her.

Lindsey had grown up poor and worked her way through college as a waitress at Hooters. She had been pursued by more men than she could count, but all of them either wanted only to get her into bed or lacked, in her estimation, the potential to help her achieve the life of fame, wealth, and influence she had always dreamed of. Lindsey was not above using her allure—and her bed, if necessary—to further her goals, but she was judicious with both.

She was beginning to make her mark on the local news scene and with Universal. The network suits had noticed her work and were enthusiastic about her future. Even though she might never make it to the anchor position on the network's nightly news, there were many other opportunities for an attractive, articulate young woman like her.

Since the first interview with Danny at the scene of the accident, Lindsey had considered his story to be *her* story. She had avidly read the articles about him in the newspapers and believed that this could be a big shot in the arm for her career—that is, if she could get her boss, Bill Carpenter, the news director at Channel 14, to let her run with it.

She had approached him several days after the death of the Mexican teen with an idea for a documentary about Francisco Ramos, Jr., and Danny Chambers: The young Latino gangbanger and the all-American hero. She wanted to research Danny's background, taping interviews with old friends, military associates, the people he worked with, and his immediate family. She intended to do the same type of interviews with the family and friends of Francisco Ramos, Jr.

Her aim was to lay out the events that had led these two unlikely adversaries to a deadly face-off on a busy Atlanta intersection. Carpenter had told her he had too much on his plate and had serious reservations about whether she was the right person for the job. Besides, he said, he wasn't sure he could even find the money in the budget for the research.

One week later, Lindsey walked into his office and sat down without being asked. Carpenter was reading something on the CNN Web site and didn't see her come in. After a few seconds, he looked up.

"Good afternoon, Lindsey," he said. "I didn't mean to keep you waiting, but I didn't hear you knock."

Lindsey flashed her brilliant smile and said nothing.

"Okay, I'll bite. To what do I owe the pleasure of your company on this fine winter day?"

"Come on, Bill, don't be coy. You know exactly what I want to talk about. When are you going to give me the go-ahead on my story on the hero and the gangbanger?"

"Lindsey, we've talked about this before, and you know how I feel. I just don't know if you're ready yet. I think you've come up with a good angle for a story, though, and if we can find the money, I'll want you to work with Doug Altman on it. He would be the lead, but you'd be heavily involved." Altman was the evening news anchor who had been a fixture on Atlanta television screens for more than a decade. He was rich, arrogant, and powerful—everything Lindsey Adams aspired to be. He was also good-looking and had hit on Lindsey more than once, so she was sure that if she wanted, she would have no problem getting him to accept her as his assistant on the story. But that was not what she wanted. She wanted the whole thing for herself and was determined to get it any way she could.

"I don't know what my responsibilities on the story would be," she said sarcastically, "but I can guess who'd get all the face time on the air."

"Come on, Lindsey, you know how it works," her boss said, trying to settle her down. "Doug is the face of Channel 14. Our viewers will expect him to do the story."

Yeah, he's the face of channel 14, but not forever. Lindsey thought to herself. "Bill, I can do this," she pleaded. "I know I can. It was my idea. Why should Doug get it? He's already the star. This story needs a fresh approach, a fresh face. Look, I know you're busy now, so why don't the two of us meet for dinner tonight and talk it out. What do you say, boss?"

Carpenter glared at her. "Lindsey, I'm a married man, and a happily married one at that. Dinner with you would get me in a lot of trouble with my wife. I make business decisions at work, not over candlelight and wine." Lindsey started to protest, but he continued talking. "You're a pretty girl, and I've seen how men react when you flash those baby blues at them, but I need to make decisions based on what's best for this station, not what's good for me or for you. Do you understand?"

"Of course, I understand," Lindsey said. "I'm sorry, but I think you misinterpreted my dinner invitation. All I wanted was some time with you away from the phone so we could discuss this documentary in depth."

"Really? Where did you plan on eating?"

"How about a good steak at McKendrick's?" Lindsey asked, sensing victory.

"Great," said Carpenter. "What time should I tell my wife to meet us?" Lindsey's face turned red, and Carpenter laughed. "See how easy it is to get yourself in trouble? You're going places in this business, Lindsey, but I don't want you to do it on your back. Just do the grunt work like everyone else, and you'll get there soon enough."

Lindsey clasped her hands in her lap and stared down at them, trying to hold back tears of shame. No one had ever called her out like this before, and she didn't know how to react. Carpenter saw that she was embarrassed and began to feel bad that he had been so rough on her ego. *Oh, what the hell,* he thought. *She has to get her feet wet sooner or later.*

"Okay, girl," he said, " the story is yours, but with a few caveats."

Her mood brightened immediately. "Whatever you say, as long as it's my show."

"First, you tell how much air time you think you'll need. I'll cut that figure by seventy-five percent, then you can proceed. Second, you keep me informed all the way, and if I see you're getting off track or the story's going nowhere, I pull the plug. Finally, you have to scale this thing down. You can interview anyone you want about Chambers, the dead kid, or his father, as long as they live in the area. I don't have a budget for travel, and I'm not authorizing any. If you feel you have to do any traveling, it will come out of your own pocket. Does all of that work for you?"

"Absolutely," she said, eager to get started. "Thank you so much for giving me this chance, Bill."

"Just make me proud and make the station look good. That's all I ask." Lindsey got up to leave. "Oh, one more thing," said Carpenter. "Remember me when you're in New York anchoring the evening news, little lady."

Lindsey winked at him and floated out the door.

CHAPTER TWENTY FIVE
NEWSPAPERMAN

LINDSEY ADAMS WAS not the only news hound who saw great potential in a series about Danny Chambers. Joe Goddard, senior staff reporter for the *Atlanta Record*, had received high praise from his editor for the first article he wrote about Danny. The *Record* was a distant second in circulation to the venerable Atlanta Journal-Constitution, commonly referred to as the AJC. The *Record* tended to chase the more sensational stories and often tried to make them even more sensational, whether they deserved it or not. If there were any paparazzi in Atlanta, they most likely took their photos to the *Record*.

Goddard watched Lindsey's first interview with Danny and saw, even before Lindsey did, that this story was gold. In an America that appeared to be growing increasingly uncomfortable with the invasion of Hispanic immigrants, this story could be huge. Though they worked as hard as any other ethnic group, Hispanics were perceived by some as dangerous and not to be trusted. To a casual observer seeing groups of them standing around every other street corner in certain areas of Atlanta, they came across as bums looking for a handout, or worse, looking for trouble. In reality, most of them were waiting for a bus or hoping to be picked up for day work on a construction site or with a landscaping crew.

A story about a football coach stopping a young Hispanic gang member from brutally killing a woman in broad daylight, was a godsend for the *Record*, especially in light of its lagging circulation. It did not matter at all to Goddard that it was the AJC that uncovered the military hero angle. He knew the larger paper would lose interest in the story, as bigger more important ones cropped up. But *he* was not going to lose interest. He was going to fan the flames and make this story bigger than anyone else could imagine. Joe didn't know that Lindsey Adams planned to cover this story from both sides, but even if he had known, it wouldn't have changed his approach. He was going to make Danny Chambers larger than life, and if he had to bend the facts a bit here and there about the dead teenage gangbanger, so be it.

His first order of business was to send an email to every one of his contacts in the city, saying he would pay for any significant information about Danny Chambers, Cisco Ram, or the Latino Death Lords.

∾

CHAPTER TWENTY SIX
FORT MCPHERSON

LINDSEY ADAMS CONTACTED the commanding officer at Fort McPherson, which is located in East Point, Georgia, a small town on the southwest border of Atlanta. Though the installation and it's subpost, Fort Gillem, housed fewer than three thousand active duty U.S. Army personnel and about forty-five hundred civilians, it happened to be the fort that Danny's reserve unit had been assigned to. It was, in short, the perfect place to uncover more facts about Danny Chambers' military background.

The administrative assistant to Colonel Omar Kinkaid, the post commander, informed Lindsey that the colonel could spare her thirty minutes, and not one minute more, at 1000 hours on Wednesday morning, five days after she got the go-ahead from Bill Carpenter. She was processed onto the base, had her picture taken and imprinted on a visitor's pass, and handed over to the colonel's adjutant, a second lieutenant fresh out of Virginia Military Institute named Jamie Preston. The Lieutenant told her the colonel had been delayed but had instructed him to occupy his guest with a quick overview of Fort McPherson and its mission.

Listening to this wet-behind-the-ears 22-year-old lieutenant who couldn't keep his eyes off her breasts, ramble on about the mission of the U.S. Army Installation Management Command was the last thing on Lindsey's agenda for today or any other day. But, she knew the value of contacts, so she listened attentively, batted her eyes at the appropriate times, and asked the young pup a few innocuous questions such as, "How dangerous is it to be a modern-day soldier?" while she waited to see the colonel. Twenty minutes later, she was sitting in front of his enormous desk, declining the colonel's offer of coffee and accepting instead a Diet Coke. While he was on the phone ordering her soft drink, Lindsey surveyed the room. The walls of the office were festooned with relics of the colonel's military career. When her drink was brought in, she asked Col. Kincaid a few questions about his background and military adventures. She had no interest in any of this, nor would any of it appear in her story, but she knew the fastest way to get the man talking and on her side was to let him talk about himself. It was a tactic that had never failed her, and it did not fail her now. After going nonstop for fifteen minutes, the colonel looked at his watch.

"I beg your pardon, Ms. Adams," he said, "but I've wasted a lot of your time with a bunch of old war stories. Excuse me a moment." He turned to the credenza behind his desk and punched a button on the intercom. "Molly, contact Captain Morrison and tell him I've been unavoidably detained and can't make our meeting this morning. Ask him if he can come by today at 1500 hours. Also, please and hold my calls until further notice." He swung back around to face Lindsey and stole a glance at her well-formed legs, which were crossed demurely, and asked, "Now, young lady, what can this old soldier do for you?"

Lindsey told him about the story she was doing on Danny Chambers, with no mention that the story would also be about Francisco Ramos, Jr. or his father. Without telling any outright lies, she did her best to imply that the story would be about how Danny's military training and experiences had prepared him to do what had to be done, on that fateful day, to save the life of an innocent woman.

When Colonel Kinkaid said he would do everything he could to help, she asked him how she could obtain information about Danny Chambers military service, including dates of service, types of training, places where he was stationed, who his buddies were, and what type of performance ratings he received. The colonel told her he could immediately get some of this on-line from Washington and other parts of it in a few days time from the National Archives and Records Administration in College Park, Maryland. He then informed her that certain aspects of her requests, were not available to the public since they dealt with the private records of a living individual. Lindsey then asked if he could help her find any of the men Danny served with.

"Since Danny was in the Reserves and not regular Army, all the men in his outfit were locals," the colonel said. "They're all from north Georgia. They served together one weekend a month and two weeks each summer. When they were called up to active duty and sent to the war zone, they went as a unit."

"That's fantastic!" Lindsey said. "Can you give me the names of the men in his unit so I can interview them?"

"Actually, Ms. Adams, there were men and women in Danny's unit, and no, I can't give out the names of any military personnel assigned to this base, past or present."

Lindsey batted her eyelashes and pouted. "Well, what good does it do me that they're all local, if you won't tell me who they are, Colonel?"

"It's not that I *won't* tell you. I'm prohibited by Army regulations. What I can do is contact some of the troops who spent the most time with Lt. Chambers, advise them of your interest, and have them get in touch with you if they're willing to speak with you about him."

Lindsey's pout turned to a smile. "That works for me, Colonel. How long would that take?"

"One more thing, Ms. Adams. Is Mr. Chambers okay with you doing this story about him? I mean, he's not going to be upset that you're tracking down his old friends to ask them about their association with him, is he?"

This was a question Lindsey had been afraid the colonel would ask. Based on the one interview she had done with Danny Chambers, she was quite sure he wasn't interested in any publicity about the incident. She was equally sure he wouldn't approve of her interviewing his friends, either. But she had prepared herself to answer this question with a lie. A lie she hoped the colonel wouldn't bother to check out.

"Absolutely!" she said with all the false sincerity she could muster. "Maybe you saw the interview I did with him on the nightly news? Danny is certainly in favor of anything that puts the value of the military, the National Guard, and the Army Reserves in front of the public."

"In that case, I see no problem with helping you contact a few people from his past," said the colonel. "I can reach out to most of them this afternoon or in the morning. As for how long it will take them to get back to me, I couldn't say. I doubt that any of them are still serving, so they're under no obligation to respond."

By the time Lindsey left Col. Omar Kinkaid's office, she was well on her way acquiring the background she needed on Danny Chamber. *Now, let's see what we can find out about the little thug,* she thought to herself. She gave the guards at the main gate a big smile and a little glimpse of leg while she was punching numbers into her cell phone. Then she pulled out of the base and onto the highway.

෮෨

CHAPTER TWENTY SEVEN
JUDGE THORNTON

"THE SUPERIOR COURT of the County of Gwinnett is now in session," the bailiff intoned solemnly, "the Honorable Judge Ronald Lewis Thornton presiding. All rise." The defendant, his attorneys, the assistant district attorney who had tried the case, and the small group of spectators rose as one. The judge swept into the room like a king proceeding to his throne, and with a swirl of his black robe, took his seat. Everyone else followed suit.

"The defendant will rise," said the bailiff, and a young black man dressed in prison-orange coveralls stood up slowly, wearing a look of casual disdain for the business at hand. His attorneys stood beside him. The taller one leaned over and whispered something to his client. The defendant laughed behind his hand and whispered back.

"Do you find something about these proceedings humorous, Mr. Taylor?" the judge bellowed ominously.

"No, your honor," replied the defendant.

"Then what are you laughing about?" asked the judge.

"Your honor, I believe that's a...how you say it?...*privileged* conversation between me and my attorney, and I don't think I need to answer that question."

The judge glared at him for a moment, and the man defiantly stared back at him. Finally the judge said, "Althenal Shauneen Taylor, you have been found guilty by a jury of your peers of the crime of armed robbery. We are here today to hand down the sentence of this court. Since this is your third offense, the court sees no reason for leniency, and since it appears that you do not show any remorse for your crime or any respect for this court or it's officers, there will be none granted. Furthermore, I personally think you are a blight on this city and county, and we would all be better off if you were banished from decent society for as long as possible. Therefore, I am sentencing you to the maximum penalty under the law. You will be taken to the state penitentiary at Milledgeville where you will be confined for a period of twenty-five years without parole." He banged his gavel down. "I hope you find your sentence humorous, Mr. Taylor. Bailiff, take him away."

There were cries of anger from some of the defendant's relatives. A woman shouted, "That's not right! He never done this robbery, anyway. Now you saying no parole. It was someone who looked like him. You wouldn't have done this to my boy if he was white."

The judge, who was himself an African American, banged his gavel again. "Madam, I don't know who you are, but if you want to join Mr. Taylor behind bars tonight, disrespect my court again." The woman was about to do just that when she was dragged from the courtroom by other family members.

Judge Ronald Lewis Thornton had a reputation as a modern-day hanging judge, meting out the strongest sentences of any judge in the Georgia superior court system. He lectured the guilty unmercifully about their crimes and exacted the harshest sentences possible for those he deemed "unacceptable" to society. His sentences were also reduced on appeal almost twice as often as his colleagues, but this never deterred him. He had recently been elected to his third consecutive four-year term by the voters of Gwinnett County, Republican and Democrat alike, because he was who he was—a judge who put the bad guys away for as long as the law would allow. The people loved him for it, so he didn't care that his sentences were often overturned. He knew he had done his best to punish the guilty as fittingly as possible.

Judge Thornton not only had a reputation, he also had a secret. He was a sex addict. And though he had been married to his college sweetheart, Marilyn Seashole Knight, for more than twenty years without a hint of scandal, the judge kept a mistress and visited prostitutes as often as three times a week. He managed to keep this quiet because of two factors: one, his wife knew about his dalliances and had long ago decided it was better to be the wife of a celebrated judge and live a life of prestige and plenty than be just one more divorced woman; and two, she had never cared much for sex, even less so after losing a breast to cancer. Despite his infidelities, her husband had always been a kind and caring man who provided well for his family. He was also a loving father who spent as much time as he could with his children. Marilyn Thornton loved her husband and felt that since he was still a strong, virile man in his late forties, he deserved to have some sex in his life. It didn't matter that it wasn't with her, although the number of his paramours likely would have astonished her.

To protect herself from acquiring a sexually transmitted disease, she had made it part of their pact that she would not have sex with him again. So, as long as he was discrete, she never asked questions about his comings and goings. Besides, she often told herself, there were the children's feelings to consider.

Another reason the judge could indulge his taste for expensive women was that he never had to pay for them. They were furnished free of charge, any time he wanted, by a man who had once stood before him in court accused of running a prostitution ring—Francisco Miguel Ramos, street name: Cisco Ram.

As soon as Cisco was indicted on the prostitution charges, he had instructed his contacts to dig into the personal life of the district attorney, Dalton Gray. Specifically, they had reached out to every dope dealer, porno dealer, and call girl they knew to see if the D.A. had anything he might want to hide. They found nothing on him that would be useful, but they did find something even better: Judge Ronald Lewis Thornton's secret. One of the whores told Cisco she had never seen the D.A., but she knew a judge who really liked the ladies.

Cisco's attorney, fearing that the "hanging judge" might prove impossible to blackmail and would throw him in jail for trying, refused to approach the judge. *Cuchillo*, however, called the judge at home one night from a pay phone, disguising his voice with a handkerchief and promising the judge two things: one was that if Francisco Miguel Ramos was found guilty, the judge's secret life would be all over the papers; and two, if he was found not guilty or the case was dropped, the judge would never have to pay for sex again. It was the promise of unlimited free sex more than the fear of being exposed that won him over. The judge discreetly suggested to Cisco's lawyers that they should seek a trial by judge with no jury. At trial, to the surprise of everyone in the courtroom except Cisco and his defense team, the judge ruled that certain key evidence was inadmissible and that he therefore had no choice but to find the accused not guilty.

The Judge had availed himself of Cisco's special escort service ever since. Cisco sent him only the cleanest, most trustworthy, and most beautiful girls, instructing them to do whatever this "special" client wanted and never, under any circumstances, ask him any personal questions. The arrangement had worked out well for both parties. The judge satisfied his cravings, and Cisco had a friend on the bench when he needed it. He was careful to call on Judge Thornton only when there were some legal grounds, no matter how obscure, that the judge could employ. Sometimes the help came in the form of an outright dismissal of charges; other times, it might be a reduced sentence, a smaller fine, or a shorter probation period. Because of the leniency he showed toward Cisco's friends, Judge Thornton had to become even tougher on the other criminals who came before him in order to maintain his hanging-judge reputation.

CHAPTER TWENTY EIGHT
PROMISE LAND

WHEN MANUEL OSORIO left Veracruz, he left as a 15-year-old boy who had already murdered three people in cold blood. He did not leave just to escape the law but because he had a vision that *Los Estados Unidos* was the promised land. Based on the many stories he had heard from the American merchant seaman who docked in Veracruz, it was a place where a young man like himself, someone unafraid to take action, could become rich.

He no longer thought of himself as a boy or as Manuel Osorio. He was now a man, and his name was *El Cuchillo*, a name he would make famous somewhere in the United States. He did not know where he was going when he left. All he knew was that he was going across the border into the promised land. It took him eight days to hitchhike from Veracruz to Matamoros, Mexico, which was just over the border from Brownsville, Texas. Simply by asking around, he found one of the many criminals who specialized in smuggling Mexicans into the United States, and he paid the man $100 of his savings to let him join his next group.

Some of these criminals used elaborate schemes, such as dressing as Mexicans soldiers and pretending to be arresting the illegals they were smuggling if they were stopped by U.S. authorities. Others hid their human cargo in freight trucks or in secret compartments in tanker trucks that carried gasoline, milk, or even liquid fertilizer. Some of them used their intricate knowledge of the border to lead their flocks to a section they knew was lightly guarded, then gave them a life jacket and ordered them to swim across the Rio Grande.

The most lucrative schemes involved collecting on both ends of the deal. The Mexican nationals, seeking a better life in the United States, paid the smugglers not only to get them across the border but also to hook them up with an employer once they reached the promised land. The U.S. employers also paid the smugglers as much as $1,000 per head, for furnishing them with cheap labor that was not likely to complain about low pay and bad working conditions.

Collecting $1,100-$1,200 each, for twenty or more unfortunate souls, was financially rewarding enough to attract hard-core criminals who were willing to take greater risks and who had no qualms about ditching their clients in the desert, locked inside a blisteringly hot truck, if that's what they had to do to avoid being captured. On more than one occasion, trucks were found abandoned less than a mile from the U.S. Border filled with men, women, and children who had died excruciating deaths in temperatures that often surpassed one hundred-thirty degrees.

The villain Manuel signed on with was called Juan Garcia, but Manuel had no doubt that the name was a lie. He refused to pay his money until the truck was loaded and actually leaving Matamoros. Garcia told Manuel that for another $1,000 U.S., he could guarantee him a job in a T-shirt factory in a place called Atlanta, Georgia. Manuel knew one thing about Atlanta, Georgia: it had a baseball team called *Los Bravos*. He had seen the Atlanta Braves on satellite TV in more than one bar in Veracruz. Although he had no intention of working in a T-shirt factory, he decided that Atlanta, Georgia, would be his final destination. Now all he had to do was get across the border. He trusted his own ingenuity to get him the rest of the way.

No one can say for sure what percentage of Mexicans attempting to enter the United States illegally are successful on their first try because no one has any idea how many are turned back before they get across, or even get to, the border. The best guess is that it's a 50-50 proposition. *El Cuchillo* was lucky. His entry was flawless. Less than eight hours after the truck carrying him and sixteen others left Matamoros, he was safely in the United States.

Having lived in a thriving port city such as Vera Cruz and watched American television, Manuel had picked up enough English to get by. When he found a truck stop outside of Brownsville, he had no trouble making a deal with a fat old trucker who was heading to Laredo. Manuel agreed to unload the truck in return for a ride. When the truck pulled into a warehouse district in Laredo that night, Manuel opened the door, jumped out, and disappeared into the night, leaving the driver to unload his own truck.

Manuel was a quick-witted, entertaining boy who had asked enough questions during the trip up to learn that U.S. Interstate 35 ran north from Laredo to Dallas, where he could then pick up Interstate 20 and follow it all the way east through Louisiana, Mississippi, Alabama, and straight into Georgia's capital city. Although he was small for his age, Manuel was strong and had little trouble working for rides and hitching the rest of the way. It took him less than three weeks to go from the docks of Veracruz to the streets of Atlanta.

But as clever as he was, he was also naïve. It didn't take him long to hook up with two other Mexican boys who were a few years older. It took them less than a month to get Manuel involved in everything illegal that they were doing. This included petty theft, car theft, breaking and entering, and even extorting money from the street vendors who worked the *barrios* of east Atlanta. It was the small-time extortion that caused Cisco Ram to take notice of the boy. Some of Cisco's merchants had complained to *Borracho* that three punks were giving the LDL a bad name by extorting people the gang was supposed to be protecting.

Borracho bragged to Cisco about how he was going to make an example of these three boys, but Cisco instructed him to hold off. He asked *Borracho* how old the boys were, and *Borracho* told him that one of them was barely sixteen. "It takes a lot of balls to do what these *chicos* are doing at their age," said Cisco, who was always on the lookout for new talent. "Tell these boys to leave our 'clients' alone, but other than that, don't mess with them. Just keep your eye on them—especially the youngest one—and let me know what you think in a couple of months or so."

Six weeks later, certain the proprietor had left for the day, Manuel and his buddies broke into a small pawn shop. Unfortunately, the owner was still there. When they first came through the back door, the two older boys sent Manuel downstairs to the basement to see if there was anything of value they could carry out. Meanwhile, they would check out the main floor of the shop. Manuel's accomplices surprised the old man who owned the pawn shop—and themselves—as he was doing inventory in his office. Because the boys thought the shop would be empty, they had not bothered to put on their stocking masks, and the proprietor recognized one of them and called him by name.

"Jesus Morales, I know you," he shouted. "I've seen you hanging around the *barrio*, harassing people all day. You have no job, no money, and you're just a punk. Now, you get out of here, boy, and maybe I won't call the cops." Jesus hit the old man across the face with the crowbar he used on the back door, causing him to stagger backwards, trip, and fall. He lay there on the floor looking up at them, dazed.

"Man, we got to get out of here *now*," said the other boy, Juan Montalvo. "He knows you, man."

"Well, that's too bad for him, isn't it?" said Jesus, raising the crowbar to strike again as the old man reached under the desk and hit the silent alarm button. The store owner tried to rise and shield his head with his arm, but the boy's first blow shattered his forearm. The second one caved in the side of his head.

"*Jesus Cristo!* Are you crazy, man?" yelled Juan before he sprinted for the door. Jesus, pumped full of fear and adrenaline, was right behind him. In their haste to escape, neither of them gave a thought to their new young friend "*Manuelito.*" Two uniformed patrolmen, responding to the silent alarm, burst through the back door, guns drawn, just as Manuel was emerged from the basement.

"Police! Hands behind your head and don't move!" one of them ordered. Less than an hour later, Manuel was being booked into the Gwinnett County Jail pending his arraignment on multiple charges that included murder. Although Manuel was very young, he was an old hand at dealing with police and wise in the ways of the law. He knew the best thing to do in this situation was to deny, deny, deny, and keep on denying anything and everything until someone could prove different.

The next day, the court-appointed attorney, a pasty-faced young man with thinning hair, a pencil-thin mustache, and little actual courtroom experience, met with him before the arraignment. Because most of his clients were, in his words, "guilty as sin," anyway, he almost always pleaded their cases out to avoid the wrath of a judge. He had earned his degree from a local college at night and aspired to be on the other side of the courtroom, an assistant district attorney who would put scum like Manuel *in* prison rather than keep them out. But for now, while his application for employment with the county was pending, his lot was with the defense, and he felt his best chance of making it into the D.A.'s office was to impress the prosecutors every chance he got. Impress them by simplifying their case load with accepted plea bargains.

He and Manuel sat across from each other in the interview room. Manuel tried to appear bright, alert, and innocent. He puffed on a cigarette while his attorney meticulously laid out two yellow legal pads, two pencils, and a small pocket calendar.

"Mr. Osorio," the public defender said, "my name is Ray Malfurs. I have been appointed by the court to handle your defense. Let's get right to the heart of the matter if we can. Also, please remember that I am your attorney and I am on your side. If you tell me the truth, I can help you far easier than if I am burdened by trying to sort through a bunch of self serving lies. Now, did you have anything to do with the death of Mr. Solomon Stein?"

Manuel stuck with his strategy of denial. "No, man. *Hell* no. I liked the old dude. I wouldn't hurt him."

"What were you doing in the basement of his shop on the night of his death?"

"Old dude gave me twenty bucks to move some footlockers and other heavy stuff around for him."

"Can anyone verify that Mr. Stein actually hired you to work for him that night?" the attorney asked.

"I don't know who he might have told," said Manuel. "All I know is, I come in that morning to see if he had a boom box I could buy. He asked me if I wanted to make twenty bucks for some heavy lifting that night. I didn't know what he meant, so I asked him if the stuff I would be moving was legal, you know? He said absolutely it was all his stuff. So I say I'm in, and he says come back after he closes. I come back that night, and he takes me down to the basement and shows me some stuff to move. That's all I know. Next thing I know, the cops have me."

"Do you know anything about who may have killed Mr. Stein?"

"No way. I didn't even know he was dead until I came up stairs and the cops grabbed me," Manuel said, doing his best to sound sincere.

"Mr. Osorio, I need to tell you that the evidence is damning," said the attorney. "The back door to Mr. Stein's shop was broken open. You were found alone inside with Mr. Stein's body. You had a concealed weapon in the form of a six-inch switchblade in your pocket. You have no one to corroborate your story about being hired to move anything. You are in this country illegally, and you cannot afford a more experienced defense attorney. As your attorney of record, I strongly suggest that you plead guilty and throw yourself on the mercy of the court."

"I can't plead guilty to what I didn't do, man," Manuel said, becoming agitated. "God is my witness. I didn't kill Mr. Stein."

"Mr. Osorio, you will be facing trial in front of one of the most hard-nosed judges in the Georgia court system. He will almost certainly put you in jail for the rest of your life if you don't plead this case out. He may even send you to death row." Malfurs knew that a death sentence in this case was not a possibility, but he didn't think his client knew it. He simply wanted to scare Manuel into pleading guilty so he could be done with this case.

"I have another appointment now, so I have to leave for a while," the attorney said, his threat still hanging in the air. "I'll be back later today or tomorrow, and we can talk again. Think over what I said, Mr. Osorio."

Manuel said nothing, and the man gathered his materials and left.

At three o'clock, Manuel received a call from someone who identified himself to the officer who answered the phone, as Manuel Osorio's attorney. When Manuel got on the phone, a voice said, "*Manuelito*, this is Jesus. What's going on with you, man? Are you being a stand-up guy, *Manuelito*?"

"What do you mean?"

"You know what I mean, *hombre*. I mean, are you keeping your mouth shut about your amigos? You killed that old man, Manuelito, and we will testify that you told us you were gonna break into the shop that night. No one can prove we were there, but if both of us say you told us about it in advance, you're cooked. So just plead out and take your medicine, man. If you mention us, you're gonna fry. We will also testify that you hated the old man for dissing you and running you out of the store. We'll say you planned to kill him. Remember, man, you can't prove we were there, but we can hang

Promise Land

you. Plead it out, dude. Plead it out. And keep your mouth shut about us." Then a dial tone.

Manuel slowly put the phone back on the wall. For the very first time, he felt real fear. His plan all along had been to implicate Jesus and Juan, if necessary. He had been sure he could trade them for a lesser sentence. Now, he saw no way out except to take that dumbass gringo attorney's advice and try to cut the best deal possible. Either way, he was sure he was going to jail for a long time. Manuel had no way of knowing that *Borracho* had been watching him, Jesus, and Juan for six weeks and asking questions about them. Or that *Borracho* had decided that the other two were just dumb punks but that the one who called himself *El Cuchillo*, was bright, cunning, and fearless. He had reported all this to Cisco only a day before the boy was arrested.

Cisco instructed *Borracho* to put in a call to Judge Thornton and let him know that Manuel Osorio was one of Cisco Ram's "friends" and, therefore, a friend of the judge. Before *Borracho* contacted the judge, he paid a visit to Manuel at the county jail.

"Amigo, I am here to tell you that you have a good friend now," *Borracho* told him through a two-inch-thick pane of glass in the visitors room, "a friend who is going to get you out of here, a friend who will make sure you are released without being convicted or serving any more time than it takes to get you out. How do you like that, *Manuelito?*"

"My name is *Cuchillo, hombre,*" the boy responded boldly. "*Cuchillo* is a man's name. *Manuelito* is a boy's name. I am not a boy."

Borracho didn't care what the boy wanted to be called, so he just shrugged his shoulders. "All right...*Cuchillo.* How do you like that?"

"I like it fine, but who is my new friend and why is he helping me?"

"You will meet him soon enough, amigo. He's helping you because he likes to hire young men such as yourself to work in his businesses. He knows that if he helps you, then you will be loyal to him and work hard to make money for him. He is a good man, and he would hate to see one so young as you spend the rest of his life as the punk of some nigger in jail."

"I will be no one's punk," Manuel said defiantly. "I will die first."

"Very good. Then you will be very thankful when my friend has you released from this jail, won't you?" It was more of a statement than a question.

143

"*Si, hombre, si.* I will be very thankful to the man who frees me."

"Good. Now just stay cool, keep your mouth shut about anything we've talked about, and, most important, take no deals from your attorney. He doesn't care if you live or die. He just wants your name off his case list."

"No problem," said Manuel. "I will be as quiet as a mouse, and I will wait for my new friend to free me. But you have not told me the name of my new friend."

"Don't worry about his name, amigo. As I have already said, you'll meet him soon enough. Just stay cool."

Later that evening, a lovely young woman, recently a resident of Juarez, Mexico, was delivered to the motel where Judge Ronald Lewis Thornton awaited. Earlier, the judge had had a private conversation with *Borracho* and agreed that since Mr. Osorio was armed only with a small knife that was not the murder weapon and since Mr. Osorio's fingerprints were not on the murder weapon, the police had insufficient evidence. He also told *Borracho* that there was no way to disprove Mr. Osorio's assertion that Solomon Stein had hired him to work in his storeroom that night, which meant there was insufficient evidence even to indict. The judge then told *Borracho* that the boy would be released when he appeared before him the next day at the arraignment.

Once again, the wheels of justice had been lubricated to allow a friend of Francisco Ramos to walk free amid allegations of police incompetence, specifically their failure to secure the necessary witnesses. One hour after his release from jail, Manuel Osorio met Francisco Miguel Ramos. The Ram had a new and deadly knife in his arsenal, a fierce young man who would come to believe that in Cisco Ram he had found the kind of father he never had.

That night, *Cuchillo* phoned a bar that Jesus Morales had told him to use to leave messages for him. "Hey, *hombre*", *Cuchillo* said to the bartender who answered, "tell Jesus Morales that his friend *Manuelito* is free and ready to go back to work. Tell him I will be at the Waffle House on Peachtree Parkway at midnight tonight and that I have a very good opportunity for us. Tell him to bring Juan with him."

The next day, the bodies of Juan Montalvo and Jesus Morales would be found in an alley behind a bar in east Atlanta with their throats cut. *Cuchillo* never forgot a friend—or an enemy. These boys had betrayed him and left him to rot in jail for a crime they had committed. In his mind, there was nothing for him to do except what he had done. With their lifeblood still draining from their necks, *Cuchillo* stood there feeling no remorse. He was already thinking about his new friend and his new life.

CHAPTER TWENTY NINE
INTERVIEWS

AFTER LINDSEY LEFT Fort McPherson, she went directly to Northwest High School, where Francisco Miguel Ramos, Jr. had been a student. She went to the main office and asked to speak to the principal. The power of the press—in this case the even greater power of television—opened the door for her. She told the receptionist she wanted to do a special report on the problems facing high school faculty and staff. When the woman passed that along to the principal, he agreed to see her immediately.

William B. Enders had been the principal at Northwest High for ten years. As always, Lindsey had done her homework. She knew he had been a football star at Florida A&M and for one year in the NFL before a serious knee injury ended his career. He had gone back to A&M, a predominantly black university in Tallahassee, and obtained a master's degree in education and then on to Clark University in Atlanta, where he earned his Ph.D.

After she introduced herself, Lindsay started off by asking Enders about his football days to loosen him up. This time her tactic did not work as well as it had with Col. Kinkaid. Dr. Enders answered her questions politely, but when she persisted with the football talk, he patiently waited for her to finish her next question.

"Ms. Adams, I'm sure we both have more important things to do today than talk about my football career," he said coolly. "I'm told you're doing a story on the problems faced by the faculty and staff of today's urban high schools. Is that correct?" Lindsey was taken aback by his no-nonsense approach.

"Yes, it is," she said, trying to regain control, "but I want to be a bit more specific. I'd like to talk about problems you've faced with gangs and gang members—Francisco Miguel Ramos, Jr. in particular." Dr. Enders sighed softly and leaned back in his chair. He looked at Lindsey for a moment then stood up.

"Ms. Adams, I will not discuss a former student, especially one who is recently deceased, with anyone except his parents," Dr. Enders said firmly. "Whatever problems this school or its students may have had with that young man, died with him. Unless you have other high school problems you wish to discuss, I'll have to say, 'Good day' and get back to my duties."

"Actually, Mr. Ramos was the main thing I wanted to talk about," Lindsey stammered. Enders was already walking toward his door.

"I thought as much," he said. "I'm sorry I can't help you young lady. Nor will there be any interviews with my faculty, staff, or students on school property concerning Francisco Ramos. Are we clear on that?" Before Lindsey could think of an objection, he opened the door for her and said, "Have a nice day." As soon as she stepped out, he closed the door.

Lindsey Adams was not accustomed to being dismissed so quickly, especially by a man. She took a moment to gather her wits. In the hallway outside the school offices, she saw one of the students, a cute boy who looked young enough to be a freshman or sophomore. He was wearing a red and white letterman's sweater with a large "N" on it. She walked up to the young man and tried to charm him.

"Hi there, big guy. You look like the captain of the football team, so I just know you can help me out."

The boy blushed and said, "Oh, no ma'am, I don't play football, I run." He turned redder. "I don't mean I run from football....uh, I love football," he stammered. "Uh...I mean, I'm a distance runner."

"A cross-country runner! What a coincidence. I was a runner in college myself." Lindsey often lied to get what she wanted and hoped the boy wouldn't pursue the topic, but he did.

"Cool," he said, honored to be in the presence of a college runner. "What was your best time in the mile?"

Having no idea what a reasonable answer might be, Lindsey fell back on what worked best for her and smiled broadly. "Oh, forget about what I ran. How about you? I see you're a letterman. And you are so cute that I bet you have to beat the girls off with a stick, don't you?" The boy's face was deep crimson now and Lindsey seized the advantage back. "Say, I wonder if you could do me a favor?"

"Sure, I'd be glad to," he said. "If I can."

"Oh, this is easy," Lindsay said. "I'm doing a report for Channel 14 on gangs at high schools, and I'll be right outside the gate with my cameraman when school lets out this afternoon. If you or any of your classmates want to be on TV, just meet me there this afternoon. I'll be asking a few questions and taping some interviews."

"What kind of questions?" the boy asked.

"Just background stuff. Like are there a lot of gangs on campus, and do the gangs start fights or bully other students?—you know, easy questions like that."

"And if we do an interview, we'll be on TV?"

"Not all of the interviews will make the final program, but a cute guy like you, in your letterman sweater, would certainly look good on TV. Please pass the word around to your friends, okay?"

"No problem," the boy responded eagerly. "I'll definitely be there." Lindsey gave his hand a firm, lingering shake and then headed for the parking lot. Three hours later, she and her cameraman were surrounded by a sea of smiling high schoolers, all hoping to be seen by their friends on TV.

Lindsey knew who to target. Because she knew most high school gangs were made up primarily of minorities, typically blacks and Hispanics, she wanted to interview an average white kid. Her vision was to show that gang-bangers like Francisco Ramos, Jr., were a cancer in inner-city public schools. She felt that white parents would be far more interested in the story if they felt that the minorities were disrupting their children's education. If there were white gangs, Lindsey had no desire to mention them. She wanted to talk about Francisco's gang.

Had Lindsey done the proper research, she would have known that the dead boy had not actually been a member of a gang. He merely was allowed to hang around with the Latino Death Lords because his father was the leader. Even if he had been a member, the LDL was by no means a high school street gang. Like many of the viewers who had seen her on-the-scene interview with Danny Chambers, Lindsey assumed that a Hispanic kid with tattoo-covered arms who was driving a pimped up car and attacking a defenseless Anglo woman in broad daylight, had to be a gang member.

She was careful to pick a few black kids and a few Hispanics to interview to give an impression of being unbiased, but she planned to cut anything they had to say that wasn't spectacular. Her first subject was a petite blonde with blue eyes and a ponytail. *Just perfect*, Lindsey thought to herself.

"Hi, young lady," she said energetically. "What's your name?"

"Mandy Simmons," the girl answered.

"What year are you in, Mandy?"

"I'm a senior, and I've already been accepted at the University of Georgia. Go Dawgs!" she said, then made a barking sound. Some of the kids behind her took up the barking. "*Go Dawgs!*" they shouted.

"That's great, Mandy," Lindsey said, ignoring the commotion behind her. "Do you think there are gangs here at Northwest?"

"Yeah, I guess there are gangs at most schools," Mandy responded, "but they don't bother us much. They mostly fight with each other." This was not what Lindsey wanted to hear, and it would definitely never make it into her report. She took another tack.

"Did you know the boy who was killed several weeks ago when he tried to drag a woman out of her car on the highway?"

"Oh, you mean Francisco Ramos? Sure, I knew him. He was a weird kid."

Now we're getting somewhere, Lindsey thought. "Weird? In what way?"

"He was always pissed off about something. Oops, I guess I can't say 'pissed off' on TV, huh?"

"Don't worry, we'll edit it out," Lindsey said. "But try not to use any profanity if you can help it. Go on."

"Well, the jocks said he was on steroids. He was always pumping iron, and they said he had 'roid' rage."

"What's that?" Lindsey asked, even though she knew the answer.

"I'm not sure," Mandy said. "I think something in the steroids makes boys go nutty."

"And their nuts shrink too," a male voice from behind Mandy yelled, producing a roar of laughter from the crowd.

"Well, Mandy, did you ever see Francisco Ramos do anything violent?" Lindsey asked when the laughter subsided.

"Yeah, I saw him punch kids a few times at football games, that kind of stuff. But here's something maybe you should know. He asked this girl Meredith Stanford to go out with him, and she said no and kind of laughed at him. Well, he got really mad at her, and I think he was going to punch her in the face, but a teacher walked up."

Lindsey wrote Meredith's name down on her pad. "Is Meredith still a student here?" Mandy turned and looked over her shoulder at the other kids.

"No, she disappeared a few days after Francisco asked her out," the girl said. "And her boyfriend got killed."

Jackpot! Three bars on the slot machine just hit, Lindsey thought, fighting hard to conceal her excitement from the camera. "Really? So only days after an argument with Francisco Ramos, a girl disappears and her boyfriend is mysteriously killed? Tell me more."

An hour later, she was back in her office, going over the taped interviews. She talked to seven other kids after Mandy, but none of them had anything memorable to say. Lindsey called the Gwinnett County Sheriff's office and verified that a young woman named Meredith Stanford had been reported missing by her parents and that the young man she had been out with on the night of her disappearance, had been found stabbed to death in the parking lot of a local movie theater that same night. This was shaping up to be a far bigger and far better story than Lindsey had hoped.

The next day brought her even more good news. She received phone calls from eleven different former soldiers who had served at home or overseas with Danny Chambers and were more than happy to talk about the young man they held in high regard. The following morning, Lindsey met the first of them for breakfast at a Denny's restaurant. The man, who introduced himself as Johnny Avery, appeared to be in his late thirties or early forties. He had been a medic and assigned to the same company as Danny during

Operation Desert Storm. Danny flew the choppers and medics like Johnny tried to keep the wounded alive until they could be transported back to their base to receive proper medical treatment.

After he and Lindsey exchanged a few pleasantries, they ordered. Lindsey opted for half a grapefruit, yogurt, and black coffee, while Johnny decided to have the Grand Slam, which consisted of eggs, pancakes, sausage, and bacon.

"Did you know the Army awarded Danny a Silver Star for Bravery in Desert Storm?" Johnny asked after the waitress had gone.

"Yes, I read that in the paper," Lindsey said. "He must have been a very brave man."

"Let me tell you something, ma'am. They could have given him ten or fifteen of those things. Danny Chambers is the bravest man I've ever known. The kind of thing the Army singled out for the citation to accompany his Silver Star was the rule, not the exception, with Danny."

"Really? That's amazing. Mr. Avery, if you don't mind, I'd like to ask you some questions, but I'll need you go over your recollections of Danny Chambers again when my cameraman gets here. I'd like to get this on tape."

"Sure, we can talk now and do it again later," said Avery, jovially. "Hell, we can do it three or four times if we need to. When it comes to Danny Chambers, I have all the time in the world. And call me Johnny, if you want to."

"Thank you, Johnny. That would be wonderful."

"There's something about bravery most people don't understand, but Danny did," he said.

"What's that, Johnny?"

"Well, in my lifetime, especially in the military, I've seen some crazy bastards—excuse me, I mean I saw some crazy guys—do some seriously brave things. But the truth of it was that sometimes they just didn't know how great the danger was when they did them. A lot of them would tell you after the fact that if they had known what they were doing, they would have never done it. Does that make sense?"

"Kind of," Lindsey said. "Please, go on,"

"Okay, what I mean is that a man who is fearless is not necessarily brave. Not having any fear can mean you're ignorant of the facts or just plain crazy.

True bravery is all about knowing exactly how bad your situation is and being scared to death, but going ahead and doing your job the best you can anyway. That was Danny Chambers."

"How can you be so sure that Lt. Chambers knew how dangerous the things he did were?" Lindsey asked. "Couldn't he have been one of the crazy guys you mentioned?"

"Danny was different. He held a little prayer meeting beside the chopper before we took off on every single mission I ever flew with him. I can tell you for sure that he knew what we were flying into because he always told us in advance when we were about to get really deep in the shit… oops, there I go again, sorry. Anyway, he knew because he always prayed for all of us except himself. I always wondered about that. Danny prayed for us and the rest of the company, and he prayed for God to comfort his wife and folks if something happened to him. He always ended his prayers by saying, 'Your will be done, Lord'. The incident he won his Silver Star for is a good example. He told us we were supposed to wait until dark to try to go in and get some guys out. He told us that was correct U.S. Army procedure for that situation. He probably figured we already knew the procedure, but he told us just the same. Anyway, he said he was afraid some of the wounded wouldn't survive until dark, so he was going out to get them. If we wanted to come along, it was our choice. You know, he was the aircraft commander and in charge of every mission, so he could have ordered us to go if he wanted. Or he could have simply said we had to follow procedure and wait until dark."

"Did all of you go with him?"

"That mission was flown with a full crew, ma'am. Pilot, co-pilot, and two medics. Any one of us would have walked through a wall for Danny and still would. I'll tell you one more thing about Danny Chambers. He never lost a crewman."

"What do you mean never lost one?" Lindsey asked.

"Just what I said. Danny flew more than six hundred missions into Indian Country while he was part of Desert Storm, and he never had a single crewman wounded or killed."

"Indian Country?"

"Sorry, ma'am, it's military lingo for any territory not controlled by friendly forces. When I say we flew into Indian Country, I mean we were on our own if we were shot down or disabled."

"I'd say you were all quite lucky, then," Lindsey said.

"You can call it luck if you want to. Everyone who flew with Danny knew it wasn't luck."

"What was it, then?" Lindsey asked.

"We figured it was just God looking after one of the good guys, and the rest of us were just riding his coattails home."

They finished their breakfast, and when Lindsey's cameraman showed up, she and Johnny Avery went through it all again. His story was even more powerful the second time. For the next two days, she heard variations on the same theme over and over again. She had half expected that at least one person would show up who had a beef with Danny Chambers and wanted to air his complaints. She wouldn't have included it in her story, but she thought it would have been interesting to hear anyway. But everyone she interviewed told the same story. Danny Chambers was an honest-to-God hero and family man.

Two days after the final interview, Lindsey completed the editing and took the finished product to Bill Carpenter. He was blown away.

"Lindsey, this is great stuff—I mean seriously great stuff. You hit the perfect balance between hero and villain. Are you sure you have all your facts straight about the Ramos kid's possible connection to the disappearance of the Stanford girl?"

"Absolutely, boss," she said proudly. "I checked it all out with at least two sources in the Sheriff's Department and the Norcross police. Francisco Miguel Ramos, Jr. was pulled in for questioning three days after the girl disappeared. The police couldn't find enough concrete evidence to get an indictment. All they had was circumstantial. The boy insisted he was at the gym lifting weights the night in question and actually had several witnesses. But he left the gym before Meredith Stanford's date was killed. The police used the approximate time of the boy's death to establish the time she was abducted. Francisco Ramos had no alibi for the actual time of death, but neither did a lot of kids from Northwest High School and a lot of known criminals in this city. The cops had to drop the case against him."

"That's all right, then," Carpenter said. "You were very careful to say he had been questioned about the murder and disappearance, and that was all. I like it, girl. I like it a lot. Get with production to work up a promo we can start airing today. Then we'll run your story as part of the evening newscast day after tomorrow."

Lindsey was somewhere high above cloud nine when she walked out of his office.

CHAPTER THIRTY
ON THE AIR

THE FOLLOWING FRIDAY evening, Cisco sat in a large recliner in front of his newest toy, a fifty-inch high-definition television. He had a glass of red wine in his hand, and the bottle it came from rested on the table beside him. He lit a cigarette, picked up the remote, and turned on the TV. *Borracho* and several other gang members had told him that Channel 14 had been running promos for the past two days about a special segment airing on tonight's news that would deal with Francisco Miguel Ramos, Jr. and Danny Chambers.

Cisco decided he would watch the show alone in his secure, comfortable home rather than surrounded by the gang at the clubhouse. He had no idea what the angle of the story would be, but he doubted it would cast his son in a favorable light. As the screen came to life, Cisco punched in Channel 14. The anchor was just starting the broadcast:

"Good evening, Atlanta, I'm Doug Altman, and thanks for joining Channel 14 for Eye On the News. We open tonight's edition with the first segment of a three-part series about the recent death of Francisco Miguel Ramos, Jr., son of a reputed gang leader known to police as Cisco Ram. The series will also examine the life of Daniel Chambers, the local high school coach and teacher whose intervention in an alleged car-jacking attempt by the young Ramos, resulted in the boy's accidental death.

In part one of our series, Lindsey Adams is interviewing students at Northwest Senior High School who knew Francisco Ramos."

Lindsey appeared on the screen and began to speak. *"Good evening Doug. I am speaking with Mandy Simmons, a senior at Northwest, who has been in school with Francisco Ramos, Jr. since the two were in middle school. Mandy, what can you tell us about Francisco Ramos?"*

"He was a weird kid."

"Weird? In what way?"

"Well, the jocks said the kid was on steroids. He was always pumping iron, and they said he had 'roid' rage."

"What's that?"

"I'm not sure. I think something in the steroids makes boys go nutty."

"Well, Mandy, did you ever see Francisco Ramos do anything violent?"

"Yeah, I saw him punch kids a few times at football games—that kind of stuff. But here's something maybe you should know. He asked this girl named Meredith Stanford to go out with him, and she said no and kind of laughed at him. Well, he got really mad at her, and I think he was going to punch her in the face, but a teacher walked up."

"Is Meredith still a student here?"

"No, Meredith disappeared a few days after Francisco asked her out, and her boyfriend got killed."

Lindsey was then seen interviewing several more teenagers, each one painting a similar picture of Francisco Ramos as a bully, a trouble-maker, or worse. Lindsey ended the segment promising that tomorrow night she would air interviews with soldiers who had served in the Gulf War with reluctant hero Danny Chambers.

When the anchorman reappeared to read the night's headlines, Cisco turned off the set. His anger was palpable, and it was burning a hole in his heart. His son was dead and this bitch was dragging his name through the mud. To make matters worse, the reporter had promised that tomorrow night there would be even more praise for the man who had killed his son. This was too much to bear. He picked up his cell phone and punched the speed dial for *Carnicero,* who answered after the first ring.

"Carni, I have an important job for you," Cisco said, trying to remain calm, "a job I can entrust only to you because of my faith in your loyalty."

"Yes, *jefe,* whatever you need," *Carnicero* responded. "You know I'm your man."

"Did you see the news story tonight about my son?"

"*Si, jefe,* I saw it, but I did not like it."

"That reporter is going to pay for her words, Carni, and pay with pain. I want you to get one of the girls from the LDL who you can trust and who you don't mind seeing disappear. Have her call this reporter, this Lindsey Adams, at her work tomorrow and say she has information about what happened to Meredith Stanford. Tell her to say that if the reporter will give her five hundred dollars, she will tell her where the girl's body is and who killed her." Carnicero said nothing. He always knew when Cisco didn't want to be interrupted with questions.

"Have this girl tell the reporter to meet her at noon on the lower level of the parking garage at Lenox Mall," Cisco told him. "When she gets there, you and some of your *muchachos* will be waiting out of sight in a van next to the car your girl is driving. When the reporter comes over to the car, you grab her quickly and quietly. Leave her car where she parks it. You got that, amigo?"

"Yes, *jefe*, I understand. What do you want me to do with the reporter after we grab her? "

"Do whatever you want, then give her to our friends who took little Miss Stanford." Cisco's mood turned evil. "The two of them can be roommates in a Columbian whorehouse."

At ten the next morning, Lindsey was at her desk working on the final edit for part two of her story, which was scheduled to air that night. Her morning had been interrupted by co-workers dropping by her desk to congratulate her on a great feature and phone calls of praise from family and friends. She almost did not answer the next call, but the high she was getting from all these compliments was too good to resist, so she picked up the receiver.

"Lindsey Adams," she said cheerily.

"Is this the lady who did the special about Francisco Ramos on TV last night?" asked a female caller.

"Yes it is. How may I help you?"

"I think I can help you, *senorita*," the voice said.

Lindsey sat up straight in her chair. "And how can you help me?"

"If you pay me five hundred dollars, I will show you where the body of the girl you talked about last night is buried and tell you who killed her."

"Are you talking about Meredith Stanford?"

"Yes, that's the girl."

"Who am I speaking with?" Lindsey asked.

"My name is not important," the voice said. "The only thing that's important is that for five hundred dollars, I can make you famous."

"How will I know the information you give me is true?" Lindsey asked.

"Because you don't have to pay me the money until you see the body."

"May I ask how you came to know all this information?" Lindsey didn't expect the woman to say, but she had to ask the question.

"Let's just say Francisco did a lot of pillow-talking, and he liked to brag about what happened to people who crossed him."

That was all Lindsey needed to hear. "When and where can we meet?"

"Today at noon. I'll be parked on the lower level of the parking garage at Lenox Mall. I'll be sitting in a green Toyota with a tennis ball on the antenna. Wear jeans and sneakers or hiking shoes if you want to see the grave today. Do not bring the police. If you do, I'll say I don't know what you're talking about and you won't be able to prove any different. If you want the story, come alone."

"All right, I'll be there," Lindsey said. "I'll be driving a white BMW convertible." There was no response, and a few seconds passed before she realized that the person on the other end of line had ended the call. Lindsey Adams was not stupid, and she considered herself to be reasonably cautious. But, her desire to meet this girl and break this story far outweighed her normal bent toward caution.

She thought about going to Bill Carpenter for the five hundred dollars and for guidance. But what if Bill decided the story was too big for her and gave it to Doug Altman, or worse, decided to call in the police? Either way, Lindsey would end up with nothing. She had slightly over six thousand dollars in her bank account, so she could afford to pay the five hundred herself. If the story was as good as she hoped, she could always ask Bill to reimburse her. She decided that the parking garage at a major mall like Lenox was a safe enough place to meet, especially at high noon. The comment about wearing jeans and sneakers made the whole thing sound even more legitimate, which was exactly what *Carnicero* intended when he told the girl exactly what to say to the reporter. Lindsey changed the greeting on her voice mail, picked up her purse, and walked to the receptionist desk.

"Susie, be a doll and tell Bill I'm taking an early lunch and then follow-ing up on a lead I just got." She walked out of the station with no reason to think that she might never return.

She stopped by her apartment, changed her clothes as the girl had sug-gested, then went by the bank and cashed a check for five hundred dollars. As she drove toward the mall, she began to have second thoughts. *Was this smart? Was this safe? Was this worth the risk?* She answered the first two questions with maybes, but the last one with a resounding yes. It was definitely worth some risk. *After all,* she thought, *if I'm not willing to take some risks, what will I ever accomplish in life?* Lindsey knew that if she broke the story about who killed Meredith Stanford and where her body was buried, she would be able to write her own ticket in Atlanta—and maybe even New York. A story like this would certainly be picked up by the national wire services. She might be able to ride this rocket all the way to the network news. No more covering traffic accidents and school board meetings for her. She would be a big-time media star.

Lindsey pulled into the parking garage and followed the winding ramp down to the bottom level. There were plenty of cars, and the area was well lighted. She even saw a few people moving about. She cruised up and down the lines of cars until she saw an older green Toyota Camry with a tennis ball on the radio antenna and a young Hispanic woman in the driver's seat. The woman appeared to be alone. The parking spaces next to the Toyota were occupied by a late-model silver Lexus on the right and a black van with tinted windows on the left, so Lindsey was forced to park several spaces away. She got out of her car and walked up to the driver's side of the Camry. The win-dow was down, and the young woman sitting inside was smoking a cigarette.

"Hi, I'm Lindsey," she said tentatively. "Were you waiting for me?"

"Yes, I'm the one who called you," the girl replied. "Did you bring the money?"

"The money is in cash and it's close by," Lindsey told her. "But, we agreed that you don't get paid until I see the grave and you tell me who killed her."

Suddenly, the side door of the black van slid open and two men grabbed Lindsey, dragged her into the van, and pulled the door shut. It all happened in less than four seconds. The men held Lindsey tightly, and one of them put duct tape over her mouth. When they had abducted Meredith, the men had worn masks hide their faces. This time, however, they figured that no one was going to be around later to identify them anyway.

"So, miss smart ass reporter, you wanted to find out what happened to Meredith Stanford, did you?" asked the man in front of her. "Well, we're gonna help you find out. In fact, I think you and Miss Stanford will become very good friends, maybe even roommates. You want to know where she is, so I'll tell you. She's working in a whorehouse in a little village in the heart of the Columbian coca fields. The men who harvest the leaves get very lonely for female companionship, so we sent her down to entertain them. I think you and Miss Meredith will be the most popular girls there. Cisco Ram sends his regards and says to tell you that you never, ever should have spoken ill of his son."

Lindsey struggled to try to free herself, but she quickly saw that it was futile. She felt a sharp pain in her arm and looked down to see one of the men pushing the plunger of a syringe filled with a clear liquid. Two minutes later, she was unconscious.

Carnicero got out of the van and walked around to the window of the Toyota where the Hispanic girl was still sitting. "You did good, Marlena. We're proud of you. Cisco said to give you this." He put a pistol against her head and pulled the trigger, sending .25-caliber bullet through her temple. The silencer on the automatic weapon muffled the sound. He caught her head as it fell forward so it wouldn't hit the horn. *Carnicero* continued to lean into the car as if he were talking to the girl until he was sure no one had seen or heard anything. He gave her shoulder a shove, and the body toppled over into the passenger seat. He got back in the van and drove slowly out of the garage, as always, leaving no loose ends.

By four in the afternoon, Bill Carpenter was beginning to get a little worried about the whereabouts of his new star reporter. He called Lindsey's cell and left a message, then did the same on her home phone. When she still had not returned his calls by six that evening, he called the police and reported her missing. The next morning, two policemen came to the station to tell him that Lindsey's car had been found at one o'clock that morning, in the parking garage at Lenox Mall, by a mall security patrol. The mall security officers had also found the body of a young Hispanic woman, who had been shot, in a car parked near Lindsey's abandoned vehicle. The policemen told Bill they would be around most of the morning to question him and Lindsey's other co-workers about her disappearance.

That night on the news, Channel 14 Anchorman Doug Altman made an impassioned appeal to his viewers, asking that anyone who had any information concerning the whereabouts of reporter Lindsey Adams contact the station or the Gwinnett County Sheriff's Department immediately. Directing his remarks to those responsible for her disappearance, he said that the Federal Bureau of Investigation had now joined in the search and pleaded with the perpetrators to release Ms. Adams unharmed. He informed his viewers that Lindsey's car had been found abandoned in the parking garage at Lenox Mall and asked that anyone who had been in that area yesterday, report anything suspicious that they might have seen to the police. He also announced that the station was offering $25,000 reward for information leading to Lindsey's safe return and asked viewers to pray for her well being.

Because Lindsey had failed to tell anyone where she was going, who she might be meeting, or even which story she was following up on, the authorities had to assume that her disappearance was somehow linked to her story about Francisco Ramos, Jr. Francisco Ramos, Sr. was promptly called in for questioning and came willingly, along with his attorney. The attorney told the police that Mr. Ramos knew nothing about the reporter's fate and had been in a day long business meeting at a local Marriott Hotel, where a number of reputable witnesses could confirm his presence. The police took down the names of the witnesses, advised Cisco not to leave town, and sent him home.

Having found a dead woman in the car near Lindsey's, who turned out to be a known associate of members of the Latino Death Lords, and knowing that Lindsey had broadcast a scathing indictment of Cisco Ram's son, the police and the FBI decided to continue to focus their investigation on Cisco and the LDL. But unless a witness came forward, they all knew they had no case.

Since Cisco's *Tres Tiburones* were also well known to the local police, they were each called in and questioned, all three claiming to have been involved in a marathon session of Texas Hold'em poker at their club, using their partners, as well as other gang members, to corroborate their alibis. Two of the three sharks were telling the truth, but the police were going to have to get very lucky if they hoped to connect the one who was lying, to the crime.

CHAPTER THIRTY ONE
FATHER AND SON

DANNY'S PARENTS, ROGER and Sarah Chambers, lived in a tidy, comfortable three-bedroom ranch-style home in Alpharetta, Georgia, a suburb of Atlanta, situated northwest of Norcross. Roger had retired after thirty-one years as a jet engine mechanic with Delta Airlines. His pension was good, and he had been frugal all his life, so their retirement was unmarred by the financial woes that plagued many seniors.

Roger was very proud of his son, but the news of Danny's promotion to assistant principal had been clouded by the highway incident that led to the death of a young man. Five days after his meeting with Cisco at the strip club, Danny called his father and told him he would like to come over for a chat, if his father wasn't busy. Roger appreciated that Danny called first, but he reminded his son that he was always welcome. Danny said he would be there in time for lunch.

When Danny arrived, his father was in the detached garage tinkering with an old power lawn mower and cursing quietly under his breath. "Come on now, Pop, you know Mama don't allow that kind of talk around here," Danny said, smiling. It was an old joke between them, and Roger chuckled.

"Boy, as long as your mama don't hear it and you don't tell her, it will be no problem." Roger Chambers was not nearly as mature a Christian as Danny was, but he had never in his life used profanity in the presence of a woman. *Words are just words to men,* he would always say. *They can't hurt you. But they take on all kinds of meanings as soon as they enter a woman's ear, and then they get all mad and insulted.*

Danny laughed. "I know what you mean, Pop. Where's Mom?'

"She went down to the market to get some smoked ham for our sand-wiches. She won't be long."

"Good," Danny said. "Because I have something I want to talk with you about before she gets back." His father stopped what he was doing and looked at his son's face. He could tell that this was serious. He wiped the oil and grease from his hands.

"Okay, Son. You want a cold drink?"

"No thanks, Dad. But you go ahead and have whatever you want."

"Suit yourself. Have a seat, Danny and I'll be right back."

He returned with a bottle of domestic beer in one hand and a can of peanuts in the other. They pulled a couple of folding lawn chairs down from a wall rack and sat down in a shady spot near the entrance to the garage.

"That was some kind of a crazy accident you were involved in last week, Son," Roger said. "If I've seen you on TV once, I've seen you twenty times."

"Yeah, Dad, crazy is the right word, and that's what I need to talk with you about." He began with the first phone call and laid out the whole story. His father did not say a word until Danny was finished.

"Son, I know you said you talked to the police, and they said they couldn't help, but surely there's some government agency that can. I just can't believe we're at the mercy of people like this with no protection."

"Unfortunately, Pop, it's true. The police made it very clear that unless I can prove that Ramos is stalking us or that he is actually the one who is threatening my family, there's nothing they can do. And I can understand that. I mean, what would they say to the judge when they ask him for an arrest warrant—that they think he's threatening me because I said so? No, I've come to the conclusion that I only have two options."

"What do you mean, Son?"

"I either have to attack him before he attacks my family, or I have to sit back and wait until Sheila or one of the kids is hurt or killed. Then I can go to the police, and they can try to prove it was this psycho, Ramos. And I'm not going to do that. So I really only have *one* choice, Pop. I have to believe that this man means what he says when he promises to kill my children—and I have to kill him first."

"Kill him?" Roger was incredulous. "Are you *serious?*"

"Yes, sir, kill him," Danny said calmly. "Do you see any other option, Pop?"

"Well, I don't know, Son," said Roger, struggling to face the harsh reality his son had just presented to him. "I never imagined I'd hear my son talk about killing someone, so I guess I'm a bit flabbergasted right now. I have often wished for a faith as strong as yours, Son. I've been amazed at the peace it brings you, and I hope to get there myself one day. I say this because I don't believe you could actually kill this animal, even if you got the chance. Why don't you just take Sheila and the kids and leave Atlanta? Get the government to put you in one of those witness protection programs or something?"

"I thought of that, Dad, but the man told me that if I try to run away, he'll kill you and Mom and anyone else who's part of our family or one of my friends. Besides, you didn't raise me to run away, and the government isn't going to put us in a program just because we've been threatened. I have no choice, Dad. I think you know me well enough to know how hard it is for me to even consider taking a life, much less to actually do it. But I can't sit around and wait for this lunatic to kill somebody I love before the authorities step in. And who's to say they'll even be able to prove he did it anyway? No, I have to do this."

His father was in shock, his mouth wide open. It took him a few moments to compose himself. "He said what? He said he would kill your mom and me? Why, that son-of-a-bitch...I have a good mind to...."

"You see what I mean, Dad," Danny interrupted. "I have no choice but to kill him before he kills my family. And not just him. I may have to kill the entire leadership of the gang, or they'll just come after us for revenge."

"How many people do you think that is, Son?"

"Maybe as many as twelve, but I don't know for sure yet."

"Could you be at peace with yourself, Son—I mean, after the fact?"

"I think so," Danny said unconvincingly. "I know one thing for sure. I could never have peace if I sat by and let him kill my family."

"What does Sheila think about this, Danny?"

"She doesn't know about this, and she won't know until it's over, one way or another. Ramos wants to hurt me. I'm the one he blames for his son's death. The only reason he wants to hurt Sheila or the kids is to hurt me. If

I fight him and win, he won't be a threat anymore. If I fight him and he kills me, then he won't have any reason to hurt my family, because I wouldn't be around to see it and suffer."

"What can I do, Son?" Danny's father asked.

"Nothing, Dad. I just wanted you to know what was going on and see if maybe you had any advice on how I should go about it."

"Well, right off the top of my head, let me ask you a question: If you're going to fight a shark, would you rather fight it in the water or on land?"

"That's a no-brainer, Dad. I'd have a much better chance if we were on land."

"Well, if you want to fight this particular shark, you need to make sure the fight happens someplace that's advantageous to you and not him."

"Any thoughts on where that might be?" Danny asked.

"Somewhere that's unfamiliar ground. Most of these thugs are city kids, so don't fight him in the city. That's my advice."

Danny's mother's van turned into the driveway.

"We better drop this for now, Dad, but I'll keep you up to date. And, Dad, please be alert for anything or anyone that seems out of place around here. Keep your eyes and ears open, okay? And thanks."

Roger nodded, then the two of them got up from their chairs and went to help Mrs. Chambers with the groceries.

ൟ

CHAPTER THIRTY TWO
BOBBY

"...AND SO, LADIES and gentlemen, once again, your final score from Philips Arena in Atlanta: the Cleveland Cavaliers 106, and the Atlanta Hawks 99. Thanks for watching, and good night."

Bobby Pendleton kicked over the coffee table his feet had been resting on, spilling the remains of his beer, his Chinese take-out, and an ashtray full of cigarette butts onto the carpet.

"Choking, puking dogs!" he screamed to the walls of his empty apartment. "You can't even cover at home when you're getting points. For Christ's sake, *nobody* gets points at home in the NBA and loses."

His hands were shaking as he picked up the phone and punched in a number. "Yeah, is he there? Tell him it's Rico." Rico was the code name he used with this particular bookie. Bobby heard the sound of the phone being dropped onto something hard. In the background, he could hear people laughing and talking. Behind the voices, he could hear music. Then he heard someone pick up the phone.

"He said to tell you he's closed for the night and not to call back until tomorrow," the voice said.

"Closed? Come on, man, I need to get a play down on...." The voice had been replaced by a buzzing of a dial tone. Bobby Pendleton was a very bright man—in every area of his life except handicapping sports. He was a gambling addict who bet on any sport and every sport. He did it for the high, not for the money he might win. His civil-service job as an accounting supervisor at the Georgia Bureau of Investigation in Atlanta paid more than enough for him to live in a better home than the tiny two-bedroom, one-bath ranch he rented and to drive a better car than his six-year-old Toyota. Unfortunately, Bobby sent far too much of his $68,500 annual salary to his bookie, Big Jack Niehaus. Bobby told himself it was seed money, an investment he would one day, when his luck changed, get back ten-fold.

☙

The evening after Bobby lost on the Hawks, he was sitting in front of his computer studying the records of the college and pro basketball teams that were playing that night. When he had made his picks, he called the bookie he sometimes played with in New Orleans, an old high school pal he liked a lot more than Big Jack. He had his schedule open and his pencil poised when the bookie's voice-mail answered, and a recording began giving out the latest lines on the night's action. It was a common practice smart bookies used to make the most of their time. While the recording gave out the lines, the bookies accepted bets on a separate line. After he had the information he needed, Bobby ended the call and punched in Big Jack's number.

"Yeah?" There was no mistaking the gravelly voice on the other end.

"Rico here. What you got tonight?"

After Big Jack gave him the NBA numbers, he started with the college games: "Providence, three and a half; Indiana, ten; Louisville, five; Syracuse, fifteen...." Bobby's heart skipped a beat. Did Jack say Syracuse was a fifteen-point favorite over Boston College? Bobby always wrote each bookie's line down in a column on the schedule next to the other bookie's line for quick comparison, and he saw that the book in New Orleans had Syracuse as only a three-point favorite. Somebody had screwed up a line, and Bobby wasn't about to straighten it out for him. He missed the lines on the next three games because he couldn't concentrate on anything but the Syracuse game. Jack finished, reading off the lines.

"Let me check a few of these to make sure I got them right," Bobby said. "We got a bad connection." He asked about a few meaningless games and then asked the only question that mattered to him right now. "And what was Syracuse?"

"Fifteen, for Crissakes," Jack said, sounding annoyed.

"Okay, I'll call you back in a minute." Bobby couldn't disconnect from Jack and make the call to New Orleans fast enough. He fidgeted as the voice on the tape droned through the games again. Finally, he heard what he was hoping for: "Syracuse, three."   His heart was pounding. This was it. Every player's dream. The chance to middle a game like this came along once in a lifetime. Bobby could bet as much as he could get down on Boston College plus the fifteen points with Big Jack then turn around and bet the same amount on Syracuse minus three with the New Orleans book. If Syracuse won the game by four to fourteen points, Bobby would win both bets. If Syracuse won by three or fifteen, he would win one bet and push the other. If they won by less than three or more than fifteen or lost the game outright, Bobby would win one bet and lose the other, a scenario that would cost him only the "juice" on the losing bet, typically ten percent for football and basketball.

Bobby's mind was racing. *How much will these guys let me play?* he wondered to himself. He knew he had to act fast before someone noticed the mistake. He knew from the line listed in the newspaper that the New Orleans line of three points was probably right and that Big Jack had somehow picked up the wrong line. He would make his bet with Big Jack first, since it was the one most likely to change. Niehaus answered on the second ring.

"Big man, how much do you want to take on one game?" Bobby asked.

"I can cover anything *you* can bet, you nitwit, and you know it." Jack was making it clear that while some people might roll too high for him, little Bobby Pendleton wasn't one of them.

"How about we bet ten thousand on one game—that is, if you've got the *cojones*." Bobby knew he needed to challenge Big Jack a little to get him to accept a wager this large. In fact, the wager would be twenty times larger than any single game bet Bobby had ever made with him. Bobby had never risked more than a thousand dollars in total bets, out at any one time, in his gambling career. He knew ten thousand would be no problem for the man in New Orleans.

"You ain't got ten thousand if you lose, you little weasel," said Big Jack.

"Oh yeah I do. I wouldn't have had it yesterday, but I got a big fat check from the IRS today," Bobby said, hoping Big Jack would believe the lie. "They've been trying to screw me out of my refund since I filed last February, and it finally came through, a smooth eleven thousand three hundred and seventy-four dollars."

"Eleven dimes? How does a donkey like you get an eleven-dime refund? That's what I want to know."

"What is this, Jack, an audit? You working for the IRS now? Damn, man, you want the play or not?"

"All right, kid, you got a bet. Ten dimes. What's the game?"

Bobby knew this was the moment of truth. Jack may have already discovered his mistake on the Syracuse line, or worse yet, Bobby's big play might make him suspicious enough to check the line. "Put ten thousand on Boston College at Syracuse." He waited for Jack to say that line had been a mistake, but the fat man didn't hesitate.

"You got it. Ten thousand on BC plus fifteen. If you lose, I want the whole ten dimes plus the juice on Monday, numbnuts. I got bills to pay myself. And, Bobby boy, you don't even want to know what will happen to you if you ain't got the money. No ifs, ands, or buts—no excuses. So, if you're up to something, don't think you can hide from me, either. If you stiff me, you better disappear forever to a desert island, kid. You get my meaning?"

"Yeah, I hear you loud and clear," Bobby said. "You just have my money ready, because I feel this one in my bones." Bobby hung up the phone and wiped the sweat from his palms before he dialed the New Orleans number.

The phone rang once, then the shrill tone of a phone-company recording filled his ears: "We're sorry. All circuits are busy. Please try your call again later." Bobby looked at his watch. He had fifteen minutes until the New Orleans bookie closed for the night. No reason to panic yet. He hit the redial button and waited. "We're sorry," the recording said. "All circ...."

He hung up in mid-sentence. "What is this crap!" he said out loud to no one but himself. He hit redial again and got the same recording. He punched in a zero for the operator.

"AT&T," the operator said. "May I help you?"

"Yes, operator, I'm trying to get through to New Orleans, and I'm getting a recording about all circuits being busy. I was wondering if you could help me. It's kind of an emergency." Bobby said, trying to convince her he was worried, which, in fact, he was.

"What number are you calling, sir?"

Bobby gave her the number. "Please hurry," he said, pacing around the room.

"One moment, please, while I try to connect you."

The phone began to ring. "All right," Bobby said aloud, "now we're cooking."

"We're sorry," the recording said again. "All circuits are busy. Please try your call again later." The operator came back on again. "Just a moment, sir. Let me see if I can find out what the problem is." She sounded so calm and professional while Bobby's blood continued to rise. She was gone for thirty seconds before he heard her voice again.

"Sir, I'm putting the long distance operator on the line, and she'll try to assist you." Bobby tried to say something, but the new operator was already on the line.

"I'm very sorry, sir, but one of our main switching stations is down between Atlanta and New Orleans and a big winter storm in the Midwest has knocked out some of our other switching stations, I'm told. We're having to reroute calls all over the country, and it's backlogging everything."

"Thank you," Bobby mumbled and put the phone down. He now realized that he would not be able to get down the other side of his bet and that he was in danger of owing eleven thousand dollars he didn't have—and could not get—to a very dangerous man. He had one chance to save himself: call Big Jack and bet another ten thousand, only this time it would be on Syracuse. He dialed the number.

"Mulroney's," a voice answered with the name of the bar where Big Jack hung out after he closed his business for the night.

"Let me speak to Big Jack," Bobby said.

"Jack just left. Sorry, but you missed him by thirty seconds."

"Just left! Are you kidding me? He's always there till eight."

"Yeah, well tonight he got tickets to the Hawks, and he left a little early. You wanna leave a message?" Bobby's whole life was passing before him. He could no longer think or reason, just beg.

"Hey listen, if he just left, maybe he's not in his car yet. Maybe you could run out and try to catch him."

"You're putting me on, right, pal? I'm gonna leave the cash register and run out into the street looking for Jack so one of his addicts can make a bet. Get real." The man's voice was replaced by a dial tone. Bobby cursed Big Jack, his own bad luck, and his life. He tuned his television to ESPN. The network was showing highlights from the night's NBA action, but Bobby did not care. The only thing he was interested in was watching the score scroll across the bottom of the screen. First the NBA scores, followed immediately by the NHL scores. Who cares about hockey anyway. Dumb game. All they do is fight. After the hockey came the only ones Bobby cared about – the NCAA men's basketball scores. He watched the scores as they slowly rotated through the night's games. It took exactly seventeen minutes and thirteen seconds for the score to come back around to the Boston College – Syracuse game. At twenty minutes until eleven o'clock, the score came across the bottom of the screen. Syracuse 66 and Boston College 60 with three minutes and forty seven seconds remaining. If BC could avoid being outscored by 10 points or more, he would win or at worst, push the bet.

"Yeah baby, yeah! That's what I'm talking about. Hang tough Eagles!" Bobby screamed to the empty room.

Seventeen minutes and thirteen seconds later, the score appeared again. Syracuse 76 – Boston College 60. The dreaded word 'Final" appeared next to the score. Bobby just stared at the screen, his mind willing the score to change, praying with every inch of his being that the score was wrong. He went to his PC and tried to get on-line with CBS Sports to verify the score, but his internet was down and all he got was a message telling him that a connection could not be made. But, in his heart, he knew the score was right. He had known from the moment he was unable to get through to New Orleans that he was doomed. His mind was racing through every possible way to get out of the mess he was in and he knew he could not sleep without help. He took a sleeping pill and went to bed. He asked himself why he had lost. Then supplied his own answer. He lost because that's what losers did.

The next morning, after trying to get on-line and failing once more, slipped on a robe and went out the front door and down the walk to his mailbox. Under the box was a cylinder that held the daily newspaper. He grabbed the paper and searched for the Sports section, dropping three other sections to the ground in his haste. He found the scores from the previous night's college basketball games. Each was accompanied by a few paragraphs about the games.

Syracuse 76, Boston College 60. The unranked Orangemen overcame a five-point halftime deficit and won going away. Boston College shot a season low 20 percent from the field and went scoreless in the last four minutes of the game.

The story hit Bobby like a freight train. "Just perfect, just freaking perfect," he said out loud. "Scoreless in the last four minutes. One lousy basket, and you lose by fourteen, not sixteen." One basket was the difference in being up ten thousand and being down eleven thousand. He began to wonder how it would feel to have two busted knee caps. "I am in it deep now," he said softly to himself as he started back to the house.

"Mr. Pendleton, oh, Mr. Pendleton?" Bobby stopped and looked to his left. It was Mrs. Rosenblum from two houses over. The old lady and her five cats had lived in that house since before Bobby was born, and she had long ago appointed herself as the neighborhood watchdog for everything from suspicious cars to peeping toms. "You dropped some of your newspaper, and it's blowing all over the lawn."

Bobby just stood there looking at her. He was torn between telling her where she could stick the newspaper and going to pick it up. He did neither, and instead glared at her until she scurried back into her house in fear. After she was gone, he went down to the street and collected the errant papers. He could see Mrs. Rosenblum peeking through her curtains. He resisted the urge to give her the finger and went back inside.

ༀ

CHAPTER THIRTY THREE
FATHER AND DAUGHTER

WHEN DANNY CAME home from school the next day, Melissa was in the front yard playing with the family pet, a feisty little bundle of energy named Scruffy. When the family had rescued the pure-blood Wheaten Terrier from the pound five years earlier, the vet had speculated that the dog was more than likely pedigreed animal and probably between six months and one year old. He also told them that Scruffy likely had cost someone between eighteen hundred and twenty-five hundred dollars when purchased. Apparently, the dog had run away and ended up in the pound. The Chambers family named him Scruffy because of his disheveled appearance when they first saw him.

Melissa was tossing a tennis ball on the lawn for Scruffy to retrieve. While his back was turned to chase the ball, she would hide behind a bush or tree and make the dog find her. Because Terriers are scent hounds and not sight hounds, the dog always sniffed her out in a matter of moments. Although the dog was primarily the responsibility of DJ and Melissa, Danny and Sheila had come to love the little animal as much as the kids. By the time Danny pulled into the garage and got out of his car, Scruffy was at his feet, tail wagging, waiting for a tummy rub.

"Ok, Scruffster, roll over." The dog immediately obeyed and Danny slipped his foot out of the brown loafer he wore and began to rub the animal's stomach with his foot. Melissa came in and wrapped her arms around her father's waist.

"Hi, Daddy. Did you have a good day at school today?"

"I sure did, sunshine. How about you?"

"Oh, it was okay, I guess," she said. "But Jimmie Edmondson can be such a pest. He took my books and put them up on a shelf where I couldn't reach them. I had to stand on a chair to get them back. Boys can be so immature, you know."

"Well, shame on him for that. But you know why he does that to you don't you, baby?"

"Because he's a pest and he's immature," she answered emphatically.

"Nope. It's because he likes you. That's his way of getting your attention."

"Oh Daddy, that's so dumb, if it's true. Jimmie Edmondson is kind of cute, but if he wants me or any of my friends to like him, he needs to grow up."

"Well, honey, your mom and I have told you before that girls mature faster than boys. He can't help it if he's not as grown up as you. I bet he has a crush on you for sure. Just be nice to him. One day you might just think he is the cutest boy in school."

"Hah!" Melissa said, folding her arms. Then she thought about it and softened a bit. "Well, maybe by the time he's fifteen—but only maybe." She stood closer to her father, put her arms around him again, and hugged him fiercely without saying a word. Scruffy alternately nuzzled her leg and sniffed at the well-worn tennis ball she was holding. Danny put his hand on his daughter's head and ran it through her hair.

"Are you all right, sweetheart?" he asked. She didn't answer at first. Then she pulled away from him, turned, and tossed the ball into the yard, keeping her back to her father. Scruffy shot out the garage door and across the lawn to retrieve the ball. Danny put his hands on her shoulders and turned her around to face him. He saw the tears in her eyes.

"What is it, honey? Why are you crying?"

"I don't want that man to hurt my brother!" she blurted out and began to weep.

"Who told you that, honey?"

"I heard DJ talking to one of his friends on the phone. I heard him say that the man whose son got hit by the car and died was going to kill him to hurt you. Daddy, please don't let him kill DJ." Her words were barely intelligible through the sobs.

"Now, now, little one, you know your daddy is not going to let anyone hurt your brother or you or Mommy. You stop crying now or you'll upset Scruffy. You know he hates to see you cry." He took his handkerchief from his pocket and wiped her cheeks.

"Go on, now, and play with him, but maybe you guys would be better off playing in the back yard, though."

She was still sniffling a little. "The backyard isn't big enough, Daddy. Scruffy can't get a good run back there."

"Well, I'm afraid he might chase the ball into the street if you play out here, so do me a favor and go in the back, okay?"

The girl looked at him suspiciously. "We play out here all the time, Daddy, and you know it. I don't think that's what you're afraid of."

Before Danny could say anything else, Melissa signaled to the dog. "Come on, Scruffy, let's play ball in the back." She was out the door of the garage and gone in a flash.

She's growing up so fast, Danny thought to himself. *She's just my baby, and she shouldn't have to have this worry in her life. I have to do something to put an end to this. No, that's not strong enough. I* will *put an end to this.*

〆

CHAPTER THIRTY FOUR
THREATS THAT BACKFIRE

THAT NIGHT, THE phone rang at fifteen minutes past eleven. Danny had not gone to bed yet. Ever since the first call from Cisco, he was lucky to get to sleep by three in the morning most nights, so he usually sat in his recliner and read or watched television. He kept the shotgun on the floor beside him. After the kids went to bed, he would load the weapon and put the safety on. Sheila had asked if he truly was having that much trouble sleeping or if he was really just on guard duty. Danny had merely grunted, and she let it go. He wasn't sure what the truth was, either. He was sure of one thing, though: When he sat in this chair, with his back to the wall, the doors and windows locked, the alarm system armed, and the 12-gauge at his side, he felt better about the safety of his family than at any other time during the day.

The ringing of the phone didn't startle him anymore. He picked it up.

"Hello, Cisco. I was just thinking about calling you, but you called before I had the chance."

"You were going to call me, Hero?" Cisco said incredulously. "Why would you call me? I thought you didn't like me, Hero."

"I don't like you, but I found out some information today that I wanted to share with you."

"Oh yeah? And what would that information be, Hero?" Danny had been thinking about this conversation all day. When he spoke with GBI Agent Don Livingston earlier, Danny asked him if Cisco had any other family in Atlanta. Livingston told him Cisco's mother, Eldemira Santos, lived in Hapeville, near the airport.

"My friends at the police department told me your mother only lives thirty miles from me, Cisco."

"So what? I know where she lives. What...do you think you can go see my mother and ask her to make me leave you alone?" Cisco laughed. "Is that what you think, Hero? You think my mother can save you?"

"No, that's not what I think, Cisco," Danny said with a lot more bravado than he felt. "What I think is that if anything happens to anyone in my family, I will pay your mother a visit. Whatever you do to my family, I will do to her. *Comprende*, amigo?"

"Is that so? So, if I kill your wife, you gonna kill my mommy?" Cisco sounded amused. Danny had no intention of harming the poor woman who had given birth to this animal. He knew he couldn't do something like that to an innocent person, no matter what the provocation, but he continued with this line of attack.

"Yes, that's *exactly* what I meant." Danny said.

"Well, let me ask you this, Hero," Cisco said. "Did your friends at the police department give you her street address?" Before Danny could speak, Cisco answered his own question. "Because if they didn't, I can give it to you right now." All the humor, in his voice disappeared. "When you kill that rotten old bitch, tell her I said, 'Hello.' Tell her I'll see her in hell, Hero."

Danny was completely caught off guard. This wasn't what he expected to hear from Cisco. "You don't mean that," he said, trying to regain control, "so don't try to bluff me."

"My mother turned me in to the police, Hero. She turned her son over to the cops, and they sent me to prison. I should have killed her myself a long time ago. You made a big mistake, Hero. You threatened Cisco Ram. I don't care about her—but you didn't know that. You threaten me, you threaten the Latino Death Lords. So now, Hero, the rules have changed. I'm not just going to kill your son and then you; I'm going to kill your wife and your daughter first. That way you can feel all the pain, Hero. I hope you sleep well." Danny heard a dial tone.

Still holding the receiver, he stared at the picture of Sheila, Melissa, and DJ that sat on the mantle. He hung up the phone, leaned forward, put his head in his hands. Oh God, he groaned softly, what have I done?

⁊

CHAPTER THIRTY FIVE
HEART ATTACK

TWO DAYS AFTER his son's visit, Roger Chambers was trimming the azalea bushes near the front of his home. Roger was not a large man at this stage of his life. In his younger days, he had carried more weight and muscle, but after a minor heart attack at sixty-two, he had gone on a diet and lost almost thirty pounds. His doctor had told Roger that a six-foot-two man his age, who had a history of heart problems, should weigh no more than one hundred and seventy-five pounds, which is exactly what Roger now weighed.

Maintaining his weight at that level accomplished two things: one, he felt better; and, two—and almost equally important—being able to say his weight was exactly where the doctor had prescribed allowed him to eat peanuts or drink a beer several times a week without catching hell from his wife. Roger still had a good head of hair, even if it was almost completely white, and his hands were large, strong, and scarred from his years as a mechanic. It was impossible to work on airplanes engines for any length of time without getting a few nicks and cuts, and Roger wore these scars proudly as an emblem of his trade.

He still had a few friends working at the Delta shops in Atlanta and occasionally attended union meetings. He wasn't really concerned about the doings of the union, but he did like to sit in on the poker games and have a few beers with the guys afterwards. Roger Chambers was, and had always been, "a man's man" who loved the outdoors, an accomplished bird hunter and a competitive fisherman who had won several of the bass-fishing contests that were frequently held on the lakes around the Atlanta area. He played football and baseball in high school and coached Danny's first baseball team when the boy was only seven years old.

Roger and Sarah attended their own church regularly and often visited at Victory with Danny, Sheila, and the grandchildren. Roger was continually asking the Lord to help him control his temper, which could only be described as volatile with a low flash point. Only a few things set him off now—such as rude drivers, people who talked during a movie, and, especially, anything he considered a personal affront to his wife, any of which could instantly bring him to a boil. Roger wasn't proud of this shortcoming and had worked hard to correct it, in part because his doctor had told him more than once that it wasn't good for his heart. Sarah, in fact, recently told him she thought he was getting better at controlling it.

Roger heard the music before he saw the car. He stopped trimming the bushes and turned around to see a jet-black late-model SUV with tinted windows turning the corner onto his street. The front windows were down and rap music blared through them, with bass notes almost powerful enough to rattle the fillings in his teeth.

Damn hoodlums, he thought. *You don't live on this street, so get the hell off it, or turn your radio down.* He was surprised when the big SUV eased to a stop at the curb in front of his house and three young Hispanic men got out and came up the walk toward him. They were each dressed almost the same—very low-slung denim jeans, jerseys representing a football or baseball team, baseball caps or brightly-colored bandanas, and dark or mirrored sunglasses.

Roger didn't wait for them to get any closer. "What can I do for you, fellas?"

"Are you Senor Chambers?" a man who appeared to be the youngest of the three asked.

"Yeah, I'm Roger Chambers. Who wants to know?"

The man took a toothpick out of his pocket and stuck it in the corner of his mouth. Using his lips and tongue, he rolled the toothpick from one side to the other and back again before he spoke. He didn't respond to Roger's question.

"Senor Chambers, the father of the hero we keep reading about in the papers?" he asked.

"My son *has* been in the papers a few times lately," Roger said calmly. "What's it to you?" The man didn't answer this question, either.

"The father of the phony hero who killed the sixteen-year-old boy for no reason?" the young man asked, causing Roger's temperature to rise.

"Now you see here, sonny. My son didn't kill anyone who didn't need killing, sixteen years old or not. Now you get the hell off my property before I call the police. I mean it. You git!"

With no warning, the man slapped Roger in the face, hard, with the full palm of his hand. The blow caught Roger high on the cheekbone, causing him to stagger but not fall. One of the other men, using both hands, shoved him backwards violently, and this time he did fall.

"You sons of bitches are going to pay for this," he sputtered, trying to rise. Before Roger could finish his threat, one of the young men kicked him in the side, and he thought he heard something crack. He fell back to the ground, crying out in pain.

"Tell your son, the hero, his time will come soon," said the leader. "And before it does, maybe we'll come back and visit his *madre.*" The three men turned and walked leisurely back to their vehicle and climbed in. The power windows slid up and they disappeared behind the tinted glass. The SUV slowly pulled away from the curb and headed up the street, leaving Roger curled up on the ground.

When he tried to get up, he felt a crushing pain in his chest, as if someone were sitting on him and forcing all the air out of his lungs. He recognized the feeling and struggled to find the nitroglycerin pills in his shirt pocket, praying he could get one in his mouth before he passed out.

∽

CHAPTER THIRTY SIX
HOSPITAL

DANNY WAS IN his office going over some papers when his cell phone rang. He picked it up and looked at the screen. It read "Emory Hospital." His heart was racing as he flipped open the phone.

"Hello?" he said tentatively.

"Danny, it's Mom. I'm with your father at the hospital. He had another heart attack, but the doctor says he's going to be fine. There's no sign of a stroke or any paralysis, so that's a great blessing."

"Thank the Lord," said Danny. "When did this happen, Mom?"

"About an hour ago, hon. I found him passed out in the front yard when I came out to bring him a glass of iced tea. What a shock that was. I thought I was going to pass out myself when I saw him lying there in the flower bed. I called 911, and they got there in a flash."

"That's good, Mom. Sounds like we were really lucky you were home. What was he doing when it happened? He wasn't trying to climb back up on the roof to clean the gutters again, was he?"

"I don't think so, hon. He said he was going to work on the azaleas for awhile. I told him it was too cold to be out there, anyway. But you know your father. Once he puts his mind to something, it's hard to change it."

"Yeah, I know him, Mom. Sheila says I didn't fall far from the tree on that one. I'm going to go home, pick up Sheila and the kids, and we'll be at there soon. What's his room number?"

"Maybe you shouldn't bring Sheila and the kids tonight, honey. Your father's very tired, and I don't think he needs a room full of visitors."

"Whatever you say, Mom. I'll get there as soon as I can."

"That's good, son. Your father said he wanted to speak to you as soon as he could, so I hope you can get here before they give him a sedative or something." She gave him the room number and told him not to speed because his father wasn't in any immediate danger. Danny buzzed Jonathan Evans' secretary and told her where he was going, stuffed some papers in his briefcase, and headed to his car. *Why is Dad in such a rush to talk to me?* he wondered aloud on his way to the hospital. *And about what?*

CHAPTER THIRTY SEVEN
EDITORIAL COMMENT

LIKE ANY GOOD reporter, Joe Goddard kept a number of sources, known as stringers in the business, in his contact list. These people did not work for the *Atlanta Record;* Goddard paid them only when they called with something that interested him or fit into a story he was following. How much he paid for each bit of information depended on how useful he thought it was. His stringers were smart enough to read his articles and occasional editorials in the *Record* and look for information that related to stories he had written.

Fortunately for Goddard, Herman Weatherell was one of his sources and was an EMT who worked for Gwinnett County Fire and Rescue. Weatherell had been dispatched to the home of Roger Chambers when the emergency call came in.

As Weatherell sat in the back of the ambulance, monitoring Roger's vital signs, and administering oxygen, Roger mumbled something about being attacked by a bunch of damn Mexicans. Goddard's informant had followed the story of Danny Chambers on television and in the newspapers and immediately connected the name Roger Chambers, to Danny. Doing his best to calm his patient, Weatherell tried to change the subject.

"Take it easy, Mr. Chambers. You aren't doing yourself any good getting upset, and you aren't making my job any easier. By the way, your son wouldn't be *Danny* Chambers, the guy I read about in the paper who saved some lady's life?"

The mention of his son's name had the desired effect. Roger settled down and began to talk about his son, the hero. When Weatherell commented that Danny probably would be angry when he heard about what had happened to his father, Roger decided to say nothing more about the Mexicans until he could speak to his son face to face.

Herman Weatherell had already heard enough. After he delivered his patient to the Emergency Room and filled out the required forms, he got a cup of coffee from the hospital cafeteria and stepped outside for a smoke. His driver, Millie Jones, had gone to use the restroom, so Herman was in no rush. He took out his cell phone and called Joe Goddard. When Goddard answered, Herman told him that the father of Danny Chambers had been attacked by several Mexicans in his own front yard and that he had just delivered him to the ER at Emory.

"That's worth fifty bucks, Herm," said Goddard. "If I scoop the AJC on it, it's worth a hundred. Thanks, buddy."

The EMT flipped his phone shut, took a draw from his cigarette, and headed back to his vehicle. Other than his hope that the old man would recover, Roger Chambers and his problems were no longer of any interest to him.

Meanwhile, Joe Goddard was hunched over his laptop, feverishly typing his story for the next edition of the *Record*.

CHAPTER THIRTY EIGHT
ROGER TELLS THE TRUTH

WHEN DANNY WALKED into his father's hospital room, he found his mother sitting at Roger's bedside, holding his hand. He went over to her immediately, bent down, and kissed her cheek. Then he shifted his gaze to his father.

"How you doing, Pop?"

His father looked very pale and tired. "Well, the doctors say I'm going to live," he grunted, "so I guess, I'm better than a lot of guys would be in my situation, Son." His voice was weak and nasal because of the oxygen tubes in his nose. Danny moved to the opposite side of the bed and took his father's hand.

"Give my hand a good squeeze, Dad," he said.

"What are you now, some kind of doctor?" his father asked playfully. "I thought you were a football coach."

"Actually, Dad, in case you've already forgotten, I'm now assistant principal and dean of boys," Danny said, feigning smugness. "Just humor me, Pop, and squeeze my hand so I'll know you're still the hardest man in Delta's machine shops." Roger Chambers squeezed his son's hand as hard as he could. It wasn't as firm a grip as Danny was used to, but it was better than he had feared. "Okay, Pop, you're still the man." Roger smiled, and some of the color returned to his face.

Danny's father turned to his wife. "Sarah, girl, I want you to go home and get some rest. You're exhausted, and I don't want you to end up in the bed next to me, so just give me a kiss and go on home."

"How can I leave you here all alone in this big hospital?" she asked. "I wouldn't feel right about it."

"Well, I won't feel right if you don't," said Roger. "Besides, Danny can stay until I doze off, can't you, Son?" He turned back to his son and winked at him with the eye Sarah couldn't see.

"You bet, Dad. I was planning on staying awhile anyway. Mom, you need to go home like Dad says. You need to rest so you can come back tomorrow and tell the doctors and nurses what to do, right?"

"All right, all right," she said. "I'm being double-teamed by my own family. I guess I'll go home and let you boys talk your man talk." She leaned over and kissed her husband tenderly on the lips. "I love you, old man. Don't you go anywhere without me." Danny came from the other side of the bed, put his arm around her, and walked her out into the hall.

"I'll stay until he goes to sleep, Mom. Don't worry about him. God is watching over him and guiding the doctors' hands."

With tears in her eyes, she stood on her tiptoes and kissed her son gently. "I'm glad you're here, Son. I love you, Danny. See you tomorrow." Danny watched her all the way to the bank of elevators. When the doors opened and she stepped inside, he went back in the room and sat down beside his father.

"When Mom called to tell me about your heart attack, she said you needed to talk to me. What's up, Dad?"

"Sit down, Son, and I'll bring you up to date. Give me a little sip of that water before you do though," Roger said, pointing to a plastic cup with a straw in it. Danny handed it to him, and his father took a few sips. "First off, I didn't have a heart attack pruning azaleas."

Danny leaned forward in his chair and grinned. "All right, Dad, how *did* it happen?"

"I had a visit from some of your friend Cisco's gang. Hell, for all I know, one of the sons of bitches might have been Cisco himself." His face was turning red.

"Calm down, Dad. Calm down. I don't want you to have another heart attack while you're telling me about the last one. Just pretend you're working on the engine on a 757 and have a tight deadline. Be that calm, cool Roger Chambers."

"Well, I was working out front, and these three Mexican punks pull up at the curb and come up to me in the yard. I asked them what they wanted, and they started making a lot of cracks about you killing that kid. Well, I told them to get the hell off my property before I called the police. They made a few threats about what was going to happen to you and your family, then the one doing all the talking slapped me in the face. Can you believe that? He slapped me, damn his soul. Another one pushed me down, and somebody kicked me. I don't know what happened next because I was starting to black out. I remember trying to get my nitro pills out of my pocket, and that's it. I guess I must have gotten one in my mouth. Otherwise, I wouldn't be here now."

Rage was building in Danny's heart like nothing he had ever felt before. But he didn't want to upset his father, so he tried his best to appear calm.

"Did you tell the doctors any of this, Dad?"

"Hell no! I haven't told anyone but you. The doctors asked me about the mark on my face and the bruise on my side, and I told them I must have landed on a rock or a tool when I fell. I figured I'd just wait and tell you, and then you could decide what to do."

"Do you think you could identify these guys if you saw them again or from a mug shot, Dad?"

"I don't know, Son. Maybe the one who slapped me. He was the one running his mouth, so I was looking at him most of the time."

"That's good. As soon as you feel up to it, I'm going to bring a detective from the GBI around to talk to you. Is that all right, Dad?"

"Sure. I expect to be going home tomorrow or the day after, anyway."

"How about talking to him in the morning? Maybe look at some pictures? That is, if the doctors say it's okay."

"I don't see why not. I'm just a little tired. Other than that, I feel fine, Son."

"Great. I'll talk to the doctor before I leave, and if he gives me the go-ahead, I'll be back in the morning between ten and eleven."

Danny changed to subject to the upcoming Super Bowl and he and his father chatted about football until the old man's eyes began to flutter. Danny lowered his voice, but continued to speak until Roger's eyes closed and stayed closed.

He gripped his father's hand gently, leaned over, kissed his cheek and whispered, "I love you, Pop." Then he left the room in search of the attending physician.

CHAPTER THIRTY NINE
LOOKING AT PICTURES

WHEN HE LEFT the hospital, Danny called Don Livingston to advise him of the attack on his father. As soon as Danny told him what had taken place, the lieutenant began a series of rapid-fire questions.

"How's your father now, Danny? Is he going to live?"

"He seems to be doing pretty well. I spoke with his doctor before I left the hospital, and he says Dad should be able to go home in a day or so."

"Does he think he can identify any of the men who attacked him?"

"He says he would know the one who did all the talking if he saw him again," Danny responded, "even though the guy was wearing sunglasses and a baseball cap."

"That's good news, Danny. I'll get some mug shots of Cisco and his crew and be down at the hospital tomorrow morning. Can you meet me there at eleven?"

"That works for me, Don."

The next morning, Danny stopped at the hospital gift shop to look for something for his father to read. The newspapers were neatly arrayed in stacks on the floor in front of the magazine racks. He picked up the *Atlanta Record* and absent-mindedly flipped through it. The headline of an opinion piece on page three caught his eye: COACH'S FATHER PAYS FOR SON'S HEROICS. Danny let out an audible sigh, refolded the paper, and tucked it under his arm. He grabbed a golf magazine for his dad, paid for it and the newspaper, and went across the lobby to the cafeteria. He went through the breakfast line and got a cup of coffee, then took a seat at a table in the corner and began to read Joe Goddard's column:

When Danny Chambers came home a decorated hero from Operation Desert Storm almost twenty years ago, he probably thought his fighting days were over. He settled comfortably into civilian life as a high school football coach and history teacher. He started a family and became an active member of his community. Life was good for the young man and his family, until one day several weeks ago when he saved an Alpharetta woman from almost certain death at the hands of a youthful gang member. The young Hispanic man was struck and killed by a passing car as Danny Chambers attempted to pull him away from the woman he was savaging. Our readers are familiar with the story of Danny Chambers and his heroic actions that day, so I will not repeat them here.

Unfortunately, such acts of heroism often come with a heavy price. The family of Danny Chambers is beginning to pay that price. Yesterday morning while he was working in his garden, Roger Chambers, a sixty-three-year-old retiree from Delta Airlines, was brutally attacked by three Hispanic men. Confidential sources at several area law enforcement agencies tell me that the perpetrators are part of a violent street gang, which operates all across metro Atlanta, known as the Latino Death Lords.

The motive for the attack was clearly revenge. Francisco Miguel Ramos, Jr., the youth who died accidentally when Chambers intervened as he attacked Ms. Holly Langman, was the son of the gang's leader and had a violent history at his school and with the law. He had been a crime—or an accident—waiting to happen for a long time. Unfortunately for Danny Chambers and his family, the boy's father, Francisco Miguel Ramos, Sr., known on the street as Cisco Ram, may already have begun exacting vengeance on the family of Coach Chambers for the death of his son. Danny Chambers, a hero twice over, is not likely to be intimidated by these street thugs.

But where does that leave the rest of us law-abiding citizens? The likelihood of additional budget cuts to state and local law enforcement agencies means that these street gangs will become an even greater menace to our safety. Even at current staffing levels, the police appear unable to protect us. Where were they when a helpless old man was beaten in his front yard in broad daylight? Where will they be if another member of Danny Chambers' family is attacked? Only time will tell.

When he finished reading, Danny tossed the paper into a nearby garbage can and began to massage his temples with his fingers. The column was so over the top that Danny couldn't believe anyone would take it seriously—anyone except Cisco Ram. He knew that these words would only further infuriate the man and cause Danny and his family a lot more problems. He took a last sip of coffee, picked up the magazine he purchased for his father, and went upstairs.

He had decided against mentioning the newspaper column to his father. Danny knew that Roger was a proud man and that seeing himself referred to as a "helpless old man" in a newspaper, even one as small as the *Record,* wasn't going to sit well with him.

Promptly at eleven o'clock that morning, Lt Livingston and another GBI agent came into Roger's hospital room. After Danny introduced Livingston to his father, Livingston introduced his associate to both men. Roger was sitting upright in his bed and looking considerably better than he had the night before. His eyes were clearer, and he had regained some of his color.

"I'm so sorry for your discomfort, Mr. Chambers," Livingston began. "We'll try not to take any more of your time than we need to."

"Thanks," said Danny's father, "but call me Roger. That way when you say 'Mr. Chambers,' I won't have to tax my brain to figure out if you're talking to me or my son. And don't worry about taking up too much of my time. As soon as I start to feel bad or just get tired of talking, I'll push this little button here on the side of the bed, and that cute little nurse down the hall will come in here and run you all out." The other men smiled.

"Good enough," said Livingston, getting down to business. "We have a group of photos here of various men. Some are criminals; some are not. Some are Hispanic; some are not. I want you to look very carefully at each one to see if you recognize any of the men who came to your home and assaulted you."

Roger Chambers put on his glasses and took the four-by-six-inch color photos from Livingston's assistant. There appeared to be roughly twenty-five in the stack. He held each picture up to the light coming in through the large windows in his room and studied it closely. After he looked at a picture, he put it in one of two piles beside him on the bed. He made no comments about any of them, until he had finished looking at all of th pictures. One pile contained twenty-one photographs; the other held seven. He handed the larger stack back to Livingston.

"I've never seen any of these fellows before," Roger said. Both Danny and the lieutenant were disappointed to see the photograph of Francisco Miguel Ramos on top of that stack. Danny more so than the detective, who had hoped but not expected that Cisco Ram himself would have come out in the open for this type of blatant attack. It would have been completely out of character.

Roger went through the remaining seven photos a second time. He kept looking at them and shuffling them around, occasionally handing one of them back to Livingston. Finally, he held two photos, one in each hand. He extended his right hand and said, "This guy might have been there, but he didn't say a word and he isn't the one who slapped or pushed me." Extending the photo in his left hand, he said, "This is the SOB who did the talking and hit me."

Taking both photos from Roger's outstretched hands, Livingston held up the second of the two and said, "You're sure that this is the man who attacked you in your front yard yesterday?"

"Yep, he's the one alright. I pray to God I get to meet this bastard again when he doesn't have his buddies with him."

Danny took the picture from Livingston's hand and looked at it closely. "Who is he?" he asked.

Livingston's associate, Agent Wayne Mercer, took the photo, flipped it over, and looked at a number on the back. He matched the number against a list of names in his notebook. "His name is Victor Garza," he said firmly. "He's one of of Eduardo Aguilar's guys. Aguilar, better known on the streets as *'El Carnicero,* the butcher, is also reputed to be one of Cisco Ram's top three lieutenants and he also just happens to be the man in the other photo that your father said may have been at his home."

"Yeah, I recognized Aguilar's picture when I saw it," Livingston said. "That would make sense. Cisco wants the job done right, so he sends one of his best people along to supervise. He doesn't want to risk having a top gang member identified, so he tells him to stay in the background and let someone else deliver the message."

"Can we arrest the one who hit my father?" Danny asked.

"Of course we can do that—if we can find him," said the lieutenant. "But I suspect that Mr. Victor Garza has already left Atlanta for a little vacation in Mexico."

"How about the other one?" Danny persisted.

"As long as your father says he can't positively identify the man as having been part of the group who attacked him, we can't touch him," Livingston said. "But, who knows, maybe we'll get lucky with Garza. Cisco is getting a little reckless, and maybe he's getting a little overconfident. I'll request warrants for both men. If we can bring them both in, we might shake Cisco up a little, even if we have to release Aguilar as fast as we bring him in." Danny thought he detected a glimmer of hope in Livingston's eyes.

❧

CHAPTER FORTY
FRIENDS IN HIGH PLACES

THAT AFTERNOON, DON Livingston requested and received warrants for the arrest of Victor Garza and Eduardo Aguilar. Officers from the Gwinnett County Sheriff's Department, accompanied by GBI agents, went first to the LDL clubhouse, which served as the gang's headquarters, and found Victor Garza playing cards with three other men. Garza was taken into custody and read his Miranda rights without incident. Eduardo Aguilar was not there, and all of the LDL members who were present, said they had no idea where he was. The GBI agents informed them that Aguilar was wanted in connection with an assault and battery and that if any of them spoke with him, they should advise him to surrender to the authorities immediately. The officers went next to Aguilar's last known address, only to find that, according to the occupants of the apartment, he had moved out three months earlier. Further questioning yielded only that Aguilar had left no forwarding address.

Don Livingston was waiting at the Gwinnett County Jail when Garza was brought in. Livingston attempted to question him about the attack on Roger Chambers, but all Garza would say was, "I want to talk to my lawyer."

Livingston then called Danny to give him an update on Garza and Aguilar. An hour later, Livingston's office called to tell him that Eduardo Aguilar had turned himself in at GBI Headquarters downtown, and was waiting there with his attorney. This concerned Livingston because he knew that if Aguilar came in voluntarily, he must be confident that the authorities could not tie him to the assault. Heading out the door, Livingston told the deputies to advise him as soon as they knew when Victor Garza would be arraigned.

County District Attorney Dalton Gray was waiting outside the interview room. Livingston had called him when he learned that Garza was being brought in. Livingston gave the D.A. a quick but thorough update on everything that had happened to Danny Chambers family since the death of Francisco Ramos, Jr., and asked that Gray request that Garza be held without bail. The D.A. said he would do his best to keep Garza behind bars, at least until Roger Chambers could come in and identify him.

When Livingston arrived at GBI Headquarters, he went straight to the interview room where Aguilar and his attorney were waiting and sat down across the table from them. "My name is Don Livingston. I'm a lieutenant with the Georgia Bureau of Investigation. I have some questions for you concerning an attack on a gentleman named Roger Chambers at his home in Gwinnett County at approximately ten o'clock in the morning on the twentieth of this month."

The attorney spoke for his client. "We're pleased to meet you, Lieutenant Livingston. I'm Jorge Rivera, and I represent Mr. Aguilar. He is here of his own free will and has nothing to hide. As his attorney, I have instructed him to answer any and all of your questions truthfully. So, please, go ahead." This was exactly what Livingston had expected. He knew he would get nothing but lies, but he had to go through the motions.

"Mr. Aguilar, where were you on the twentieth of this month at ten in the morning?" Livingston asked.

"I was taking my sister and my niece to the shopping center to buy some birthday presents," Aguilar responded smugly.

"Can anyone other than your sister attest to that fact?" Livingston asked.

"Si, si. I'm sure the saleslady at the store will remember me," Aguilar said playfully. "She was very pretty, and I tried to get her phone number. You know how it is, amigo."

"By any chance was this saleslady Hispanic?" Livingston asked.

"Why, yes—yes she was," said *El Carnicero*. "Why do you ask? Do you have a problem with Hispanic people, amigo?" Livingston ignored the question and shoved a pad and pen across the table to *Carnicero*.

"Please write down the names and contact information for your sister and your niece, the name of the store, and the sales clerk's name," he said.

"Give it to the officer at the door. And don't leave town without clearance from me." Livingston got up and left the room. Two hours later, D.A. Dalton Gray called to say he had failed to get Victor Garza remanded. Judge Ronald Thornton had released him on minimum bail, ruling that the man had no criminal record and had only been identified by a photograph, not in person.

"That's outrageous," Livingston said, fuming. "I can't believe Judge Thornton let this guy go. No criminal record my butt. We haven't even had time to run his prints through NCIC to see how many crimes he's committed and how many times he's been arrested under other names. This is very disappointing."

"I'm really sorry, Don," said the D.A. "It's all my fault. I could have held Aguilar in custody for 72 hours before I even had to bring him before a judge. Based on Judge Thornton's reputation, I figured there was no way he would let this guy go."

"I'm not blaming you, Dalton. I didn't see it coming, either."

"I appreciate that, Don, but it gets worse."

"You're kidding."

"I'm afraid not. It turns out that Senor Garza is in this country illegally. Big surprise, huh? Anyway, at some point, Judge Thornton asks to see his passport, a visa, or a green card, and Garza can't produce one. Here's where it gets a little strange. For some reason, it only occurs to the judge after Garza had departed the premises that the State of Georgia should petition a federal judge to immediately initiate deportation proceedings against Garza. Judge Thornton sent a note to my office to get this moving. The problem is, I doubt we'll ever see Garza alive again."

"That's usually how anyone who poses a threat to Cisco ends up, isn't it?" Livingston said, shaking his head. "Poor slob probably thinks he'll just have to disappear until things cool down a bit. What he doesn't know is that Cisco will more than likely make him disappear forever."

"One thing puzzles me, though," said the D.A.

"What's that?"

"If the judge had wanted to, he could have ordered Garza held as an illegal alien."

"So why didn't he?" Livingston asked.

"Who knows? Maybe the judge doesn't want to get on the wrong side of this whole immigration issue. Maybe he's getting old, or just getting soft? Your guess is as good as mine."

"Well isn't this just grand," said the lieutenant. "With Garza gone, unless Roger Chambers suddenly has a marked improvement in his memory for faces, we have no chance to get Aguilar to talk. I was hoping to use Garza's testimony as leverage against him."

"Sorry, Lieutenant," said the district attorney. "I guess it's back to the grindstone."

Livingston cursed under his breath. *More like back to square one*, he thought to himself.

℘

CHAPTER FORTY ONE
DISAPPEARANCES

DANNY HAD ALWAYS loved dogs. He once heard it said that you can own a dog, but you can never own a cat because cats don't have masters, they have staff. Danny felt you could never really own a dog, either. He couldn't understand how anyone could say you owned something you loved.

His first dog, an almost purebred German Shepherd, was a good southern dog, appropriately named Rebel. When Danny was eleven years old, he found Rebel wandering the streets without tags or a collar and brought him home. He convinced Roger and Sarah to let him keep the dog if no one put up any posters saying it was lost. Being dog lovers themselves, Danny's parents really didn't need much convincing. When Danny took Rebel in for a checkup and shots, the vet said the animal was somewhere between twelve and eighteen months old.

Danny had found the dog on July 5, so that became Rebel's official birthday. Danny also decided that since the vet wasn't sure about Rebel's age, he would choose to believe the dog was twelve months old, hoping to add six months to his new friend's life. Rebel died of liver cancer when Danny was in his second year of college, and although Danny was brokenhearted, he resisted the urge to get another dog until he and Sheila were married and had a home with a fenced yard.

He rescued his next dog from the pound when it was six months old. Rommel, his second Shepherd, had recurring health problems and passed away at age ten, when DJ was ten and Melissa seven.

The family waited more than a year after that before they saw Scruffy at the pound. The little Wheaten Terrier quickly wormed his way into their hearts and played no favorites. In fact, it seemed that the dog instinctively knew when he had been snuggling with one family member for long enough and that it was time to leap from one lap to another. Danny was particularly fond of Scruffy, feeling at times that he might actually love this dog more than Rebel or Rommel. He told Sheila he didn't know if it was because he was getting older and more sentimental, or because Scruffy was such a lovable little lap dog.

The back yard at the Chambers home was fenced, and so that the animal would have a shady place to rest, the screen door on the back porch was always left open whenever Scruffy was left in the backyard. Because he liked to run and, like all terrier breeds, sniff out the world around him, he was left in the fenced back yard whenever the family was away and the weather was suitable. Three days after the attack on Roger Chambers, Danny was at work, the kids were at school, Sheila was out running errands, and Scruffy, as usual, was in the back yard.

When Sheila got home, she went to the screened porch and called the dog's name. When Scruffy didn't respond to her third call, she went out into the back yard to look for him. First, she checked the gates on both sides. They were closed and latched. Then she checked the shady spot under the steps, which was one of his favorite haunts, and the azalea beds along the back fence. Scruffy was nowhere to be found.

Starting to feel uneasy, she went back inside and called Danny at school. When he answered, she told him that Scruffy was missing. Even though he had already missed a great deal of time from work lately, this news was serious enough to cause Danny to drop everything and head home. When he got there, he went straight to the back yard and walked along the entire fence looking for cracks or places where the dog might have tunneled its way out. Nothing.

"You're absolutely positive he was in the yard when you left this morning?" Danny asked Sheila.

"I'm positive, Danny. I put fresh water in his bowl and stood here and watched him drink some so I could refill it before I left. He was here for sure."

"Don't worry," Danny said, trying to reassure his wife and himself. "We'll find him." He started running toward the driveway, motioning for Sheila to follow. "You take your car and go east on Oakwood, and I'll go west. Keep your cell phone on and call me if you spot him."

"Aren't we avoiding the obvious, Danny?" Sheila shouted to him.

"What do you mean?" Danny shouted back, stopping to wait for her answer.

"I saw you checking the fence for breaks or places he might have dug out," she said, "but you didn't find any, did you?"

"No, I didn't."

"Well, think about it," Sheila said. "The gates were closed, and he was here when I left. He isn't here now, and he didn't fly away. Someone must have taken him—and we both know who." Her eyes began to fill with tears. Danny came over and put his arms around her shoulders.

"Let's not jump to conclusions, honey. There may be another explanation." Danny tried to sound confident, but he couldn't think of one. Sheila buried her head in his chest and began to sob.

"The only explanation is that those bastards took our puppy," she said.

"Maybe you're right, angel," Danny said. "But I don't know what else to do right now, but look for him—so let's get on with it."

After an hour of searching, they returned home, having seen no sign of Scruffy. When DJ and Melissa got home from school and learned that Scruffy was gone, they asked to join the search. Melissa rode with her mother, and DJ slowly cruised the neighboring streets on his bicycle, calling Scruffy's name. By dinnertime, everyone was back at the house. The four of them sat quietly around the table, pushing the food around on their plates. Finally, Melissa broke the silence.

"We can put up posters in the morning," she said enthusiastically. "I have lots of pictures of Scruffy we can use." By now Danny had resigned himself to Sheila's earlier assessment of what happened to the dog, but he didn't have the heart to tell his daughter that the posters were a waste of time.

At seven thirty the next morning, the phone rang. Danny picked up the receiver and looked down at the recording equipment to see if the light was on.

"Hello?" he said softly.

"Good morning, Hero. How are you?" Maybe it was the same voice as last time. Danny couldn't tell anymore.

"What do you want?" Danny asked.

"I hear you lost your little dog, Hero. Is that right?" Danny wanted to scream at the voice on the other end of the line or threaten him, but he knew either would be useless. Instead, he chose to beg.

"Please, if you have our dog, just let it go, and tell me where it is," Danny pleaded, trying to keep his voice down. "It's just an innocent animal. It has nothing to do with this. Please, just don't hurt him."

"Oh no, Hero. I don't have your dog. But I heard he was lost, so my boys and I went out to help you look for him. In fact, we already found him and put him back in your yard. He's there now. Have a nice day, Hero." Then a dial tone.

A cold dread gripped Danny's heart like a vice. Without saying anything to Sheila or the kids, he went out to his back porch and looked around the yard. There, on a medium-sized silver maple in the back corner of the yard, he spotted Scruffy's lifeless little body hanging by its neck, turning slowly in the morning breeze. Danny raced back inside and told Sheila to keep the kids out of the kitchen and stay in the front of the house with them. He picked up a knife and one of Scruffy's old blankets and ran over to the tree. Hot tears were pouring down his cheeks and a fire born of pain was growing in his soul, a fire that would not be quenched until the people who did this died.

After he cut the animal's tiny body down, wrapped it in a blanket, and put it in the trunk of his car, he dialed Lt. Livingston's number and left a message. He told him what had just happened and informed him that there was a new conversation on the recording equipment. Then he called his family together to tell them that Scruffy would not be coming home. Danny had flown hundreds of missions into combat zones to rescue wounded soldiers, but he knew that this was going to be one of the most difficult things he would ever have to do.

෧෨

CHAPTER FORTY TWO
GOING TO THE MALL

MELISSA CHAMBERS HAD most of the same interests as any other thirteen-year-old girl: boys, clothes, music, and hunky, young movie stars. She played volleyball for her school and had dreams of being varsity cheerleader when she got to high school. Her only regret was that being three years younger than her brother, she wouldn't be able to cheer for him because he would have graduated before she was eligible for the varsity squad.

When her father told her about the man who was angry at him over the accidental death of his son, it had frightened her considerably. But she was afraid for her father, not herself. When she heard her brother tell his friend that the man wanted to hurt him, too, this frightened her even more. Now she was afraid for her brother and her father. It never occurred to her that this man might hurt her. Her father had told her that Scruffy had tunneled under the fence and got hit by a car. She wasn't sure she believed him, and she strongly suspected that what happened to Scruffy had something to do with the man who had threatened her dad and brother. Still, the absence of fear for her own safety and the passage of a few days caused her to discount the warnings her father had given her, when tempted to ignore them, by her best friend, Erin Nichols.

The two of them had been planning a trip to the mall for over a week. Their trip was to be the next afternoon, and when Melissa called Erin to cancel, Erin wasn't happy about it.

"Melissa, come on," she said. "Get over it. Your dad's exaggerating. You said that Scruffy's death was an accident. You know how parents are? They make a big deal out of every thing. What can happen to us at the mall?

There'll be, like, a thousand people around us. Please, please go with me. Don't make me go with Shelly."

The Shelly in question was Shelly Perry, a girl Erin had been good friends with through elementary school until Melissa replaced her as Erin's BFF in middle school. Being a typical thirteen-year-old girl, Melissa was very concerned about who was whose "best friend forever," and she desperately wanted to be Erin's.

"I don't know how I can go," Melissa said. "Mom said we have to come straight home after school, and I'm riding with DJ. I know he won't drop me off at your house without permission, because he's so serious about everything he does, especially when it comes to obeying mom and dad."

"Ask your mom if you can come to my house to study after school," Erin suggested. "Tell her my dad will bring you home after we finish. We can go to the mall and then go back to my house. Daddy will take you home, and your mom will never even know we went."

Melissa had a strong stubborn streak that Danny said she got from Sheila and Sheila said she got from Danny. Melissa wasn't a spoiled child by any stretch, but she liked to have her own way whenever she could. She was also very susceptible to peer pressure and immediately began to waver in the face of Erin's persuasive arguments.

"I really shouldn't, Erin," she said halfheartedly. "I'm sorry, but my mom and dad will get really mad with me if I disobey. Maybe we can go this weekend? Can't you just wait until then?"

"I can't wait until this weekend to get the new Britney album for my iPod," Erin said, sensing weakness. "I just *have* to have it tomorrow. If you can't go, I'll just have to ask Shelly to go with me." Erin knew the right button to push.

"Okay, okay," Melissa said, bordering on panic. "Don't call Shelly yet. I'll ask my mom and call you back." That night at dinner, Melissa brought up the subject of a big biology test she had coming up in two days. Then she casually mentioned that she and Erin would be studying together at Erin's house the next day after school. Both Danny and Sheila said they didn't think it was a good idea and suggested that Erin come to their house to study. Melissa had not foreseen this alternative, and for a moment she was at a loss for words. Then she thought of something.

"Oh, Mom, two of the other girls in the class are coming, too, and Erin's mom promised to make cookies. I don't want to call everyone and say they have to come to my house now. Wouldn't that be rude?"

"I don't like it," Danny said. "I'll feel a lot more comfortable if you're right here at home or at school." Melissa made a face and looked pleadingly at her mother.

"Danny, we can't keep her locked up here and at school forever," Sheila said. "I think she'll be fine at the Nichols if DJ drops her there after school. I can pick her up when they're done."

"Erin said her dad will bring me home, Mom," Melissa swiftly cut in. "You won't have to come out." Sheila looked at Danny and cocked her head to the side, waiting for his response.

"I still don't like it," he said, "but I guess it'll be all right as long as DJ drops you off and watches you go inside and Erin's dad brings you home. But you be home before dinnertime—and no stops along the way."

"And don't eat so many cookies that you ruin your appetite for dinner, either," Sheila added.

Even though Melissa had gotten her way, the lies she told her parents at the dinner table began to bother her when she tried to go to sleep that night. She had attended Sunday School, worshiped regularly at Sunday services, and participated in youth activities at her church, for most of her young life, so the seeds of the Christian faith had been firmly planted in her heart. But she had not yet felt the call to truly surrender her life to Jesus Christ. She wrestled with her conscience and weighed her feelings of guilt against her desire to go to the mall with her best friend. In the end, her friend and the mall won out.

The next day, soon after the last school bell rang, DJ waited patiently behind the wheel of his mother's car for his sister to appear on the front steps of the main entrance of Nathan B. Forrest Middle School, where Melissa was an eighth-grader. Her school was only a block from Lee High School, and their school days ended at the same time, so it wasn't a problem for DJ to pick his little sister up when he didn't have football practice.

The season had been over for more than a month, and Sheila let him drive her car to school this day because she didn't need it and because she preferred, considering the threats to her children, that they have their own transportation rather than have to wait for a school bus.

Melissa had clear instructions from her father that she was to leave the school only by the main entrance and only when she saw that her brother was waiting for her. If DJ was not there, she was to wait inside, near the main office, until she saw him. When DJ spotted his sister coming through the double doors, he rolled down the window.

"Come on, Mel, let's roll," he shouted.

When she got in the car, DJ said, "Did you have a good day, squirt?"

DJ loved Melissa, but, like most older brothers, he also loved to annoy his little sister. His favorite way was to call her "squirt," a nickname he gave her when she was five or six. At first she actually seemed to like it, but by the time she was ten years old, she had decided that it was insulting and had asked her brother to stop using it. Of course, the more vehemently she protested, the more often DJ used it. Melissa scowled at him.

"DJ, I'm not a squirt," she said firmly. "Daddy says I'm a young lady and that you should stop calling me that."

"Okay, okay," DJ said, having gotten the desired reaction. "I'm sorry, squirt. Now let's get going. I have things to do besides being your taxi for the day."

As instructed, he pulled into the driveway at the Nichols house and watched his sister skip up the sidewalk, knock on the door, then disappear inside when Erin opened it. His passenger safely delivered, he backed out of the driveway and drove away. The radio was blasting out a song from his favorite band, and his mind was on a girl in his chemistry class. He didn't notice the black van parked at the curb two houses down.

കൈ

Carnicero was in the driver's seat, wearing his usual day-time attire; Los Angeles Dodgers baseball cap pulled low over his mirrored sunglasses, and Oakland Raiders sweatshirt with the sleeves cut off, and floppy denim jeans. The windows of the van, as in all of Cisco's gang vehicles, were tinted as dark as the law allowed.

Carnicero was smoking a cigarette and listening to an Hispanic radio station while the three young men in his crew were dozing. One of them, Juan Madrigal, was slouched low in the front passenger's seat, his head resting at the intersection of the seat back and the window ledge. The earphones from his iPod were jammed in tightly, and he was softly humming along with the music. The other two, Ricky Montalvo and Benito Valdez, were stretched out on a pile of carpet remnants and dirty clothes in the back of the van.

The four men had followed DJ and Melissa home from school for the past three days, waiting for the right opportunity. Today, it appeared that opportunity had finally come. The brother was gone, and the *chica* would have to come out of her friend's house sooner or later. *Carnicero* guessed it would be sooner, and certainly no later, than the dinner hour.

After following the two teenagers to the Nichol's home, they kept going when DJ pulled into the driveway, but stopped the van two houses further down the street. *Carnicero* kept puffing while he watched the house from his side mirror. The van had stolen plates and an easily removable, magnetic sign which read; Southeastern Carpets and Flooring. The sign had a fake web address and phone number.

Carnicero was about to interrupt Juan's musical interlude and tell him to keep watch for a while when he saw two girls come out of the house where the Chambers kid had been dropped off. They were carrying books and walking quickly in the direction of the van. *Carnicero* started the engine and eased away from the curb.

"Hey, amigos, wake up," he said. "It's time to go to work."

The presence of a second girl was an unwelcome development for *Carnicero*, but he had his orders. He would have to grab them both or suffer Cisco's wrath. The girls were walking in the opposite direction from the Chambers' home, so he figured that they were either going to another kid's house or to Southland Mall, which was only three blocks away. He knew they would have to grab the girls before they got too close to the mall or there might be too many witnesses.

Carnicero did not see a single person anywhere on the street or in a yard in this quiet neighborhood. He had also noted that very few cars had gone by during the past hour. He decided it was time to act. He sped up pass the girls and turned right at the first intersection, then made three more right turns that brought him around the block and behind Melissa and Erin. Unless a neighbor happened to be looking out of her window at the exact moment the deed was done, he thought, they should be able to pull this job off cleanly.

"Just like we talked about it, amigos," *Carnicero* said. "Ricky, you and Benny get out here and walk fast enough to catch up to the girls. Juan, you throw the doors open when we come up beside them." He pointed at Ricky and Benny.

"You two put the bags over their heads from behind and throw them in the van. If you move fast enough, they'll never have a chance to see your faces."

When the two men got out of the van, *Carnicero* started moving forward again at the same pace Ricky and Benny were walking. He kept one eye on his rear view mirror to make sure no cars were coming up behind him. If a car did approach, the plan was to accelerate past the girls, which would signal Ricky and Benny to wait until he came back around the block for another pass. But the street was clear. As the van came up alongside the girls, who were lost in conversation, *Carnicero* turned his head to the left so they couldn't see his face. When Juan saw his amigos come up behind the girls and quickly slip large black cloth bags over their heads, pulling the drawstrings tight, he pushed open the side doors of the van. Ricky and Benny roughly threw the girls in, and Juan pulled the doors closed and *Carnicero* slowly picked up speed. He didn't want to risk drawing anyone's attention. If someone *had* seen them, he knew they were as good as caught. If not, there was no need to rush. He heard the muffled screams of the girls through the cloth bags.

"Shut them up, amigos," he said, trying to disguise his voice.

Immediately, Juan took control. "*Chica*, I have a knife to your friend's throat. If you make another sound, I will slit it from ear to ear." Neither girl felt a knife at her throat, so both of them assumed he was talking to her and holding the knife to her friend's throat, just as Juan intended. The screaming stopped.

"That's much better," said Juan. "Now, if you'll be good little *muchachas*, you might get home alive." It was twelve minutes before the hour of four o'clock in the afternoon. The abduction had taken less than ten seconds.

Melissa was petrified. It was pitch dark inside the bag and the voices she heard were intelligible, but muffled. She heard one of the men say, "You *chiquitas* look like you're old enough for us to have some fun with. What do you think, amigos? Shall we have a little fun with them, or do we just cut their throats?"

Melissa had already been crying softly; now she began to sob. "Stop the crying!" a voice shouted. "Are you little girls, or are you ladies? I don't really care because I like them both. Which is it?"

Melissa didn't understand why he was asking this question and sensed that her answer would have no impact on her fate. Her mind replayed the scene from less than an hour ago when she gotten in the car with her brother and told him she wasn't a squirt, but a young lady.

Suddenly, she felt someone put his arms around her waist and pull her close. Even through the bag, she could smell cigarette smoke, body odor, and the remnants of the man's lunch on his breath. She felt something press against her ear, then the voice again, now even closer. The man said what he wanted to do to her, something more disgusting than she could imagine. She began to scream and heard Erin screaming, too. Melissa could not hear the four men laughing at them.

❧

CHAPTER FORTY THREE
TRACKING THE CELL PHONE

AT FIVE MINUTES after six, Danny walked into the house and asked Sheila if Melissa was home yet. When he found she wasn't, he said he was going to call the Nichols house and offer to come get her. A male voice answered.

"Joe, this is Danny Chambers. How are you doing?"

"I'm fine, Danny. How about yourself?"

Danny had decided that sharing his problems with anyone who didn't need to know didn't help things and put a burden on those he told, so he responded as if nothing was wrong.

"I'm about as good as a man can be, Joe," he said cheerily.

"Glad to hear it."

"Listen, Joe, you obviously haven't left yet to bring Mel home, so I thought I'd run over and pick her up and save you the trouble." There was a momentary silence on the phone.

"I'm a little confused, Danny. Melissa isn't here. In fact, Erin is supposed to be over at your place studying for some big test. I was just getting ready to call and tell her to come on home for dinner."

A deep feeling of dread came over Danny, and his hands began to shake. He was as terrified as he was the first night Cisco called claiming that DJ had been killed.

"Are you sure they aren't there, Joe?" he stammered. "Mel promised me she wasn't going anywhere but your house."

"They aren't here, Danny," Joe said, beginning to get concerned. "Donna said Erin's supposed to be at your place. They stopped here after school, and then they headed over to your house to study."

"How long ago was that, Joe?" asked Danny, the panic evident in his voice.

"Just a minute, Danny," his neighbor said. Danny heard Joe raise his voice to ask his wife what time the girls had left.

"Donna says it was a little before four. Danny, you sound upset. This can't be the first time one of your kids went somewhere without telling you." Joe tried to reassure him that everything was fine. "I'm sure they just decided to go to another friend's house to study. They'll turn up any minute now."

Danny figured there was no need to alarm Joe until he was sure they had reason to worry. "You're probably right," he said calmly. "Let me make a few phone calls, and I'll get back to you." He hung up and turned to find Sheila standing behind him.

"She's not at Erin's, is she, Danny?"

"No, honey, she's not. And what's worse, Erin told her folks they were coming here to study. No one has seen them since four o'clock this afternoon."

"Call her cell phone, Danny," Sheila said frantically.

"Good idea," he said. "I completely forgot we gave her one. I hope she has it turned on. What's the number?" Sheila went to the desk in the study and returned waving a piece of paper with the numbers for DJ and Melissa. Danny punched in the number and waited. After five rings, a connection was made, but no one spoke. "Melissa, honey, is that you? It's Daddy? Where are you, baby?"

Then he heard a low, gravelly voice. "Hey, Hero, is that you? You got a fine looking little *chica* here. We're having a little party, Hero. She can't talk now."

"If you touch her, I swear on everything I hold holy that I'll kill every one of you," Danny screamed.

"You have such a bad temper, Hero. Be calm, and maybe we'll send her back to you after the party. Or maybe we will keep her. Don't call back, Hero. We're kind of busy." The phone went dead in Danny's hand. He turned to Sheila, whose face was as white as a ghost. Tears were flowing down her cheeks.

"That horrible man has my baby, doesn't he?" she whispered.

Danny let out such an anguished scream that DJ came running down the stairs carrying an aluminum baseball bat. "Dad, what is it?" Sheila pulled him into her arms and sobbed.

"They have your sister," she said. Danny put his arms both of them. "We're not giving up yet," he said. "Mel is in God's hands, and we have to trust that He will bring her back to us." He dialed 911 and gave the operator all the information he had. Then called Don Livingston on the GBI agent's cell phone. Livingston had given Danny the number and instructed him to call anytime, day or night, and he would answer or get back to him as soon as possible. True to his word, he answered on the third ring. Danny gave him all the information he had as quickly as he could.

"You say you called her cell phone, and one of Cisco's people answered?" the agent asked.

"Yes, and for all I know, it was Cisco himself," replied Danny. "Their voices are starting to run together now."

"Well, since you called out instead of the call coming in, the recording device didn't start, so that's a dead end," said Livingston. "But we can try the cell phone locator. This is the moment we hoped would never come when you gave me permission for the subpoenas, Danny. I'll get right on this and get back to you as soon as I know anything." Livingston hung up.

Danny looked at Sheila and DJ ."The GBI is going to try to track Mel's cell phone. If we get lucky, they can pinpoint her location. Right now, all we can do is pray she's all right and that the phone is with her." Danny knelt on the floor, and his wife and son joined him. They held hands, and Danny began to pray for the safety of his child. While the Chambers family prayed, the GBI shifted into high gear. Agent Livingston already had the communications geeks on the case, and they were able to triangulate the signals from Melissa's cell phone within twenty minutes. Livingston was on the way to Danny's house when his cell rang.

"Livingston," he answered perfunctorily.

"Hey, Lieutenant, this is Agent Sellers in the Comm section. We have a location on that phone. It's in a Target Department store in Doraville. We've already dispatched the local police."

"Great work, Sellers. Give me the address." Livingston called Danny and told him they had located Melissa's phone.

"I'm on my way, Don," Danny said.

"Not a good idea, Danny," the agent said. "If she's there, we'll find her; if she isn't, Cisco or one of his goons may call you with some kind of information that could help us. So far they haven't spoken to your wife, so I think it's best that you be at home if they call. I'll call you as soon as we get on-site. I promise."

Danny reluctantly agreed. Ten gut-wrenching minutes passed before his phone rang again.

"Danny, I'm sorry, but Melissa's phone was in the middle of the parking lot in a trash can," Agent Livingston said. "We're canvassing the area for anyone who might have seen the girls or anything else suspicious. But so far, we have nothing."

"Don, can you help me with something I need to do right now?" Danny asked.

"If I can, Danny. What is it?'

"Can you go with me to the home of the other girl who was abducted and help me explain to her parents what's happening? If you're there with me telling them everything that's been done and is being done, I think they may feel a little better about the situation."

"So, you're telling me the other girl's parents don't know their daughter was abducted?" Livingston asked, sounding a bit incredulous.

"Well, *I* haven't told them," Danny said. "They know the girls aren't where they were supposed to be, but they weren't as concerned as I was because they had no idea what's been happening to my family for the last few weeks."

"How long ago did you speak to them?" asked Livingston.

"Less than an hour. In fact, I called you a few minutes after I hung up with Erin's father—right after I called 911."

"All right, Danny. I'll be at your place in about fifteen minutes, and we can ride over to their house together." Twenty-five minutes later, Danny and Lt. Livingston were knocking on the front door of the Nichols home. Joe opened the door and smiled broadly when he saw Danny. His smile turned to a look of puzzlement and then distress when he saw that not only was his daughter not with Danny, but his neighbor was accompanied by an official-looking man in a suit.

"Did you find the girls, Danny?" Joe asked with one eye on the lieutenant.

"No, we didn't, Joe," said Danny. "Can we come in? We need to talk."

"Oh my Lord." Danny heard Cheryl say from behind Joe. Danny and the detective told them the story of how and why Danny had been threatened by the Latino Death Lords and how this was connected to the abductions.

When they were finished, Joe looked at his neighbor. "Are you crazy, Danny? What the hell were you thinking when you let my daughter go wandering off with Melissa when you knew she was in danger?"

"Wait a minute, Joe," Danny said. He felt bad about what had happened, but he wanted to set the record straight. "Mel said that Erin invited her here to study and that Cheryl was going to be here making cookies for them and some other girls. She promised she wouldn't leave here and said you would bring her home. I'm sorry, Joe. I'm so sorry. I guess I'd feel the same way if I were in your shoes."

Livingston stepped in. "I'm afraid you *are* in his shoes, Danny. Both girls are gone, and it really doesn't make any difference who's to blame or if no one's to blame. We all need to keep our heads now. Mr. Nichols, we need a current photograph of Erin to put on the AMBER Alert that was already issued with her name and description."

CHAPTER FORTY FOUR
A M B E R A L E R T

ON A JANUARY day in 1996, a nine-year-old girl named Amber Hagerman was riding her bicycle in front of her home in Arlington, Texas, when a man in a pickup truck pulled over to the curb, jumped out, grabbed Amber, threw her in his truck, and drove away. A neighbor heard the girl scream and was able to report the type and color of the vehicle and provide a partial description of the driver, but little else. An immediate alert was put out for the girl and the truck. Four days later, little Amber was found dead in a drainage ditch with her throat cut. No one was ever arrested for the crime.

Later that year, someone suggested that local radio stations report the abduction of a child with repeated bulletins just as they did with severe weather alerts. In July of 1997, the Dallas Amber Plan went into effect. Amber's name was turned into an acronym for "America's Missing: Broadcast Emergency Response" system, which is now employed by law enforcement agencies in all fifty states, Canada, and a number of other countries. As soon as a child is reported to have been abducted or is suspected to have been abducted, the alert goes into effect. Notices are immediately issued on television and radio stations, electronic road signs, and the electronic advertising signs of certain businesses. In some states, the scroll boards of some lottery ticket machines are also used.

To avoid false alarms and hoaxes, strict criteria must be met before an AMBER Alert is issued. In most states, these criteria are derived from a guidance bulletin issued by the U.S. Department of Justice. This bulletin states that law enforcement must be able to confirm that an abduction has taken place, that the child is at risk of serious injury or death, and that there is sufficient descriptive information of the child, the captor and/or the vehicle. In addition, the child must be under the age of seventeen.

Less than ten minutes after Danny placed the 911 call, the AMBER Alerts for Melissa Anne Chambers and Erin Suzanne Nichols were issued to every law enforcement officer in North Georgia. Although there was no identification or description of the abductors or their vehicle, the alert was issued with only the descriptions of Melissa and Erin. Photos would follow as soon as they were made available.

Just as Danny and Lt. Livingston were leaving the Nichols home after promising to give them regular updates, Livingston's cell phone rang. He answered it quickly and listened without comment for what seemed an eternity to Danny. He could hear Livingston speaking into the phone but could not decipher the words. Two minutes later, Danny came close enough to hear him say, "Thank you, Officer." Livingston turned to face Danny. "We have both the girls," he said. "They're safe and don't appear to have been badly injured."

Danny dropped to his knees on the front lawn and bowed his head. Livingston headed back to the front door of the house to give the good news to Erin's parents. When he finished speaking with them, he came back to Danny, who was now back on his feet.

"Where is she?" Danny asked.

"They have her at Emory Hospital. Sheila has already been notified and will probably beat us there. Do you want to ride with me or follow me in your car?"

"If you use the siren to get me there faster, I'll ride with you," Danny said, smiling. "I'll worry about the car later."

"Then ride with me, and I'll tell you what I know as we go," Livingston said. Erin's parents joined Danny and the lieutenant. "Mr. and Mrs. Nichols, you can ride with me, or follow us." They opted to follow.

On the way to the hospital, the GBI agent told Danny that the girls had been seen and identified by a motorist who heard the AMBER Alert on his car radio. He saw two girls running down a side street and called 911. By the time the patrol car arrived, the girls had gone into a QuikTrip convenience store and told the manager they had been kidnapped and then released. The manager put them in his office and called 911. An EMS vehicle got there three minutes after the patrol car, and the officer directed the EMTs to take the girls straight to the hospital. The dispatcher had called the Chambers home and then, because he was lead officer on the case, Lt. Livingston.

"That's all I know right now," the GBI agent said dispassionately. Danny looked out the window and took a deep breath. He let the air out slowly and deliberately and lost himself in the wailing of the siren and the lights of the oncoming cars.

CHAPTER FORTY FIVE
BACK TO THE HOSPITAL

DR. ALVIN H. Trevor was standing at a nurses station, writing on a chart, when Danny came in. He looked up and gave his good friend an encouraging smile.

"Hey, Coach," he said. Both of the doctor's sons had played JV football for Danny at Lee.

"How's Melissa doing?" Danny asked breathlessly.

"Physically, she's going to be fine, Danny. Emotionally is another question, though. Come into my office, and I'll fill you in."

"Can I see her now?" Danny asked.

"Sheila is with her now and she is in good hands," the doctor replied, "so let's hold off on that until we talk." Danny followed Trevor down a short hall and into a small office.

"You want a coffee or something, Danny?"

"No, thanks. Just tell me how she is, Alvin."

The doctor poured himself a cup of cold coffee from the pot behind his desk, sat down, and ran his long fingers through his thick head of hair. He picked up the chart. "As I said, Danny, I can't find anything wrong with her physically other than a few bruises on her arms. Based on what she told me when I was examining her, I think that whoever did this just wanted to scare her—and they did a good job of it."

Tears were building in Danny's eyes, so he pulled a large white handkerchief from his back pocket, wiped his eyes, and blew his nose. He held the cloth tightly in his big hands and began to twist it.

"So she wasn't.....I mean. they didn't...," he stuttered, struggling to find the words. "You're sure she wasn't...?"

The doctor finished his thought. "No, Danny, it doesn't appear that she was sexually assaulted. She told Sheila she wasn't. A young girl may hide that kind of thing from most people, even her father or her doctor, but not from her mother. According to Sheila, Melissa said men didn't touch her below the waist or remove any of her clothing."

"Thank God," Danny said. He closed his eyes and relaxed his grip on the handkerchief.

"Do you have any idea who might have done this to her?" the doctor asked.

"Yeah, I know who did it," Danny said. Shifting from concern to anger, he continued, "I'm amazed, but very thankful that the girls weren't sexually assaulted, because I know the history of the vile man responsible. The police know about him, too, but so far they haven't been able to put him away. Do you think your lab guys will be able to come up with anything that might help the police identify the men who did this?"

"That will be a police issue Danny and I am sure they will try their best," Trevor replied, "but I wouldn't count on it."

"What about the stuff they're always finding on TV crime shows?" Danny asked. "There's bound to be *something*, isn't there, Alvin?"

"The police forensics people will go over her clothes Danny, and if she picked up any foreign matter, they'll find it," Trevor said. "But, unless they can find the people or the vehicle to match with whatever they might find, it won't do much good. Melissa said she fought with the men when they were dragging her into the van, but apparently she bites her fingernails down to the nub, so there weren't any nails to find anything under. She also said the men were wearing gloves. As far as foreign hair goes, I'm afraid she was contaminated as far as any evidence goes by EMTs, ER staff, and God knows who else."

Danny stood up and turned to the window that looked out on the hospital parking lot. The deputy's patrol car was still sitting there, and he could see the officer inside it talking on his radio. He turned back to the desk, picked up the telephone, and called his mother. The phone rang twice before she answered.

"Mom, something has happened to Melissa," he said. His mother immediately panicked. "No, I think she's all right. Sheila's with her now, and I'll give you the details later. I need you to get over to our house right now and pick up DJ and take him to your house. Keep the doors locked, and do not under any circumstances mention this to Dad. Just make up some story about DJ needing a quiet place to study or something. We can fill Dad in when we can actually see Melissa and know for sure that she's okay. We don't want him having another heart attack."

His mother started to ask a question, but Danny curtly cut her off. "Mom, I said she'll be fine. I can't talk now. Please, just do what I asked. I love you, bye." He gently put the phone back in its cradle and sat down.

"I'll take that coffee now, Alvin."

The doctor poured another cup and handed it to Danny, who took a big mouthful and swallowed hard. He sat very still and stared at the assorted diplomas, licenses, and certifications hanging on the office walls. He took a smaller swallow of coffee, put the cup down, and looked back at Trevor.

"So she's going to be all right, huh, Doc?" It was a hope-filled statement more than a question.

This time, the doctor hesitated. He took a sip of his coffee and grimaced. "Danny, you have to listen to me. Like I said earlier, the issue is going to be her psyche. For any woman, especially a girl as young as Melissa, to be abducted like this—frightened this badly—there's always a danger of emotional trauma. The fact that she wasn't sexually assaulted is a big plus, but who knows what they said to her or threatened her with before they dumped her out of the van?"

Danny nodded his head. Alvin Trevor and Danny Chambers had been friends for more than ten years and had watched each other's children grow up, so this conversation was hurting the doctor almost as much as it was hurting Danny, who began to pace the floor. After a moment he stopped, his face contorted in anger at Cisco Ram for doing this terrible thing and at himself for letting it happen, and asked, "What *did* they do to her, Alvin? What did they say to her?"

"I don't really know, Danny. When the EMS squad called in to alert us they were bringing in two young girls who had possibly been the victims of an assault, I didn't even know one of them was Melissa until they got here. One of the nurses spoke to her first while I was examining the Nichols girl. Melissa told the nurse that the men said nasty things to her and touched her breasts and that she never saw their faces. By the time I got to her, Sheila was here, and I left it to her to ask the non-medical questions while I watched Melissa's face to try to determine if she might be trying to block out something. I'm sorry, Danny, but that really is all I know." The doctor stood up and opened the door.

"Can I see her now, Doc?" Danny asked.

"Sure. I gave her a mild sedative, though. She'll be awake but probably not very talkative."

"Can we take her home tonight?"

"You could, but I'd really like to keep her here overnight for observation."

"Let me talk to Sheila. If I know my wife and my daughter, they're both going to want her home tonight. Where are they now, Doc?"

"In the ER in one of the curtained-off side rooms. Come on and I'll show you the way."

When Danny got down to the ER, one of the nurses directed him to the examination room where his family was. He pulled aside the curtains and found Sheila, sitting in a chair, pulled up close to the head of her daughter's bed. The bed had been elevated slightly and when Melissa, who was propped up on two pillows, saw her father, she began to cry.

"Oh, Daddy, I'm so sorry," she said. "I didn't mean to get in trouble."

Danny knelt beside her on the bed, wrapped his arms around her, and pulled her close. "It's okay, baby," Danny whispered. "You don't have to be sorry about anything and you're not in trouble. You didn't do anything wrong. What happened isn't your fault, angel."

"Yes, it is, Daddy. Yes, it is. If I hadn't lied to you and mommy about going to Erin's after school, this wouldn't have happened."

"Don't worry about that now, baby. All that matters to Mommy and me is that you're safe now and that you're not hurt. You *are* alright, aren't you, Mel?"

"I think so, Daddy. They didn't hurt me, but I was really, really scared."

"I'm sure you were, angel," Danny said. "Anyone would have been scared in your place. Did the men let you go, or did you and Erin escape?" Before Melissa could answer, Sheila stepped in, motioning to Danny with her eyes.

"I think I have the answers to your questions, Danny. Maybe we should just let her rest now." Danny looked at his daughter to see if she agreed.

"No, that's all right, Mommy," she said. "I don't mind telling Daddy."

Sheila would have preferred to let her daughter rest, but she acquiesced. "Okay, hon, go ahead."

"They let us go, Daddy. They told us to go home and for me to tell you that they could have done anything they wanted to me and you couldn't stop them. Then the man said that hurting me wouldn't mean anything to his boss if you weren't there to see it. What did he mean, Daddy? They said to tell you that this was just a taste and that next time, it would be much, much worse." She began to cry again. "Is that true, Daddy? Will they come and get me again?"

The lump in Danny's throat felt as big as a baseball and tears were starting to well up in his eyes again, tears he didn't want his daughter to see. He wiped his eyes with the sleeve of his shirt and said, "No, it's not true, honey. Those men will never, ever hurt you again. You trust your Daddy, don't you, baby?"

"Yes, Daddy. You never tell lies. I know that, and Mommy always says you're the most honest person she knows."

Danny smiled and raised an eyebrow. "Oh, she does, does she? Well, your mommy is right about one thing: I don't lie, especially to my baby girl. Your daddy promises you that they'll never hurt you again. Does that make you feel better?"

"Lots, Daddy. Lots. Can we go home now?"

Danny looked at Sheila, who nodded. "Yes, angel," he said, "we can go home now."

꩜

After they collected DJ from Danny's parents' home and put Melissa to bed, Danny and Sheila sat down at the kitchen table.

"What did they do to her, honey?" asked Danny, taking a sip of his decaffeinated coffee.

"She said someone touched her breasts through her blouse and whispered really disgusting things in her ear. She said they talked about having some fun with the girls or maybe killing them." Sheila's hand was shaking as she reached for her coffee cup. "She was scared out of her wits when I got to the hospital, Danny."

"I don't know what to do, Sheila. I'm sorry to say it, but I hate these men so much that I can't think straight," Danny said with rage in his eyes and frustration in his voice. "All my life I've been hearing pastors talk about loving our enemies and turning the other cheek, but now that it's *my* family, *my* daughter being brutalized, the last thing on my mind is love and forgiveness. The truth is, if I could find those guys right now, I'd kill every single one of them."

"Danny, you promised your daughter that these people would never touch her again," Sheila said. "How do you expect to keep that promise?"

"I'm going to kill them all," Danny said quietly. "I don't know how I'm going to do it yet, but I'll keep my family safe. I may lose my soul, but I'll keep that promise."

"Danny, my love," said Sheila, reaching across the table to touch her husband's face, "I've never known a man who had a stronger Christian faith than you do. I hear what you're saying, and I know you think you mean it. But do you really think you can kill even one person, much less a whole gang?"

Danny stared at her for a moment, shook his head, and shrugged. Then he got up from the table and walked away. That night, in bed, he tossed and turned for more than two hours before he at last fell into a fitful sleep.

He dreamed he was at the zoo with Sheila and the kids. DJ and Melissa were younger in the dream. It appeared that DJ was six or seven and Mel three or four. The family was standing in front of the three-foot fence that surrounded the South American Crocodiles pond. Danny picked up Melissa and lifted her over the fence and put her down on the other side. Then he did the same with DJ, placing him right next to his sister. Sheila was screaming at Danny, but he couldn't understand what she was saying. Suddenly, he saw a group of large, hungry-looking crocs moving toward his children. He tried to reach over the fence, but it was now twenty feet tall. He ran up and down the fence looking for a gate, but there was none. He screamed for help as he watched the crocs move closer and closer to his children, who were huddled against the fence, but the bars were too narrow for Danny to pull them through. The largest of the reptiles was now only a few feet from Melissa, its yellow eyes staring straight at Danny. The gigantic croc moved closer and opened its mouth wide. Danny screamed again and again until he was aware of Sheila shaking him and calling out to him. "Danny! Danny! It's all right, honey. You just had a nightmare."

Danny sat up in bed, gasping, his body clammy from the sweat brought on by fear. He didn't always know how to interpret his dreams, but he knew what this one meant: His children were in grave danger; and he had put them there. Now, he felt powerless to save them. He looked at the clock on the night table. It was four thirty five. He got up, went into the bathroom, and turned on the shower.

☙

CHAPTER FORTY SIX
TIME FOR PEOPLE TO DIE

SIX HOURS AFTER Danny awoke from his nightmare, Cisco called his sharks together at the clubhouse. He sat at the desk in his private office, with his three lieutenants across from him. They were all drinking strong black Cuban coffee. Cisco was smoking a cigarette, and *Cuchillo*, a small cigar.

"So, what's next for the hero, *Jefe?*" *Cuchillo* asked.

"It's time to bring this thing with my son's murderer to an end," Cisco replied. "Not too quickly, though. We've threatened him and harassed him. And we're getting to people who are close to him. But now it's time to kill people. What do you think, amigos?"

"*Jefe*, we already killed his dog and scared the hell out of his *hija*," said *Carnicero*.

Cisco gave him a withering look. "Shut up, Carni. No one cares about a stupid dog, and you didn't hardly hurt the little *chica*. I just wanted him to know we could get to her any time we wanted. Now I want people to die!" He slammed him fist on the desk. "I want people to die all around the hero. Slowly and painfully they will die. First his family, then the hero." The three men just looked at him and kept their mouths closed. *Cuchillo* blew a smoke ring and settled deeper into his chair.

"I have not told you that the other night this hero of the people did something crazier than you can imagine," Cisco continued. "Do you know what he did, amigos?" He did not expect them to know, so he answered the question for them. "He said he was going to kill my mother if I didn't leave him and his family alone. Can you believe that? This son of a whore was crazy enough to threaten Cisco. And when someone threatens me, he threatens the whole LDL and each one of you, too."

"So we kill the boy today?" asked *Cuchillo*.

"Not just yet," said Cisco. "Today, we kill the wife and grab the boy. Then he knows he can't threaten us and he can't win. When we kill her and take the boy, we show the hero that he can't protect his family. We show the hero that the police can't protect his family. Then he'll know that no one can save them from the Latino Death Lords." Because Cisco had killed his own wife but had worshiped the ground his son walked on, he believed that Danny would be hurt more by watching his children die than by seeing his wife die.

"Boss, what about your mother?" asked *El Carnicero*. "Does he know where she lives?"

"Forget about my mother!" Cisco shouted. He pulled the trash can from under his desk, leaned over, and spat loudly into it. "That's what I think of that old woman. I hate her, and she hates me. I don't care what he does to her. But the hero didn't know I hated her when he threatened me, so his insult was just as bad as if I cared about her."

"I don't know, man," *El Carnicero* said guardedly. "I mean, it's your *madre*, man. Your *madre*. How can you not care if he kills her?"

"Because she betrayed me," Cisco shot back. "No one betrays Cisco! You should never forget that, amigos."

Because Cisco was the only person in the LDL who knew the details of *Cuchillo's* hasty departure from Veracruz, he turned to him. "What about you, Cuch? Do you think I should protect my mother after she betrayed me?"

Cuchillo took another drag on his cigar, held it in for second, and blew another perfect smoke ring. "Hell no! I killed my mother with my father's own knife for betraying me," he responded.

The other two men stared at him in shock and amazement.

"You killed your mother?" *Carnicero* asked. "You're not kidding?"

"Hell no, I'm not kidding. I slit the her throat and left her to die in her bed. It was what she deserved."

No one said anything for a few moments. Finally, Cisco spoke. "Cuch, you take *Borracho* and do this thing today. Do it in the hero's house if you can, so they know they're not safe anywhere."

The three sharks looked at each other, got up, and started to leave. When *Cuchillo* opened the door, Cisco added, "Cuch, before you kill her, have a little fun with her if you want. I hear she's a good-looking woman." Then he began to laugh.

Borracho smiled and joined in his boss' laughter. *Cuchillo* did not smile or laugh, or even indicate he had heard.

ॐ

CHAPTER FORTY SEVEN
THE FIRST TO DIE

THE MORNING OF the third day since they had brought Melissa home from the hospital, Sheila was the first one out of bed. She was preparing school lunches while Danny rousted DJ, then went to Melissa's room. He knocked softly at the door and pushed it open a crack to see his daughter's small form still snuggled under the comforter. He went in and sat down gently beside her.

"Good morning, sunshine," he whispered. The girl opened her eyes halfway, then shut them again.

"Good morning, Daddy," she said sleepily.

"How are you, baby? Do you want to go back to school today?" She opened her eyes wide and sat up. She leaned over and gave him a big hug.

"Yes, Daddy. I miss my friends, and I know I'm getting so far behind on my lessons. Besides, I talked to Erin last night, and she's going back today. So, I want to go back, too."

"Are you sure you're ready, baby?"

"Yes, sir," she said eagerly. "I'm not afraid anymore. You said you wouldn't let them hurt me again, so I'm fine now." Danny fought back a tear and felt a small lump in his throat. The events of the past month had worn his emotions down to a raw edge.

"That's daddy's good girl," he said. "Okay, baby, then it's time to get up, get your shower, and have some breakfast. I'll take you and DJ to school today because Mommy needs her car for grocery shopping."

Melissa kicked her covers off, yawned while she stretched luxuriantly, and rolled out of bed. Danny closed her door behind him as he left. When he got downstairs, he told Sheila that their baby girl seemed fine. They hugged each other, then Sheila poured their morning coffee, and the two of them sat down at the kitchen table. Danny reached across and took his wife's hand, which, along with the hug and a cup of coffee, was part of a morning ritual that ended with them praying together. Danny and Sheila took turns leading the prayer, just as the family did before meals.

"Is it your turn or mine?" Sheila asked,

"I think it's you, angel," Danny answered. He held her hands in his, and Sheila began to pray. When she finished, she started to make breakfast. DJ burst in and was disappointed to learn he wasn't driving his mother's car to school that day. But, as usual, he was understanding that his mother needed her car.

After Danny left to take the kids to school, Sheila cleared away the breakfast dishes and took a shower. When she was ready to leave the house, she inspected the new keypad that was mounted on the wall next to the back door. Their home alarm system had been installed a few days before, and the red light, that signaled that the alarm was on and active, was blinking. Danny had reset it after he left. Sheila planned to do the same, but she was in a hurry to leave and couldn't remember the sequence of numbers to punch in. She scurried about looking for the instruction manual, then decided it wasn't a big deal if the alarm wasn't activated while the house was empty, as long as she remembered to reset it when she came back later. She picked up her car keys and purse, punched the "Clear" button on the keypad, and went out the door.

Fifteen minutes after she left, *Cuchillo* called the Chambers home from a public phone a mile from the house. The phone rang seven times before an answering machine picked up. *Cuchillo* hung up and got in the van where *Borracho* was waiting.

"No one answering the phone don't mean she ain't home," *Cuchillo* said. "We need to go take a look." They drove to Danny's street and parked two houses down on the opposite side of the street from Danny's house. For a while, they sat in the van smoking cigarettes and drinking soft drinks. After forty-five minutes, they decided to get out of the van, pop the hood, and pretend to be working on the engine to look less suspicious.

Out of boredom, *Borracho* opened the passenger door and reached under the seat to find a half-empty bottle of cheap bourbon. When he started to unscrew the cap, *Cuchillo* became visibly angry.

"Put that stuff away, amigo!" *Cuchillo* hissed. "Are you crazy?" Even though *Borracho* was several years older and had been with Cisco and the Latino Death Lords much longer, *Cuchillo* had asserted his personality and established his ruthlessness to the point where *Borracho* and *Carnicero* deferred to him as de facto leader of the gang in Cisco's absence. It made no difference that *Borracho* had been the one who recruited *Cuchillo*. The other sharks had watched him grow quickly and knew which of the *Tres Tiburones* was the deadliest.

"Come on, Cuch?" Borracho whined. "What's the harm in a little taste before the fun begins, huh? A little drink before we do this job?"

"So what happens if for some reason you have to drive, man?" *Cuchillo* responded angrily. "What if you have to drive, and you're all screwed up on your rotgut liquor, and we get stopped because you drifted out of your lane or some stupid thing like that? Hell no, you ain't drinking no alcohol. You drink a Coke or some water, but don't put any whiskey in it." *Borracho* began to protest again, but *Cuchillo* silenced him with a wave of his hand. "Besides, we need to get out and get ready to do it. We've been sitting here long enough, and I have a plan."

They got out of the van and opened the rear doors to expose a lawn mower and various other landscaping tools. The van was the same black cargo model they used when they kidnapped Melissa Chambers, except that both side panels and the back window were decorated with four-by-six-foot vinyl signs that read: *Vista Verde Lawn and Landscaping*, with a bogus Web address and phone number listed under the name. The van's tag had been stolen from a car in another neighborhood three hours earlier. There was no way anyone could trace this vehicle back to Cisco Ramos or the Latino Death Lords.

Cuchillo set the lawn mower down onto the street. Both men were wearing dirty baseball caps and sunglasses, overalls, and bandanas around their necks. They looked exactly like ten thousand other Latino laborers working on building sites and in yards all over Atlanta.

"Okay, I'm ready," said *Cuchillo*. "Let's go." With *Cuchillo* pushing the mower and *Borracho* following behind with a gasoline-powered edger slung over his shoulder, they walked up to the house next to Danny's, and *Cuchillo* knocked on the door. He chose this house because during their two-hour vigil, he had seen, in succession, two children come out and get on a school bus, a man open the garage and leave in a new Honda Accord, and, finally, a woman in tennis attire walk out to the street and put a letter in the mailbox, then go into the garage and drive away in her minivan. He was satisfied that no one was home, but he knocked on the door, just in case. If someone were to answer, he would ask if this was the home of Senor Oliver or some other made-up name. He would then apologize and say he must have gotten the wrong address. He knocked twice, but there was no answer.

"Okay," he said to *Borracho*, "crank up the edger and look like you're working. I think we can stay here for maybe an hour. If she don't come back by then, we'll have to split and try again tomorrow." *Borracho* complained about having to do actual yard work, but *Cuchillo* ignored him and began to slowly mow the front lawn.

Twenty minutes later, an SUV pulled into the Chambers driveway, and a woman got out. She opened the tailgate, removed two bags of groceries, and walked toward the side door near the garage.

Cuchillo motioned to his friend to follow him, and they started toward Danny's home. The woman set down one of the bags and unlocked the door. She picked up the grocery bag, pushed the door open, and went inside without closing it behind her.

Moving quickly and quietly on the rubber soles of their running shoes, the two men followed her in. After she put the grocery bags on the kitchen counter, she turned to close the door. *Borracho* hit her in the mouth with his fist, and she went down hard, barely able to utter a small sound of surprise before the blow landed. Before she could recover, *Borracho* put a large piece of duct tape over her mouth and flipped her over onto her stomach. He pulled her hands together behind her and taped them as well. During the scuffle, her skirt had ridden up slightly, exposing her upper thighs and the bottom of her panties.

"Hey, Cuch, this is going to be good, huh, amigo? She's fine." Borracho said as he began to tear at the back of the woman's skirt.

"That ain't my thing, but I'll watch the door. Make it quick so we can get the hell out of here." He stepped outside.

Borracho shrugged and knelt beside his fallen victim. She moaned and tried to turn over to face her attacker, but he drove his fist into the back of her head and shoved her to the floor again. He pulled the now ripped skirt down off her body and reached for the waist band of her panties.

CHAPTER FORTY EIGHT
A TRANSFER OF DEBT

CISCO RAM HAD managed to stay out of jail, all these years since his last arrest, by being informed. He knew that knowledge was power. He also knew that a lot of people who had very good jobs, even in the government, had problems with drugs, women, or gambling. As a result, his sharks were always on the lookout for someone to add to their contact list, someone who owed them money or a favor. Their contacts in the criminal subculture of Atlanta were legion, so it didn't take long for word to reach them that a gambler who owed Big Jack Niehaus eleven large, worked for the GBI.

Borracho had paid Jack a visit recently and negotiated a transfer of Bobby Pendleton's eleven-thousand-dollar debt from Big Jack to Cisco. Big Jack got his money, plus a tidy five percent transfer fee, and the Latino Death Lords now had a GBI employee on the hook for a great deal of money.

Bobby's week of grace from Big Jack ended one day after Big Jack sold the debt to Cisco, but Bobby had no way of knowing it. He dreaded making the call to Niehaus, but he also knew it would only be worse if Jack had to come looking for him. He was going to tell Big Jack that he was having a problem with the IRS refund, even though he knew it was a lame story that Jack would know was a line of bull. But he really had no choice other than to plead for more time.

A week without gambling was like a week without sunshine for Bobby, who was dying to make a bet. UCLA looked to be a lock giving four points at Stanford that night, but Bobby knew there was no way Big Jack was going to let him play until he had settled his debt. He lit a cigarette and dialed Jack's number. The caller ID on Jack's phone alerted him that it was Bobby.

"How you doing, high roller?" he asked jovially.

"Pretty good, Jack. How about yourself?" Bobby responded, surprised at Big Jack's cheery disposition.

"I'm great, kid, just great. In fact, if I was any better, I'd have to hire someone to help me enjoy being myself."

"Big Jack, I know I owe you a ton, but I need a little more time."

The bookie interrupted him, "You don't owe me a damn thing, Bobby. Not a dime." Bobby was too stunned to reply. Jack continued, "I sold your debt to another group, kid. I got my money, and now you owe them."

"You sold my debt? What the hell are you talking about, Jack? Who did you sell it to?"

"Don't worry about it, kid. I'm sure they'll be in touch when they want their money. If I was you, I wouldn't worry about it until I heard from them."

Bobby drew on his cigarette and asked, "So what does this mean? Am I supposed to call them when I want to make a play now?"

"Hell no, kid," said Big Jack. "Me and you are still in business together. This was a one-time-only deal. In fact, since your book is clear, you can make a bet right now, if you want."

Bobby took a moment to let this sink in. When it finally did, he almost leaped out of his chair with joy. "Okay, if it's good with you, then what do I care who I owe? What do you have on UCLA and Stanford tonight?"

"That's my boy," Niehaus said, checking his odds sheet.

♾

CHAPTER FORTY NINE
DANNY IDENTIFIES THE BODY

DANNY WAS SITTING at his desk when the student assistant stuck her head in the door. "Mr. Chambers," she said, "there are two policemen here to see you."

Danny said, "Send them back, Marcy."

Danny hoped it was just Lt. Livingston or someone else from the GBI, and not someone there to tell him that one of his family had been hurt. When the two uniformed Gwinnett County Sheriff's deputies came through the door, his alarm bells immediately went off, and he jumped to his feet.

"What's going on?" he asked anxiously. "Is my family all right?"

"Mr. Chambers, my name is Mike Roberson, and this is officer Dan Brawley."

"Is my family all right?" Danny persisted.

"Mr. Chambers, there's been an incident at your residence. We need you to come to your home with us right now."

"An incident? What the heck does that mean? All I want to know is if my family's all right."

"Sir, a woman was found dead in your home about thirty minutes ago." Danny turned pale. "It took us this long to identify whose residence it was, track you down, and get here. It's not the kind of news we deliver on the phone."

Remembering the first phone call he received from Cisco, Danny wanted to be sure this was legitimate. "May I see some identification?" he asked the officers. The policemen produced their badges and photo IDs. Danny could see that this was all too real.

"Oh my God!" he shouted. "Sheila!"

"Just a minute, sir," one of the officers said. "Our sergeant looked at some family photos in your living room and said the dead woman looks something like the woman in the pictures, but her face was ...well, her face was...." He couldn't finish the sentence.

Danny grabbed his phone. "I'm calling my wife's cell right now." He held the receiver to his ear and waited as the phone rang once, twice, three times, then after the fourth ring, it bounced over to voice-mail.

"Hi, this is Sheila Chambers, I'm sorry I missed you, but if you leave your name and number, I'll call you back as soon as I can. God Bless, and have a great day." With a sinking heart, he left a message.

"Honey, it's me," he said. "Call my cell as soon as you get this message." Then he hung up and faced the two officers. "Okay, let's go."

As they sped towards Danny's home, one of the officers explained that a neighbor had noticed the side door of Danny's home had been open for several hours, and that no one was answering his phone. Recalling that she had also seen some men cutting Danny's neighbor's grass earlier that morning and thought it strange since it was the dead of winter and no grass was growing, she had decided to call the police. The Patrolmen dispatched to check it out had found the body in the kitchen.

When they arrived at Danny's home, there were five other police cars from both the Gwinnett County and Norcross police departments, as well as two EMS ambulances. Officer Brawley led Danny through the police cordon and into the house.

"In the kitchen, sir," said one of the policeman. When Danny entered, the first thing he saw was a lifeless shape on the floor covered by a blue EMS blanket.

"Oh, Jesus, no," he moaned. "Jesus, no. Not my angel." He began to cry.

One of the policemen in the room stepped forward and said, "Mr. Chambers, I'm Sergeant Tom Stembridge. I know this is very hard, but we need you to look at this woman and tell us if it's your wife."

Danny wiped his face with the sleeve of his suit coat and took a deep breath. "All right," he said haltingly. The officer took hold of the top of the blanket and started to remove it but stopped before he exposed any of the woman's features.

"I should warn you, sir," he said. "It's pretty bad. This woman was savagely beaten before she died." Danny closed his eyes and bowed his head for a moment, silently asking God to give him the strength to face this.

"Go ahead," Danny said finally.

The policeman exposed the victim's face, which was covered with blood and swollen in several places. Her hair was matted with blood. Danny cocked his head to one side to get a better view. He had been holding his breath, but it suddenly burst forth from his lungs in a single word.

"No," he gasped.

"No what?" the sergeant asked.

"No, it's not my wife. It's her friend, Laura Henderson, who lives on the next street. They do a lot of things together and look enough alike that people often mistake them for sisters."

"Mr. Chambers, do you have any idea what Ms. Henderson would be doing in your home unless your wife was here with her?"

"I have no earthly idea," Danny answered.

"Sir, we need a good description and a current picture of your wife, as well as a description of her vehicle and its plate number." Danny was still in a mild state of shock and did not immediately comprehend what the policeman was saying.

"What...?" he said absently.

"Mr. Chambers, until we hear from your wife or verify her whereabouts, we have to assume she was here when her friend was murdered and was then abducted by the killers."

"You better have someone contact Lt. Don Livingston of the GBI," Danny said, regaining his composure. "He can give you some background on this." The sergeant nodded and spoke quietly to one of the other policemen. He turned back to Danny and started to speak but was interrupted by the ringing of Danny's cell phone. Danny fumbled for it in his coat pocket, flipped it open, and held it to his ear.

"Danny, what's wrong?" came Sheila's welcome voice. "Are the kids all right?" His sense of relief was so great that Danny couldn't speak for several seconds. When he finally did, he could barely keep his voice from cracking.

"Yeah, they're fine, honey," he said. "Where are you?"

"I'm just leaving the parking lot at WalMart. Why?"

"Don't leave the store, honey. Pull your car up to the front door and go back inside. Tell the store manager you're being stalked. Tell him to call security. Stay right there, and we'll be there in less than ten minutes. Don't hang up. I'm going to keep you on the line until we get there."

"What's going on? Who's we? Are the kids with you?"

"Just do what I said, angel. Please, just do it now. I love you, and I'll explain everything. And don't hang up."

While Danny rode with one of the detectives to the department store, he told his wife what had happened at their home. He asked her if she knew why Laura Henderson would have been there alone. In shock over the death of her friend, Sheila did not answer his question.

"It's all my fault. It's all my fault," she kept repeating. "If it wasn't for me, Laura would still be alive."

"How is it your fault?" Danny asked.

"I ran into Laura at Kroger, and we finished our grocery shopping together. She told me that Kohl's was having a wonderful sale today. There was a dress I've been wanting, and Laura said I could get it for fifty percent off. She offered to bring my perishables home and put them in the refrigerator and freezer so I could go straight to Kohl's and buy the dress. I never should have let her do it, but I was afraid the dress would be gone before I got there. Oh, Danny, if it hadn't gone after a dress that I don't even need, Laura would still be alive!" Sheila started to sob.

If you had gone home with the groceries, it would be you lying dead on our kitchen floor instead of Laura. It was a selfish thought, but somehow he couldn't feel any guilt in thinking it. But he knew that to say what he was thinking would only make his wife feel worse. He also knew she would come to the same realization herself soon enough.

As soon as they arrived at the department store, Danny jumped out of the police car and ran inside. He asked a clerk for the manager's office was and quickly found it. Sheila was sitting inside the office with a store security officer. She stood up when she saw Danny, and they hugged each other tightly.

"Sweetheart," Danny said, "I thought I lost you."

"Oh, Danny, this nightmare keeps getting worse." She hugged him tighter. "Now sweet Laura is dead, and her precious children have no mother, and…."

"I know, hon. I know. But right now, we need to get you out of here, collect the kids, and figure out the safest place for all of you until this is over."

"Does Laura's family know?" Sheila asked.

"Yes, Ma'am," one of the officers responded. "Uniformed officers went to the Henderson home and to Mr. Henderson's place of work as soon as your husband identified the body."

"Danny, we can't go anywhere until we see Stan," Sheila said emphatically. "He's our friend. We can't just run away and hide while he wonders why his wife was murdered in our kitchen."

"You're right, hon. You're absolutely right," Danny said. "But we need to go now." They started walking toward the exit.

"Danny, you said we needed to find a safe place to stay until this was all over," Sheila said.

"I did, and we do," Danny said.

"But it's never going to be over, Danny," Sheila said somberly. "Not until we're all dead."

CHAPTER FIFTY
TAKEN

DANNY AND SHEILA spent almost an hour with Stan Henderson and his children. When she felt there was no more they could do, Sheila told him they would be in touch as soon as they knew anything else. When they got back home, Lt. Livingston was waiting to escort them through the multitude of police and emergency vehicles that were still on the scene.

Before they could enter the house, Livingston was stopped by a uniformed officer who pulled him aside, out of earshot. The lieutenant returned a minute later.

"I'm very sorry," he said, "but they're just now removing the body from the kitchen, Mrs. Chambers. You'll need to stay away from that part of the house until the area has been thoroughly examined by the forensics team." Sheila started crying again as they went inside.

"We need to get your family out of here as soon as possible. It's obvious that Cisco Ram has escalated his terror campaign and is now going to make good on his threats. Whoever killed Mrs. Henderson thought she was you, Mrs. Chambers. As soon as they realize their mistake, they'll try again. They could just as easily target your children next before they make another attempt on your life."

"Oh, my God," Sheila gasped. "Where are the children now?"

"I sent agents to both of their schools with instructions to bring them home," replied Livingston coolly.

"Thank God for that," Danny said.

"Mrs. Chambers," said the lieutenant, "I suggest you start packing clothes for all of you while I get someone working on finding a safe house for you."

"How much should I pack? I mean, how long do you think we'll be gone?"

"I think a week is a good starting point, ma'am. I hope it won't be longer than that, but I can't promise you anything."

"What's going to happen in a week?" Sheila asked sarcastically. "Are the people who killed my friend going to be in jail? Are they going to stay there any longer than the man who attacked my father-in-law?" Danny could tell that his wife was starting to tip over the edge toward hysteria.

"Angel, the lieutenant didn't cause all this, I did," he said. "Let's just start packing and put this situation in the Lord's hands where it belongs." He led her toward their bedroom and returned a few moments later. "I'm sorry, Don. She's not usually like this. She's just distraught over her friend's death."

"No apology necessary, Danny. I think she's held up remarkably well under the circumstances." The front door opened, and Melissa came in followed by two GBI gents in business suits. She ran to her father and wrapped her arms around his waist.

"Where's the boy?" Livingston asked the agents with Melissa.

"The school said he left earlier today," one of them answered. "Something about getting an emergency call at the office about his mother. He signed himself out and left. No one has seen him since."

Danny groaned. He dialed DJ's cell number but got no answer.

"Cisco must have him, Don. He'd answer the phone if he could, and he knows better than to disappear like this. Maybe we can track the phone the way we did Melissa's."

"We can try, Danny," Livingston said, "but these guys are pretty crafty. They threw your daughter's phone away, and I suspect they'll do the same with your son's."

He turned to the other agents to give them instructions. "All right guys, you know the drill. Let's initiate an AMBER Alert on the boy and get some agents to Cisco's home and the gang's playhouse."

"I better go tell Sheila what's happening," Danny said.

"Danny, don't give up hope. He let your daughter go, and he may do the same with DJ. One way or the other, I think you'll hear from him soon. In the meantime, we need to get your wife and daughter out of here and to somewhere safe as quickly as possible." Danny left the room, and Livingston got on his cell phone. When Danny returned five minutes later, Livingston had already formulated a plan. "We'll be moving your family into a room at the Holiday Inn at Six Flags, Danny. Their room will be connecting with another room where two officers will be at all times. Unfortunately, this is an expensive operation, so I can't keep you there for more than a week. After that, we'll figure something out."

There was concern on Danny's face, but he just nodded.

"That's fine, Don, as long as they're safe while we look for DJ."

"They'll be safe, Danny. We've never lost a witness or anyone else in protective custody. Trust me, no one will be able to find your family."

"Thanks, Don." Danny couldn't help thinking that if Melissa and Sheila still needed protection a week from now, he and DJ would already be dead.

࿇

CHAPTER FIFTY ONE
A PROMISE OF DEATH

THE NEXT MORNING, Danny called the school and brought Jonathan Evans up to date. Evans advised him to stay home until the matter was settled and said he would be officially listed as out sick. At ten o'clock that morning, the phone rang. Danny checked the light on the recorder before answering.

"Hello," he said resignedly.

"Is this Mr. Daniel Chambers?" asked a woman with a very proper speaking voice.

"Yes, it is."

"The gentleman you have been having a disagreement with wants to meet you this afternoon at a time and place to be given to you later. He says to get in your car and and at one o'clock in the afternoon, begin driving north on I-85 from the Pleasant Hill Road entrance ramp. Have your cell phone turned on. Someone will call you and give you further instructions. He says that you are to come alone and that you can imagine the consequences if you do not follow these instructions, especially the part about coming alone. Do you understand everything I have said?"

"Yes," Danny said unenthusiastically. "I am to leave at one today from Pleasant Hill Road and drive north on I-85 with my phone on. I will receive further instructions, and I must come alone."

"Exactly," said the woman, who then abruptly hung up.

Danny briefly thought about calling Livingston, but knew the police wouldn't let him go alone. However, it wasn't their son's life that was at stake, so he decided to keep this call to himself and follow the instructions exactly.

At five minutes after one, Danny was on I-85 heading north at seventy miles an hour. His cell phone rang, and he answered it immediately.

"Danny Chambers," he said. This time it was a male speaking very proper English.

"Pull into the rest area at mile marker 141. Park in the back corner of the truck lot in the rear. Park with your car facing the woods behind the rest area. Unlock the doors of your car, and do not under any circumstances look behind you. Aim your rear view mirror and the side mirrors at the ground. You will be joined in your car by someone who wishes to speak to you. If you make any attempt to turn or to see the identity of the person who joins you, they will leave immediately and your son will pay the price for your disobedience. Do you understand everything I have said?"

Danny repeated the instructions, and the caller hung up. Twenty-five minutes later, he pulled into the rest area and drove to the place the caller had directed. He parked facing the woods and pointed all of his mirrors to the ground. He turned off the ignition, lowered his window, and waited. Ten minutes passed before he heard the left rear door open and felt someone get in. *This is the moment of truth,* he thought. *Either I'm going to get a bullet in the back of the head, or we're going to talk about getting my son back.* He didn't think Cisco would take him out this way. He had told Danny that he wanted him to suffer as he had suffered losing a son.

"You know something, Hero?" the voice behind him asked. "Even when the police came to my door and told me my son was dead, I didn't totally believe them." This was the voice of the man at Diamond Girls, the voice of Cisco Ram himself.

"Even though they said the boy who was dead was driving my son's car and carrying my son's driver's license, part of my brain still said it was a lie, still hoped it was a mistake. All the way up to the time I went down into that cold room with its dead green walls and death smells, and they pull my boy's body out of the refrigerator, I was praying it was a mistake. But, Hero, when they pulled him out, and I saw his smashed-up head, and I know for sure it's him, I felt the worst pain I have ever felt in my life. Right at that minute, Hero, I wanted to die and take my boy's place on that slab. The only thing that has kept me going since then is knowing I was going to make you pay for what you did to my boy and for the pain you've caused me.

There's something else you don't know, Hero, something your friends, the people at the television stations and the newspapers, haven't told. The day you killed my Francisco was his birthday, Hero. He turned seventeen that day. But he's never going to have an eighteenth birthday thanks to you, Hero. So I'm thinking to myself that it's fitting that your son will not have an eighteenth birthday, either. I will keep your son alive until the day he turns seventeen, which is only eight days from now, is it not? He will wake up on that morning, and I will say, 'Happy last birthday, *muchacho.*' Then I will bring him to you, wherever you are, Hero, and let you watch him die, let you watch his head be smashed in. I want you to feel the exact same pain I felt the moment I saw my boy's body and knew he was truly gone. You will watch your boy die, Hero. And then you will die. Don't try to hide from me, either, Hero. Just remember that the lives of your wife and your daughter and your mama and your papa and all your neighbors are in my hands. If I can't find you on your son's birthday, more people will die in your place. People will die every day until I find you."

Danny heard the door open and felt the weight of the man exiting the vehicle. A cold sweat ran down his body, and he couldn't bring himself to look back. What difference did it make, anyway? After Danny regained his composure and got back out on the highway, he called Lt. Livingston and told him all that had happened. As expected, he received a stern lecture about the dangers of going alone instead of calling the authorities.

"Maybe you're right, Don, but what's done is done. I made the decision I thought was best for my son's safety. All that matters now is that we have exactly eight days before his birthday to find him."

Over the next seven days, the GBI, the FBI, and the local authorities searched for DJ Chambers. They called Cisco and his *Tres Tiburones* in for questioning, and they came willingly, each of them accompanied by his own attorney and each with an airtight alibi for the night DJ disappeared. Cisco also had an excellent alibi for the day and time he spoke to Danny near the rest area at mile marker 141.

The police had no choice but to release the suspects. Don Livingston seemed to be almost as frustrated as Danny about the whole situation, but he dutifully reminded Danny, as did the FBI Agent in charge of the kidnapping case, that there was absolutely no evidence to connect Francisco Ramos or any of his employees or gang members to DJ's abduction. The FBI agent went so far as to chasten Danny for having gone alone to meet with Cisco. He patiently explained to Danny that agents could have been hidden at the arranged meeting place, and either followed his car a safe distance or tracked his vehicle. They might have been able to take photographs of Cisco entering and exiting Danny's car and planted a recording device. Danny said he understood all that, but he still maintained that he had done what he thought was best for his son at the time.

Sheila and Melissa continued to be sequestered at the Holiday Inn, and Danny spoke with them only by phone. He and Lt. Livingston agreed that Danny should not go anywhere near the hotel until DJ's birthday had passed. It would be too easy for Cisco to have Danny followed if he tried to visit Sheila and Melissa.

Seven of the eight days before the deadline were gone. Danny decided that the time for searching and planning was over. It was time for him to act.

ᕦᕤ

CHAPTER FIFTY TWO
CONFRONTATION

EL GAUCHO DE las Pampas was one of the most popular and elegant stea-khouses in Atlanta. Modeled after the great Argentine steakhouses of South America, El Gaucho featured three different cuts of steak, as well as lamb, pork, veal, and chicken, all served straight off the charcoal fire-pit, directly onto your plate from skewers carried by circulating waiters. The wine list was considered to be one of the most—if not *the* most—extensive in the city.

Cisco Ram loved El Gaucho, and the maitre d' and wait staff loved him. He appeared without a reservation every Monday night, always with his *Tres Tiburones* and always in the company of three or more voluptuous ladies, of various ethnic backgrounds.

The staff knew he would be there every Monday, and they knew which table he preferred and which wines he would choose. Because he never used a credit card or called for a reservation, the restaurant knew him only as *Senor* Francisco because that was the only name he had ever given them. When the staff addressed him, they used the title with a reverence that signified great power and prestige.

Cisco always paid for everything with large bills. He thought nothing of dropping as much as three thousand dollars a visit, which covered dinner, as many as ten bottles of wine, and lavish gratuities for the maitre d' and waiters. Dinner at El Gaucho was his one extravagance each week, and he enjoyed it immensely. Most other nights, he ate a quiet meal at home. Cisco had a simple rule about his Monday night dinners at El Gaucho: no one was to speak about business or anything related to the Latino Death Lords. The primary topics of conversation tended to be food, wine, clothes, music, and World Cup Football, especially the fortunes of the Mexican National Team.

El Gaucho was located in the prestigious Buckhead section of Atlanta, far from where the LDL operated, so no one on staff had a clue that every Monday night their biggest customer was one of the deadliest and most psychotic gangsters in the city. That was exactly how Cisco liked it, and he did everything in his power to keep it that way.

Danny Chambers learned about Cisco's weekly visits to El Gaucho from GBI Agent Don Livingston. Danny had formulated a course of action he hoped would not only free DJ, but also put an end to Cisco and his henchmen for good. He had hoped to wait for the perfect weather pattern to roll into Atlanta, but DJ's abduction eliminated that option. He would have to proceed as planned and take whatever weather he got. Danny's father had told him that because the men he was dealing with were street criminals, who were at home in the city, Danny would need to choose a venue that gave him an advantage and put them at a disadvantage. It made perfect sense, but Danny had struggled to figure out where that would be and how he would get them there.

It had been almost one month to the day since the death of Cisco Junior. Danny called the City of Atlanta Police Department and asked for someone who could assist him in hiring some off-duty policemen to act as security guards.

"Atlanta Police Association," a friendly voice answered. "This is Wendy Connors. How may I assist you?"

"I need to engage a couple of officers for tonight," Danny said.

"I can help you with that, sir," she said. "Where will you need the officers and for how long?"

"Nine o'clock at the El Gaucho de las Pampas restaurant in Buckhead," Danny responded.

"From nine until when, sir?"

"I'm not sure. Is there a minimum time required?"

"Yes, sir. The cost is thirty-five dollars an hour per officer, with a minimum of two hours, which includes travel time."

"You mean I have to pay them while they're driving to meet me? That sounds a bit high."

"I understand your feelings, sir," she said politely, "but, you have to understand that for thirty-five dollars an hour, an officer is not going to drive possibly two hours round-trip in Atlanta traffic just to earn one hour's pay."

"I see. So how much would travel time and pay for two officers be for one hour in Buckhead?"

"That would be thirty minutes each way and one hour's duty for a total of seventy dollars per officer minimum. Do you want them to be in uniform?"

"Absolutely."

"And what is the nature of the assignment, sir?"

"I'm picking up a very rare and very expensive painting tonight, and I want the officers there, in uniform, as a deterrent to anyone who might try to interfere."

"Will the officers be traveling with you while you transport the painting or just be there for the transfer?"

"Just for the transfer. Once I'm safely in my car and on my way, I should be fine."

"Very good, sir. You will be required to pay in advance with a credit card."

"That's fine," Danny said.

"I must caution you, sir, that if the officers are called to respond to a police emergency in the immediate area where you are, while they are in your employ, they will need to respond, whether or not your business is finished." Danny said he understood and asked the young woman to please send two large officers and have them meet him outside the front door of El Gaucho de las Pampas restaurant at five minutes before nine that evening. He gave her his credit card information and hung up.

At fifteen minutes before nine o'clock that night, Cisco Ram, *Cuchillo*, *Borracho*, *Carnicero*, and four women entered the restaurant. The maitre d', a middle-aged Cuban named Ricardo Perez, immediately stepped from behind his podium. "Welcome, Senor Francisco," he said fawning all over his guest. "Your usual table is ready for you. Will you want to start with two bottles of Brut Champagne, sir?"

"Yeah, sure, Ricardo," Cisco said. "Two bottles of nicely chilled Brut will be fine." He shook hands with the maitre d', transferring a fifty dollar bill to the man's palm. As Perez escorted the party to their table, he caught the eye of one of the waiters and nodded faintly toward Cisco. The man hurried to the bar to get the Champagne. He knew exactly what vintage and how many to bring. So did every other waiter in the restaurant.

El Gaucho de las Pampas was a very upscale establishment, and there was rarely any turnover in the wait staff. There were too many people waiting in line for a job there, for any of the waiters to risk showing up late, miss a shift, or—heaven forbid—deliver poor service, especially to Senor Francisco.

Perez earned over a hundred thousand dollars a year, most of it in the form of gratuities that were never reported to the IRS. He loved his job, felt very lucky to have it, and was willing to do whatever it took, as long as it was not illegal, to keep it. He didn't associate with known criminals and didn't permit his staff to do so. He would have been mortified to know who his Monday night benefactor really was.

By nine o'clock, the group at Senor Francisco's table was settled in and were enjoying their first glass of wine. Half of them were seated on a plush leather couch that encompassed half of the large circular table. The others sat in matching leather chairs around the opposite side of the table. Cisco sat in the middle of the couch. He was leaning back with his arms around two gorgeous woman and laughing uproariously at a story *Borracho* was telling about his gay nephew when he saw the two uniformed policemen come in the front door and move to each side of it. Cisco watched them for a moment but quickly lost interest. He could always tell if a cop was looking for someone or just killing time. These two appeared to be killing time. Besides, he thought to himself, tonight he was Senor Francisco, not Cisco Ram. What could they do to him?

When *Cuchillo* saw the two policemen, he caught Cisco's eye and nodded in their direction. Cisco merely shrugged.

Danny had met the two officers outside the restaurant at five until nine and instructed them to wait until Senor Francisco, who he had already pointed out to them, had been in the restaurant for fifteen minutes before they went inside. Danny told them to position themselves at the door and not to acknowledge him when he came in. They were merely to keep a watchful eye on anyone Danny talked to. He also told them that Senor Francisco was the man who had agreed to sell him the painting.

When Danny walked through the door, he immediately saw Cisco's group and headed straight for them. Ricardo tried to intercept him.

"Good evening, sir," he said smoothly. "May I help you?" Danny didn't slow down.

"No, I just need a quick word with one of your guests."

The maitre d' had a nose for trouble, so he kept pace with Danny. "I see. And which guest might that be, sir?" Danny kept moving.

"No problem," he said. "I see him right there." Before Ricardo could say another word, Danny had planted himself beside Cisco's table and was gazing directly at Cisco.

"Is this a meeting of the Latino Gay Liberation Association?" Danny asked. He wanted to make Cisco angry, and attacking a Hispanic male's sexual orientation was the surest way he knew to do that.

Borracho started to rise, but *Cuchillo* grabbed his arm and nodded in the direction of the two policemen at the door, who, even though they were too far away to hear what was being said, seemed to be watching what was happening at the table with great interest.

Danny looked from one woman to the other until he had made eye contact with all of them. "I hope you ladies weren't hoping to get lucky tonight," he said, "because these boys play on the other team, if you know what I mean. They bring eye candy like you out once a week to impress the locals and maintain their reps. But, trust me, they enjoy each other's company in the bedroom far more than they would yours."

This time, Cisco started to rise from his seat. His face was beet red and the veins in his neck stood out. *Cuchillo* reached out his arm to restraining him. "Boss, don't forget the cops by the door, man. We can't afford trouble in here." Danny saw an opening and followed *Cuchillo's* lead.

"Damn right!" he said loudly enough for the entire restaurant to hear. "The sissy boy can't afford trouble in here. The last thing he needs is word getting out that Cisco Ram is a sissy. I thought you were a real bad *hombre*, Cisco, but I know better now. You're not a man. You're a coward." He looked from one woman to another. "You know what this coward does, ladies?" he paused a moment for effect. "He beats up old men, and he terrorizes little girls, kills little dogs, and kidnaps teenage boys. What do you think about having dinner with a man who kills little dogs for fun? He's a gutless excuse for a man who's never faced another man *mano a mano* in his life. He's just a yellow Mexican dog."

The name "Cisco Ram" caught Ricardo's attention immediately. He had followed Danny to Cisco's table and was now furiously signaling his staff for some assistance.

"I'm sorry sir," Ricardo said, "but you are mistaken. This gentleman is one of our best customers, and his name is Senor Francisco."

"Yeah, Senor Francisco Ramos, better known as Cisco Ram. He kidnapped my son and he's holding him hostage somewhere right now. He's holding my son hostage because he's afraid of me." Ricardo's face went white. "He sits right here, every Monday night, like he was a normal person and not a murdering, deviant, rapist. All your other guests sit around him every Monday night, unaware that they're breaking bread with one of the sickest, most vile animals in this city—Cisco Ram himself."

An uncomfortable silence radiated from Cisco's table like ripples in a pond. Everyone within earshot had stopped eating and talking, and was staring at Cisco and listening to Danny.

"You are a worthless, cowardly piece of scum, Cisco," Danny went on, unleashing the venom he had held in all these weeks. "If you were a man, you would have met me face to face weeks ago instead of attacking innocent animals, old men, and young girls. Oh, and one more thing. It was no accident that your son died that day, Cisco. I saw the whole thing happening in front of me, and I had plenty of time to think about what I should do. Here was a wetback kid attacking a nice white lady, this kid who was probably a criminal psycho just like you. I said to myself, 'Here's a chance to rid Atlanta of at least one of these greasers and not even have to answer for it.' I could have pulled the boy away from the car and held him for the police if I had wanted to, Cisco. But I didn't want to. So I threw your kid in front of that truck. I threw him under the wheels so they could crush his greaser head. How do you like that, *amigo?*"

Out of the corner of his eye, Danny could see that his police escort was headed his way and that three burly waiters were also advancing in his direction. He picked up Cisco's Champagne glass, held it to his mouth, and spit in it. "You kidnapped my son because you want to kill him in front of my eyes and then kill me so you can get your jollies, right, you freak? Well, that's not going to happen because when I walk out that door, you'll never see me again. I know you for the liar you are. You'll kill my son and my family anyway, so why should I give you the satisfaction of playing your little sick game? The minute I knew you had my son, I knew he was going to die and that I couldn't stop it. But you won't find my wife, my daughter, or me. I promise you this, though: my son will be avenged, because when I'm ready, you won't have to find me. I will find you." Danny turned and walked toward the door. The two police officers met him halfway and asked if there was a problem.

"No," Danny said calmly, "he just changed his mind about selling me the painting, and we exchanged a few heated words. Nothing to get upset about. Let's go. We're done here." The officers escorted Danny to his car, which was parked in the restaurant lot.

"Thanks for coming out tonight, officers," Danny said.

"No problem, sir. Glad we could help." Danny got in his car and drove away.

∾

Inside the restaurant, Cisco's party was still sitting at their table in disbelief. Danny's brief tirade had forever ruined Senor Francisco's reputation at El Gaucho de las Pampas. Ricardo, not knowing whether he should apologize to Senor Francisco or ask him to leave, was back at his post by the door.

Cisco looked around the restaurant and saw that every eye was on him. As each of the diners met his gaze, they slowly turned back to their food, as if Cisco no longer existed. He violently shoved the table away from him, spilling every glass of liquid on it. He stood up, threw a large wad of bills in the center of the table, and stormed out, the rest of his group scurrying to keep up.

Cisco left El Gaucho de las Pampas in a rage. None of his three sharks could remember seeing him this angry. He screamed at the valet to get his car. When the young man retrieved the keys from the kiosk, Cisco grabbed them and shoved the attendant away, screaming that he could get his own goddamn car faster than this *burro*.

Cisco seldom drove his new Lincoln Navigator, preferring instead to have one of his followers drive him around so he could talk on his cell phone or surf the Internet. And because he often drank wine or hard liquor, he feared being stopped by the police. Cisco did whatever it took to avoid any contact with the police.

When he got to his vehicle, Cisco used his clicker to unlock the doors and started to get in the drivers seat. *Carnicero*, who had consumed very little alcohol at the restaurant, took his arm gently. "Boss, you've been drinking pretty good tonight. Why don't you let me drive?" Cisco stared at him for a moment then threw the keys at him. One of the others opened the back door for their boss and he slid in, followed by *Cuchillo* and one of the women.

Cisco put his foot in her chest and pushed her out of the SUV. "Get the hell away from me! Find your own goddamn way home, *putas*." The woman fell to the pavement and lay there in stunned silence. When the other women started to help her up, Cisco threw a several hundred-dollar bills out the door and pulled it closed. *Borracho* jumped into the front passenger seat, and the big truck screeched away.

"Take me home, Carni," Cisco said. Then he sat back in his seat and closed his eyes. His face was red and taunt and he was breathing heavily. He sat that way, not saying a word, for several minutes. When he finally spoke, his breathing was closer to normal.

"Cuch, reach out and find me four of our best people. Tell them to meet us at the club at eight o'clock tomorrow morning. I want you, Carnie, *Borracho*, and four or five of our top people. No one better be late. I pay these bastards too much money to have to wait for them when I call. This hero is a little crazy now, I think, but not crazy enough to come at me this way unless he knew his wife and daughter were safe. I don't think they'll be at his house, but check it anyway. In the meantime, call in every favor we have." He was calmer than he had been when they had left the restaurant, but still seething inside.

"I don't care what you have to do—*find out where they are*."

CHAPTER FIFTY THREE
MOUNTAIN HOME

THE FIRST PART of Danny's plan had been easy: make Cisco so angry that he would throw caution to the wind and come after him. He had decided to fight Cisco the only way he knew how and in a setting that would give him the best chance of winning. He would fight this last battle for the safety of his family in the mountains and, he hoped, in the snow.

Now that the GBI had Sheila and Melissa safely hidden away, Danny was ready to execute part two of his plan. On his way to the mountains, he had left a trail that he felt fairly confident Cisco would have no trouble following. He prayed that he had left his adversary in such a state of embarrassment and anger that Cisco would pursue him without thinking it through. As much as he hated Cisco, it had hurt Danny terribly to lie to him and tell him that he had wanted to kill his son and that he had intentionally thrown the boy in front of the truck. He only hoped that the lie had been enough to push Cisco over the edge.

From the restaurant, Danny had headed directly for the mountains by way of Georgia 400, a major artery that connects the bedroom communities north of Atlanta with the city. From downtonw Atlanta, the first twenty-five miles of the highway is five lanes wide in both directions, then it becomes a four-lane divided highway that stretches all the way to the foothills of the north Georgia mountains.

Danny knew he would reach the mountain cabin in a little more than an hour, and he calculated that Cisco would be there by mid-afternoon the next day. He figured it would take him that long to marshal his forces and drive to the mountains. If Cisco could follow the simple clues Danny had left for him, it wouldn't take him long to figure out where Danny had gone to hide.

Danny had his radio tuned to the local station that gave the most frequent weather updates. He checked the thermometer on the dash and saw that the outside temperature was already down to thirty-six degrees. The last weather report said that temperatures were expected to drop to well below freezing throughout the night, with four to six inches of snow predicted for the higher mountain elevations tomorrow afternoon. This was exactly what Danny had been praying for. If the snow materialized, it would be one more advantage for Danny. He doubted that Cisco or any of his crew had ever had to deal with weather as cold and as treacherous as it would be on the mountain tomorrow. Danny fervently hoped that there would be no snow or rain between now and early in the afternoon of the next day. Any precipitation that fell on the roads during the night or early morning hours would freeze quickly and prevent Cisco and the LDL from getting up the mountain. This was going to be a close run thing anyway and he desperately needed the weather to cooperate with his plan.

If Cisco could not get up the mountain, not only would Danny miss his best chance to end this war, but he would also be stuck on the mountain himself, for at least a few days. And although he had brought plenty of provisions, he knew he would be helpless to do anything about Cisco, who would still be in Atlanta searching for Danny's family.

Danny would have only a few hours in the morning to make his preparations. If Cisco arrived before he had time to finish, Danny knew he was probably not going to come down off the mountain alive. He also knew that his wife and daughter were merely pawns in Cisco's game. If Cisco killed Danny, they would no longer be of any use to him. Whatever was going to happen on the mountain, Danny was ready for it. He also knew that forcing the issue, even at risk of his own life, was better than waiting. If Cisco truly intended to kill DJ in front of Danny, then he would have to go wherever Danny was.

The family's mountain cabin was just over thirty-five-hundred feet above sea level and sat at the end of a dirt logging road about a hundred yards from the north rim of an abandoned rock quarry. The quarry itself stood at the end of a long, winding gravel road along which huge trucks had once rumbled down the mountain every day filled with loads of granite. The logging road branched off where the gravel road turned toward the south rim, where the trucks were once loaded.

Over the years since it had been abandoned, the quarry pit had been filled by summer rains and melting winter ice and snow. Several of the area's small streams and brooks fed into the pit, which was now over three hundred feet deep. Danny knew that on a bitterly cold, snowy February day, there should be no one but him and Cisco's crew anywhere near the quarry.

The logging road circled up the side of the mountain with numerous cutbacks. Eight hundred feet below the crest, it flattened out for a stretch and passed within twenty yards of the cabin, then took a sharp right turn up and over another ridge, sloped twenty feet down toward the rim of the quarry, then, only a few yards from the edge of the pit, turned left again to continue its path up the mountain.

Danny parked his car, in plain sight about twenty yards to the left of his cabin. The only items, aside from food and clothes, that he had brought with him from Atlanta were a shovel, a pick, a flare gun, his shotgun and all the shotgun shells.

It was a clear night, and the moon provided sufficient light for Danny to unload his gear and bring it into the cabin. Once inside, he turned on the gas and lit the pilot light for the furnace. His friend Ezra Reed, who had been the last one to use the cabin when he had come up in the fall to do some fishing, had left things just as they should be, and in less than fifteen minutes, the little cabin began to warm up.

Danny lit the small gas stove and emptied a can of beans and a can of vegetable soup into the same pot. When the mixture was hot, he took the pot off the stove, set it on a potholder on the table, opened a bottle of soda, and sat down to eat the first meal he had had in more than ten hours. He looked at his watch. It was twenty minutes after one o'clock in the morning. He needed to get to sleep soon, if that was possible, and prepare his mind and body for the next day's battle.

He went into the single bedroom, opened up a chest, and took out several blankets. He looked at the bare mattress and decided he didn't need any sheets tonight, so he spread the blankets out on the bed and put a pillowcase on one pillow. Before he got into bed, he dropped to his knees on the cold concrete floor and began to pray. He didn't pray for victory. Instead, he prayed that no matter what happened, he would have the strength to accept that God's will had been done, not his or Cisco Ram's. Then he prayed for the safety of his family and the health of his father and mother. He prayed for twenty minutes. When he was done, he felt at peace. He climbed into bed and pulled both blankets over him. He set the alarm on his watch for six o'clock, and closed his eyes. In the morning, he would prepare his welcome for Cisco and then wait. *Your will be done, Lord,* he prayed again. *Please let my son live through today, his seventeenth birthday.* Then, his mind and body exhausted, he fell asleep.

CHAPTER FIFTY FOUR
A BETRAYAL OF TRUST

THE NEXT MORNING, Cisco met with his sharks to discuss strategy. "As I told you last night, we have two tasks amigos," he said. "Number one, we must find where the hero has run to; and number two, we must find his family." There were murmurs of assent from around the room.

"Maybe they are all together, *Jefe*," said *Carnicero*.

"No, I don't think so. I have thought about what he did last night, and I still don't think our hero would have come into El Gaucho and risked getting in my face, unless he was sure that his family was safe. I hate him and I will kill him, but he's no fool. So where would his family be that would make him think they're safe from Cisco Ram?" He mused. "We know he's met several times with the GBI."

"Yeah, Boss," said *Borracho*, picking up on his thought. "Maybe the cops have them in...uh...what do you call it?...uh..."

"Protective custody," *Cuchillo* said, finished his fellow shark's sentence.

"Yeah, that's what I'm thinking, too," said Cisco. "Cuch, see if anyone we know has a source at the GBI."

"You will not have to look too far, Boss," *Borracho* said. "I bought a marker from a bookie just this week, on a guy who works as some kind of auditor at the GBI."

"An auditor?" *Carnicero* said mockingly. "What the hell good is an auditor gonna do us?"

"Well, cops always hide people in hotels, don't they?" Cisco asked no one in particular.

Carnicero looked puzzled. "So?"

"Well, hotels cost money, don't they?" said Cisco. "Someone at the GBI has to pay for those rooms, and someone has to do the paperwork." He stood up and slapped *Borracho* on the back. "Good work, amigo. Very, very good work. Reach out to our new friend at the GBI. Tell him all debts are forgiven if he can help you find the hero's family." He turned to the Butcher. "Carni, take a ride by the hero's house and see if anyone's around who might know where he is. If he thinks his family's safe, maybe he's even hiding there himself. Probably not, but it's worth a look. If you see anyone around, ask them if they saw his family leave."

∾

Bobby Pendleton was sitting in his office at GBI headquarters in downtown Atlanta, analyzing the work of some of his clerks, when the phone on his desk rang. He picked it.

"Pendleton. Can I help you?"

"Is this Bobby Pendleton?" a gruff voice asked.

"Yes, it is. How may I help you?"

"Are you the Bobby Pendleton who works in the accounting department for the Georgia Bureau of Investigation?"

"Yes, as I said, this is Bobby Pendleton And, yes, I'm a supervisor in the Accounts Payable Department for the Georgia Bureau of Investigation," he said with a hint of irritation creeping into his voice. "Now, how may I help you?"

"Good. I was just making sure I had the right Bobby Pendleton," the caller said. Bobby could clearly discern an accent, but he was not sure where it was from.

"Mr. Pendleton, I believe we have a mutual friend named Jack Neihaus. Is that correct?"

Bobby froze. "Could you hold for just a moment, please?" Without waiting for a reply, he got up from his desk and quietly closed the door to his office so his conversation could not be heard by the employees in the cubicles nearby. When he sat back down at his desk, he picked up the phone and tried to sound casual. "I'm sorry, but I think you must be mistaken. I don't believe I know anyone by that name."

The voice on the other end of the phone remained pleasant. "Are you sure you don't know him, Mr. Pendleton? I can't believe that you have forgotten a man you owed eleven thousand dollars in gambling debts. Debts which we paid and are now owed to us."

Bobby tried to bluff his way through. "Eleven thousand dollars? That's preposterous. I told you I don't know the man, and I think you should know that the Georgia Bureau of Investigation does not take kindly to having its employees harassed, especially at work. I'm going to hang up now, and I strongly recommend that you don't call back." Before he could hang up, the voice turned nasty.

"Go ahead and hang up. But if you do, I'll have no choice but to come down to your office and ask for the eleven thousand in front of your employees and maybe even your boss. You can try explaining to them that you don't know Big Jack Neihaus, if you want. We both know you owe the money, Pendleton. You know it, and I know it, so quit screwing around and wasting my time. Now I'm going to ask you one more time: Do you know Big Jack Neihaus?"

Bobby knew it was useless to deny it. "Yeah, sure, I know him. I just needed to make sure you were on the up and up and that you knew him, too. Betting on sports is not the kind of thing a person would want talked about, especially someone who works for the GBI."

"Good. Now that we have that crap behind us, let's get down to business. As I said, My associates and I purchased your debt from Jack, so now you owe us. I'll be by later today to pick up the money. You *do* have the money, don't you, Mr. Pendleton?"

Not only did Bobby not have the money, he had lost another eight hundred to Big Jack after he learned that the debt had been sold and that his slate was clean again. "I'm sorry," he said nervously, "but I don't have the money here at the office. Maybe we could get together later this week and discuss this?"

"No, we ain't going to get together later this week to discuss it because there is nothing to discuss, Mr. Pendleton. You owe us eleven thousand, and we want it today. If you don't got it at the office, then a few of our nastier friends can drop by your place tonight and pick it up. Is that better for you?"

"Not really," Bobby said. His palms were beginning to sweat as he said, "You see, I don't have the money—at least not all of it, right now. What I meant by discuss it was that maybe we could discuss some kind of arrangements to pay it back a little each week."

"Sorry, Mr. Pendleton, we don't run that kind of business. We want our money today, or your life is going to become very, very unpleasant. *Comprende, amigo?*"

Bobby was on the verge of a full-scale panic attack. "I'm sorry, but I can't pay you if I don't have any money," he said plaintively. "I don't know what else I can say."

"Okay, Mr. Pendleton, don't blow a gasket. You wanted to make some kind of arrangement to pay it back, so I have a thought. My associates and I are very interested in finding out the whereabouts of some people the GBI is currently hiding from the public eye, so to speak. I think these people are in a hotel or a motel somewhere in the Atlanta area, and I think you can find them for us. If you help us, your debt of eleven dimes will be completely wiped off the books. How does that sound?"

Bobby was intrigued but puzzled. "If this is about witness protection, it's really not my area. I'm in accounting. I don't get involved with witnesses or talk to them or about them. I don't see how I can help."

"These hotels and motels that the police use to hide people don't give out free rooms to witnesses, do they, Mr. Pendleton?"

"No, of course not. We get a discount, but we still have to pay for them."

"That's what we thought. We also thought it wouldn't be hard for you to look through the current bills and find what motel or hotel is charging you for a room for some people named Chambers. That shouldn't be too hard, should it, Bobby?"

A cold sweat was spreading all over Bobby's body. His gambling had finally gotten him in over his head. Now his job was in jeopardy, and maybe even his life. *Who knows what these people might do to me?* he thought to himself.

"I'm sorry," he said. "I wish I could help you, I really do, but I'd lose my job and possibly face criminal charges if I gave out that information."

"Bobby, here's how you need to look at this," the caller said calmly. "If you tell us what we want to know, there is a slight chance you could get caught giving out confidential information. You would probably get fired and maybe go to jail—*if* you get caught, which is a big 'if'. On the other hand, if you don't tell us what we want to know, you will definitely lose your job for associating with gamblers because we'll turn you in to the GBI, along with you buddy Jack Neihaus. Big Jack won't want to go to jail, so he'll be glad to throw you under the bus, Bobby. So, you either take your chances with us that you don't get caught, or we'll turn you in and you'll get caught for sure. What's it gonna be, Bobby, I don't have all day."

Bobby quickly weighed his options: don't help them and my career at GBI is over; help them and maybe I'll get away with it, keep my job, and get rid of the huge debt that's hanging over my head. Not really a hard choice at all, he decided.

"Okay, I'll see what I can find out. If I locate them, who do I call?"

"Call the number I'm going to give you and ask for Jose. If Jose isn't there, just leave the name of the hotel and the room number. If it all works out, this is the last time we'll ever need to speak, Mr. Pendleton."

Borracho gave Bobby the number to call and hung up without saying good-bye. Bobby immediately turned to his desktop PC and typed in a file name. In a moment, he was looking at a listing of the hotels and motels the GBI routinely used to house witnesses or other individuals in protective custody. Then he opened another file that contained open accounts. Each account was cross-referenced by the names of the individuals being housed and the department or agent within the GBI who had authorized it. Twenty-five minutes later, he picked up the phone and dialed the number the caller had given him. Someone answered after the third ring.

"Let me speak to Jose, please," Bobby said.

୭ඉ

CHAPTER FIFTY FIVE
SECRETS EXPOSED

WHEN *BORRACHO* TOLD Cisco he had found Danny's family, his boss was ecstatic.

"Excellent work, *Borracho*, excellent. Call Carni and see if he found anything interesting at the hero's house."

"But we already know where his wife and kids are," Borracho said. "So why do we need him?"

"Don't be such an idiot, man!" Cisco yelled in frustration. "One minute you do excellent work, and then with one question, you become an idiot again. What good is his family to me if I can't find *him*? I don't give a shit about his family except to kill them to give him pain. If I can't find him to tell him that I have his family, they're no good to me. We leave them where they are until we know where he is."

"I have someone watching the motel, *Jefe*, just in case they try to move them," Borracho said.

"Good. Now you're thinking, mi amigo," Cisco said. "Make sure they don't slip away while we look for Papa." He took his cell phone from his pocket and hit the speed dial for *Carnicero*, who had done as he had instructed and gone to Danny's house. After circling Danny's block twice, he had left the neighborhood and was parked at a fast-food restaurant. He was sitting in the parking lot, eating a breakfast sandwich, when Cisco's call came through.

"What did you find out?" Cisco asked.

"I don't see nothing going on around there, Boss. If he's inside, he ain't showing no signs of life, and he ain't answering the phone."

"Okay, go back and if you see anyone, ask them if they know where Coach Danny Chambers is. You're a smart guy, and I know you'll think of a good reason for asking. Don't go up to his house, though. After the mess Cuch and *Borracho* made by killing the neighbor instead of his wife, the cops might be watching." Only after Cisco had ended the call did he realize that he had not told Carnicero that Borracho had found the Chambers family.

Carnicero went back to Danny's street and passed the modest split-level one more time, hoping no one had noticed him cruising the block. Nothing had changed. No lights were on, the garage door was closed, and there didn't appear to be any activity in the house. On his way back to the neighborhood, he had stopped at a pay phone and called Danny's number again. There had been no answer. As he was about to leave Danny's street, he saw an old man puttering around the front porch of a house three doors down from Danny's. *Carnicero* stopped the car and walked up to the house.

"Good morning," *Carnicero* said warmly.

"Good morning yourself, young fella. What can I do for you?" The man appeared to be in his mid-sixties, tall and slim, with thinning gray hair. He wore a pair of denim jeans and a flannel shirt. A dirty Atlanta Braves baseball cap sat back on his head. He had a hammer in one hand and an electric drill in the other.

"I'm hoping you could help me get in touch with your neighbor, Mr. Chambers," *Carnicero* said. The man looked at him more closely now, then smiled pleasantly.

"Get in touch with him? What do you want with Danny Chambers?" Before *Carnicero* could answer, the man turned crusty. "I don't like talking about my neighbors to strangers, young man. Exactly what do you want?"

"Mr. Chambers hired me to do some carpentry work on his porch. I told him I'd give him a really good price if he could let me do it now because I have no work in the winter. He said he wanted to wait until the spring, but I really need the money now, so I was hoping to see him and offer him an even better price if he changed his mind and let me do it now."

The old man continued to stare at him, as if he was trying to deciding whether or not to trust this young stranger. Finally, when *Carnicero* was about to say something, the man spoke up. "He ain't home now. He went up to their place in the mountains for the weekend. They got a real nice little place up there that they share with Sheila's parents. Sheila, that's his wife you know. She's a real sweet girl too. Family is salt of the earth and..."

Carnicero cut him off without trying to be to obvious that he didn't care about Sheila's family.

"A mountain cabin, huh? Man, that sounds nice. I wish I could have me a mountain place. I'll be lucky to keep my apartment unless I get some carpentry work soon. So, did he take his family, or is Mrs. Chambers at home? Maybe I could talk to her about the carpentry work."

"No, he didn't take Sheila and the kids this trip. I think he was going to do some work on the place. I saw him when he was leaving, and he just told me where he was going and asked me to keep an eye on his house."

"So, do you think his wife is home?"

"I don't think so. Sheila's a neighborly kind of gal, and if she's home, the garage door is usually open and there's a fire going in the fireplace. I don't see any smoke from the chimney, so I think you can assume that she and the kids are gone somewhere, too."

"Okay, thanks," said *Carnicero*. "By the way, where is this mountain place?"

"It's up there north of Dahlonega on Wolfpen Ridge," the old man said. "Wolfpen isn't really a mountain, just a ridge. But it's almost a mile high, and it's part of the Blue Ridge Mountain chain. There's a whole lot of ridges like that up in Towns and Union counties. I had an aunt that used to...."

Carnicero could see that the old man was going to talk forever if he didn't stop him. "I guess a mountain place like Mr. Chambers has would take a long time to get to and be hard to find, wouldn't it?"

"Oh, hell no. You just take 400 until it runs out, go east on Route 652, and follow the signs to Stillman's Quarry. Hard to miss unless you're a complete idiot."

"Stillman's Quarry?"

"Yeah, just follow the signs to Stillman's Quarry. Danny's place is right on the site of the old quarry. In fact, the house is the old quarry office. They just turned it into a hunting and fishing cabin."

"Well, thank you, sir, for the information," *Carnicero* said politely. He decided to ask one more question to maintain the charade. "You wouldn't by any chance be needing any carpentry work done around your home, would you?"

"Nah, not me. I do all my own stuff around here. That's what I'm doing out in this cold today, getting ready to replace a plank on my porch before my old woman falls though it and breaks her neck. Say, you aren't planning on going up to Danny's place, are you? He don't like to be disturbed, and he would be madder than hell if he knew I even told you about it. I wouldn't go up there if I were you. He'll be back by Monday anyway."

"No, sir, I'm not going up there. I was just curious about his place. Maybe he might need some work done on it if it's that old."

"Well, you'd have to ask him that when he comes back. I have to get back to my project here, so you have a good day, young man."

"Thanks. You, too." *Carnicero* was smiling on the way back to his van. *This is going to be even easier than I thought.*

A half hour later, he was back at the clubhouse. He wanted to save his best piece of information for last, so he simply told Cisco that the Chambers house was quiet and dark and that there were no cars in the garage or driveway. Cisco cursed and smashed his fist down on the table.

"Don't worry, *Jefe*," *Carnicero* said with a sly grin. "You know I don't let you down. I know where the hero is hiding." He then gave Cisco the details.

"So the hero has become a rat and gone into his hole," Cisco said, barely able to contain his glee. "Well, he can't hide from Cisco Ram. Okay, get everyone loaded up, *muchachos*. We're going to the mountains for some fun—everyone but you, Cuch. I have a special job for you. The rest of you get out and get ready. Cuch, you stay here a minute."

෭෨

CHAPTER FIFTY SIX
NORTH TO THE MOUNTAINS

WITHIN AN HOUR, two of the Latino Death Lords' black Lincoln Navigators were rolling north on Georgia 400. Cisco rode in the lead vehicle while *Carnicero* drove. Juan Madrigal, Ricky Montalvo, and Benito Valdez, the same three who had been with *Carnicero* when he abducted Melissa and Erin, were in the back.

Borracho drove the second vehicle, accompanied by three of his best crew members. The temperature was just above freezing, and the forecast called for precipitation and colder air. Cisco was wired on Puerto Rican rum and the two lines of cocaine he snorted before they left the clubhouse.

"Are you sure you know how to get there, Eduardo?" It was one of the few times he had referred to *Carnicero* by his given name in several years.

"Si, *Jefe*, I have it all right here," he said, tapping his temple with his right index finger. "We can ask for directions when we get closer, if you wish, but I think something as big as a stone quarry will be easy to find."

"Okay, good," Cisco said. "Turn the heat up, amigo. It's getting cold in here. You know I don't like the cold."

"It will be colder in the mountains, *Jefe*," *Carnicero* said. "Maybe we should go home and come back when it's warmer. Man, we could freeze our asses off up there."

"We ain't going back home, so forget that. It don't make a difference if it's freezing on the mountain," Cisco snarled. "We won't be there long enough for you to catch a cold." Cisco was the only one who had thought to wear an overcoat. The rest of his gang members were wearing suits or sweaters and light jackets, and all of them, including Cisco, were wearing street shoes.

"Okay, okay," *Carnicero* said. "I just think maybe there's a better...."

"Shut your mouth, Carni!" Cisco shouted. "Do you think I can let one more day pass without killing this *gringo* after what he said in the restaurant? He insulted my manhood. He insulted all of us. How can we ever go back there after what he said? No, I am finished waiting. Today the hero dies."

Carnicero cast a sideways glance at his boss but said nothing. Cisco sat up stiff as a ramrod in his seat and stared straight ahead. His jaws were clenched. *Carnicero* knew it was time to stop protesting and just drive. About an hour after leaving Atlanta, they came to the end of the four-lane highway. *Carnicero* studied the signs at the intersection with the smaller roads and made the turn toward the quarry. Two miles down the road, they came to a small convenience store and gas station.

"Carni, stop here and ask if we're going the right direction," Cisco ordered. "Ask if they know Mr. Daniel Chambers. Tell them you're going up to do some carpentry work or something. Jose, while he's inside, I want you to open the rear hatch, get out the two gas cans, and fill them up at the pump. We'll have a little surprise for the hero, I think." *Carnicero* and Jose did as they were told. A few minutes later, *Carnicero* got back in the SUV.

"Damn, it's cold as hell out there, amigos," he said, briskly rubbing his hands together.

"Would you shut up about the cold, and tell me what the man said about our hero?" Cisco snapped.

"He says we're on the right road," *Carnicero* answered. "He says we make only one more turn and we'll be there. Maybe another ten minutes or so."

"Does he know the hero?" Cisco asked.

"Si," replied *Carnicero*. "He says Coach Chambers came in to pick up some groceries this morning."

"Excellent! Excellent!" Cisco said with satisfaction. "We have the rat cornered now!" Jose put the filled gas cans in the rear of the vehicle, and the SUV pulled back out onto the roadway. Cisco took out his cell phone and tried to make a call. He held the phone to his ear for a moment, then took it away and glared at it. The display read "No Service." He tried again and got the same result. "Damn, I have no cell service up here. The rest of you try your phones and see if you get a signal."

The rest of the men tried with no success to connect.

"When we get to the turnoff for the hero's hideaway," Cisco said, "pull off the road and wait for *Borracho*. I can't get him on the phone, and we need to make our final plan." When they arrived at the last turn-off, *Carnicero* eased the SUV onto the shoulder of the road. He saw *Borracho* in the rear view mirror pull in behind him.

"One of you in the back, get out and go tell Borracho to come up here," Cisco directed. No one moved.

"Somebody better get moving, or you will all be standing out in the cold," *Carnicero* shouted impatiently.

Juan Madrigal, who was sitting on the passenger side in the second row of seats, reluctantly opened his door and stepped out. He took one step, slipped on the ice that had formed on the dead grass beside the road, and fell down hard on his backside. The others were afraid to laugh, fearing that they would be the next one sent out into the cold. Juan struggled to his feet and walked cautiously back to the driver's side of the other SUV. A moment later, *Borracho*, walking on the paved road, got into the back seat of *Carnicero's* vehicle.

"When we get to the hero's cabin," Cisco said, "here's what we do. If we don't see the hero anywhere outside, then, *Borracho*, take your men and Benito, and put them around the sides of the building so he can't escape through a window or a back door. Then you knock on the door, and tell him to come outside, or we'll burn the cabin with him in it. If he still won't come out, pour some gas on the door and light it. We'll smoke him out. When he comes out, grab him. I want him alive so he can enjoy what I have planned for him."

Borracho was skeptical. "*Jefe*, what if the hero has a gun when he comes out? How can we grab him if he has a gun? You don't want us to shoot him I know."

"He won't have a gun, *hombre*," Cisco assured him. "Don't you read the papers? He's a school teacher. Besides, when he was in the army, he chose to fly helicopters instead of fight. I think the hero is a coward who can only fight school boys like my Junior. Don't worry about a gun. Anyway, he won't come out of the cabin until it's filled with smoke, so he'll be blind when he runs out. Just drag him to the ground as soon as he's outside."

Borracho got out and walked gingerly back to his vehicle. When he got in, he checked the instrument panel: the outside air temperature was twenty-nine degrees. The snow was falling faster now, and he had the same thought he had had earlier in the day: *This is a bad idea. A very bad idea.*

CHAPTER FIFTY SEVEN
NO PLACE TO HIDE

THREE YEARS BEFORE the Disney World boom hit central Florida, a 230-acre amusement park opened on the west side of Atlanta. Six Flags Over Georgia was modeled after its sister park, Six Flags Over Texas, which had opened in 1961. The name was inspired by the six flags that had at one time or another flown over all or part of the state of Georgia: the flags of Spain, the United Kingdom, France, the United States, the Confederate States of America, and the State of Georgia.

The park was an immediate success, drawing hordes of visitors from all over the southeastern United States. The once-barren stretch of Interstate 20 that ran west from Atlanta toward the Alabama border now teemed with hotels, motels, restaurants, gas stations, and anything else a weary traveler or bored vacationer might desire. The Georgia Bureau of Investigation routinely used hotels and motels near the giant park because of the vast numbers of people who were out and about at all hours of the day and night.

Sheila and Melissa were set up in a Holiday Inn, one mile from the main gate of Six Flags. They had a three-room suite that consisted of one bedroom on each side of an attached parlor. Each of the bedrooms had a connecting door into the parlor. Their bedroom connected to the parlor through a door on the right side of the room; the other, which housed two uniformed Georgia Highway Patrolmen, connected on the left side.

At six o'clock in the evening on the second day of their stay, Corporal Jody Patton of the Georgia Highway Patrol asked his partner, Delano Riggs, if he wanted some Chinese food. Riggs readily agreed, and the takeout order was placed at a nearby restaurant. Riggs had suggested that the food be delivered, but Patton needed cigarettes and said he would pick up the food while he was out. After Patton left, Riggs turned on the evening news. Meanwhile, Melissa was playing a video game in the parlor, and the noise of the game and her loud narrative of the action prompted him to get up and partially close the door between the parlor and his room. There was a knock on the parlor door.

"Pizza delivery," a male voice said. Melissa, who had just told her mother she was starving, jumped up to answer the door.

"Wait," Sheila said, "I didn't order a pizza. Did you?"

"Must have been the policemen," Melissa said, reaching for the handle.

"Wait a minute, Mel," Sheila said, "Let's ask the officers if they ordered it." Just then, Patrolman Riggs came through the adjoining door, unsnapping the strap that held his 9mm pistol in its holster. At the same instant, Melissa saw the familiar red and blue pizza logo through the peephole and pulled the door open. The deliveryman pushed Melissa backwards and shot Riggs twice in the chest. The officer, who had removed his uncomfortable bulletproof vest and hung it on the coat rack in his room, dropped to the floor immediately. The silenced gunshots could barely be heard above the sounds of the video game.

Sheila ran over to her daughter and put herself between the girl and the man with the gun. The intruder raised his finger to his lips and made a shushing sound. Keeping the gun pointed at Sheila and Melissa, he stepped into the doorway of the room Riggs had come from and quickly scanned it. Crossing to the other bedroom door, he did the same. Seeing no one, he turned back to the cowering females. "We leave now," he said. "Do what I say, and nobody gets hurt." He looked at Sheila. "If you give me any trouble, I kill the little one."

He checked the breezeway and seeing no one in sight, motioned for them to go ahead of him down the stairwell to a waiting SUV. The gunman pushed them into the back seat, closed the door, and got into the front passenger seat. He turned in his seat to point his pistol at his two terrified passengers, and said, "*Vamos amigo*" to the driver. The vehicle slowly pulled away from the hotel and was soon lost in traffic.

CHAPTER FIFTY EIGHT
PREPARATIONS FOR WAR

THE ALARM ON Danny's watch woke him from a restless sleep at six in the morning. He washed the sleep from his eyes with cold water and brushed his teeth. Then he set about preparing himself for the day. First, he put on a pair of long thermal underwear and a long-sleeved thermal top, then two pairs of wool socks and a pair of denim jeans. He added a flannel shirt and a thick sweater. Finally, he pulled on a pair of insulated hiking boots with large treads on the soles. He was confident that, no matter what else happened today, he would be better prepared for the weather than his enemy.

He put a small pot of water on to boil, then drank some water and ate two protein bars. When the water was ready, he poured a cupful and added two spoons of instant coffee and one spoon of sugar. He took his cup over to the window and watched the sun rise slowly over the peaks of the nearby mountains.

When he finished his coffee, he rinsed the cup with water and placed it in the rack beside the sink to drain. He immediately realized that this was purely force of habit and grinned a morbid grin. *What would it matter to anyone if this coffee cup was clean or dirty when this day was over?* he thought to himself. He briefly considered straightening up the kitchen and the bedroom but decided that the condition of the cabin, like the coffee cup, would be meaningless at the end of the day.

Danny put on his fleece-lined insulated jacket and his gloves, then went outside and removed the shovel and pick from the trunk of his car. So far, he thought, the weather was cooperating. Snow was lightly falling, and the thermometer that was tacked to the exterior wall beside the door showed that the temperature was now below freezing. If the weather reports were correct, the weak winter sun would not be sufficient to offset the cold front that was predicted to roll into north Georgia by midday. With the pick and shovel over his shoulder, Danny followed the road over the rise and down to the rim of the quarry. The sun was still partially below the horizon, but there was enough light for him to work. He took his shovel and began to dig.

It was closing in on mid morning when he completed his first task. He went back to the cabin and drank more water and ate another protein bar. Then he set about his work on the propane furnace. After he extinguished the pilot light, he used a wrench to disconnect the incoming gas line.

Danny knew from his college and high school chemistry classes that, in their natural state, both propane and natural gas have no odor, taste, or color. As a result, gas suppliers add an odorizing agent so consumers can tell if there is a leak. The odorant in propane is ethyl mercaptan, a sulfur-based compound that smells like rotten eggs. While natural gas tends to rise into the atmosphere and disperse, propane sinks to the ground and tends to collect in low areas and enclosed spaces, behaving more like water, hugging the ground and flowing downhill toward the lowest spot it can find, such as a basement, cellar, or crawl space. Propane can even flow underground if it leaks from buried pipes.

Like water, propane can seep through a foundation into the space beneath a structure and has a propensity to accumulate and pool. When mixed with the proper proportion of air, propane is highly explosive, and propane explosions can cause severe structural damage and in many cases completely level a building. The other thing that Danny knew about propane gas was that, in certain situations, the odorant begins to fade, making it difficult to detect the presence of the gas. He was counting on this today.

When his work inside the cabin was done, he turned off the lamp, took one last look around, and went back outside. He closed the door but left it unlocked. His preparations were almost complete. All he had left to do was to find the best place to await his adversary. He took the shotgun and the flare gun with him and began to look for a vantage point that would give him a view of Cisco's approach and put him in the best position to execute the second part of his plan.

After twenty minutes of checking various locations along the road and the rim of the quarry, he found it. He would be able to rest here in the prone position and look out over the quarry while he waited for Cisco to emerge on the logging road, then quickly move ten feet back down the road and have excellent ground cover and a clear view of the cabin, which was thirty yards to his right. He laid out a camouflage-colored tarp, stretched out on one side of it, then pulled the other side over him like a blanket. At the rate the snow was coming down now, he knew he would be completely covered within fifteen minutes. Everything was in place, and he felt as ready as he would ever be to face Cisco and his men. He watched the road across the quarry and began to pray.

∞

CHAPTER FIFTY NINE
ARMAGEDDON

AT TEN MINUTES after noon, Danny saw the first of the big black vehicles round the curve on the other side of the quarry. The snow was falling heavily now, but it had not completely obscured the opposite rim of the quarry. The waiting was finally over. Danny remembered how it had been in the deserts of Iraq, how nervous he had been just sitting and waiting for the radio call to come in requesting Medevac choppers on the battlefield. His anxiety always vanished when the call actually came and Danny was in his chopper with his hand firmly on the stick. As soon as he lifted off, he felt calm, peaceful, and ready to do his job.

As he watched a second SUV come into view, that same familiar feeling of peace came over him. What was going to happen, was going to happen; and, as always, Danny's survival was in God's hands. He watched the two vehicles wind slowly up the gravel road, then make the turn onto the dirt logging road. He waited a few moments longer to see if there was a third vehicle behind them. When he was satisfied that there wasn't, he crawled backwards down the small hill beside the road and tucked himself into the hiding place he had chosen between two large chunks of granite and a small Fraser fir tree. He checked the shotgun for the fifth time to make sure he had a full magazine and that the safety was off. Then he waited.

The two SUVs rolled up into the gravel yard in front of the cabin. At this distance, Danny could see them clearly, even through the heavy snowfall. The doors of the lead vehicle opened simultaneously and five figures appeared. One of them moved out of Danny's view behind the building, and two others split up, each taking a position on either side of the cabin. The two remaining men approached the building slowly, stopping only when they reached the small deck that served as a porch at the front entrance.

"Hey, Hero," one of the men shouted, "company's here! It's time for you to meet your God, Hero. Come out and face Cisco Ram." A few seconds passed, and the man shouted again. "Hero, if you don't come out, I will burn the cabin down, and we'll have roasted hero for lunch." Another thirty seconds passed, and the man doing the shouting turned to his companion and said something. The other man went back to the SUV, opened the lift gate, and brought out two red gas cans. He took them over to the man on the porch and handed him one. Both of them began to slosh the gas from the cans onto the porch, the front door, and the front walls of the cabin.

"Last chance to come out and meet your maker, Hero!" the man shouted. When there was still no response, he took out his cigarette lighter, stepped up to the door, ignited the lighter, and pushed the door open. Then he tossed the flaming lighter inside. Instantly, there was a blinding flash of light and a deafening explosion. The small wooden-frame cabin that had served as the family's vacation hideaway for so many years, simply ceased to exist, along with the five men who had surrounded it. Pieces of wood were blown a hundred feet or more into the winter sky, followed by a plume of pure white smoke that looked like a tiny atomic mushroom cloud.

As the pieces of wood rained down with the snow flakes, Danny waited and watched the second vehicle. For a moment or two, there was no movement. Then the front passenger-side door opened, and Cisco Ram stepped out, holding a pistol in his hand. He stood beside the SUV, keeping it's bulk between him and the fire that was raging where the cabin had once been.

"*Borracho!*" he screamed, as if he could not believe the man had just disintegrated. Cisco stepped slowly around the front of the vehicle and gazed at the fire. Finally, he spotted what might have be the remains of a body about thirty feet from where he had last seen *Borracho*. As Cisco moved toward it, Danny felt he had waited long enough.

He leaped from his hiding place and fired at Cisco. The shotgun jerked in his hands and the butt of it smashed into his shoulder. He had never fired a shotgun before and had not expected the recoil to be so strong. His shot missed Cisco, but that was not his primary objective in firing from such a distance. He wanted to get the attention of the men in the SUV. When the sound of the shotgun blast reached Cisco's ears, he turned and saw Danny on the hill. He pointed in Danny's direction and screamed something to the men who were still in the vehicle.

Danny ran up the road toward the top of the hill. He looked over his shoulder and saw the SUV roaring up the road behind him like an enraged bull. Cisco was running behind it. When Danny went over the crest in the road, he was only thirty-five feet from the rim of the quarry. As soon as he was out of sight below the crest, he dove off the road and hid behind a small fir tree. Three seconds later, the SUV came flying over the crest in the road, traveling far too fast for the terrain and the weather conditions, but the men inside did not know that—at least, not yet.

The truck went airborne momentarily, and when it touched down, it was less than fifteen feet from the quarry rim. Danny couldn't tell if the driver ever hit the brakes. It would have done no good, anyway. The speed and the weight of the vehicle, combined with the downward slope of the road and the natural lubrication of the snow, sent the SUV sailing out into the quarry. Danny heard the transmission scream as the tires cleared the edge, and seconds later, the huge splash the vehicle made when it hit the surface of the lake.

He looked back to his right just as Cisco was lumbering to the top of the rise. Cisco stopped and looked to his right then to his left, and Danny realized that the leader of the Latino Death Lords had no idea where his men or their SUV had disappeared to. Danny stepped from behind the tree.

"They're gone, Cisco," he shouted. "Over the edge and into the lake. It's a hundred-foot drop, and the lake is three-hundred-feet deep. Your friends are not coming back." He raised the shotgun and fired. As Danny pulled the trigger, Cisco dove for the snow-filled ditch beside the road. When his head appeared again, Cisco fired his pistol at Danny.

CHAPTER SIXTY
REDEMPTION

ON THE ROCKY hillside overlooking the campsite below, the man seated himself on a smooth rock behind a large fallen tree and rested his rifle on one of the limbs. He carefully adjusted the telescopic sight and peered through it at the figures below. Although they were more than six-hundred yards away, they appeared to be no more than twenty-five feet away through the scope. The snow was falling steadily now, but not hard enough to obscure his vision or to distract him from his purpose. He could see Danny Chambers standing by the roadside holding a shotgun. Danny's back filled the frame of his sight, and the crosshairs centered on a point between his shoulder blades. The rifleman slowly swung his gun left to focus on Cisco Ramos, who was on his hands and knees in the mud and snow. He tested his sights one more time by centering them on Cisco's forehead, then moved them back to Danny and relaxed his grip on the rifle. He raised the binoculars that hung from his neck and surveyed the entire area below him. At this distance, a 7.62 mm bullet, traveling at a speed of twenty-eight hundred feet per second, would reach it's target in six-tenths of a second. The maximum effective range of an MI4 rifle equipped with a telescopic sight was slightly over eight-hundred and seventy-five yards. As he sat perfectly still and waited, his mind drifted back to another time and place.

❧

By now, Cisco had crawled to his knees near the edge of the cliff, his eyes fixed on Danny and the shotgun. "Did you think you could sneak off up here and hide from me, Hero, like a rat in it's hole?" he said as he slowly climbed to his feet. "You were easy to find. Your neighbors? They like you, Hero. They told us about your little hideaway in the mountains. The man down the road at the little gas station? He likes you, too. He gave us very good directions to your rat hole, Hero. I guess you think it's just me and you left to fight, don't you? You think God has eliminated all my friends and left us to face each other *mano a mano* to settle this. You are a fool, Hero. I have a little surprise for you. I still have a few cards to play, amigo. I have more friends you have not yet met."

"I don't care anymore," Danny shouted defiantly. "This ends today."

Cisco removed a handkerchief from his pocket, wiped his hands with it, then raised it over his head and began to wave it slowly back and forth. "That's for some more of my friends, Hero. They were waiting on the other side of the pit. I think they have seen what you did to their amigos and I don't think that they ae going to be very happy with you, Hero. What do you think?"

Sixty seconds later, a third large black vehicle that had been hidden from Danny's view by the trees on the far rim of the quarry, rolled slowly into view and stopped fifty yards from where Danny was standing. The driver's side door opened, and man got out and walked around to the opposite side. He opened both the front and rear passenger side doors, reached in, and roughly pulled out a woman and then a young girl. Danny's heart sank.

No longer worrying about the pistol Cisco held, Danny stepped farther out into the road and looked back at the SUV where the man stood holding Sheila and Melissa. They were both bound with heavy tape, their hands secured behind their backs, and their feet tied at the ankles. Neither of them seemed to be struggling, which made Danny conclude that they might have been beaten or drugged. Had Cisco's henchman not been holding them up by their hair, they most certainly would have fallen to the ground.

Danny turned his gaze back to Cisco and knew he was beaten. *This evil, vicious man is going to win after all,* he thought to himself. He had hoped he would at least be able to save his family. He had hoped that one day his life and the lives of his family would be back to normal. In that instant, the words from an Emily Dickinson poem popped into his head: *Hope is the thing with feathers, that perches in the soul.* He felt as if that thing with feathers had just taken flight from his soul.

He thought about how arrogant he had been to believe that he could ignore God's laws and kill all these people. He thought about how his arrogance was going to result in the death of his entire family. He didn't know where DJ was, but if Cisco had Sheila and Melissa, he must have brought DJ along, too. Danny knew he would be forced to watch his son die, and there was nothing he could do about it.

"What are you going to do now, Hero?" Cisco asked mockingly. "You can't shoot my friend *Cuchillo* with that shotgun, can you? No, of course you can't, because the pellets will also strike your wife and your daughter. Your shotgun is of no use to you now, Hero. Toss it away. Do as I say, or I'll tell him to cut your daughter's throat."

He turned to the man who was holding Sheila and Melissa. "Cuch," he shouted, "if he shoots me, kill them both as quickly as you can." Then he set his eyes back on Danny. "He is my man, Hero, my man. And he will do exactly what I tell him. So, if you're thinking about shooting me and then trying to deal with him to save your women, forget it. They'll be dead before my body hits the ground."

Danny knew Cisco was right. The shotgun was useless in this situation. He could shoot Cisco, but that wouldn't save Sheila and Melissa. He also knew that even if by some miracle he managed to kill both of these men, he wouldn't know where to find his son. Cisco's shouting interrupted his thoughts.

"Hero, I said for you to toss the shotgun and get down on your knees," the gang leader ordered. "Maybe you want to pray before you die, huh, Hero? Be sure you pray for the women, too, because you will watch them die before you do unless you do as I say. The only way you can save them, Hero, is to do what I say. Then, only you and your son will have to die."

Danny was frozen in place. He couldn't feel his legs or his hands. His heart was racing and his chest pounding.

"I said on your knees, Hero," Cisco commanded. "Do it now, or the women die before your eyes. If you want to save them, drop the gun."

Danny knew that this cruel, godless man was going to kill his family whether he dropped the gun or not. He knew Cisco was lying, but he also knew he couldn't bear to actually watch his beloved wife and daughter die. He pitched the shotgun into the snow in front of him and dropped to his knees.

He had a vision of Sheila snuggling close him in his old Chevy when they were dating, leaning her head on his shoulder. He could almost smell her hair. He pictured holding Melissa's hands when she was learning to skate on the sidewalk in front of their house when she was five years old. He thought of how fragile his son had looked the first time Danny saw him in the hospital nursery when DJ was barely twenty minutes into this world. He looked at Sheila and mouthed the words, "I'm so sorry. I will always love you."

Then Danny prayed out loud. "Lord, I am truly sorry I have offended Thee. Please show mercy on my family. Give them peace, and let then die quickly."

Cisco was walking toward him. "Hero, you're not very smart," he said, laughing. "Did you think I would let them live? They only serve one purpose now, Hero, and that is to give you pain. You must watch them die before I kill you. I told you that you would feel the pain I felt when I lost my son." He turned to *Cuchillo*. "Cut the girl's throat first, Cuch," he shouted, "then do the woman."

Cuchillo hesitated a few seconds, and Cisco screamed at him. "Do it *now*, Cuch. Do it now!" *Cuchillo* maintained his strong grip on Melissa's hair, but released Sheila's, and she fell sideways to the ground. He reached into his pocket and brought out his knife. He looked down at the woman lying at his feet, and the words she said when they grabbed her and the girl at the motel came back to him: *Please, do whatever you want to me, even kill me, but don't hurt my daughter, please. Just take me and leave my daughter alone.*

Cuchillo could barely comprehend that this woman was willing to be brutally assaulted and killed rather than have any harm come to her child. He remembered his own mother sitting passively, in a drunken stupor on a sailor's lap, while men beat and humiliated her son. But this woman was offering herself up to save her child, and Cisco expected him to kill her child right in front of her. Sheila looked up at him with exhausted, pleading eyes.

"Please...no," she whispered.

Cisco screamed at him again, "I said do the kid *now*, Cuch, *now!* What are you waiting for?" *Cuchillo* stared dumbly at the woman in the snow, the knife still poised at Melissa's throat.

At that moment, Danny heard a voice in his head. *"Have no fear, My son. They are now, as always, in My keeping. You will be together again soon. I am with you always and forever, and you have been faithful."*

At last, *Cuchillo* had made up his mind. He could not understand this woman's sacrifice or the hot tears he felt filling his eyes, but he had to do what Cisco had ordered him to do. Cisco was his master now. He was raising the knife to the girl's throat when, suddenly, his body was thrown violently backwards against the hood of the SUV like he had been punched by an invisible fist. He tried to stand erect, then swayed unsteadily and fell to his knees.

Only then did Danny hear the crack of a rifle shot echo through the quarry. He saw the growing blossom of blood on *Cuchillo's* chest before the man's lifeless body tumbled forward into the snow. The bullet that was now lodged deep in *Cuchillo's* chest, had arrived almost a full second before the sound of it's firing reached Danny and Cisco on the road. Danny, struggling to get his mind around what he was witnessing, stared dumbly at the body.

But Cisco Ram, a veteran of so many street fights, understood immediately. He was stunned when *Cuchillo* fell, but he knew when he heard the crack of the rifle that someone else had joined this party. He dove off the road and rolled into the shallow ditch again. Danny was slower to react, but Cisco's movement spurred him into action. He lunged for the shotgun, picked it up, and aimed it at Cisco, who was at least twenty-five yards away. Cisco raised his pistol and pointed it at Danny, who was still on his knees. Danny was trying to decide what to do next when Cisco suddenly tossed his gun into the snow. Cisco knew his chances of hitting Danny from that distance with a pistol were not nearly as good as Danny's chances of hitting him with the shotgun, and there was still the other shooter to consider. He climbed out of the ditch and stood in the road with his hands above his head.

"Who is your friend, Hero?" Cisco shouted.

"I have no idea," Danny said numbly. "Maybe it's God."

"Whoever it is, Hero, it looks like you win. My men are all dead, and you're pointing a shotgun at me. I would say it's over. We are finished with each other. So you can call the police now, and they can come and take me away."

Danny got to his feet and began to walk toward Cisco, who began to retreat slowly down the slope toward the edge of the cliff. Danny continued to hold the shotgun in the firing position, the butt of it pressed firmly against his cheek and the barrel aimed at Cisco's head.

"Where is my son, you worthless scum?" he asked.

"Oh, the boy? I had forgotten about the boy, Hero. Yes, of course. You need to know if he's safe. Maybe we can make a bargain after all, can't we? You let me go, and I tell you where the boy is. Do we have a deal, Hero?"

In that moment, Danny hated this man more than he had ever hated anything or anyone in his life. He wanted to pull the trigger and blow Cisco Ram's head off, but he wanted his son to be safe even more.

"I don't trust you any farther than I can throw you, Ramos," Danny yelled. "If you can show me that my son is safe, then I'll let you walk away."

"You don't trust me, Hero? Well, that's all right because I trust you. You are a hero and a good Christian man. So, we have a deal?" Danny nodded. "He should be in the back of the SUV, tied with tape, just like your women."

Danny motioned toward the SUV with his shotgun. "Start walking," he said.

Cisco walked past him down the road toward the vehicle. Danny followed ten feet behind until they reached the spot where his wife, daughter, and—if Cisco was telling the truth—his son were waiting.

"Sit down on the ground, Ramos, and put your hands behind your head," Danny said when they got to the SUV. Cisco did as he was told, and Danny tried to peek into the back of the vehicle but couldn't see anything through the tinted windows.

"DJ, are you in there?" Danny shouted.

"Dad, get me out of here!" came the muffled response.

"Are you all right, son?"

"Yes, sir. Just scared."

Keeping his eyes trained on Cisco, Danny moved to where Sheila and Melissa were lying. He picked up the knife that *Cuchillo* had dropped and cut the tape that bound Sheila's hands. Then he handed her the knife. "Cut Melissa loose," he said, "then get DJ out of the back." Then he walked over to where Cisco was sitting.

"Get up, Ramos," he said. Cisco got to his feet. "Start walking back up the road toward the quarry."

"What do you mean? Hero, we had a deal. Your son for my life. You have your son, and now you must release me."

"That's what we're going to talk about when we get up the road, Cisco," Danny said. "Now get moving." Cisco walked back toward the curve in the road that lead down to the rim of the quarry. When he got to the bend, he stopped. "Not yet, Cisco, keep going until you're over the hill." Ten more steps and both men were hidden from the others by the crest of the hill and the snow-covered bushes.

"Now what?" Cisco asked impatiently.

"Now, you die."

Cisco panicked. "We had a deal, Hero. I trusted you."

"And I trust you, Cisco," Danny said calmly. "I trust that when you got back to Atlanta, your lawyers would keep you out of jail long enough for you to recruit some more of your gang members and come after my family again. I can't let that happen."

"I swear, I won't do that," Cisco pleaded. "It ends here today, Hero."

"Yes, it *will* end here today, Cisco."

"You can't kill me. You're the hero, the all-American good guy. Heroes don't kill people in cold blood. Hell, you didn't even kill my men. The idiots blew themselves up or drove off a cliff. You can walk away with a clear conscience, Hero. Turn me over to the police if you're afraid I'll come after you again." Cisco stopped four feet from the edge of the cliff. He looked back at the quarry rim, then back at Danny. He stood there with his palms outstretched and shrugged as if he didn't know what else to say.

Danny lowered the shotgun to his waist but kept it pointed at Cisco. "So you think I was easy to find and your men all died by accident?" Danny asked, a forlorn smile spreading across his face. "Did you ever stop to ask yourself *why* it was so easy to find me? How convenient it was that my neighbor told you where this cabin was—and even gave you directions? How helpful the man at the gas station down the road was to direct you to the cabin and tell you I was already here? That's what I *told* them to do, *muchacho*. I led you here, Cisco, like the Pied Piper of Hamelin led the children. And another thing, did you ever think to ask yourself why the cabin exploded instead of simply catching on fire? It blew up because it was filled with propane gas. I turned on the gas and left it on. If your man hadn't used his lighter to torch the place and saved me the trouble, I had this flare pistol ready." He pulled the flare gun from his pocket and held it up. "I was set to fire it through the window to ignite the gas. I even parked my car near the cabin so you'd think I was inside."

Cisco looked confused, and, despite the below-freezing temperature, began to sweat. Danny continued to explain.

"Oh, and the SUV full of your men that went over the cliff? It wouldn't have gone over yesterday because a set of large metal guard rails would have stopped even a vehicle as big as yours. I dug out those guard rails this morning. I knew that once I started running up this road, you'd follow me, and you did. My only concern was that your men might be on foot instead of in a vehicle. But, just as I expected, the cold and snow kept them in their truck. I knew that by the time your SUV came over the crest of the hill and the driver saw the cliff edge, it would be too late to stop because of the ice and the slope of the road. By the way, I intended to use this shotgun to kill anyone who survived the explosion or the plunge over the cliff. And, finally, the snow. This lovely snow. How did a city punk from Mexico like you end up dying in the snow in the mountains of north Georgia? Can you figure that, Cisco? It's because this is where I wanted you to be. I brought you here in your expensive silk suit, your five-hundred-dollar cashmere overcoat, and your fancy leather-soled Italian shoes. You can't move very well in the snow in those shoes, can you, Cisco? You're freezing your butt off in that expensive suit, aren't you? And your cell phone has no service, so you weren't able to call any of your friends to bail you out or do your dirty work this time. You see, Mr. Ramos, I knew that you and every single one of the men you brought up here with you were going to die on this mountain, so there would be no one left to threaten my family, or I was going to die up here."

Cisco could see that he had badly miscalculated. "But that's different from you just shooting me in cold blood as I stand here," he said, trying to appeal to Danny's sense of decency, "very different. I'm a human being, and I don't think this is something you can do, Hero. Your conscience will not let you. Your Christian beliefs do not permit it, do they? Jesus will not be happy with you if you kill me this way. Am I not right, Hero?" Cisco's voice was quaking.

"That would be true—if you were a human being," Danny said menacingly. "But you're not. You're a rabid dog, a vicious, cruel, and very evil man. The world will be much better off when you leave it. You terrorized my family. You almost killed my father. You killed my innocent, helpless little dog. You put your hands on my daughter. You killed my neighbor and abducted my son. You're not going to walk away from all that because your lawyers and corrupt judges set you free. As for my Christian beliefs, that's between me and my Lord. He will deal with me as He will, and into His hands I gave up my soul before I climbed this mountain to meet you."

"You are not a judge and jury, Hero," Cisco said desperately. "You know you can't do this. You're a Christian, and you'll have to look me in the eyes when you pull the trigger. I know you can't do that."

Danny thought of his family just around the bend. In his heart, he longed to run to them and to hold them tightly to his chest. But in his head, he knew that this must be finished now, and finished for good. Visions began to race across his mind of his sweet angel daughter being manhandled and terrorized by Cisco's thugs on Cisco's orders; his father being beaten and kicked in his own front yard; the brutalized body of Sheila's friend, Laura Henderson, lying on the floor of his kitchen; and, finally, his little dog hanging from a tree like a side of meat. Danny raised the shotgun and aimed it at Cisco's chest. His heart was pounding, but, for the first time in many years, it was pumping pure ice water through his veins.

"One last thing, Cisco," he said. "I didn't mean to kill your son. I would give anything if I could to go back and relive that day so it could end another way. I said those things at the restaurant to make you come after me, but I didn't want the boy to die. It truly was an accident." Danny took a deep breath before he finished what he had to say. "May God have mercy on your soul, and may He, in his infinite mercy, forgive me for what I am about to do. As you say, Cisco, a hero wouldn't do this. But like I've been telling you from the beginning—I'm no hero."

Danny pulled the trigger, and the six-inch pattern of double ought buckshot hit Cisco square in the chest, lifting him off his feet and thrusting him backwards over the cliff. Danny didn't move until he heard the splash. The sound of the shotgun blast was still echoing through the hills as he walked over to the edge and looked down. Cisco Ramos was floating face down in the black water. He was startled by familiar voice from behind him.

"You did the right thing, Mr. Dan. You did what I should have done all those years ago." Danny turned to see Ezra Reed standing a few feet away. The old man had a large rifle with a telescopic sight cradled in his arms.

"Ezra, where did you come from?" Danny asked excitedly. "How did you know I was here?"

"I called your house when you weren't at school today, but no one answered. Your kids weren't in school, either. Principal Evans said he didn't know where you were and he was pretty worried. I called your father and told him I knew you were having some trouble, and I wanted to help. He didn't know where you were, but he said he told you to fight your fight on your own ground. Finally, I went to your house, and your neighbor said you were probably up here. So I took a chance and came on up. I got here about an hour ago, and I've been watching and waiting up on that hill." He pointed to the spot where the rifle shot had come from. "Your daddy said you would defend your ground as best you could, and this is your ground, isn't it, Mr. Dan?"

"Yeah, Ezra, it's my ground," Danny said. "Thanks to you, I'm alive to say it, and thanks to you, my family is alive as well. I need to go see how Sheila, Melissa, and DJ are doing. Then I have a lot of questions for you."

"Yes sir," Ezra said, "then we got some cleaning up to do, too." Danny was already running toward Sheila and the kids, who were huddled together hugging each other beside the SUV. When he got to them, he wrapped his arms around their necks.

"It's finished," he said solemnly. "You're safe now, and he'll never bother us again."

Sheila started to ask him what happened, but he just kept hugging his family and telling them how much he loved them. While they were all crying and hugging, Danny noticed Ezra standing off to the side. He went over to the old man and found him smiling and teary-eyed.

"Are you okay, Ezra?"

"Yes, sir, Mr. Dan, I'm about as good as I can be. I finally made the shot I was late on a long time ago. It don't bring back my wife and kids, but it does my heart good to see yours safe from that man."

"God sent you, Ezra, and I thank you with all my heart. My plan didn't work out as well as I thought it would. If you hadn't come up here, my whole family would be dead—and so would I." He put his arms around the old man and pulled him close. "How can I ever thank you, Ezra?"

"Mr. Dan, you might bring me an extra ham and swiss once in a while," he said jokingly. "I'm so tired of those little sausages. But they's cheap." The two men started to laugh. It was the first time Danny had laughed in months.

"You said we had some cleaning up to do, Ezra, but I don't think we should disturb any of this until the police get here."

"Who's going to call the police, Mr. Dan?"

"I am, Ezra. I killed that man, and I broke the law. The police will have to come and sort it all out."

"Mr. Dan, if the police come, maybe you'll be going off to jail?"

"If I do, then I do," Danny said. "I didn't want to break the law. I just wanted to protect my family. I have to face the music and take whatever the law gives me."

"Mr. Dan, do you think the Lord brought you through all He's brought you through just so's you could go to jail? If you go to jail, who's gonna support your family? Who's gonna help Miss Sheila raise them young'uns?"

"I don't know, Ezra. I guess I hadn't thought about that."

"Well you better start thinking, Mr. Dan. Jail's a bad place to be at any age, but especially yours. Watching yo kids grow up once a month through two inches of Plexiglas ain't the way it ought to be." Danny looked down at the ground and slowly shook his head.

"I guess I'll have to trust the Lord on this one too, Ezra," said Danny, his voice beginning to quiver with emotion.

"Well, Mr. Dan, the Lord helps those who help themselves, so I say we clean up here a little bit and get out of here. If the Lord wants you in jail, he'll send someone to put you there soon enough." Danny shook his head again and seemed resolved not to try to hide what had happened, but Ezra kept on.

"What about me, Mr. Dan? I shot that man, and he wasn't no threat to me. Heck, I didn't even have no business being up here. I think you gonna get me put in jail, too, Mr. Dan. Is that what you want?"

Danny looked deep into the old man's eyes. "No, Ezra, of course that's not what I want. I'm so sorry. I wasn't even thinking about what might happen to you. I guess since I owe you my life and my family's, I have no choice. Okay, let's clean up and get out of here. What do we do?"

"Well, sir, it looks like we have five or six bodies and two mighty big vehicles to get rid of. I say we put the bodies in the trucks and push them into the quarry. If we weigh them down enough, they'll be at the bottom of that quarry until Jesus comes for us all. The first thing we need to do though is to git on down there to shore and git that Cisco fella's body out of the water before he sinks. If it sinks now, with nothing to weigh it down, it will just pop back up in a day or so and we can't have that."

"Wait here for just a minute or two," Danny said. He went back to where Sheila and the kids were waiting.

"What happened over the hill, Danny?" Sheila asked him. "Is Cisco dead?"

"Yes, he's dead," Danny said. "I *had* to kill him. He gave me no choice." He knew the words he spoke were technically true, even though they didn't tell the whole story. Danny truly believed that Cisco had given him no choice. "I'll tell you all about it when I get home. Now I want the three of you to head back to Atlanta. I'll be there when I'm done up here. Don't stop and don't talk to anyone until I get home, hon." Danny handed DJ the keys to his car, which was still parked near the remains of the cabin, and told him to take his mother and sister home.

When his family drove out of sight, Danny and Ezra found the path down to the shore of the lake and went down to retrieve Cisco's body. Fortunately, the prevailing winds were in the right direction to push the body close to the shore. After they pulled it out, they went back up to the top and began to collect the charred bodies of the men who were killed when the cabin exploded and load them into one of the black SUVs. When they were done, Danny got in and drove up to the edge of the quarry. He carefully wiped his fingerprints from the steering wheel and doors with his handkerchief and put the transmission in neutral. He and Ezra then went around to the rear of the vehicle, leaned their backs against it, and pushed. With the road sloping downhill, it didn't take much to get the SUV rolling. A few seconds later, it tumbled over the edge and fell a hundred feet to the surface of the lake, where it created an enormous splash. At first, Danny feared it might simply float out to the middle of the lake and just sit there, but Ezra had been right about leaving the windows partially open. The water began to pour into the SUV, and it quickly sank beneath the surface. Air bubbles continued to rise for a while after the truck disappeared. Then the water was calm again.

Danny and Ezra put *Cuchillo* in the third SUV and went through the same routine. When it disappeared beneath the surface of the water, Danny went to the storage shed and came back with several links of heavy chain he had once attached to his tractor to remove stumps. With all the other vehicles and bodies now safely resting deep under the lake, it was time to deal with the last piece of the clean up.

They went back down to the shore where they had left Cisco's body. They placed the body on the bow of a small row boat, that they had often used for fishing, and while Ezra held the body on the boat, Danny rowed them fifty yards off shore. He stowed the oars and they wrapped the heavy links of chain around the body several times. When he was satisfied with their efforts, Danny pushed Cisco's bulky form off the bow and watched it sink rapidly out of sight.

"I hope that be the last we ever see of that man." Ezra said.

"As do I Ezra, as do I. The water is hundreds of feet deep here so I think it will be." Danny said as he picked up the oars and began to paddle back to the shore.

It took them longer to clean up the area than Danny thought it would, but when the task was accomplished, he and Ezra climbed back up the hill to the logging road that ran above the property where Ezra's old pickup truck was parked.

Before Danny could get in the truck, his stomach began to cramp and he suddenly dropped to his hands and knees and began to throw up the meager contents of his stomach. He remained in that position for a minute or two after the last spasm passed, then sat down and rested his back against the truck's wheel. His face was white and even in the chill air, he could feel the perspiration on his forehead.

"You just sit there awhile Mr. Dan. You will be alright shortly. I know how you feel. I did the same thing after shooting the first three Viet Cong I killed in the war. It will pass."

"Wow, I thought I was handling it pretty well until just now." Danny said.

"It's okay. Just a delayed reaction to the killing. It ain't never easy to kill someone, but if anybody ever needed killing, it was that Cisco."

"It might pass like you say Ezra, but it is something I will never forget."

"You ain't supposed to forget it Mr. Dan. If you could, you wouldn't be the man you are. But you done the right thing and you will learn to live with it."

Another five minutes passed without any further conversation before Danny stood up and opened the passenger door of the old truck.

"Ezra, I still don't know how to thank you." Danny said.

When they got in, Ezra reached out his hand to Danny. "You already thanked me fine Mr. Dan. You my friend. You my good friend, and I don't have a lot of friends. Here's a souvenir for you, Mr. Dan, something to remember this by and something you don't want the police to find." Danny opened his hand, and Ezra dropped a spent shotgun shell into it. Then he reached into his jacket pocket and pulled out the empty shell casing from a 7.62-caliber U.S. Army issue M14 rifle. Ezra held it up and looked at it for a moment. "Ten bad men dead and only two shots fired. Now, you tell me the Lord didn't have a hand in this business, Mr. Dan. You just try and tell me that."

Danny didn't say a word as Ezra put the truck in gear and started down the mountain.

❧

CHAPTER SIXTY ONE
ABSOLUTION

WHEN DANNY GOT home, there were two messages on the answering machine from Lt. Livingston. Danny replayed the first one:

"Danny, this is Don Livingston. I need to speak to you as soon as possible. Somehow Cisco's men found out where your family was being sequestered and abducted them. Apparently, one of Cisco's men pretended to be a pizza delivery man, and your daughter let him in before the officer in the adjoining room could react. Cisco's man shot him using a pistol with a silencer on it. The officer lived long enough to tell his partner, who had gone out to pick up dinner, what happened. I'm sorry about your family. Please call me if you hear anything from them or from Cisco." Livingston's second message simply requested that Danny call him as soon as possible.

It was late, and Danny didn't have the energy to try to explain things to the GBI, so he put off calling until the morning. When he reached Livingston at half past nine the next morning, he still wasn't sure if he should confess. The only thing keeping him from doing so, was his desire to protect Ezra. He had not been able to fabricate a story he thought anyone would believe about how he had managed to kill Cisco Ram and every single one of his top people all by himself. Even the part about the cabin blowing up and the car crashing into the quarry sounded manufactured to him. As heavily as his conscience was weighing on him, he couldn't bring himself to put Ezra in jeopardy. Danny dialed the direct line Livingston had given him when they first met, and the lieutenant picked up on the first ring.

"Lieutenant Livingston, this is Danny Chambers. My family is safe. They're all with me right now."

"All of them? You mean you have your son, too?"

"Yes, Don, they're all home safe."

"That's wonderful, Danny. I've been really worried about you. Where have you been the last two days, and how did your family manage to escape?"

Danny was at least prepared for this part of the conversation. "I've been in hiding trying to come up with a plan to deal with Cisco," Danny said, trying to sound convincing. "As far as my family escaping, they didn't. Cisco's men let them go. Sheila said the guy who appeared to be in charge of the group that took them from the motel got a call from Cisco saying they needed to lay low for a while and to let them go."

"What about DJ? How did he get free?" Livingston sounded more incredulous with each word he spoke.

"Same deal, Don. They just let him go."

"Uh huh...I see," Livingston said.

Danny knew that the lieutenant wasn't buying any of this. "Did your wife or either of the kids get a look at the men who abducted them?" Danny did not answer right away because he realized how lame his story sounded. His lies had seemed a lot more plausible when he was rehearsing them in his mind. Finally, he broke the silence.

"No, Sheila said they all wore masks the whole time," Danny told him. When the detective spoke again, his voice was dripping with suspicion.

"So, they kidnap your son, promise to kill him on his birthday, go to the trouble of searching the city to find your wife and daughter, kidnap them, kill the patrolman who was guarding them, and then they change their mind and release them all?"

"I know it sounds crazy," Danny said defensively, "but that's what happened."

"All right, Danny. I'm glad they're safe. I'll be in touch with some follow-up questions in the next day or so. I hope you have a nice day." The line went dead, and Danny knew he was in trouble. Livingston didn't believe his story for a minute, and Danny didn't blame him. He realized too late that while he might be able to cover up the deaths of Cisco and his men, he was going to have a very difficult time getting anyone to believe that his family had been voluntarily released by a man as vicious and cruel as Cisco Ram. Sheila had been standing beside Danny during the entire conversation.

"Danny, why did you tell him I said they wore masks the whole time?" she asked him.

"He wanted to know if you or the kids got a look at your abductors," he replied. "I told him no."

"If he believes that, he must think we're a bunch of complete idiots," she said.

"Why is that?"

"Don't you think we'd have to be idiots to open the door without at least looking through the peephole to see who it was? And if we looked and saw a man in a mask, we never would have opened the door." Her logic was flawless, and Danny felt like an even bigger fool for thinking he could lie his way through this.

❧

Two days later, Lt. Livingston called and said they would be coming over to Danny's house within the hour, if that was convenient. Danny said it was and hung up the phone wondering who the "they" was that the detective was referring to and why anyone but Livingston needed to come. The only answer he could come up with in his paranoid state was that it must take more than one policeman to arrest him. The pressure of the last two days had been almost as intense as the pressure of having his family terrorized by Cisco and his gang.

Danny didn't think he could continue the charade much longer and felt that the only way he would ever be at peace again was to confess. The lies were eating away at his conscience, and he had told so many lies that he was having trouble keeping his story straight. Sheila's comment about opening the door to a masked man had really shaken him.

He couldn't bear the thought of living another day looking over his shoulder and waiting for the authorities to unravel all of his lies or maybe find Cisco and his men in a quarry lake on his family's property. He had decided to say that he had killed all the men himself, that he blew the cabin up without any help and that the SUV went over the cliff by accident. He knew his real problem would come if the authorities retrieved the bodies and discovered that Cisco had been killed by a shotgun blast while his henchman *Cuchillo* was killed by a rifle. This fact alone would raise a lot more questions, but Danny knew that if he stuck by his story—even though the authorities might be suspicious—they wouldn't be able to connect Ezra Reed.

If the police didn't believe him, that was fine. They couldn't put him in prison for any longer than they were going to put him in for anyway, whether they thought he was lying or not.

When Lt. Livingston arrived at Danny's home, he was accompanied by a uniformed officer who came along to remove the recording equipment from Danny's phone.

"I'm sorry the recording equipment was so ineffective, Danny," the lieutenant said.

"We analyzed every call that came in against voice prints of Cisco Ram and his top people. The only ones we could match up to Cisco himself, were the calls that didn't contain any direct threats, so they are of no value. It was worth a try, though."

"I understand, Don," Danny said, "but we truly appreciate the effort." Danny had realized as soon as Livingston told him why the other officer was there that Livingston must be changing his approach. *If I don't ask him why they're removing the recording equipment*, Danny thought, *Livingston's going to think I know that Cisco's no longer a threat. And the only way I could know that is if I killed him.* But since Danny intended to confess everything anyway, he did not follow through on the thought.

Danny showed the officer where the phone was and then asked Livingston to come into his study. The lieutenant sat down, and Danny closed the door. "Don, you've been very kind to me and my family, and you did your very best to help us. I'm so sorry for the family of the officer who was killed attempting to protect my family. I'm prepared to answer any and all questions you have about what happened after Cisco's men snatched my family from the motel."

The detective held up his large hand, signaling Danny to stop. "Danny, I don't think I have any more questions for you. What I do have is a huge case load to work today and very little time to do it. So I apologize, but I have to tell you that I no longer have any interest in this case. As far as the Georgia Bureau of Investigation is concerned, it is closed. I've spoken to my counterpart at the Gwinnett County Sheriff's Department, and they feel the same. I just came by today to get the equipment and to tell you that I'm very happy that your family is safe."

Danny was dumbfounded. He was all set to be dragged away to prison, and now the authorities were saying the case was closed? "I don't understand, Don. I thought you wanted to know how my family escaped from Cisco's men. I'm willing to tell you the whole story." The detective held up his hand again.

"Danny, we have all the information we need about what happened to Cisco Ram. Our contacts on the street have been collecting information for the past couple of days concerning his whereabouts. Let me tell you what we've learned and then I really must go.

According to our best sources, Cisco Ram and all of his top people have disappeared. None of them has been seen or heard from in almost three days. None of them has been anywhere near the gang's headquarters nor has Cisco Ram been seen at his home. We have had both sites under constant surveillance ever since your family was abducted. Our best information is that Francisco Miguel Ramos, his top lieutenants, and most of the rest of the mid-level leadership of the Latino Death Lords, were killed by Columbian drug dealers who they double-crossed.

Apparently, the LDL is no longer operating in the state of Georgia, and unless they start up again, I don't expect the GBI to be conducting any investigations into their whereabouts. We will continue to pursue investigations of past crimes committed by their members, but as far as we are concerned, since there are no outstanding warrants for any of the missing leadership, their disappearance is not a criminal matter. For all we know, they've all gone home to Mexico."

Danny tried one more time to explain what had happened, but the detective stood up and shook his head. "Danny, please keep in mind that the first day we met, I told you that I really, really wanted Cisco. Now, if Cisco Ram is gone...I am a happy man," he said. "So listen up. I understand your desire to be forthcoming about this matter, but you don't seem to get the point I'm trying to convey to you, sir, so let me make it crystal clear.

The LDL is gone. Francisco Ramos is gone. If he's dead, I don't care who killed him. Do you understand now, sir? I don't care what happened to him or his gang members as long as they are gone and will never harm anyone again. What I know for sure—just in case you still aren't clear about what I'm saying—is that the night before he disappeared, you confronted Cisco Ramos and his three sharks in a restaurant called El Gaucho de la Pampas. Harsh words were exchanged, and you left in a hurry. Ramos and his friends followed you and appeared to be quite angry. One of the policemen you hired to escort you that evening saw the old APB on Cisco that was issued along with the AMBER Alert for your daughter, and remembered the incident in the restaurant. He didn't remember your name, but he described you perfectly. It wasn't difficult to find the credit card information you gave when you paid for the officers' time. The officer said you were supposedly picking up a rare painting but that you did not, in fact, pick up anything. All you did was have a verbal altercation with Cisco Ramos. I can piece the rest together for myself."

"You can?" Danny said, his voice quavering.

"It's obvious to me that you created a situation that was sure to enrage Cisco Ram to the point where he would follow you from the restaurant. I don't even want to speculate on where you wanted him to follow you or for what purpose. But that is neither here nor there. When Cisco and his men left the restaurant in pursuit of one Danny Chambers, they must have run into the Columbians along the way and met with foul play.

We suspect they were taken to a small cabin in the mountains north of Atlanta and disposed of. A forest ranger heard an explosion in the vicinity of Wolfpen Ridge but observed no subsequent fire, so no attempt was made to check on it until after the snow stopped falling and the roads cleared. When the rangers did go by the area, they found the remains of a small vacation cabin that had been destroyed by what appeared to be a gas explosion. County land records indicate that the property where the explosion occurred is deeded to a man named Samuel Taylor, who has no criminal record nor any apparent ties to the Columbian drug cartels or the Latino Death Lords. We do not believe Mr. Taylor was aware that his property was being used as a meeting place by criminals. That's about it Danny. We've done quite a bit of work over the last two days, and we're comfortable with our hypothesis that the

LDL was eradicated by members of one of the Columbian Drug cartels. Is that how you see it, Danny, I mean, the part about the Columbians?"

Danny looked at Lt. Livingston for a few moments without saying anything.

"Well, isn't that the way you see it, Danny?" Livingston asked again, almost pleading with him. "Wouldn't that be the best thing for all involved?"

Finally Danny responded. "Yes, sir, that would be the best thing for all of us," he said, a surge of relief rushing through his body like a flash flood through a dry river bed. The GBI agent knew everything up to and including the explosion on property owned by Sheila's father, Samuel Taylor. But for some reason he was trying to tell Danny to just shut up and get on with his life. Livingston smiled for the first time since Danny had met him. He extended his hand out to Danny, who gripped it tightly and shook it warmly.

"I have to go now, Danny. Please give my regards to your wife."

"Lt. Livingston…I don't know what to say," Danny stuttered. "I don't know why you're doing what you're doing, but God bless you for it. All I can say is, thank you."

"You're very welcome, Danny, and God has blessed me many times over already. It's been a pleasure getting to know you, sir. I only wish we had met under different circumstances."

"Thank you, Lieutenant. I feel the same, and I don't think we could have made it through this without your help. If you ever want to see a good high school football game, just give me a call. I may not be coaching anymore, but I can still get good tickets."

"I'll keep that in mind, Danny," Livingston said as he turned and opened the door to the study. The lieutenant walked out and joined the other officer, who was standing in the hallway near the front door. As they stepped out onto the porch, Don Livingston looked back at Danny.

"I saw a movie the other night, Danny, about soldiers and war. Near the end of the movie, one of the characters says to another, 'Don't hold your breath for someone to come along and save our butts, buddy. There are no heroes left in this godforsaken world.' Danny, people like you give me hope that he was wrong. There *are* a few heroes left. Have a good life."

CHAPTER SIXTY TWO
SAMSON

DANNY CHAMBERS AND his family had been weighing heavily on the mind of David Shieldman over the past few weeks. He was concerned about anyone in his congregation who was hurting, either physically or emotionally. However, it was natural that he would be closer to some members of his flock than others. The needs of those who participated in the life of the church and opened themselves up by confiding in their pastors, were always going to be better known than those who seldom attended services and rarely, if ever, spoke with their pastor.

Because he had always been active in the church and had an outgoing personality, Danny was someone who all the clergy at his church liked and respected, especially David Shieldman. The problem that Danny had shared with his pastor was one that Shieldman had never encountered in all his years as a clergyman. After Danny had unburdened himself, Dr. Shieldman had tried to tell himself many times that things like this just did not happen in real life, they happened in the movies or on TV. And even if they did happen in real life, they happened to someone you didn't know.

Danny's pastor had not spoken to him in several weeks and had noticed that Danny and his family had not been in church the previous Sunday. Considering the pressure Danny was under, the pastor found it both amazing and gratifying that the Chambers had not missed a Sunday until now.

Danny had told Shieldman emphatically that he did not want to involve him in anything that broke the laws of God or man, and the pastor had respected his wishes. He had sent Danny a few encouraging emails and scripture readings, but he had neither called nor attempted to engage Danny in any conversation about the situation when he saw him at services. They had not talked face to face about the problem since the day they had lunch together. When he did see Danny after services, he would always hug him warmly and whisper, "You and your family are in my prayers, and I am here for you." Danny would always mumble an emotional "thanks" and move on.

Because the family had not attended church last Sunday, Shieldman felt he could no longer refrain from reaching out. For all he knew, the entire Chambers family might be lying dead in their home right now. He got up from his desk and closed the door to his office then dialed his secretary. "Joanie," he said, "I need to make an important call, so please hold my calls and guard the drawbridge."

"Yes, sir, I'm on duty as always," Joanie responded. "Guard the drawbridge" was their special code for "Please don't let any of the clergy or other visitors come wandering in my door, until I tell you otherwise." Shieldman dialed the Chambers home number and was delighted to hear Danny's voice after only two rings.

"Hello, Danny Chambers, this is your pastor calling," he said, trying to sound as lighthearted as possible.

"Hello, David, I was just thinking about getting together with you," Danny said.

"That's wonderful, Danny. When do you want to do it?"

"Would it be possible for you to come over today?"

"If it suits you, I can be there in half an hour."

"That's great, David. I really appreciate it. We'll see you shortly, then."

"Danny...is everything all right?" Shieldman asked.

"We're good, Pastor. We'll tell you all about it when you get here."

After he hung up the phone, Shieldman realized that Danny had said "we" instead of "I." He guessed that meant whatever Danny had to say, Sheila would be involved. He locked the door to his office as he was leaving and told Joanie he would be gone for a while. It wasn't long before he was sitting in Danny's family room with a cup of hot chocolate in his hand.

"Okay Danny," he said, "I'm all ears. I've been concerned about you and the family."

Danny and Sheila sat side by side holding hands on the couch across from their pastor, who was seated in an overstuffed easy chair. David leaned forward to hear the story.

"David," Danny said, "our family is safe, and the man who threatened our safety is no longer alive, nor are any of his associates. For fear of somehow involving you in my misdeeds, I will tell you no more than you need to know." Shieldman felt a mixture of curiosity, relief, and a desire to somehow be of help to his friends, but he wasn't sure how to proceed. He nodded his head slowly, then took a sip of his hot chocolate.

"Danny, I don't *need* to hear anything more," he said, "but I'm willing to hear anything you want to tell me. The bond of confidentiality between clergy and confessant is sacred and cannot be broken. You can't tell me anything that will in any way involve me in things that have already occurred. If you want to talk, I'm ready to listen. Is there anything you want or need to tell me?"

Danny and Sheila looked at each other for a few moments, then Sheila gave Danny a slight nod.

"I'm not sure where to start, David, so I'll just go right to the worst of it," Danny said. "I killed ten men and buried them under three-hundred feet of water where I hope they'll never be found."

David thought he had prepared himself for the worst, but he never expected to hear his friend confess that he had killed ten men. He sat there staring at Danny with the cup of cocoa poised halfway to his lips and his mouth hanging open. Then he looked at Sheila, who did not look away, and tried to think of something to say.

"David," Danny continued, "do you think the Lord can ever forgive me?"

"Danny...Sheila...my goodness," he said incredulously. "You know I'm never at a loss for words, but I have to tell you that right now I am." He studied Danny's face. "You killed ten men?"

"Well, actually, David, I only killed nine," Danny said, "but I'm also responsible for the other one's death."

"These were the men who were threatening your family?" the pastor asked.

"Yes, sir, those were the men."

"Do the authorities know about this?"

"They know that the man and his friends are dead, but they actually went out of their way to tell me they don't care who did it, won't be investigating any further, and don't want to hear anything more about it from me. I tried to confess, but the officer in charge of the case stopped me before I could. Then he made it pretty clear that he knew exactly what happened. So you see, David, I'm at peace with the law. It's my soul I'm worried about."

The clergyman's mind was racing. His agile brain was rapidly sorting through its vast knowledge of the Bible, seeking the words that might comfort this good man and his wife.

"First and foremost, Danny," he said, "you already know the answer to your question about the Lord's forgiveness. If you humbly and honestly repent and ask God's forgiveness, he will forgive any transgression—even causing the death of ten men. Now let me ask you a question. Do you suppose that Samson is in heaven?"

"Sir?" Danny responded, puzzled by the question.

"How many Philistines do you suppose Samson killed when he pushed down the columns that held up the roof of their temple?" Sheildman asked. Before Danny could respond, the pastor went on. "I don't know either, but I'm sure it was a lot more than nine or ten. He also killed a lot of them with the jawbone of an ass before he was betrayed by Delilah."

"Yes, Pastor, but Samson's strength came from God," Danny said. "He was doing God's work."

"And where do you think your strength came from, Danny?" Shieldman asked. "Where do you think a high school teacher found the strength, the courage, and the will to kill ten violent gang members, ten men who made a profession of killing and hurting people? Do you think you did that on your own, Danny, or do you think the Lord might have been there with you all along?"

"I never thought about it that way, David," Danny said. "I guess I was taking all the credit—or, rather, the blame—myself. But the Lord did speak to me up there in the mountains. He spoke to me when I expected to die and only minutes before I killed the gang leader. God didn't tell me to kill him or that it was okay to kill him, but he spoke to me just the same."

"You're sure it was God speaking to you, Danny?" Shieldman asked.

"I've never heard voices before, David. The Lord has never spoken to me before—at least not this way. I have felt that I was being led to do or not do certain things in the past, but this was different. This was a pure, clear voice that seemed to come from everywhere at once, not just inside my head. Yes, I truly believe it was the voice of God."

"Then I believe it, too," the pastor said. "What exactly did God say to you, Danny?"

"I was praying for the lives of my family just as one of Cisco's men was about to kill Melissa with a knife, and God said, 'Have no fear. My son. They are now, as always, in my keeping. You will be together again soon. I am with you always and forever, and you have been faithful.'"

"What did you feel when you heard those words, Danny?" Shieldman asked.

"I felt at peace. I felt that my family was going to die but not suffer. I felt I was going to die with them and that we would all be reunited in heaven in a twinkling of God's eye. That's what I thought."

"Did you think that God might strike these men dead?" the pastor asked.

"I had thought that and prayed for that before," Danny answered, "but that's not what I was thinking at that moment."

"Well, he *did* strike them dead, didn't he, Danny?" Shieldman asserted. "Except he used a devout, loving family man who coaches football and teaches kids history, rather than a Samson armed with the jawbone of an ass. And I imagine that soon after the last one was dead, you were reunited with your family, just as the voice of God said you would be."

"Yes, David, I was," Danny said, trying to absorb what his pastor was telling him.

"Then what is it that's troubling you, Danny?" Shieldman asked. "Do you think you need absolution? If so, it's not mine to give. Even if I could, I don't believe it's necessary. Your prayers were answered, and your Philistines are all dead. Accept it, Danny. Give the Lord thanks for His power and His mercy, and get on with your life."

Danny and Sheila stared at him through misty eyes. "Maybe this is a good time to go to the Lord in prayer," said David. The three of them knelt around the coffee table and took each other's hands to form a circle.

"Our Lord in Heaven, we thank you for the lives of this family," the pastor prayed. "We thank you for the strength you've given them to endure this trial. As only you can provide, we ask humbly and with loving hearts that you give them the comfort they need, heal their scars, and take away their pain. Help us always to remember that our scars, like the scars on your hands and feet where the nails were driven and the scar on your body where the spear was thrust in, should not remind us of where we've been but where we're going. Bless us and keep us near you forever, Lord. In Jesus' name we pray, Amen."

When he had finished his prayer, the pastor returned to his seat and smiled at Danny and Sheila, who were locked in a warm embrace, tears streaming down their cheeks.

As Danny held his wife, he thought about how much he cherished her and his children, and how they now were safe from harm. Sheila thought about her husband, about his strength and his faith. David Shieldman sipped his cocoa and thought about evil men, collapsing columns, and crumbling temples. He thought about Samson and other heroes.

⁓

EPILOG

WITH THE DISAPPEARANCE of Cisco Ram, his *Tres Tiburones*, and the other leaders of the gang, the Latino Death Lords ceased to exist. Without Cisco to instill both loyalty and fear, many members of the gang, who were arrested for crimes they committed over the next several months, gave local police and the GBI extensive information about the gang's past activities in return for reduced sentences. This information led to the successful resolution of many open cases and was sufficient in some instances to initiate search warrants for the homes of Cisco and many of his top aides.

Information found at Cisco's residence lead authorities to Maria Elena Santana, the Diamond Girls dancer whose stage name was Tequila. Maria, who had been forced to grant sexual favors to Judge Ronald Lewis Thornton on numerous occasions, told the police everything she knew about the judge. Thornton was disbarred and convicted of corruption in office, bribery, and numerous other offenses. He is currently serving a ten-year sentence at a minimum-security prison in south Georgia.

Maria no longer dances at Diamond Girls. After Cisco's disappearance, she took her daughter and her hard-earned savings and left Atlanta to pursue the American dream in California. She is currently studying to be a court reporter.

Holly Langman completely recovered from the injuries she sustained during the attack by Cisco Jr. Due in no small part to the notoriety and free publicity she received as a result of the incident, her real estate career has soared to new heights.

The Georgia Bureau of Investigation promoted Lt. Don Livingston to the rank of captain for the role he played in the follow-up investigations that put away so many criminals, including a sitting judge. Although Livingston had recommended that the case of the LDL and Cisco Ram be closed, the absence of an official report explaining the disappearance of Francisco Miguel Ramos compelled his superiors to instruct the new captain to keep the file open. Captain Livingston said he would be happy to do so and added that he looked forward to arresting Cisco Ram should he ever "resurface."

The disappearance of Meredith Stanford and the death of her boyfriend, Sammy Wright, as well as the disappearance of Lindsey Adams, were never solved. Meredith's family, with the help of friends, posted a fifty-thousand-dollar reward, but no one ever came forward. Channel 14 posted a similar reward for information about their missing reporter, but did not receive a single legitimate lead.

The Georgia Bureau of Investigation never discovered who told Cisco Ram where Sheila and Melissa were hidden in protective custody. Bobby Pendleton remained on the job for another two years before he added a drug addiction to his gambling addiction and was terminated. His last known address was a halfway house in Las Vegas.

Dr. David Shieldman turned down a promotion to District Superintendent, preferring to minister to his own flock. He continues to be the senior pastor at Victory United Methodist Church, close friends with the Chambers family, and an ardent Georgia Bulldog.

Roger Chambers quickly recovered from his heart attack and still putters with his azaleas and plays an occasional game of poker at the union hall.

Melissa Chambers has been undergoing counseling and attributes her steady improvement to her faith and the prayers of her parents and brother. She seems to be a happy, well adjusted young teen, but the doctors have told Danny and Sheila that trauma, of the type she suffered, can take a long time to heal.

DJ Chambers is on scholarship to play football at the University of Georgia. Sheila Chambers has recurring nightmares about the death of her friend Laura, and, though she prays about it often, continues to wrestle with feelings of guilt. Whenever she asks Danny why she's still alive and Laura isn't, Danny hugs her close and tells his wife that he doesn't know for sure but that maybe it's because God isn't finished with her yet.

Epilog

After a number of prayerful sessions with his pastor, Danny Chambers finally accepted God's forgiveness for killing Cisco and his men. Danny's faith was strengthened by the ordeal, and he is using the unsolicited fame he gained through the accidental death of a teenage boy, as an opportunity to give his testimony in churches in and around Atlanta.

When the head coach at Robert E. Lee Senior High School left after only two years to accept a position on the coaching staff at the University of Tennessee, Jonathan Evans asked Danny if he wanted the job that should have been his two years before. At this point in the season, the Generals and Head Coach Daniel Chambers are 8-0 and appear to be a lock for a playoff birth. Danny has lunch once or twice a week with his best friend, Ezra Reed, who is still making sure that the power stays on at Robert E. Lee.

Thomas Conway Fishburne

∞

Purchased at public sale
surplus materials

CPSIA information can be obtained at www.ICGtesting.com
Printed in the USA
LVOW011746270313

326354LV00020B/1086/P